eyes

Robert Mayer

eyes

Cover design by Rhonda Ward
Photos by Rhonda Ward and the author

ISBN-13: 978-1936404-35-3

Published by Combustoica, a prose project of About Comics.
WWW.Combustoica.COM

For rights inquiries, contact RIGHTS@ABOUTCOMICS.COM

Published September, 2013.

eyes

Robert Mayer

Combustoica, a prose project of About Comics
Camarillo, California

Acknowledgments

This book could not have been written without the expertise and grace of Kristin Reidy, D.O., of Eye Associates of New Mexico. Despite a densely packed schedule of patients and surgeries, Dr. Reidy took the time to tutor me in the practices and principles of ophthalmology, as well as to read the manuscript for errors. The anecdotes she volunteered would have gladdened the heart of any writer.

Robert Fauret of Taos filled me in on the history of glass eyes, and gave me permission to photograph part of his collection, as seen in the photograph on the cover. I am grateful to the rotating officers of the United States Marine Corps recruiting office in Santa Fe for answering my every question about Marine training and weaponry. Jana and the other second floor nurses at St. Vincent Hospital were forthcoming about their jobs and emotional strains. Numerous articles available on the Internet have described the growth of Oriental gangs on the West Coast.

Ann Kelley of the *Daily Oklahoman* was a combined cheerleader, inspiration and fount of information on several subjects. She and Cheyenna Villareal described the harassment faced by fair-skinned girls growing up in a Mexican-American neighborhood. Dr. John Talley told me of the abundance of Jewish families in California adopting Oriental babies.

As first readers, Karen Chavez, Alma Garcia and Jane Kepp offered helpful suggestions. Margaret Walsh did her usual superb job of editing the copy. My longtime agent and friend, Philip Spitzer, was always in my corner, as he has been for 38 years.

Finally, I owe publication of the book to Nat Gertler of Combustoica, a rare ethical publisher who innately values words above dollars — whether he wants to or not.

To Ann Kelley Weaver

(1971—2012)

whose lovely light was stolen from us

much too soon

Wine comes in at the mouth,
And love comes in at the eye;
That's all we shall know for truth
Before we grow old and die.
I lift the glass to my mouth,
I look at you, and I sigh.

—W. B. Yeats,
A Drinking Song

If I maintain my silence about my secret it is my prisoner.
If I let it slip from my tongue, I am its prisoner.

—Arthur
Schopenhauer
Suffering, Suicide and Immortality

A Brief History of Sight

(Poster in the lobby of the Coastal California Regional Medical Center, Santa Clara County)

Free lecture series for the public, by our staff.
Saturdays, 10 AM, Community Room

Aug. 27: "When Were Eyes Invented?"
Until 544,000,000 years ago, no creature on earth had eyes ....F. Pike, D.O.

Sept. 4: "The Cambrian Explosion"
How the evolution of eyes changed the world .... C. Reiter, M.D.

Sept. 11: "What the Ancients Thought"
Wise men explained sight in ways that seem quaint today ..... R. Leventhal, D.O.

Sept. 18: "Candid Camera"
How eyes are not like your old film camera.................................. F. Heller, M.D.

Sept. 25: "It's a Colorful World"
But dogs, cats and rats see everything in black, white and gray. G. D'Anna, D.O.

Oct. 1: "Want Eyes on the Sides of Your Head?"
That's where most animals have them..L. Fisher, M.D.

Oct. 8: "Rods, Cones, the Rabbit and the Dead Man"
It's about the retina. But leave the kids at home ....M. Hewitt, M.D.

Oct. 15: "Fear and the Eyes"
Your frightened friend, the amygdala ....M. Klonsky, M.D.

Oct. 22: "When Your Eye Hurts Too Much."
Advances in prosthetic eyes.. V. Vigil, D.O.

Oct. 29: "Distortions and Illusions"
You swear that's what you saw. But is that the way it was ? ....M. Lee, M.D.

Part One

Chapter 1: Mona

The women began to taunt me yesterday, in the eye of a little boy.

Afternoon, not quite four o'clock. Twenty-two surgeries completed, a twelve minute average. No problems. Like a plumber fixing a sink, a ballplayer catching a fly. Cataracts, mostly old folks. Routine. Slip blade under the sclera, chop up the nucleus, the yellowed lens, tweezer the pieces out. Both hands acting in concert, like a pianist seated at the keys. Insert a new lens. *Voile!* I could do it blindfolded.

Well, not quite. False modesty conveys false security. Every human eye is different. Once you've sliced your way in, you have to be alert for the unexpected. Be prepared for complications.

Within reason.

The Coastal California Regional Medical Center sits in white virginal glory south of Palo Alto and north of San Jose. It was opened in 1988, allegedly to ease congestion at the Stanford Medical Center and at clinics serving immigrants in the area. As if anyone cared about the brown illegals from Mexico. Real reason? The young millionaire geniuses of Silicon Valley wanted a chop-chop private hospital only minutes away. To save their white and brown and yellow asses in case of sudden ills.

We're rated second only to Stanford by the Western States Hospital Group. Despite the dotcom debacle (I lost my share), hordes of intel companies in the valley are still pumping out unnecessary junk of self-described brilliance. They're also still producing more than their share of stress-related illnesses: ulcers, migraines, heart attacks, strokes, glaucomas. My job — after 40 years, even surgery is just a job — is to operate on cataracts, and to detect a scurvy roster of eye diseases with euphonious names: chalazion, trachoma, scleritis, keratoconus, uveitis, retinopathy, retrolental fibropasia, glaucoma. Names so mellifluous they could be poetry. Cataracts fail the poetry test only by being prosaic. Eye cancer is too brutal to mention, unless we call it uveal melanoma. Which sounds soft as a caterpillar.

Michael Alton Lee. That's me. Hoping to replace the Chairman of Medical Services when he retires next month. Credentials? The usual internships, residencies, fellowships, honors, consultancies. (Failed poet, but that's not on my resumé.) Sixty-three years old, tall, still slim from riding Eyeful, my sleek black colt, mature good looks (intellectually prominent nose, perhaps) gray-blue eyes, hair more graying than disappearing. A necessary stylish goatee strictly clipped. I eat mostly fish and salads, no desserts, when I'm being good. I could still model for Harrods, I did so one summer at Oxford in my youth. The tweeds. Reading/ surgery glasses on a brown cord are always around my neck. A trademark gray wool vest against the air conditioning. I probably resemble a tenured English professor at an erudite college in the Berkshires. Slip me into a sport coat and I'm the perfect image of a board member sipping cocktails and picking the pockets of potential donors while mingling with Palo Altoans. I'm said to be on a fast track for the chair.

Maxie Klonsky, my Jewish rival from neurology, agrees. With his iconic daily outfit of loose-fitting, almost droopy dungarees — on Max they are not jeans — held up by wide red suspenders, over a long-sleeved T-shirt in red or brown or black, the whole topped by thick curly hair riled and white as an unsheared sheep. He never wears a jacket of any kind, on a cool day a fierce red wool cable scarf is his only protection from wind or rain. Maxie, chief neurosurgeon, dresses and shuffles in old shoe comfort, never mind success. He's as well-loved for that as for his brilliance. There's talk this could be the year Klonsky and I share the Nobel, for work we did in our late twenties at neurOptics, illuminating key aspects of the visual pathway. Such rumors arise each year as the calendar nips at October, while our breakthrough discoveries fade into the past. We grow old together, Maxie and I, two friends glancing at the receding years with weakening eyes. World class thinking is for the young. Should we ever win, raucous betting at the hospital would focus on whether Maxie would buy a suit to accept his share of the money, or *schlep* to Sweden and back as himself. If it were not such a cliché, the two of us as Don Quixote and Sancho Panza would have a certain visual truth. Maybe deeper than visual.

So. Chairman of Medical Services for me? That's a stuffed tiger at a carnival compared to the Nobel, but it recognizes you as top doc in the hospital, maybe in all of California. It's not as devoutly to be wished as a month in Oaxaca with Miss Lompoc.

I stood a surefire chance for the chair. Until yesterday.

Yesterday, during the day's final surgery, a dead woman's face appeared in a child's blue eye. An eye in which my steel blade still probed.

The boy, Jimmy Doyle (real name used with parental permission) was eleven years old, rusty hair, freckles. He was the last patient of the day. He had a story. Playing soccer for his school team, he was goalie, filling in for a taller kid. They're leading their cross-town rival one-zip as the game winds down. A kid on the other team is on a breakaway, beats a defender, is charging right at Jimmy. He knows he's gonna get beat. There's only one thing to do. He dives at the ball just as the other kid is kicking it. The ball deflects off Jimmy's head, goes wide of the goal, but he takes a shoe in the eye. Teammates surround him, cheering, he saved the game. Jimmy Hero. But there's a price. A bruise at first, with swelling. His father, a police captain, homicide squad, name of Stennis Doyle, makes an appointment, brings him over. In the slit lamp the retina looks white, not red, as it should. A week later a traumatic cataract develops. Thick yellow fluid clouds the lens. The kid's Irish eyes are no longer smiling. He can't see out of the left one.

In the holding room he absorbs a light tranquilizer through an IV. Like all patients. To calm the natural fears. A light blue drape covering every inch of his body above his knees, except for the left eye, which is visible through a small round hole. He's wheeled on a gurney into the adjacent operating room. A metal bridge under the drape gives him breathing room. Oxygen tubes in his nose. EKG clips taped to his chest. We have to monitor all functions, just in case. He's put to sleep by the anaesthese . . . you know who I mean. Forty years a doc and I can't pronounce the damn word right. I probably had a quiet TIA once. The point is, adults can stay awake through cataract surgery. Lidocaine, a gel that deadens just the eye, is squirted with a syringe into the sul de sac at the base of the eye. They don't feel a thing. Kids have to be put under. They can't be trusted to keep still. We can't have them squirming, bolting the point of a needle-sharp keratone into the retina.

If you Google lasers you'll find a Picadilly of advertisements for bladeless Lasik surgery. My wife, Morgan, took pride in being a second cousin of Ted Maiman, who made the first working laser back in 1960. Maiman died in 2007, still waiting for his own Nobel. But despite his achievement, Lasiks is a triumph of marketing. Not all optic surgery is bladeless. Cataracts — by far the most common — still are sliced apart with steel. Which can make even ER docs squeamish. I've seen them fall like trees in a storm while watching. But a laser beam is still a cutting tool. Set it too strong and it can slice and dice.

So, there lies Jimmy Doyle under the blue drape. Unconscious. Anesthese doc standing by in case the kid needs more. Technician at my right to hand me instruments. All of us in pale green scrubs, matching caps, sterile gloves — a photo spread for Medical Vogue. My RN, Victoria Chen, sits at the foot of the bed, ready to take surgical notes. To make sure the tech hands me the right power lens.
—How's Maya?
—Good. Her cold is gone, she went back to school today.
Cute little girl.
I adore Vicky, but she's in the operating room only because it's required by law. Mostly she'll watch a one-man show. Mine.

It's the end of the day, I'm a little weary, could use coffee but that's not allowed, not even for breakfast, on surgery days. Tuesday, Thursday, Friday. You've got to have a steady hand. No alcohol the night before, same reason. Food is necessary, bites of a sandwich while moving between the two surgery rooms. To keep the energy up. Finish one eye, toss the gloves, pull on a new pair, stride into the other room. The next victim is ready to be cut. I get protocol nods from Vicky, the tech, the gas man. The captain has boarded the ship.

With the Doyle kid things go smoothly at first. A lid speculum to keep his eye open. I sit beside his head, slit through the sclera and the cornea, three millimeters, make the incision, cutting down, at the limbus. A bit of blood trickles to the bottom of the eye, not enough to be a concern. I cut a groove with the keratone blade. The tech hands me the phaco. Its steel tip vibrates at ultrasonic frequencies, emulsifies the nucleus, the yellowed lens. He hands me a chopper. Anticipating my needs. Normally I would talk to the patient, tell him he's doing great, everything's going fine. Not with the boy, he's out of it.

I hear a siren from down in the street. An ambulance coming in. I'm surprised I notice the sound. I'm surprised I'm aware of my surprise.

The phacoemulsification does its job. I scrape my way through the nucleus of the lens, scrape and crack, till it starts breaking into smaller pieces. The cracking pieces often take on shapes — mountain range, rock faces, angry waves slapping the sandy shore.

That's when I see her. As clear as King Hamlet's ghost. Inside the eye of Jimmy Doyle. Shimmering with watery light. Looking angry. Or is it hurt? A thin face, pointed nose, mousy hazel hair. My knees slacken, they could not support me, it's a good thing I'm sitting. Last bite of ham and cheese upchucks into my mouth. Sour, acidic. I clench my teeth to keep from spewing over the patient. I struggle to keep my fingers from trembling. The chopper is still penetrating the boy's eye. It could blind him if my hands suddenly stutter. I look again, my heart vibrating like the phaco. Will the face speak? My forehead drapes in cold sweat. I glance away for an instant to let her disappear. Look back. She's still there. Only worse. No hair. No nose. A bleached, wet skull.

Mona Drew, Buffalo, New York.

I could have killed her.

Again.

I feel the eyes of the others upon me. They're thinking, What the hell is he waiting for? If there were another doc in the room, I could turn it over to him. But that would be recorded by Vicky, and how could I explain to the brass? No matter, no other doc is present. It's up to me to continue.

I don't know what goes on inside our heads when we dream. I don't know what goes on in people's heads when we knock them out with gas so we can cut. I hope Jimmy Doyle is dreaming soccer. Scoring goal after goal. I hope he can't see through his eyes from back to front, that he doesn't know that inside his head he's carrying a corpse.

Three million cataracts are removed every year. How many reveal the dead? The surgery's been done since fifth century B.C. India. Recorded in Sanskrit. How many faces were discovered in prehistoric eyes?

I summon Vicky closer, though she isn't scrubbed.

—Tell me what you see.

—Is something wrong, doctor?

—Just look, and tell me!

—The usual, doctor. Pieces of cracked nucleus. Am I missing something?

— No, that's fine. Thank you.

I'm not much relieved. I don't know what's happening. Or why. I have to suck it up, finish this. Bury the dead. I hold my breath, scrape and crack, scrape and crack, break the segments into smaller and smaller pieces. The skull warns, *I shall return tonight*, and drowns in the sticky cortex.

I continue with the surgery. Vicky is breathing more easily. The other two are squinting at me, as if I've told a monstrous fib. Or passed monstrous gas.

I pull out remaining pieces of the nucleus with tweezers. Slip the new lens in through the slit at the edge of the cornea. A new lens that will let him see again. It's why I still do cataracts. It's tricky, getting the lens to sit just right. I edge it around until it does. I close everything down, make sure the incisions are waterproof. Some need stitches, Jimmy won't. I rim the eye with disinfectant.

—Done.

A single word is all I can speak. Sign Vicky's operation form. Shaky as I leave the room, knees still wanting to buckle. They surely noticed. I leave the others behind. Vicky and the gas doc will wheel the boy into the holding room, wait for him to wake. Scrub tech will clean the instruments for the autoclave.

Need to be alone, figure out why this happened. Need a drink, lurch dizzily as if I've had three, make my way to my office. Lucky that at that moment the corridor is mostly empty. I glide close to the wall, to grab hold if necessary. Maggie Moore, the silver-hair-in-a-bun doyenne of pediatrics, is approaching. We exchange courteous smiles.

—Just had a seven month preemie with detached retinas, she says. What a day!

She moves on without quite stopping. I don't think she noticed anything. Nor does a stocky red-faced fellow pacing like a smoker in need of a puff. He asks if the boy will be all right. Somehow I recognize in civilian clothes Jimmy Doyle's father, who last time had been in uniform.

—Jimmy will be fine. You can take him home as soon as the drugs wear off.

He pumps my hand several times, as if it's the handle of a slot machine. Sometimes it seems like it is, though rarely with cataracts.

—Basketball practice starts in a month, doc, will he be ready?

—He'll be ready in a week.

—That's great, great. If you ever need help with police business, I owe ya.

—I'll remember that, Captain.

Right now I'm remembering dead women. Eleven of them.

Are they all, like Mona, stirring?

Chapter 2: Yessenia

What the hell does Nia have to do with it?

Real name Yessenia. Named by her mother in San Diego. Who is the only one who still calls her that. Her mother and the United States Marines. Staff Sergeant Yessenia Ruiz.

She's called Nia by Mickey, my son, who brought her home for dinner one evening a year ago. Captain Michael Alton Lee Jr., United States Marine Corps. Some day they will marry, that is the plan. Some day in a month or a year when he gets back from doing recon somewhere we cannot know. The Middle East, we imagine, but we can't be sure. Called Nia by me and her father and all her friends and by her underlings at the largest Marine recruiting post in San Jose. She's informal, she encourages that. Unless potential recruits are present, then it's Sergeant Ruiz.

I sit in the leather chair behind the desk in my office, the chair turned the other way, my back to the door. Look out the window at the hospital parking lot. Years ago when I came west for my internship and residency at Stanford, Santa Clara County was mostly fruit orchards as far as the clear eye could see. Since then the apples have been replaced by the Apple Corp. and its thousand and one sisters. The worker bees with their slick degrees and their foreign accents needed places to sleep. Silicon Suburbia was born.

Perhaps cataracts are Nature's way of protecting us from seeing what we have wrought.

A bright flash when a piece of sunspotted chrome bumper or rear window assaults my eye. My scrubs are in a pile on the floor. I'm wearing tan chino pants, blue oxford shirt, no tie. My uniform through Harvard (varsity swim team), Columbia Med School, Stanford. After my residency was done, I worked at half a dozen state clinics in the worst poverty pockets in California. East L.A. to the Mission District. Doing penance. Those five years I played seeing-eye dog for the poor. At the salary of a grocery clerk (nonunion), while doing research with Maxie Klonsky at night. Morgan, my wife, didn't care much for that. I saw up close in the clinics the daily suffering, the hourly terror behind the faces in the streets. Morgan, for all her charity balls, turned away when I brought slum stories home. For years I'd thought my five years of penance were enough. Now, if the dead are coming back, I'm not sure.

I wonder how much they noticed in surgery. My pause only momentary, blink of an eye, but Jimmy wasn't blinking, his eye held open by lid clips. Without blinking, human time stops, relatively. Dr. Michael Lee's improvement on Albert E.

Vicky won't mention the incident to anyone. The others might start a rumor: Dr. Lee is getting too old for surgery. Nonsense. Jack Beecham, never a star, more a utility infielder around Coastal Cal, still is fixing glaucomas at 74. The only one I might confess to is my wife. Who is in a coma, ninety cents dead on the dollar.

The untimely return of Mona Drew. Why?

Retinas, even of the dead, can retain images. Gustave Eckstein wrote about it in his droll 1969 work, *The Body Has a Head*. Turquoise and black cover, easy to find on the shelf. A wonderful book to thumb through at rare restful times. I've marked the passage:

An unpleasant dramatic experiment dates back to the last century. A rabbit was kept in the dark, then for an instant one of its eyes was exposed to an old-fashioned daylighted laboratory window with bars, the next instant the rabbit killed, an eye removed, its retina immersed in a solution of alum, as a photographer immerses a film in a developer, and there on the retina was the window, dark bars and the bright blotches, the unbleached and the bleached. Almost the same experiment at almost the same time was performed secretly upon the retina of a guillotined criminal. A Frenchman did that one. . . . A detective story written at almost the time of the rabbit and the guillotined criminal did have a detective getting evidence about a murder from the retina of the victim. All murderers since then have practiced how to work from behind.

Eckstein has a way with words. Could little Jimmy Doyle have somehow acquired an image of the skull of Mona Drew? Retained it? Not possible. He's ten years old. He's alive. A million images would have washed her skull away, even if he had somehow seen it. Which he couldn't have.

What, then? Was I merely hallucinating? If so, why Mona Drew, after all these years?

I get nowhere trying to understand it logically. I learned long ago you cannot reason with the unconscious. It doesn't speak English.

Still, during every crisis, I try.

Pull another book, *Eye and Brain*, off the shelf. Hands shaking as I turn the pages. R.H. Woodworth suggested that during hallucination, the observer identifies with the figure being observed, and becomes emotionally involved, so that his vision is distorted. The way emotion can distort an intellectual judgment. I had been involved, that's for sure.

Fifteenth century philosophers believed that light emanated from the eyes, and was reflected back by the object we saw. That could make sense in this instance, because though Jimmy Doyle could have no image of Mona, alive or dead, I do. Was my eye projecting her image onto his nucleus?

R.L. Gregory: *Hallucinations are similar to dreams . . . They may even combine several senses at once, when the impression of reality may be overwhelming.*

At least I didn't hear her screaming. Gurgling.

Gregory again: *Extreme emotional stress may upset the system, much as stress can distort intellectual judgment, giving . . . terrible but false reality.*

False reality. But what was the underlying stress? Why today, after all these years?

I turn in frustration to what does sometimes rappel down the dendrites to the truth. Meditation. Imaging. The silent languages of brain country. I try to relax, trembling hands in my lap. Both feet in brown loafers flat on the floor. Eyes closed.

Beneath the lids I see fields of random colors. Dark green. Blue. Red. Purple. Nothing to make of these. No shapes beyond amoeboid. No mountain range, no sea. Then as in a conjurer's kaleidoscope a face emerges. Not Mona. Nia. The most seductive face I have known since Addie Judd. Nia. The only body I have hungered desperately to know since Addie. Nia with her Anglo skin and Mexican sultriness. Dark hair, bright brown eyes, well-shaped inviting lips, one slightly crooked tooth, barely noticeable, which when she smiles suggests her vulnerability beneath the confident surface. A hint of cheek bones, not as severe as Indian but enough to propel her across the line from pretty (Marilyn Monroe) to beautiful (Jeanne Moreau.) A proudly developed chest, a slight belly she hates — visible only when she is seated, perhaps the flaw that highlights the perfection of the rest, which somehow adds appeal, and therefore is no flaw. Nia. Outgoing, curious, swift-moving, smart. Half the men she meets fall in love with her. The other half are blind.

So why is Nia conjured here? What has she to do with Mona?

A recollection. This very morning. While buttoning my shirt before the mirror in my bedroom. The water running in the shower. Nia. She's been living in Mickey's old room since my auto accident six months ago. Moved in temporarily to drive me around town from one lab's mechanical eyes to another. Cat scans, MRIs. Me gripping the world at the end of a walker, with a fractured pelvis and two collapsed vertebrae. Nia used leave time from the Marines to help me. She's comfortable in Mickey's room. And realizes that when I am well, if she gives up her apartment in San Jose and stays with me, paying less rent, she could accumulate a nest egg for the two of them. If that would be okay with me. If I wouldn't feel crowded.

It's better than okay. Sweet cells of the young waft invisibly into the air we breathe, and keep the old from aging. Especially cells of the achingly beautiful. I have one condition for Nia. Forget about rent, you're practically family. Instead, once a week you fix us a real Mexican meal. Deal? Deal! She throws her arms around me in a familial hug. Her soft chest pressed to mine.

The noise from the shower trickles away. She's drying herself. I picture small dark hairs cleaving, dripping. The bathroom door opens, Nia is padding down the hall toward her room, a large white bath towel wrapped around her, covering her slightly tan body from underarms to knees. Left hand holding the taut top of the towel in place. She's passed my doorway just so a hundred times. It's not for me to suggest a robe, she's 27. And there's always hope of a glimpse.

Like today. Was it oddity or luck or female calculation? Just as she's passing my open door she yelps, the way my dog Butler does if accidentally I step on his tail. Apparently a carpet tack, or a biting spider, penetrated her right foot. Hopping on the other leg she bends at the knee and reaches down with her left hand to remove whatever is stinging her. As she does the towel droops. Just a bit. The upper left part. Revealing for a moment her left breast. In an instant she recovers and covers herself and hops the rest of the way to the cover of her room. Flinging the door shut loudly behind her. In petulance or tease.

Mickey's a lucky boy. Lucky man. He's 29, and special even among Marines. Top sharpshooter in his platoon before they assigned him to Recon for another eight months of special training. Jumping lessons at Fort Bennett. It's in his genes. My father was a Marine pilot, 130 sorties in Korea before his engine failed over the Yellow Sea. Missing in Action. Still.

With me the warrior genes had a cynical laugh. Sorry, son, flat feet.

I remember the day clearly. So do you. Four hours later, Jack Kennedy, Class of '40, was shot. In Harvard Square, doe-eyed coeds sobbed in the arms of guys they didn't know. I couldn't tell my friends about my Marine rejection, not for at least four days. Not till after the kid saluted the coffin. The kid who like his dad would die young.

I had planned on studying literature. But I watched Kennedy's brain exploding on the tube a hundred times. Is that what planted in me the seed of pre-med?

The unspoken reason? Essays on Crane and James would hardly pay the rent.

Reading for pleasure usually stops at the scalpel's edge. Trying to defeat that fact is an unwinnable war with time. After a tense day at the hospital, reading requires too much attention. Most docs don't even try. But for me, it is my succor, my escape. From them.

Was I jealous when Mickey was accepted by the Marines? Not so's I admit. We drove to Monterey to celebrate. A seaside feast for three on the marina. Bass stuffed with lobster and crab. A full moon nodding assent in the ripples of the sea. Dark otters frolicking near the pier. I intended to get him good and drunk. Instead he wound up driving me and Morgan home. I always felt he exhibited a certain smugness, a superiority, that night. At least towards us. But perhaps it was there all along, and I didn't notice.

Six months after Dad disappeared into the sea, Mother died of loneliness — abetted by a dozen barbiturates. So I was led to believe. I was eight, my brother 12. We were taken in by an aunt and uncle in Connecticut, Dan and Clara Winslow.

A dentist and his hygienist. A generous, childless couple. Who are long gone. For years after my mother's death, I feared girls. Women. They could too painfully abandon you. Until ten years later, when I learned the truth of why my mother bailed (the bitter word my brother uses still.)

The Winslows were solicitous. They decided it would be good for me and Carl to learn to play musical instruments. A musical escape from orphanhood. Carl chose the piano — the Winslows had an upright in their living room. I picked the drums. Not to be ornery — already by then I had a need to let frustrations out. Beginners' drum sets were $59.95 in the Sears, Roebuck catalogue. But the Winslows drove me to Manhattan, an emporium called Wurlitzer, which sold every kind of instrument from flutes to grand pianos. Also juke boxes. Right on Forty-Second Street. The Winslows watched my eyes alight and bought the set with which I fell in love. Lots of silver and brass. Grown-up drums I'd have to grow into. It cost more than they'd intended to spend, I'm sure. They had it shipped to Connecticut, installed in a storage shed they didn't use much. They bought me a music book as well, but I did not want lessons, did not care about following music notes. I wanted freedom to bang my heart out. Like Gene Krupa, Buddy Rich. A homemade one-man jazz band born of frustration. Music or noise, it eased my pain. The Winslows never complained, they just wore ear plugs. A fact I did not learn until much later. In high school four of us formed a band and played at school dances. Later I lugged the drums up to Harvard and caught on with a student jazz group, played three nights a week in The Cambridge Cafe. Till the day the music died. Not for Buddy Holly, for John Kennedy. The Cambridge Cafe where JFK hung out as a student went quiet for a week, then another. By the third week we didn't care to play anymore. Mourning became eternal, like the flame. I put my drums in storage, did not take them out till after med school. After Morgan and I moved to California. I had them shipped out then, the need to bang away overwhelming in the wake of eleven dead. I set up the drums in the garage, lined the walls with mattresses so as not to drive Morgan crazy. One year a few of us brought instruments to the annual Christmas party. *The Jazz Docs*. Not very imaginative and not very good. Our one and only drunken performance. The drums are still in the garage today. Before Nia moved in I would sidle over there after dinner and play themes for the dead women who inhabit my head. Theme for Francesca. Theme for Gretel. Sometimes loud and pounding, sometimes soft riffs. Morgan, too, used ear plugs — she had no choice, she knew the women's story. With Nia, I much prefer to spend the evenings talking, reading.

To this day I don't understand why inserting Dr. Scholl's into Marine combat boots would not have corrected flat feet. I imagine sometimes having been a jungle rat in Nam, descending into the twisting tunnels of the Black Pajamas, tossing hand grenades to kill them or rout them out. The path my feet would not allow: possibly getting killed myself in the booby-trapped underground. Then the women would still be alive.

Before Mickey brought Nia home I was ignorant about recruiting. I assumed that the soldiers, sailors, Marines perched on their butts in recruiting offices in desultory malls and flag-brightened store fronts across the country were bottom of the barrel, couldn't cut it in the field. From her I learned that the truth was the opposite. Those who scored highest in training and looked the sharpest were asked if they wanted special non-combat duty. Those who volunteered were interviewed from here to Thursday. Those who made the best impression were chosen. The services all want to present their best face to the public. Facilitate approval of the billions they're voted each year by Congress. Most important, keep the recruits flowing in. So. Assign the face and figure and smile of a Nia Ruiz, in uniform, to the San Jose mall, with her half Mexican heritage. A strapping 18-year-old kid stepping into the office, maybe just to glance at a recruiting folder, is duck soup. The same for male recruiters. The brass would like all Steve McQueens. The military's not as dumb as the civilians who've been running the show have made them out to be.

The last time Mickey came home for two weeks, before he shipped out to he knew not where, to be the distant eyes of America, he approved our *de facto* money-saving arrangement, Nia's and mine. No prissy maiden, she met him at a motel in San Diego. I don't know if they ever left the room. Mickey came to visit me on the last day. He wouldn't be calling or e-mailing, he said. Except maybe once every few months, if he's pulled back from the front line. Or from behind it. For a few days R&R, someplace that has the Internet, or telephones. He won't be saying where he is, or they'd pull the plug and break his rank.

The contours of Nia's breasts I had envisioned long ago, beneath almost every blouse she wore. Praise God to whomever devised the cleavage look women and girls have been wearing these past few years. Unimaginable when I was young. Strike that. Only imaginable. Except in her two uniforms — dress blues, desert cammies — which seem to flatten her. But the luscious details I could only guess at. Aureoles sprawling like a pink ink spill, or round as a quarter? Smooth or stippled? Pink as bubble gum or brown as nuts? Same for the nipples. Shyly hidden, introverted, waiting for a tongue's invitation? Or reaching out on their own and saluting? Her secrets were revealed in the instant the towel slipped. Round and smooth, shy and pink. Which was surprising, but should not have been, from her female heritage. Her mother, Margaret McNeil, a school teacher in San Diego, is a light-skinned, freckled redhead. It was she who chose the Mexican name Yessenia, perhaps to win over Grandma Ruiz. Her father, Sergeant Valentin Ruiz, a police officer, supplied the Mexican genes. Black hair. Dark brown eyes, penetrating, in the photos I've seen. Being a doctor, I should look on female breasts merely as bags of tissue. Fatty tissue, prone to problems. Cysts. Tumors. If I were an oncologist perhaps I would. But as I heal only eyes, mine roam like any other man's.

I finish buttoning my shirt. A gush of buttery emotion floods through me, a wave of fine French wine, carried on floating platelets to every cell from cortex to groin. Candlelight flares in my brain. The big brown rat of denial scurries away, carrying its blind eyes to a darker nook. I hover just above a pond covered with water lilies. Friendly fish bump wet noses against my toes. Bug-eyed frogs frolic, sing Hallelujah, joy to the world. Repressed truth is asserting itself, repressed, I know, for many weeks. Telling me to face the fact. At 63, for the first time in forty years, I am in love.

With my son's girl.

I refuse to listen. I try to deny this with my reason, heart, soul. Call it obsession. Infatuation. Fixation. Call it what you will. But do not call it love. I will not, cannot be in love with my son's intended. That is borderline obscene. Borderline incestuous. Disloyal to the nth degree. Even traitorous. A person could be shot for less.

And yet . . . .

I curse God's monstrous whimsey. Life is sadistic humor. Milton Berle, the bastard king of comedy, has supplanted Jesus at His right hand. Jokes? He's got a million of 'em.

Imaginary blasphemy, of course. My belief is in determinism, not in a God who acts, who cares about human beings. It's the same faith as Jefferson, Franklin, Einstein. Once the universe was set in motion — give God credit for that, if you insist — all else followed like a train on tracks. We do what our genes and the past have programmed us to do. The most terrifying yet illuminating sentence in all of philosophy is by Schopenhauer: *A man can do as he wills, but not will as he wills.*

We have few choices. If a giant computer had been present at the creation, it could predict that you will eat cold cereal for breakfast tomorrow morning. You would get to choose between Cheerios and Rice Krispies. That's the extent of free will. This cosmic computer would decide who will get cataracts. Or cancer. Who will die young. The computer, not God, would be all-knowing. And neither of them would give a damn.

I cut into people's eyes and pretend it is my choice. Just as you pretend.

If I had no choice back then, why do I still feel guilty? Why do I see their dead and dripping forms every day? At least I do not hear screams. My tinnitus is loud and common, and in a way it is comparable to seeing figments in the eye — sounds in the ear when there are no sounds. But no one heard their dying screams as they succumbed. Only, no doubt, each other.

Passion is unfathomable wonder and joy at the presence, or mere thought, of the beloved. But unless it is returned by the party in question, it is velvet imprisonment. A nude statue draped in black. In this instance, waiting for me to sweep the drape away, at 63. Can she possibly love me in return?

There is a jauntiness to Nia, a kind of perpetual motion, which I have rarely seen in others. Sticking last night's dishes in the dishwasher, folding the laundry she hauls out of the dryer, talking to a friend on her cell phone, laughing, conversing with a person in the room, throwing items together effortlessly for a superb casual dinner, each activity gliding into the next with no visible shifting of gears, all to a jaunty inner music no one else can hear. This is, for her, the essence of life — not frantic, but a conquering of time, in the same way that when she says she is going to bed she is asleep almost at once. Her bedroom door left ajar not in invitation or tease, I think, but a certain recklessness, to catch the late summer breeze. And yet perhaps it is, in its way, slightly frantic, masking an inner turmoil, a restless, ambiguous sorrow she allows few to see. This is suggested at times by overheard pillowed sobs in the night.

Every one of her traits, except the turmoil, I lack, and thus perhaps overly admire.

My favorite cartoon appeared in *The New Yorker* years ago. A toothless old man is sitting in his rocking chair on the porch of a rustic cabin — he's got to be over 70, could be 80 or even 90. A bird has just landed on the porch railing, is chirping gaily to the stoic old guy: *Hi, Billy! I'm the bluebird of happiness. Sorry I'm late.*

Eyes did not exist until 544 million years ago. Creatures had organs that could distinguish between light and dark, but that was all. They could not see anything. Earthworms still function that way. Seven million years later, in the Cambrian period, real eyes suddenly were everywhere. Hundreds, perhaps thousands, of new species appeared on earth, giving one another the once-over. Eyes became the in thing to have — on the earth, in the sky, under the sea. A passing fad that has lasted. Evolution's rock 'n' roll.

Thorius, a miniature salamander, is the smallest land vertebrate living today. It has eyes only a millimeter in diameter, believed to be the smallest eyes that can provide precise vision. Today one of them has settled, wriggling, in my stomach. To monitor incestuous desire.

But this one is Precambrian. Ahead it sees only darkness.

Emerging from her room, Nia was wearing her dress blues, bright red stripe down the trouser leg, red piping on the jacket.

—Brass coming to visit today?

—No, I just felt like dressing up. The cammies make me feel like a fraud some days. Michael, tomorrow you go in late, right? How about we go riding with Eyeful in the morning?

—Don't you have to work?

—I had this idea a while back. The recruiting office is open nine to five, Monday through Friday. I would assume that recruiters in every mall in America work those hours. So who does that exclude from coming to see us? The best students, who are in school full time and play sports afterwards. Also kids who are working full time. Just the ones we want to recruit. The daytime hours cater to dropouts and mall rats. If we stayed open till nine a couple nights a week, we might attract a better recruit.

—Makes sense to me.

—Two month ago I wrote to the brass at San Diego. No answer. Last month I wrote to Parris Island. No answer. I decided, what the hell? Starting tomorrow I'm going in at noon and working till nine, Wednesdays and Fridays. On my own authority. If it works, if recruits increase in number and quality, I'll make sure they hear about it at the Pentagon. If things don't improve in a few months, I'll go back to the old hours. No harm, no foul. Which is why I can ride with you in the morning. If you want.

—It's a date.

I give her the perfunctory half-hug goodbye as she heads to her car. Feel a rush of heat. Was I pressing extra hard? Was she? Neither of us mentions the slipped towel. But look what she has proposed? Time alone together in the mountains.

All very innocent, of course.

Chapter 3: Victoria

A knock on the door to my office. I can tell through the opaque glass it is Vicky. Deep breaths, try to calm myself. I must reveal nothing of why I stalled in surgery like a dilapidated automobile. The door cracks.

—May I speak with you, doctor?

Closing the door behind her she steps to the middle of the room, bends her slight form, picks up my tossed scrubs. Places them in the basket beside the door.

—You didn't have to do that.

—The orderlies work hard enough, she says.

She's that kind of person.

—You want to ask what happened in there?

—Do you know you're still wearing your scrub cap?

—That must be a sight. Larry, Curly, or Moe?

I pull it off and toss it to her. She catches it like a point guard at Stanford.

—I want to talk about something else. But what did happen in there?

—Just a momentary aberration of my eyes.

—When was the last time you had them checked?

—God knows. They're not a problem.

—I'll make an appointment for you with Dr. Beecham. He usually has time.

—Not Beecham. He hates office exams. It's surgery or bust with him. Get Lacey Roberts.

—The pretty blond? She's only a resident.

—She has just a few more weeks.

—She'll need a supervising doctor.

—She can handle an examination. I'll be there, remember.

If you say so, doctor.

— Besides, Beecham has bad breath.

—Besides, you like pretty women.

Will plead guilty to that. Vicky sees all her fellow humans as fellow humans. My eyes too often go blank, except for the pretty ones. The medical center, like the rest of world, is weighted heavily with the plain — nurses, doctors, residents, interns, orderlies. In one sense we are a vast community, nearly a thousand employees, scrub smiling at passing scrub, and I understand what they — the nurses, for instance — are going though. Those just hired out of nursing school are extra careful to read twice the label on every vial of pills, of blood, read every word on every chart with extra care. As they should. They take their patients, three or four a day, to heart, often take them home into their dreams, sometimes take home phone numbers, call to see how they are doing after they have been discharged. As time passes they must get over this to protect their own psyches, their own emotions, yet every so often a patient will penetrate their defenses, and sometimes the nurses welcome this, they never want to get hardened to the profession. I understand, yet mostly we — me and the unpretty ones — pass in different orbits. Inhabit different galaxies. Indifferent galaxies. Except for the patients, who must remain the centers of our universe.

During working hours.

So I concede, I prefer the company of the funny and the warm and lovely, especially the lovely. Is that a crime? I have saved a hundred thousand eyes, most of them in routinely plain faces. Shouldn't that count for something?

My hero, Einstein, the most astonishing intellect since Shakespeare, had a thing for pretty ladies — and he spurted often inside them. His wife was not even AWOL — yet he remains an icon for the ages. I still only look, don't touch. Why must I be defensive?

Because of my fantasies?

Vicky doesn't know the half of it. Last summer two stunning dark-haired young bank tellers appeared, one at each of the two banks I frequent. Marisol at First National, Vanessa at California State. Standing in line, I always hoped fervently that Marisol or Vanessa would be my teller. The odds were one against three. But they came up often. This allowed me to kid with them, tease them, complement their outfits. Momentary mental diversion. Both were 23, exquisite. Then tragedy struck. After Christmas Marisol showed up wearing a small diamond and a wedding band. Is that new? Of course it was new. A car salesman in Palo Alto. Lucky man, I tell her. Shy grin. Thank you. Then last month Vanessa one morning is wearing a rock as big as Beverly Hills. He must like you a lot. Wider smile, gleaming white teeth, nod. A landscaper. Her black hair hanging low like a weeping willow. Has he already fertilized her? I don't know, she seems like a good Mexican girl, but what is good these days? A Peter Handke title comes to mind: *The Envy of the Depositor at the Teller's Window*. Have you set a date yet? Oh, no, it's not like that. There's no big hurry. So my pool of personal beauties is shrinking. I still hope to approach their windows, but the spark is not as bright.

Variation on an old joke: 63 goes into 23 how many times?

But the pathetic little thrill isn't gone altogether. Friday, depositing half my paycheck in savings, half down the block in checking, I scored both. Vanessa and Marisol, shy smiles in quick succession. It felt better than hitting the double at Golden Gate.

Sitting on the pavement outside one bank or the other there is usually a beggar of sorts. Filthy hair, unshaven, dirty woolen shirt, torn jeans, torn red sneakers, no socks. In front of him an open violin case which he salts with a few dollar bills, sometimes a five, though most people, despite feeling guilty going into the bank to make a deposit or coming out with a wad of cash, usually toss into his case only silver. Beside him is the bow of a violin, as if to suggest his instrument has been stolen, though he does not say that. He rarely speaks. On the other side of him lies a thin beggar's fold-up cane. As if between the two he is imprisoned by life. One eye is covered with a bloodstained filthy bandage, the other with a black eye patch. He is supposed to be blind but I can tell he is not; there are tiny pinholes among the bandages. I can also tell in other ways. He is quite attentive to the passing in or out of the bank of either Vanessa or Marisol. Or other beauties. Sometimes he rubs at such times the inners of his thighs. As if he has selective fleas.

    —What's your name, I asked him once, having time to kill, holding a dollar bill.

    —Oedipus.

    —Interesting.

I took a card from my wallet.

    —I'm Dr. Michael Lee. An ophthalmologist. That's an eye doctor.

    —I know what an ophthalmologist is.

    —If you want, I probably could fix your eyes.

    —Already tried that, he mumbled, head looking down.

    —You did? Where? At Stanford? At Santa Clara?

    —In the rest room.

    —It wouldn't cost you a penny. I'd operate free of charge. Then you could get a job, wouldn't have to beg.

No response. I had him dangling on a conversational rope. I hate fake beggars. They think they're so smart. But they siphon money from those who really need it.

    —If you're passing yourself off as Oedipus, why not be the real thing?

I regretted my words immediately *First do no harm.* What if the guy went and blinded himself? Not very likely, I decided. He wouldn't have the guts.

He raised his weary head and looked at me with invisible eyes.

    —Why don't you bug off, Doc?

    —I tossed the dollar into his case and returned to work. Never saw him again at either bank. I don't know where he went to ply his fakery.

I wonder if he, too, is haunted by guilt. Probably not.

Without warning Vicky collapses onto the leather sofa. Suddenly sobbing. Pounding petite fists into a cushion. I jump from my chair, rush beside her, put my hands on her shoulders.

    — Victoria, what is it?

I smooth her black hair off her face. She's got high cheekbones, sparkling dark eyes, is slim as a fashion model. Size petite.

    —You're as white as I am.

Through her sobs she is looking at me like an immigrant off the boat. I envision her wandering in a fish market, looking for something, lost amid the sacred smells, the shimmering scales, the shining eyes. Odd old images. That would be her mother or grandmother. Half the intel valley is Asian now.

— It's nothing, doctor. I'm sorry.

—Don't say it's nothing. Look at you.

She tries to dry her eyes with a small yellow handkerchief. The stanched tears keep coming. The handkerchief darkens in her hand.

—Will you talk about it?

—I lost control for a moment, she says, weakly. That's not good for a nurse. Please forgive me. I need my job here. I can't talk. I have to figure things out for myself.

—Your job is as secure as mine, Victoria. And mine is secure as they get. Tell me what's the matter. What can't you talk about?

She straightens herself on the couch, but seems to have shrunk in size because of her outburst. Or thinks she has, and thinking makes it so.

—I can't involve you in my personal life, Dr. Lee. These people are creepy. It could be dangerous for you. It's not hospital business. Unless . . . maybe it is, I suppose. They want me to steal hospital drugs.

I let her compose herself, breathe more easily.

—Of course stealing drugs is a hospital matter. Who are we talking about?

—My husband's brother. They've threatened to hurt my daughter.

—Why? When did this happen?

She's trying to choke back a second wave of sobs that jolt her chest like hiccups. I hand her a box of tissues from my desk. She takes one but doesn't use it.

—Last night. Gangs. Chinese. Vietnamese. I don't even know. Asian gangs.

—They want to hurt Maya? When I watched her dance recital last month she was an angel. I remember thinking, the next Maya Plisetskaya. What is she, eleven? Her name is a wonderful coincidence.

—Not a coincidence. I watched ballet videos when I was pregnant. I loved Plisetskaya in *Don Quixote.*

She's drying her eyes again with the single tissue. Natural delicacy.

—Tell me exactly what happened. We'll call the police.

—No police! They warned me.

She lifts her slight frame against the back of the sofa. Gains more control. Folds a leg under her. White blouse, short black skirt, black stockings, soft black shoes embroidered with yellow roses. Still pressing the tissue to her eyes. At last she tells me the details.

Met her husband, Lenny Chen, when she was 19. Just starting nursing studies at Santa Clara. He working for a dot.com, entry level. Fell in love, were married, had Maya. The cutest little girl, with dancing feet. Dot.com crash. Layoffs. Lenny lost his job. Could not find work. He got depressed, more depressed, started going to San Francisco for days at a time. Hanging out with his older brother, Kenneth, who heads a small Asian gang, the Golden Swords. Ken-Chen, they call him. They threaten other gangs with his violence: Ken-Chen will come. This went on for years, she said. Her salary at Mercy in Oakland was their only income. Lenny came home now and then. Until he did not come back. Not for days, weeks. No calls. She went to the police. Mr. Chen is an adult, there's nothing we can do, she was told. She hasn't heard from him since.

—I know that gang killed him, Vicky says. I don't know why. This year I got the job here. It's more money, and a more peaceful atmosphere for Maya.

—You still wear a ring.

—I don't know for sure that he's dead. Ken-Chen says he doesn't know. But he has my new address, he started coming to our house. He is scary. Mean. Tall. When he hugs me it is too tight. I can feel him.

—This is personal, Vicky. You don't have to answer. Has he . . .?

—No. He says he would if I were not his brother's wife. That's forbidden. But sometimes the way he looks at Maya, I'm afraid.

—What happened yesterday? Why did he threaten you?

—I shouldn't be talking about this. But I have to. Asian gangs along the coast smuggle heroine from Afghanistan. Cocaine from somewhere. Through Mexico. They make lots of money. His gang, Golden Sword, is small potatoes. They act like big shots, but they're small fry. Then someone saw in the newspaper, in the last ten years prescriptions for pain killer drugs are up eight hundred percent. Morphine. Codeine. Hydrocodone. Others. People are getting older, living longer, they need more pain pills. Or want more. Sometimes doctors say no, you'll get addicted, you don't need them. But people have money, it's okay if they are addicted. So the black market in pills is growing fast. The Golden Sword dummies want in. They know Ken-Chen's brother's wife is a nurse. Make her get them for us, they say. Ken came over last night. He told me all this. He said I have to do it. If I don't get them painkiller drugs, they'll break Maya's ankles. With a baseball bat. Ichiro model. No more ballet. If I still don't do it they'll break her knees. Last chance, they put out my eyes. Can't be a nurse. I tell him if I get caught I'll lose my job, go to jail. He says don't get caught. I tell them we don't use those drugs in eye surgery. I don't even know where they're kept. The hospital is large. He tells me to find out. To make arrangements. I have ten days to deliver the first batch. After that, a batch every week. No police, or they share Maya and me with the whole gang. Many times. Many days. Much pain. Before they kill us.

—Jesus!

—Ken Chen says they approached someone else as well. I don't know who.

Nia. Mona. Now this. My niece Annabel in Santa Fe would tell me which planet is in retrograde. Sounds like Venus and Mars at war, if I had to guess. That's not my specialty.

Vicky is dropping silent tears like diamonds. I take her hand. What can I do for her? She speaks impeccable English but in telling me about these bastards some of the words pour out in primitive vernacular. Who can blame her? It's a primitive tale.

—I don't know what to do. Can't go to police. What will the police do? No evidence. They arrest some gang member, others will still be around to rape my child. To break her legs.

I'm stymied. Brain dead. She is turning the gold band on her ring finger nervously, back and forth. She manages a small smile.

—That keeps you from getting hit on?

—Maybe my husband will come home one day. But he won't. I know he's dead. He would not just go away, not without saying goodbye to Maya. The ring doesn't really help. The old men still watch me in the hospital gym.

—The Fishing Hole.

—They really call it that?

—Old docs do. Easy stretches they could do at home. They come to watch shapely legs in shorts. Breasts in sports bras. Tight butts.

—Not you.

—I haven't sunk that low. I'm a face man. If I go to the gym, which is not often enough, I go to sweat, not to drool. But what have old men to do? Their wives are gone, or no longer interested. The men still are. So they pick out pretty interns to fantasize about.

—What do you mean, you're a face man? I can probably guess, but . . .

—Back in college, in some class — sociology — we got this odd assignment. Find out what men look at first in women. Really. We went into the streets of Boston at lunch hour. Loads of lady lawyers and secretaries and bank tellers were walking through the streets. I took up position on a street corner, and watched closely the eyes of men standing or passing. I had a form to check off. What they looked at first, second if we could tell. Some men focused on passing faces. Others on breasts, legs, ankles. Some on the view from the rear. It was a warm spring day, so shapes were visible. I forget the winner. Breasts, I would guess. It was not very scientific. But I became self conscious, literally, and took note of what I myself was doing. The face came first, every time. Then ankles, which surprised me. Then back to the face for a second look. Face, ankle, face. Hardly paying attention to breast size. Maybe I'm a freak. The other thing that struck me is obvious: most of our appreciation of beauty comes through the eyes. There's beautiful music, lovely aromas, so on, but mostly when we say beauty we mean physical beauty, whether a flower or a woman, and it's conveyed through the eyes. Any five year old could tell you that, but in a *sub rosa* way it directed me into this specialty. In my innocence I thought, when people lose their ability to see beauty, and you restore it to them — no profession could be more noble.

—You don't believe that anymore?

—It's hard to make the case, when so much of what we see is terrible.

—We can always close our eyes.

—Most people do. But let's not get political.

—Let's not. I'm glad you're a face man.

I grin. Vicky's breasts seem just right for her size. Slim women rarely think they have enough. Their mothers too often make it a contest. Mommy wins!

—Can I be nasty, say something about your survey?

—Feel free.

— I'll never put Harvard on a pedestal again.

Another smile wrinkles my face. Vicky gets bolder.

—When you were talking about the gym, you made it sound as if you're old. You're not old.

—What are you, Vicky, 29, 30? Would you want to be with a man who's 63?

—I'm 32.

I look at my left hand. No ring. For 37 years there was one. No point telling Vicky this. Though I feel her looking at my naked finger. Probably I am imagining this. Surely she knows I have a wife. Everyone does. Vicky joined us six months ago. Maybe gossip already had petered out by then. How long can people be solicitous, ask How is your wife doing? When she's been in a coma for two years.

—How did you concentrate today? With these gang threats on your mind?

What else could I do? Work is therapy.

I try to stand up from the sofa. Stumble, grab the desk.

—Are you okay, doctor? Is your pelvis acting up.

—My pelvis is healed. So's my back. No thanks to the girl in the red car. I'm just tired.

She's standing now, picking up the wet tissues, putting them in the waste basket.

—Thank you for listening to me. It's a cliché, but I feel a little better just from telling someone. You never know whom you can trust.

—Victoria, we'll figure something out. The police will know what to do.

—No police! Can I trust you, Dr. Lee, or not? No police. Let the police find my husband!

—All right. You can trust me. With anything. As your boss, sort of, I feel responsible for you.

—You're nice, doctor. But you're not responsible for me.

—This Ken-Chen sounds like a real shit. But one thing is strange. Why would he threaten you, when this other person might supply what they want? Why not wait?

—I don't know. Ken is not the biggest brain on the block.

I try to let it go, but still it puzzles me. It sounds as if they're pretty sure the first person will fail.

—Another thing. If you could get a few drugs for them — for their personal use — that's one thing. But how do they expect you to steal enough to run a black market? It's ridiculous. They'd be better off hijacking delivery trucks.

—That would take brains. And guts. They're good with guns and knives. Maybe baseball bats. They're not good with brains and guts. Ken-Chen likes to frighten women. To be in control. To hurt them. This makes points for him as leader of the gang.

Many hospitals have problems with drug pilfering. We must have some here. To paraphrase Willie Sutton, this is where the painkillers are. It's well known that some doctors and nurses become addicted. How much leaves the building for resale I have no idea. One case I read about, in Illinois, cops found a tractor-trailer carrying 16.6 million tablets of Vicodin — street value about $80 million.

A hospital in Indianapolis discovered that one pharmacy employee stole 623,843 tablets of hydrocodone for resale. They don't know how he did it. I don't know who counted them. But he at least worked in the pharmacy. This Golden Sword gang might be nibbling at the edge of a big underground business, but threatening to break the legs of children? I'd like to get this Ken-Chen flat on his back, with his eye under my blade. See how threatening he is then.

For the first time ever, I just thought of a surgical blade as a weapon. Something that could destroy sight as well as save it.
File and forget.

Sunlight is still visible through the window over the thinning acres of cars. It's been a long, strange day. I don't want to leave Vicky alone with her fears. Nia's going to dinner and a movie with a friend. Why rush home to an empty house?
—Are you in a hurry, Vicky?
— Not really. Maya has ballet after school.
—I could use a drink. I wish the cafeteria served beer. Or Scotch.
—We might lose a few patients.
—How about coffee? It will calm us down, or freak us out.
—Sure. I like to gamble.
—After coffee, let's walk around to the other side of the building. I don't think you've met my wife. I'm feeling bad, I haven't visited her the past few days.
As we leave my office our hands touch lightly. Accidentally.
—Where is your wife?
—Room 101.
She glances at me, has caught the reference. Obscure, I would have thought, to her generation.
—They call it 103. Someone with appreciation of Orwell designed the place. There is no 101.
—Except inside us, Vicky says.

The cafeteria is a good one. Subsidized. Decent food. Which is smart, it keeps the staff close to home at lunch time. We're on the first floor, large windows imbibing the lowering sun. A vast room of wooden tables and chairs almost empty now. We carry coffee in paper cups to a table in the corner. There is no one within fifty feet.
—You've been with us half a year, right? This is the first time we've been out of ophthalmology together. Tell me about your life.
—It's not very interesting. Until last night.
—Tell me anyway.
—I grew up in San Francisco. Chinatown. My parents run the best restaurant in the city. You'll have to come try it. Mr. and Mrs. Ling's. Next door is a big chain, Chinese Heaven, which has bright red wallpaper, golden dragons, long fluorescent lights. Waitresses in black pants, white shirts, chopsticks and little red umbrellas in their hair. A big room, half the size of this. But it's never more than half filled. My

parents' place fits only thirty people. Small tables, crowded, no dragons. There's always a line outside. Lunch time, dinner time, all the time. The locals know about it. Tourists wonder what's going on, but they don't want to wait. And papa has a firm rule: no take-out.

—I never heard of a Chinese restaurant without take-out.

—Mr. Ling says good food should be hot out of the kitchen, on real plates. Not half cold from paper cartons.

—That must cost him a fortune.

—He doesn't care. He stands for quality. Next time you're in San Francisco, you try it. My two sisters work there, they wait tables in blue jeans. They're twins, younger than me, prettier than me.

—I doubt that.

—Sonia and Madeline. If you meet them, you'll see.

—What are their names, your parents?

— I can hardly remember. They've always been Mr. and Mrs. Ling. Even to us kids. To instill respect. They were happy I became a nurse. In Oakland. A good profession, they said. Help people. They were not so happy when I married Lenny Chen. But they loved it when Maya came.

I sip my coffee, speak over the rim of the cup.

—Are you happy here?

—The truth? I would rather be a doctor. A psychiatrist. Well, it's too late to be a doctor. A psychologist, maybe.

—You'd be a good one.

—Why do you say that?

—The way you look at people. You see through them. Into them.

—My parents are not happy that now they rarely see Maya. They work seven days a week. I try to get her up there once or twice a month. Tomorrow night I'm taking Maya to the San Francisco Ballet. A preview called *Danse Macabre*. With Samantha Eberle in red as Marie Laveau, Sam Reed in black as Death, and Patty Dehlers in white as The Moon. Plus dancing skeletons. We get the program in the mail. Maya looked through it and chose that one. Then supper on grandma's lap.

I recall I always liked the Saint-Saens music. Watching the skeletons dance might be helpful. Unless they come out wearing name tags. Mona, Jolene . . .

—Sounds nice.

—You want to come with us, doctor? The previews never sell out week nights.

—Would that be appropriate?

—It's just the ballet, and seeing my family.

Cassandra salamander writhing in my gut. Saying no. What is Nia doing tomorrow night? I would rather be in her presence than anywhere else. She has gravitational pull on me now.

—I'm afraid I can't. I have plans for tomorrow night. Well, tentative plans. Tell you what. I'll see if I can break them. Just to sample your parents' food.

—No pressure. I understand. Ms. Tentative is first choice.

—No, you don't understand. It's more complicated than that.

—It's okay. It was just a thought.

How can I explain? Heck, she's just my nurse, she needs no explanation. It would be easier to tell her about Mona's face appearing than about Nia. Maybe I just need to talk. I trust her. Look around. No one can hear except the walls.

—Vicky, I need to tell you something. About a woman named Mona Drew.

—You have a girlfriend? You don't need to tell me.

—Not a girlfriend. When I paused today, in surgery. When I got shaky. It was because I saw a woman's face in that boy's eye.

—In his eye?

—Her name was Mona Drew. I knew her only slightly, a long time ago. This never happened in surgery before.

Vicky touches my hand on the table. A momentary transformation from nurse to woman.

—No wonder you were upset. What do you think it was? I didn't see her. It must have been a hallucination.

—Yes. But why?

Her slim hand slips away. My thoughts are galloping like quarter horses. Nia, Vicky, Maya, Ken-Chen. Mona — who, like Jacques Brel, is dead, but also alive and well and living in Paris.

Then I have a brainstorm. The DVD!

—Vicky, do you know we record every operation? Up close, nothing but the eye?

—Doctor, I'm the one who puts the disks in and takes them out. I've wondered why we do that. For insurance purposes, I assume.

—That's not why. Ophthalmology hasn't had a malpractice suit since the hospital opened. But some doc a long time ago had the idea, and started taping. For use teaching interns. He's long gone, but the practice continues. I wonder if today's disk would show anything.

—You mean a face in the eye?

—Maybe. If I was not hallucinating.

—What else could it have been?

— I have to go look. If I can figure out the DVD player. I'm not good at that stuff.

She takes her cell phone from her purse. Her aunt Glory usually picks up Maya at ballet school and stays with her until Vicky gets home. Vicky tells her that today she might be late.

In the surgery room she pushes buttons I was not aware of. A metal arm beneath the ceiling swings to the side. She pushes another button. The arm lowers.

—Here it is, I say, finding a DVD case on a chair. Today's date. Vicky looks at it.

—That's just the first half. See, one to fourteen. I put in a new disk for the rest of the day.

She sticks her fingers into the camera box. Then pulls a chair over, gets up on her knees to peer in, feels around.

—It's not here.

—When you left the room to come talk, were the others still there? The anaetheseo? The scrub tech?

—Both had already left.

—One could have come back for the disk.

—Why would they?

—Evidence. If they want to report my . . .lapse. . . to the board. Those two guys don't like me. I'm not sure why. But by sowing doubts they might keep me from becoming chairman.

—You were about to sneeze.

—What?

—You felt you were about to sneeze. You didn't dare sneeze while cutting the boy's eye. You paused, fought it back, waited for the urge to pass.

—Vicky, you're a genius. You saw me do that?

—If necessary.

I stand, circle the table, hug her shoulders briefly. Her body feels like a Chinese bird.

Chapter 4: Morgan

It's not the sex I miss so much since Morgan lapsed into the coma. There was too much tension there anyway. She had her own bedroom, I had to schedule appointments. She actually wrote them on her social calendar. Wednesday evening, 8:30 to 8:55. Fuck MAL. (Michael Alton Lee. Me.) She always allowed exactly 25 minutes. So she could wash herself before some TV show came on. Sometimes, if there was an early special , she watched it over my shoulder.

Simple affection is all I craved. The holding of hands. The loving goodnight. You hug and kiss a coma, you get no more response than from a corpse. But from Nia, suddenly, I want affection cubed. More than that. Love to the tenth power. With the passing hours she has become a heavenly smorgasbord: need, want, desire, fixation, ideation, ideal. The supreme attraction in the universe. From her I want everything. Even more than from Addie, back then, which I thought was not possible. Perhaps because while Addie offered a glorious beginning to life, Nia represents extra innings. A glorious end.

Mickey's girl.

An old-fashioned clock is ticking in my chest. A pendulum. Infinite passion. Infinite pain. Is consummation possible? Mutual? Or is the very thought absurd? Until I know, the clock will tick with muted cries. A Cassandra clock, boding ill.

You will think I'm exaggerating. Unless you, too, have been trapped in the quicksand of forbidden love. Then you understand.

Cassandra is on my mind. The dark Greek prophet. How old was she? She's always been an intriguing outcast. Portrayed on a wind-swept coast with rain clouds tearing at her raging hair. Did she go mad, in the end, at being ignored? I don't recall.

Jung says that when old men crave young women, it is not so much a physical desire as a religious need. Jung never met Nia Ruiz.

The sleep of reason produces not only monsters, but dreams of ecstasy. Though ecstasy itself may be a monster.

Nurses and orderlies scurry about like squirrels as Victoria and I approach room 103. For a moment I think it's happened, Morgan has died. My spirits soar, my brain screams in terror, simultaneously. Freedom's when you've got nothing left to lose. I don't want freedom that way. Do I? Maggie Olsen, the head nurse on this wing, sees me, reassures me.

—Don't worry, Dr. Lee, Mrs. Lee is fine. It's Mrs. Alperson has died. Her roommate, you know. Alzheimer's.

—Yes. Thank you.

Mrs. Lee is fine.

Large beige curtains wall off the late Mrs. Alperson's bed. But not the aromas. From the sounds I can tell the orderlies are lifting her body onto a gurney. Preparing to take her away. Others to remove the sheets. Sterilize the bed. For the next occupant. I take Vicky's hand, lead her across the room to the other bed. Morgan is lying on her back, her eyes open, as if staring at the ceiling. A thin blanket covers her to the neck.

—Vicky, I want you to meet my wife, Morgan Albright.

—Albright?

—She always kept her own name.

—Her eyes are open. Could she see us if she turned her head? Hear us?

—No.

— You're sure?

—Positive.

—That's terrible.

—Come, look into her eyes.

We do. They appear normal. The human eye is strange. The pupil is just an opening. That's what we look out of. Like looking out a window. But when we look into someone else's eyes, we can't see through the pupil. We can't see what's going on inside.

—The IV?

—Food and water. We both have living wills. No extra efforts to keep us alive. Such as breathing machines. You see, she's breathing on her own. But food and water is not an extra effort, it's required, or the patient slowly starves. That's murder, until a judge rules otherwise.

—Schiavo.

—Almost. She was a vegetable for 15 years.

—What's the prognosis for your wife?

—Nobody knows. She could have awakened in a day, a month, a year. Now it's been two years. Max Klonsky, the chief neurosurgeon, says she could start saying a few words any day. Or she could die any day. Or remain in the coma for 15 more years. The record, I think, is thirty-seven.

—What is going on in her head? Her brain? Is she thinking in there?

—I hope not. Talk about Room 101. Klonsky assures me those parts of her brain are dead. She can't see, hear, think, remember.

—Look! She closed her eyes! As if she heard everything we said, and didn't like it.

—An automatic response, Maxie tells me. The eyes open and close sometimes. As if she has waking and sleeping moments. But it's not a willed action. She's unconscious all the time.

With her eyes closed Morgan remains inert, like a specimen.

—How awful for you, Michael. How did this happen?

An orderly swings open the curtain that had encircled Mrs. Alperson's bed. Another patient is being wheeled in on a gurney. I've got her back, you have her legs. Okay? Now!

An emaciated, gray-haired woman is moved into the newly made bed. A nurse covers her with a blanket, pulls the curtain around her.

—I'll give you folks some privacy, doctor.

Einstein once said, *Subtle is the Lord, but malicious he is not.*

Standing in this room, it is hard to agree with either proposition.

Morgan Albright. What I also missed for 38 years was an affectionate nickname to use. Morg didn't work, obviously. Nor did Morgie. I suggested Marge, but she hated it. It was so . . . pedestrian. Morgan would rather die than be pedestrian.

—How did it happen, you asked. It was unexpected, frightening. We slept in separate rooms, as I've said. That was Morgan's choice, a long time ago. Sometimes, if she couldn't sleep she'd get up and fix herself a bourbon. One morning I woke up, went into my office to check for messages. Morgan was sprawled on the floor, in her nightgown. Not moving. Beside my computer table there's an old box, a small wooden chest covered with colorful Mexican paintings. I picked it up in Vera Cruz a long time ago. I throw stuff into it — clippings from medical journals, notes for a book I hope to write some day, *A Brief History of Sight.* Old newspaper clippings. The usual stuff. At the bottom was an old revolver my dad left. Morgan's head and neck were lolling on the edge of this chest. Just hanging there. In her motionless right hand was a pair of sunglasses that must have been in the chest for years. I checked her pulse, it was very faint. Also her heartbeat. I called the emergency room. They must have flown, the ambulance was there in five minutes. The medics gave her injections, IV. Onto a wheeled gurney, off to the ER. I told them I'd be there as soon as I threw on some clothes. I knew it was either a heart attack or a stroke. I couldn't tell which. To make a long story short, she'd had a massive stroke. With no help for hours, because I was sleeping. She was already in a coma. February 14, it happened. Valentine's Day. An extra sick joke, we had stopped exchanging Hallmarks years before. I keep saying two years ago, I guess it's two and a half already. For months I came to sit by her every day. Read the newspaper to her. Poetry. Studied her eyes. Never a response. No sign at all of comprehension. My visits slackened after a while. Slackened into guilt. Guilt into acceptance. There's nothing I can do. Then into anger. Why me? You hear that, Vicky? Not why her? Why me? That's the kind of person you're working with.

—Don't put yourself down, doctor. It's normal. Life has to go on. So you started seeing other people when? Women, I mean.

—I haven't. She's still my wife. It would feel like betrayal. Anyway, most good women won't date a married man. And it's too embarrassing for me to ask. To explain. I took my ring off last month. That's as far as it's gone. To be honest, it does get frustrating. I do have some life left. I never signed up for a monastery. But there I go again, as if it's about me, with poor Morgan lying here.

—It's just like with my husband. No one can prove Lenny's dead. I don't know what that gang did to him. But there is a difference. If I wanted to date, I could date. Men would sleep with me married or not. Then go merrily on their way.

Very merrily, I imagine. But dare not say.

—I seems we're two peas in a pod, Vicky. Who would have thought that? Look, let's get out of here. I have no surgery tomorrow. Let's get a real drink.

No surgery tomorrow. Just me and Eyeful and the fresh morning air. And Nia in riding britches.

The sun as it lowers is glaring. I reach absently for the sunglasses in my sport coat pocket, then realize I left the coat in my office. I stretch for the spare glasses in the glove compartment of the Camry, keeping one eye on the road. It's ironic, given my profession, that I always had ultra-sensitive eyes in the sun, even as a kid. Or maybe it's not ironic. Maybe it's cause and effect. Determinism.

The place is called The Half Moon. Half a mile from the hospital. We take separate cars. There are closer bars, where hospital people congregate, but this is more discreet. Red leatherette booths. The ceiling a dark sky with stars and the requisite half moon. Tasteful, not overdone. At the bar a few middle-aged people are intent on getting drunk this Tuesday night. All the booths are empty. I choose one in the middle instead of the back. No point in seeming to hide. Dewars on the rocks for me. Scotch sour for Vicky. I find that endearing. Teenager at a wedding bash.

—Tell me about your marriage, she says.

I'm weary, but what the hell.

—You want to know about Morgan and me? Early on she bought a collie. It looked just like Lassie. She named it Lassie. When it died after twelve years, she got another. Looked the same. Named it Lassie Too. Last year, with both Lassies dead and Morgan comatose, feeling lonely I bought a camel's hair pit bull. Sweet, not nasty. He slobbers his tongue on people who come to the door. I named him Butler. That was our marriage.

—Do I also hear Yeats in there?

—I take back what I said. You can see right through my eyes, into my brain.

—I have good peripheral vision.

—His *Collected Poems* on my desk?

—*The ceremony of innocence is drowned.* I like Yeats, too.

Her quotation startles me with the images it raises, as if from underwater. Quickly I continue.

—Okay. Morgan Maiman Albright, 101. There's that number again. Born and raised in Oyster Bay, Long Island. That's an enclave of wealthy Wasps. Her mother was a society trendsetter. Father a well-known psychiatrist. Plenty of family money. She went to Sarah Lawrence College. Art history, what else? Had an apartment in the city, a trust fund at 21, did not have to work. But she discovered that at parties in the city, for better or worse, people always ask what you do. She was doing nothing much. This was no way to answer, or to interest an interesting man. So she took a job with Lightmares. It's on Long Island, near Grumman Aircraft, near Roosevelt Field. Lindbergh took off from there on his famous flight. The company developed lasers, which had not yet come into public view. They were cutting edge, so to speak. Her uncle owned the company, so getting a job was not a problem. She became his executive assistant, whatever that meant. At least he had a sense of humor in naming the company. Morgan thought it was silly, would discourage investors. She was probably right. But she had small talk now. Lindbergh could lead to historical riffs about anti-Semitism, all sorts of things. We met a party, and she latched onto me. I'm not sure why. Perhaps because at 5-10 she was too tall for most guys. and I had two inches on her. I also had a resumé she could brute about to her friends — Harvard, Columbia med. I'd just started my second year. I was so busy studying I had no time to scope out girls. I drank myself silly at one party, from any bottle that was open, after thinking I'd flunked a practicum. I woke up in Morgan's bed. Her face was not stunning, but better than plain, in an angular sort of way. We began dating.

—An easy lay.

—That's one way to put it. But she convinced herself it was love. Before I went off for a summer fellowship at Oxford, we got engaged. Her idea. To keep me pure and looking forward to my return. Neither of us could anticipate Addie.

—She being?

—Addie Judd. Oddly, she was also from Long Island. Long Beach. Not wealthy. It's by the ocean, not the bay. Which of course means nothing to you. I'm babbling. Addie had finished nursing school, was giving herself a summer fling in England before settling in to the bitchin' work. Sometimes I'd take a book and sit on the grassy slope beside the Thames, but instead of studying I'd write poems. One day Addie came along. She sat on the grass not too far from me. Not too close, but not too far. In jeans and a well-filled cashmere sweater. The most beautiful girl I had ever seen. A perfect figure. Sublime face. Dark hair to her shoulders, dark eyes. Enthralled, I whipped off a quick, terrible poem about her beauty. About hoping I would see her there again tomorrow. When I got up to leave I walked past her, dropped the poem in her lap, kept going. Twenty yards away I knelt to tie a shoelace.

—Which did not need tying.

—Hey, you! Michael A. Lee. That's the dorkiest pickup attempt ever.

—I must have blushed to my toes. But it worked. She yelled, Two o'clock tomorrow. Bingo!

I take a long sip of my Dewars, say no more.

—That's it? Bingo? What happened the next day?

—Bingo covers a summer of falling in love. Picnics by the Thames. The theater. The Tower of London. For two solid months we were holding hands. Passionate kissing, necking.

—Don't tell me you didn't go to bed with her. Did she have a problem in that area?

I down my Scotch, order another.

—I doubt it. But I never found out.

—Why not?

—I was honest with her. I confessed I was engaged to Morgan. Whom I didn't love. I told her I would break that off as soon as we returned to the States, then Addie and I would make love forever. That was the plan. I respected Addie for it. I respected myself for it. This was a long time ago, remember. We took the boat-train to Paris for two wonderful if celibate days before coming home.

—So what happened?

—I went back to school. Addie started her nursing job. Morgan was away somewhere. It took me a few weeks to work up the courage to face her. To break the engagement. She's a strong, determined person, used to getting her way. I did it in a restaurant called L'Orangerie, so she wouldn't start shouting. She took it surprisingly well. She had seen it coming. Maybe from the dry tone of my letters from Oxford. She didn't have my apartment key with her but said she would return it soon. With a big practicum coming up in two days, I holed up in my apartment, studying, with the phone off the hook. The bastard professors scheduled the exam right during the World Series, on purpose. It was the year of the Amazin' Mets, 1969. Before you were born. They did it to make a point: if you're going to be a doctor, medicine comes before everything. The day of the exam was Addie's birthday. October 16th. I went to the hospital where she worked to pick her up for dinner. Anticipating a sweaty celebration that night.

I take a deep breath at the memory. Fight back tears, after all these years. Have to search inside me for my voice.

—And?

—We never got to celebrate. Addie was killed that day.

—Oh my God!

Vicky touches my hand on the table. We both get damp thumbs from a residue of wet circles. She quickly pulls her hand away, as if deciding the gesture was improper. I hadn't minded.

—What happened?

I shake my head, swallow another gulp. Ice clinks against my teeth. Scotch is burning my empty stomach. I run my hand through my hair. My eyes stare beyond Vicky into the past that never leaves. Addie Judd. I would exchange one hour naked with Addie for all the future years of my life. I've been begging for that exchange since I was 24.

I do not tell Vicky I killed her.

Now there is Nia. Addie in dress blues. The same offer stands.

—I'd rather not talk about how it happened. Instead I'll quote from my most devoured philosopher, Arthur Schopenhauer. *The world is glorious to look at, but dreadful in reality.*

—If you believe that, Doctor, you could argue that our eyes are deceitful organs.

—You could.

—Which might lead you to question everything we do.

—It might.

—That would be upsetting to such as you.

—It is

She rubs my thumb with her finger, comforting me, the woman, not the nurse, but quickly pulls it away.

—You seem confused about what you do, doctor. After so many years.

—These days I'm confused about a lot of things.

I'm hopeful and terrified at once, I could tell her. About my sudden passion for Nia, my son's girl. Joyful at the hope and terrified of the pain it will leave in my gut and my brain when it shatters. As, fulfilled or not, one day it must. I'm a wanderer lost in a forest, eating a mushroom, not knowing if the nourishment is a 'shroom illusion or a poison that twists knives in your gut.

—Well, the heck with that, Vicky says. Remind me never to read that guy.

I notice a dimly lit aquarium along the side wall of the bar. I had not been aware of it before. I need to lighten the mood.

—Do you know that the eyes of fish have lenses that move around, unlike ours, which only change shape? That helps them pick up more light underwater. Which is a problem deep down. At the time of the dinosaurs, there was a reptile shaped like a dolphin, more than ten feet long. It used to plunge pretty deep. Scientists call the fossils *Ophthalmosaurus.* You know why? They had eyes the size of soccer balls.

—Ophthalmosaurus? I think one of them is our head nurse.

I can't help grinning. Out of the office Vicky is fun.

I bury the thought. How many women can I fall for in one day?

On the other hand, might I fight passion with fondness? Fight love with like? Might viewing Vicky not only as a fine nurse but a lovely woman dilute my fixation on Nia? Spread the pain around, like digging a thumbnail hard into my forefinger to diminish apprehension of the dentist's drill? Ken-Chen's threats have opened the door to amity. Dare we walk through?

—I was devastated by the loss of Addie. Devastated enough to marry Morgan. I knew I would never truly love again, so what did it matter? One-love marriages may be more common than we think. I was accepted as an intern at Stanford. Morgan liked the idea of California. I buried myself in interning, residency. She bought art, got involved with charities, golf tournaments. And here we are. But I left out the one good thing. My son Mickey. Michael Alton Lee Jr. Captain, U.S. Marine Corp. Somehow our genes clicked. I'm grateful for that.

I look at my watch. Gold on gold-link band. A gift from Morgan.

I'm a silver person.

—Are you hungry? How about we order some burgers?

—I just had the strangest thought, Vicky says. It's like that tree falling in the forest. If you hadn't told me your story, would it really have happened?

Our cars are side by side in the parking lot under a real half moon slithering between clouds. An illusion that the moon is moving rapidly, not the clouds. Neon reflections on my midnight blue Toyota, her gray Chevy. I stand beside her as she unlocks it. Blue light from a fake half moon atop the bar is not flattering, it changes our faces to Picassos.

I realize there is no Ms. Tentative tomorrow night. Nia can go riding in the morning because in the evening she'll be recruiting at the mall.

—About the ballet tomorrow. I accept your offer. I would like to escort you and Maya. If the offer is still open.

—You're sure?

—Absolutely. I'll pick you up. But I don't even know where you live.

She fumbles in her small purple purse, changes her mind.

—I can give you the address in the office tomorrow. Don't eat a big lunch. Mr. and Mrs. Ling will stuff you. Some people have been unable to walk after dinner, if my parents like them. Meeting my boss, they will feel honored.

I reach for her hand as she is about to slide behind the wheel. The result is not even a tepid handshake, it's a tepid finger touch. We both pretend not to notice.

Blowing gray clouds hide the moon and darken her face to a deeper blue as she speaks.

—Thank you, Dr. Lee. For hours I have not thought of Ken-Chen and his threats. That was a wonderful gift.

—Have you told your parents about that?

—No. Why worry them?

—We'll figure something out. I won't let you or Maya get hurt. I promise.

Two Scotches talking. She bends back out of the car, straightens up, kisses my cheek. Disappears behind the wheel before I can react. Hesitates.

—I'm not used to alcohol, she says.

But I catch her sly grin as she turns and drives off, engaging her headlights belatedly.

I stand alone in the parking lot like a drunk, gazing at dozens of stars revealed by the scooting clouds. My friend Fletcher in Pasadena — telescope land — says there are more than a hundred billion galaxies. A hundred billion! Galaxies! He accepts this and still is content with his wife, with raising four kids. He sends me Hubbell pictures. My favorite is the Sombrero Galaxy (part Mexican, like Nia?) It alone has 800 billion suns. I mentioned this to Nia one night. She said it sounds like a great place for a vacation. I told her I know she likes the beach, but the Sombrero Galaxy is 28 million light years from Earth. She conceded that we'd have to get an early start.

So. Are we each a grain of sand in the eye of God? No, not that big. An atom? An electron? A quark? I swing sharply into my driveway, almost miss it. I think: desire is the quantum mechanics of emotions. Everything random, invisible, unpredictable.

What if every galaxy has its own God? Why not? A hundred billion Gods.

While the best and the brightest of us are busy improving the iPad.

Chapter 5: Monique

—Michael, are you all right?

—Wha? What?

I open my eyes, look around, feel a tightness in my chest. A split second of worry. Then realize it's my seat belt. Smell Nia's light perfume. Her head seems huge through the driver's window. Where are we? Jeez, the driveway? Guess I fell asleep before I got inside. She leans in, her cheek pressed to mine, her body twisted, reaches across my chest, does something twisty with her hands. Pulling the key out of the ignition. The engine stops. She pulls back slightly, turns the headlights off. I manage to unhook the seat belt by myself.

—You must have had a busy day.

Withdrawing, she kisses the rim of my ear.

—Let's get you inside and to bed.

To bed?

—I must have had a hundred mall rats hanging outside the recruiting office today. Giving me the eye. Two made obscene gestures. I grabbed the slower one by the ear and marched him to mall security. The next one who does that gets shot, I told them. They laughed. It seems that's against the law. Also, I'm not armed down there.

She's talking through the closed door to her room as she changes into pajamas. I fix a small Scotch for myself.

—See you in the morning.

The light under her door vanishes.

— If I were you I'd hit the sack, too, Michael. Don't forget we're going riding in the morning. I can be pretty mean when I'm disappointed.

I take a sip of Scotch.

—Sweetheart, you couldn't be mean to the Taliban.

I hear bare feet hitting the floor. Her door flies open. Her pajamas are purple. Her face nearly so.

—You going sexist on me, Dr. Lee? Or just stupid drunk? It's a good thing you're Mickey's father, or I'd deck you. What do you think I was doing for eight months at Parris Island? Making tortillas?

—Let me come in and explain . . .

—Keep away from my room. Lest you forget, I have a rifle in there. I do know how to use it.

She whirls and stomps into her bedroom, slams the door.

Jesus! I was just trying to say something nice.

I don't know how long my nap had lasted with the motor running and the headlights on. I'm not sleepy now, too much in the day's events to ponder. The missing disk comes to mind. At first hoped it would show Mona's face. Prove I was not going mad. Now that the board might see it, I have to hope there is no face. It would be too difficult to explain. It would lead to all sorts of questions. Who is she, what happened to her? There is no Fifth Amendment at board meetings. Better a normal disk showing a slight delay and using Vicky's brilliant idea. Kerchoo!

Mona. I have to get tough with Mona. So she doesn't interfere with my work again.

First, I should explain what I have done. When you kill, the guilt is almost intolerable. At least with most of us. Kill more than one, the guilt increases geometrically. Mona to the tenth power. Unless you're a pure psychotic, like Bundy, Gacy those others, with no human feelings. You have to do something to release the pressure, relieve the anxiety: confess, stay drunk, drug out. None of those appealed. I wanted to live my life. That suggested the answer — a unique solution. Keep them alive, too. Continue their life stories as if they had not died. These second acts are in my mind, of course. But fantasies are real. Any shrink will tell you.

So, Mona. From Buffalo, New York. There was no other information in the newspaper. Well, she certainly had a life in that chilly town. Mona Bradshaw. Graduated from Cheektowaga High, went to nursing school in Ocean Park. Got pregnant by a long distance truck driver named Otis Drew. Married before she was showing, sweet little white-painted country church. First time he came home from a cross-country drive, she was more visible. Muscle-shirted son-of-a-bitch got drunk, accused her of cheating on him, beat the hell out of her till she lost the baby. Beet soup down the toilet. Don't you dare do it again. A few trips later he accused her again. Beat her up worse: face, head, back. She had just gotten her nursing degree. When the coast was clear she loaded up her old Dodge with her clothes and scrammed the hell down to New York City. Answered an employment ad for nurses at Rikers Island Hospital. A notorious prison island in the East River. A prison infirmary with 500 beds, always short of nurses. She had put in five years when she died. A bed check found no inmates missing. The culprit was never identified.

But that's not the end of her story. She always liked to sing, even as a kid. Chorus in high school. Sang around the house, drove her husband wild. Think you're Rosemary Clooney? That what you sing to the guys at the diner when I'm off on the road? *C'mon a My House*?

One evening, in Greenwich Village, where she was sharing a small apartment with another nurse, she went to a movie called *La Vie en Rose*. The life story of Edith Piaf. Mona was bitten, smitten. Dead or alive, she quit her job on Rikers, withdrew all her savings from the bank and bought a ticket to France on The French Lines. One way. She was not coming back. The first night out the movie they showed was *Gentleman Prefer Blondes*, Jane Russell and Marilyn Monroe. Not by coincidence — it was shown on every voyage, as the film happened to feature The French Lines. Convinced, Mona bought hair dye at the ship's commissary and became a blonde. Decided her name in Paris would be Monique. One word. Much sexier than Mona Drew. Why carry her son-of-a-bitch husband's name into Paris or eternity? Monique. No last name.

The rest of the five-day crossing she ignored the movies and hung out in the lounge. A Catskill Mountains piano player name of Bennie Beserk, something like that, entertained the passengers while they drank free Champagne. Old favorites each night. Passengers crowded around piano, joined in. At first Monique stood quietly in the rear. But when Bennie segued smoothly from *Maria* into *Summertime*, she joined in the singing. Half way through the song the other passengers stopped, hearing this beautiful voice slicing through the air, a beatified hummingbird. She was singing alone. When it ended the others burst into applause, bravos. Bennie Beserk nodded, asked what other songs she knew. Most of Billie Holiday she said, and off they went, *Strange Fruit, What a Little Moonlight Will Do,* her notes soaring out the portholes into the North Atlantic. The next three nights the lounge was mobbed, to listen to Monique from Cheektowaga High baring her soul.

The last night out a large Frenchman, looked sort of like Gerard Depardieu, approached her. Asked if she is going to Paris — she was — and did she have a place to stay. Of course, she said, lying, and Monsieur Maurice Levan said that if she wanted to save money from the overpriced Paris hotels he would be happy to put her up. I'm not that kind of woman, Mona-Monique snapped. Monsieur Levan says a thousand pardons, dear lady, I did not make myself clear. You would be staying not only with me but with my lovely wife Sophie and our two daughters and our maid. You sing beautifully. I own several small cabarets on the Left Bank, in which I think you would be a beeg hit, as you Americans say. Also I am partner in a large new Club on the right bank, Chez Desire.

Levan was good as his word. When the ship docked at Le Havre his personal limousine and chauffeur were waiting to take them to Paris. Sophie Levan, who looked a bit like Piaf in the movie, and the two young daughters took to Monique at once. Sophie had her personal dressmaker prepare outfits that would look perfect in her husband's clubs. Before long La Monique became the toast of the Left Bank. She was born with more soul than anyone since Piaf, the critic for *Le Figaro* wrote. Not knowing her soul had been beaten into her by a drunken truck driver.

That was long ago. Of La Monique's lovers I know little. Perhaps Levan himself. I have no interest in that. A year ago she moved across the Seine, began opening at Chez Desire for Diana Krall.

That's the problem.

I open my eyes, startled There is Mona — Monique — looking much as she had this afternoon in the eye of the little boy. But larger. With her left eye hidden by a black eye patch. Her face is hanging in the air like the bloody dagger in Macbeth. Or Salomé's dripping prize. My mouth is dry as I speak.

—What's the problem? And what's with the eye patch?

You don't know about that? Last year I climbed the Eiffel Tower. Never did that before. A sudden wind came up, drove a cinder deep into my eye. Docs removed it, put ointment in, bandaged the eye, told me to wear the patch for a few days. I sang that night wearing the patch and people loved the effect. They said it added atmosphere, the look more German than American. That gave me an idea. I learned Pirate Jenny, *other Lotte Lenya songs. Kurt Weill. Now my repertoire includes three languages. My eye is fine, but the eye patch has become my trademark on stage. I get more bravos than Krall. She's old hat. She should be opening for me.*

—That's why you interrupted my surgery? Why you endangered that little boy?

To get your attention. Your mind is too full of that Nia woman. There's hardly room for us to breathe. You never let Morgan displace us. Not a day of your marriage went by when you didn't think of us. But now you have this Nia fixation. It's nonsense. You're 63, she's 27. Why would she be interested in you? Mon Dieu, *she's your own son's paramour.*

—This is not about me. Krall is an international star. I've got three of her albums. Can you top *The Girl in the Other Room?*

That one's good. But mostly she's too girlie-girlie. Not enough Weltschmerz. *I guess she's never worked in a prison ward.*

—You've traveled a long way from Buffalo to Paris. Maybe I did you a favor.

I wouldn't go that far. The point is, Krall just covers. I'm writing my own tunes. Dark and weary. The way life is. And death. Soon it will be time to do an album. We've neglected that part of my career.

—Me, me, me! Don't bother me about that! Not until you're ready. And dammit, stay the hell out of my operating room. It's not a complaint box.

A warning, Michael. I'm not the only one who's angry. After what you did you have no right to love. You don't even play the drums for us any more. You may get other visitors. Including Addie Judd.

I think not. Addie is the one who will never come.

Like a snuffed candle Mona flickers, disappears. I swallow a swig of burning Scotch. Upset with myself. I've never gotten pissed with any of them before.

You think, perhaps, that I am psychotic, schizophrenic. Not fit to be a surgeon. You're wrong. You perform the same denial of death all the time. You call it Heaven.

Behind me, the door to the hall bathroom clicks. I don't know how long Nia has been standing there, watching me speak to the air.

Chapter 6: Nia

Driving southeast. Polk State Park, largest in California, is twenty minutes away. Named after the president who fought the Mexican War and acquired California. Manifest Destiny. Maps still show Polk State Park, but that will change next year. The legislature recently renamed it Destiny State Park. Both political parties, facing an increase in Mexican voters, showing sympathy with complaints that Polk killed thousands of their countrymen to confiscate California. Personally I like the change. It has a literary ring, an air of expectancy. Unlike Destiny as a name for all those little girls running around burdened with it. Destiny Chen? Destiny Klonsky? Any day we'll see a TV show for teens. *A Date With Destiny.* Or, more recently, as I've noticed with some of my younger patients, Destinee. Or Destinie. Polk is where I stable Eyeful.

—Do you mind if I ride her today? Nia asks.

—Of course not.

Though the request does upset me. Perhaps she's getting even for my Taliban remark. Though neither of us has mentioned last night.

—I feel like riding bareback. You can't do that with the rented horses. Insurance rules.

—Did I ever tell you why I named her Eyeful? Her dam was Madame Bovary. Her sire was Tower Magic. A landmark in France — Eyeful was obvious. Morgan wanted to call her Black Beauty. But she was mine, so I had naming rights. Morgan called her Black Beauty anyway. But it's no problem, I'll take out Grits. She's a nice strawberry roan. Calm disposition. I rented her for Morgan the few times she came with me. I'm not feeling hell bent for leather today.

—Michael, your pelvis. Your back. I forgot about that. Have you been on a horse since the accident?

—There has to be a first time. It's been six months already. The doc says I'll be fine if I don't overdo it.

—The first time back up, you should ride your own horse.

—I prefer to see how you ride bareback. I'll be careful.

Six months ago. Pause at red light. Begin turning left on green arrow. Girl in old red Mitsubishi is flying down hill, doing fifty at least, through a red light, no intention of stopping. She must be stoned. A UPS truck in front of me, a Hummer behind me. I can't budge in the two seconds I see her hurtling toward me like a heat-seeking missile, aimed at the driver's door. I see the top of her brown hair through her windshield, she's driving blind as she flashes through the red light, never brakes, never swerves. I grip the steering wheel tight with both hands and close my eyes against flying glass. Whamcrunch! A flash of bright white light fills my brain. I'm rolling backwards. I open my eyes, my back is killing me, I wriggle my toes. Same with my fingers. No severed spine, thank God. Hunched forward over the steering wheel, I can't straighten up. Quasimoto. The bells of Notre Dame should be ringing. I was hit so hard I spin across three lanes, the Corolla rolling backwards even though it's in drive. One of the witnesses must have hit 911, because the cops are there in minutes. They try to get me out of the car but the door is buckled in, the side post bent. They have to call for the Jaws of Afterlife to cut through the metal and get me out. Medics lift me into an ambulance. Dozens of X-rays. Hours pass. After one, I'm amazed to see Nia watching me. With Morgan in a coma, Mickey overseas and my brother in Connecticut, she's my emergency contact. She must have done a hundred driving up from San Jose. I spend six hours in the ER, then instead of admitting me they send me home. Doc, you're lucky, you've only got a bad muscle strain, the young ER doc says, and gives me a pain pill that doesn't work. You're a monkey's asshole, I want to tell him, if this pain is from a muscle strain then I'm Donald Duck. Nia and an orderly excruciate me onto a gurney of porcupines, then bend me into the backseat of her Volvo for the ride home. Holding the side of the dresser I inch and wince myself into pajamas as she scoots to a drug store for stronger pain pills. The best thing about being a doc, you can write your own prescription. I ease into bed. In any position except lying flat, a mountain lion is gnawing at my spine.

I'll stay in Mickey's room tonight, Nia says. We'll get you to a specialist in the morning. She takes a few days of family leave. The next day, Maxie Klonsky, seeing how I walk, orders assorted scans. They show a fractured pelvis and two compressed vertebrae. Nia drives me from one X-ray lab to the next for days, and moves in temporarily in case I need help. Vicky, new to the office, checks with me by phone every day. I catch up on stacked journals. I'm on a walker four weeks, then walk with pain for three. I don't report the ER doc for missing the fractures, not everything shows on X-rays. The fucking girl in the red car, who was not hurt, turns out to be 18. She gets off with tickets for speeding, running a red light, driving with a revoked license, driving without insurance. Four small fines. No criminal charges. If I'd been killed she'd have been up on vehicular homicide. If her car were taller than a Mitsubishi my brain would have been bouncing on the passenger seat. You were lucky, each doc tells me. Without even knowing that Nia would move in.

In the annals of time, going back to the Big Bang, what exactly determined that the girl in her mother's Mitsubishi and I in my Toyota would try to occupy the same molecules of space simultaneously?

Dear Abbey: I'm 63 and passionately in love with a 27 year old woman who is engaged to my son. While my wife lies in a coma and my son in the Marines is overseas defending his country, I am desperate to make love to his fiancee. I'm not sure how to ask her. What should I do? —Michael.

Dear Michael. Soak your head. Leave it in the toilet bowl. Flush.

—Where's your head, Michael?

Just after I slam on the brakes, two feet more and I would have knocked over the wooden railing of the parking lot beside the stables, which is just across the road from park land. Grits is led out of her stall by Larry, Eyeful by Harry, the twin black stable boys. They look about 14, but Lynn, the owner, says they're 25, have been with her for 10 years. Nia reaches into the pocket of her black Western shirt, pulls out two baby carrots, gives one to each horse. Reaches in again, gives a second one to Grits. Eyeful looks hurt. He nuzzles his large head against her chest, extends his long pink tongue, comes up with not one more carrot but two. Chomps those, pokes his tongue into her breast pocket again, seeking another. Even my horse is getting more than me.

Nia is dressed all in black — jeans, the shirt, a black bandana as a belt, a shorter one across her forehead. Barefoot. Pancho Villa with curves. I'm in my habitual khaki — doesn't show much trail dust — brown riding boots, necessary sunglasses. The only black is my baseball cap. Two orange letters. I followed the goddamn Giants for 55 years, that coast and this, NY and SF. All we got for it after Willie Mays was the Steroid King, a chubby faced role model. Ken-Chen probably worships him. There seems to be a culture clash, however. He'll use an Ichiro bat to break Maya's legs.

Larry carries my stored saddle over to Grits, lifts it on, cinches it. Nia takes hold of Eyeful's neck and swings easily onto his back. Eyeful turns his head as far as he can over his shoulder, as if saying, *What's this? No saddle? Just girl? Feels good.*

Nia's legs spread wide astride the horse. She makes no mention of what if anything she heard me say to Mona.

—How'd you learn to ride bareback?

—When I was a kid my father took us across the border every Sunday to visit my cousins. They all rode bareback. And barefoot.

—Sounds Indian. Is that the Mexican culture?

—It's the Mexican border culture. There's no money for saddles. Or shoes.

I mount Grits, walk slowly out of the saddling area, up a slight incline to the park entrance, from which a mesa a mile long spotted with ponderosa pines leads to an upsurge of craggy ridges, down to rocky valleys yellow with chamisa, up sharp hills that make up most of the park's miles and miles of trails. It's the most underused park in the state, according to the guidebooks, because of its ruggedness and primitive facilities. Only three roads, all dirt, trisect the vast acreage. Only one percent of those who do use the park are equestrians (the guidebook's word.)

That's why I chose it to stable Eyeful. It's a good retreat from the hospital, which is all people and facilities. This is a place to ponder the natural realities.

Nia inhales deeply of the morning, filling her lungs with it.

—I love riding bareback, she says. In your thighs you feel every rippling muscle of the horse. You hardly need the reins. You communicate what you want with your own taut muscles. It almost feels like . . .

—Like what?

—Never mind.

She's a healthy young woman. She's been without for a year, except for those two weeks of F & F in San Diego. How could it not be on her mind?

The eyes of horses are twice as big as ours. Yet they see less than half of what we see, in terms of resolution. Their pupils are horizontal — look closely as they thunder down the stretch — for a wide aperture, letting in more light. A horse can pick its way along a dangerous path in light so dim the rider can barely see the ground. But their retinas are not as sharp as those of birds of prey, or carnivores that stalk.

Grits and Eyeful know the way. They've been on these trails for a lifetime. A worn rocky path climbs onto a low ridge, just wide enough for both. We loll easily on their swaying four-legged rhythm, reins resting light as cotton candy in our hands. Scaly lizards either freeze in place or scurry off the hoof-marked trail as we approach .

—All the times we've talked, I say, I've never asked why you joined the Marines.

—You want the short form or the long?

—Is there a medium?

I'm riding closer to the edge. Gallantry. Grits dislodges a small rock into the canyon below.

—My father was both Mexican and a cop. You know that. Makes for a very conservative person. And my mother was white. In high school I was called a weda. It means white girl in Spanish. One girl in particular would always ask me, Why are you so white? When I made the basketball team, I wasn't picked on anymore, I became known as a good player rather than just a white girl in a mostly Hispanic school. But there were some kids who always believed I was rich. I remember once — I think I was 8 or 9 years old — when I was pushed to the ground by a black boy and called a rich white bitch. I've never forgotten that. Obviously. Anyway, when I graduated I wanted to go off to college. Mom was okay with it, but my father said absolutely not. A girl lives at home until she's married or pregnant. I was not interested in being either. So I got an idea. I went to the nearest recruiting office and joined the National Guard. When I came home with the paperwork I felt triumphant. I had figured out a way to go to college on my own, and get out of the house. My father felt betrayed, but I was 18, he couldn't stop me. Now that I'm older, I can see that he was scared. He himself had served in Vietnam. Anyway, the argument became so heated that I packed my stuff that night and stayed with a friend for two weeks until I shipped out for boot camp. I actually liked boot camp. Pitting myself against others. The Guard paid half my tuition at Santa Clara Junior College, in return for one weekend a month and two weeks in the summer. A good deal. I wanted to get a bachelor's degree, but I didn't have the money. Instead, I gambled on solving the image problem that had tormented me all my life. I joined the Marines. They grabbed me up, what with my Guard experience. Off to South Carolina. I still hope to get a bachelor's degree some day.

—Do we have a war in South Carolina I haven't heard about?

The horses reach the end of the ridge. They hesitate, not knowing if we want to return lower or hang a switchback right and go higher. We urge them on with our thighs.

—Marine boot camp is there. San Diego for Westerners, Parris Island in South Carolina for Easterners. Except that all women go to Parris Island. I guess that saves money on showers. But the training is the same for men and women. They say Marine boot camp is the worst of the services, but I reveled in it, came out stronger. More confident. I was tops in my platoon in sharp shooting. They asked if I wanted to be an NCO — drill sergeant, recruiter, things like that. Why not? Better pay, live closer to home. Sergeant Yessenia Ruiz. Now Staff Sergeant.

—This torment you mentioned. What was that?

—Like I said. My mixed heritage. When I was with a group of white people, I felt Mexican. With Mexicans, I felt white. I was always an outsider. I never belonged. This played havoc with my head. It made for lots of depressing days. Want-to-stay-in-bed kind of days. Black hole days.

—The Marines changed that?

—In the Marines there are only three colors — olive drab, dress blue, service green. It doesn't matter if you're white, black, brown, yellow, you're part of something bigger. You don't give a crap what others think. You're good, and you know it. You always belong. Because you're a United States Marine.

—Did that help with you and Mickey? Him being white, you mixed.

—*Semper Fi.* We're both Marines.

—You never wear civvies to work, even though it's allowed. Same reason?

—I tell myself it's out of respect for the office. Deep down, you're probably right.

Silence except for the horses' hooves clattering along the cliff as we move slowly on. Inner complications, usually hidden, are the warp and woof of souls. Nia appearing so confident. Being so not. In the middle of the night on occasion, as I have mentioned, I hear her crying through the walls. Never ask why. Yet sometimes, lying there, I softly mourn with an inner tear the comfort I cannot give her.

—But you still have your black hole days. Or nights. Care to talk about that?

—It's much too nice a day. Well, I'll tell you one thing. I signed up for non-combat because they needed recruiters. Now I feel like a fraud. A traitor to the service. I ought to go fight, or turn in my uniform.

—But you won't.

—I don't believe in Iraq, or Afghanistan. I don't want to kill civilians. So I'll keep recruiting, for the next good war.

—I think there's more to your darkness, in the middle of the night.

—Anyone with more than menudo for brains has multiple darknesses, hidden in the pockets of her soul. Never to be touched by the light. If you expose your inner secrets to the sun you wither along with them. How did someone say it? There's no *there* there. Put it another way. I'm glad I'm interesting enough to be tormented.

We reach the beginning of a higher ridge, the horses picking their way more carefully now. There's a steep drop to the valley below. Everything is brown — dirt and rock. Grits drops a load as we walk. I pull a handkerchief from my pocket, wipe sweat from my face, my sunglasses. The sun has climbed higher, the temperature is rising. A hawk circles high above. Suddenly it swoops into a valley. Best eyes on the planet. Bad news for lizards and prairie dogs. Brown on brown, but lunch nonetheless.

—Once I asked Mickey how you guys met. God sat you down on his lap, he said. I said, Not on the first date, I hope. Kidding around. But he got real annoyed and walked away. He's a hopeless romantic, that boy. I suppose I was, too, when I was young.

—You want to know how we met? I'm sitting at my desk in my cammies, hair in a ponytail, and in walks this tall, cute Captain. Spiffy in his dress blues. H takes off his cap, one look around, and he approaches me. He says: Joey was right. He told me you got to go up to San Jose and check out this hot babe in the recruiting office. Well, that's not me, I tell the Captain. I'm not a babe and I'm certainly not hot. Maybe Joey meant San Francisco. Meanwhile, we're checking each other out like heifers in heat. He says, Oh, I must have misspoke, Sergeant. What Joey actually said was, there's this really intelligent recruiter there, an okay looker, not that that matters. Uh, huh. I stand and walk around the desk. Now I'm facing him three feet away. I tell him: You ought to know, Captain, that in any relationship I'm in, I have two firm rules. The first is that I will tolerate only one lie. Then I'm outta there. You just used up yours. He's trying to hide a smile. What's your other rule? I tell him, I'm noncom, you're not. Don't get yourself killed. He purses his lips and rolls his eyes around the office as if he's thinking about it. Then he says: I can live with that — if you'll have dinner with me tonight.

—You said yes, of course.

—The crack you made that got him upset? About the lap and the first date? He probably figured I told you. Gave you a blow by blow. The truth is, I was a pretty hot babe back then. A time bomb ready to explode.

Back then. Twelve months ago. The image makes me close my eyes and breathe deeply. With pain.

We think we are God's masterpiece. The top of the chart. Yet fruit flies, *drosophila melanogaster,* which are three millimeters long, copulate for thirty minutes. It's no wonder scientists study them so much.

They also have tiny but wondrously complicated eyes. Almost as inexplicably complex as ours. Who said the following?

To suppose that the eye, with all its inimitable contrivances . . . could have been formed by natural selection, seems, I freely confess, absurd in the highest degree.

Did you say Charles Darwin? Come on down!

—Look! Can you see it? On the third ridge over.

A big cat.

—A cougar. Mountain lion. Same thing. I wish I had brought my rifle.

—This is a state park, Nia. You can't hunt here.

—I know. Just kidding. But sometimes I ignore the rules. Give in to temptation. What else is it for?

—If you really were to shoot, where would you try to hit him?

—Like a Taliban. In the widest part. The chest. Burst his heart. If you're rusty, a little high, you still rip out his throat. But not if I was showing off. That would be different.

—How?

—I'd ask you which eye you wanted him to lose.

—At this distance? You're that good?

—Some day I'll show you how good I am.

Give in to temptation.
I'll show you how good I am.
Verbal pheromones.
Uttered in innocence.
Or not.

Often at night we read in the living room, in burgundy wing chairs six feet apart that face a false fireplace. She in jeans or if it's a warm evening, shorts, leg tucked under her. Me in chinos, loafers, my ankles crossed. Nia loves spy novels. When she comes upon an author she likes she tends to go through his or her entire repertoire. She moved in near the end of Le Carré, is now deep into Robert Littell. Gets used paperbacks for twenty cents and a trade-in at the Santa Clara Book Exchange. I've read some of both, but since Mickey's deployment I find myself turning more to history and current events — Iraq, Iran, Israel, the Palestinians. He's roaming somewhere out there. I suppose I want to know why. Sometimes for a change of mood I choose a more literary novel, soak up the prose I always wished I could write. But too often I find myself distracted, eyes glancing up at her, studying her serene face as she concentrates, lamplight over her shoulder adding soft luster to her almost black hair, extra roundness to her firm thighs when she's in shorts. Several times recently she's glanced up and caught me at it. As if she could feel my eyes on her bare flesh. Me feeling worse than a Peeping Tom. Each instance her focus returned quickly to her book, as if she hadn't noticed. Her mind off in Berlin or Langley or wherever Littell has transported her. I know she has noticed. She says nothing.

—At boot camp you made sharpshooter?

—Expert. Depending on your score, there's Marksman, Sharpshooter, Expert. I was tops in my company.

—How many women is that?

—Eight platoons in a company. Each platoon has seventy. What's the math?

—You were the best of 560 Marines? Where did you learn to shoot like that?

—Guard practice helped. But mostly it was Mexico. Those Sundays we went across the border, Uncle Hector was teaching my cousins to shoot. Three boys, about 11, 12, 13. I was 9 or 10. I remember one day he came up to me holding a bunch of empty beer cans between his arms, like a baby in a blanket. He said, Yessenia, Sweetie, how come every can of Cerveza you hit, the bullet hole is right in the V? I say, Because that's where I was aiming. He says, But then you missed your last six shots altogether. The boys were laughing at you. I told him, If I didn't start missing, they wouldn't like me. They wouldn't play anymore.

—Still, that's a special talent. The sighting, the steadiness.

—My father is a cop, remember. Maybe they'll find a gene for shooting. Better for them to work on the fruit fly.

The cougar drops into a ravine. Not to head us off, I trust. In a state park, used to humans and horses, it couldn't be dangerous. But I would not want to tangle with one of those. I look at my watch. We better head home, I say, sore eyes beckon at the hospital. We turn the horses and head back down the trail. Nia's thoughts are still with the cougar.

—Did you read what happened in Santa Fe the other night? You have a niece there, right?

—What happened?

—It was all over the Net. Probably will be in today's papers.

—I was a bit smashed last night, you may recall.

—A cougar came down from the mountains. Probably hungry. It was seen stalking on the Santa Fe central plaza, about two in the morning.

—That's when the bars close there. Lots of strange things are seen in Santa Fe at that hour. Even reality, sometimes.

—There are pictures. The plaza is mostly shops and galleries, right? Well, this cougar for some reason jumps through the plate glass door of a jewelry store.

—He missed his wife's birthday?

—Somebody calls the cops, animal control, park rangers. A cop goes in to the store first, shotgun leveled. A ranger is right behind him with a dart gun. They turn on the lights, look around. They see lots of display cases of Indian jewelry, but no cougar. But something made that huge hole in the door. The rest room door is closed. They approach it, guns ready. That must have been some moment in true crime annals. They yank the door open and step aside. The cougar could spring at them. But he doesn't. They spot him in a stall, the door also closed.

—Bad burrito?

She gives me a look that could kill without a rifle.

—The ranger stretches flat out on his belly to shoot under the door. He fires, gets the dart into the cougar's shoulder. The cop is ready with the shotgun in case the cougar slips under the door and attacks. But the tranquilizer puts him out. The rangers find a cut on his foreleg from the glass door. They fix him up, haul him into a cage. They drive a hundred miles north into the forest, and set him free up there.

—They didn't charge him with breaking and entering? They probably ticketed the store owner for endangering wildlife with that glass door. It's a crazy town, but I like it. I visit once a year at least. Mostly to see Annabel. I adore that kid. A free spirit. Unlike her straight-laced uncle.

—You sound envious.

—She's living the carefree life I never did. The winding dirt road not taken.

Foster Grant. Ray-Ban. Adidas.

Most people have recurring dreams. Mine feature people wearing sunglasses.

Sometimes the men and women in dark glasses are marching troop-like on a beach toward the sea. Just as the guy with the wraparound pair that I recognize each time is about to march into the incoming waves, perhaps to drown himself, I wake up, kicking and screaming. This used to waken and irritate Morgan, asleep beside me, until we moved to California. Into separate bedrooms of our ranch style home on Blue Oak Drive. Seven minutes from the hospital.

Armani. Costa Del Mar. Dragon Optical.

Sometimes the people in sunglasses are flying, super heroes in V-formation, like geese. I am the leader. I swoop lower, the others trailing me. The Empire State Building looms before us. About to smash into it, crash to my death, I wake, punching the sheets, almost hitting Morgan.

—You hate me, she says. Trying to punch me while pretending to sleep.

—No, no, it was a dream. It's not about you.

Spy Optics. Reptile. Utopia Optics.

Last night a troop of Eagle Scouts wearing sunglasses was climbing the flagpole in front of the San Jose Mall. In which the Marine recruiting office is situated. In which Nia works. I was the leader, and as I reached the top, was about to kiss the flag, the pole collapsed, buckled in on itself, I crashed to the ground. The dream left me upset, angry at my subconscious. It should aim higher than phallic symbolism. But the message disturbs. Is it a knowing portent? Is Cassandra mocking me? Is Viagra lurking around the corner?

We don't spot the cougar again. Remain silent most of the way back to the stable, thoughts circling like that hawk. Thoughts of love, thoughts of death.

—I didn't want to mention it out on the ridge, she says, but you seem on edge this morning. Anything you want to talk about?

I could tell her I'm madly in love with her, want to hug her, kiss her, make passionate love with her, even though she's Mickey's girl. Tell her my nurse Vicky and her daughter are being threatened with mutilation, rape, death. Tell her one of my old victims, whom she knows nothing about, showed up in my operating room, almost disrupting a surgery. Not to mention my wife's continuing coma, of which she is aware, and my son's being out of touch in one of the world's shooting grounds, of which she is also aware. What is there to be on edge about? .

—I'm just a little tired.

—When was your last vacation, Michael?

—Who knows?

—Let's play doctor. I prescribe that you take a long weekend, at the least. Maybe go to Santa Fe. Eat chile, this is the season, I've heard. See that niece you adore. Come back refreshed. A new frame of mind can do wonders. And Michael?

—What?

—That's an order.

A weekend away. Not a bad idea.

Let's play doctor.

This staff sergeant will drive me crazy.

At least she's not Lolita, who was 12.

The horses, despite their large ears, do not seem to listen to any of it. Perhaps they have their own concerns.

As we drive home, mostly in silence, with cumulus clouds overhead in a deepening blue sky, an image from *Gatsby* overtakes me. The Eyes of Dr. Eckleburg — that billboard over the road, eyeglasses looking down at the people below, seeing everything, all their crimes and frailties. Like a god. My son, out of sight, out of touch in his distant bravery, has become my Dr. Eckleburg. Waiting, preparing to judge.

Chapter Seven: Lacey

I arrive at the office at 12:22 for my 12:30. Vicky informs me my 1 o'clock has canceled, she's got Dr. Roberts coming by to examine me.

—What was the rush?

—Something went wrong with your eyes yesterday in surgery, Dr. Lee, that was the rush.

—Any indication from the board that they have the missing DVD?

—Nothing yet.

Soon I'm sitting in the high-backed chair in which my patients sit, leaning forward, yellow drops in my eyes, chin on the chin rest, the mass of blond hair of Lacey Roberts surrounding my vision of her astounding blue eyes as I peer into the lens of the split-lamp so she can check the pressure. Pale freckles in a band across the bridge of her nose and under her eyes remind me of the Milky Way. One eye, then the other. She backs away, sits on my stool, makes notes on a chart.

—Your pressure is a bit high, doctor. The right is 23, the left is 29.

—That's way too high. There's no reason for that. Check it again.

—I'll be a resident for three more weeks, Dr. Lee, but I know how to check pressure.

—Humor me.

She looks in my eyes again. A great red-orange ball is what she sees, of course, like a postcard of a flaming sun going down in Maui or beyond on a Polynesian beach. The photo as if taken with the slim branches of a tree hanging in front of the lens. The red-orange color is caused by the blood in the retina. The branches are the veins and arteries going in and out. I've probably seen those inner suns a hundred thousand times.

She rolls the lens against my eyes again.

—Now I get 24 and 29. Nothing to worry about, as you know.

She holds up different numbers of fingers at different angles to my eye. Slender fingers, clear polish if any. I rattle them off. She runs through all the usual exams, checking my retinas, optical nerves, corneas, the whole catastrophe.

—When was the last time you had your eyes checked, doctor?

I laugh.

—Me?

Think back.

—That would be in med school.

—It figures. That's probably true of everyone in the department. You're long overdue. You don't have glaucoma . . .

—Good thing. Imagine going under the knife of Jack Beecham. We need to find a new glaucoma doc.

— but I want to check for a precondition.

She presses a button on her pager.

I stand from the chair. Lacey with her thick blond hair resembles that young actress, she was in Legally Blind, what's her name? Out of Dickens . . . Witherspoon! Who reminds me of a teacher I had a crush on in grade school. Odd, the images that stick. Life's eternal retina.

Isaac, one of the ophtho interns, appears.

—Isaac will administer the test. It won't take but 15 minutes, as you know.

—This is nonsense, Roberts. I have patients to see.

—You're a patient now. You'll do as I say, if you want to remain my patient.

She's right, of course. I follow Isaac down the hall to the small room, more like a large closet, which contains the visual fields machine. He gives me the usual instructions. Look only at the center of the screen. Lights will begin to flash, small circles, some bright, some dim. He places a buzzer in my right hand. I feel like a game show contestant. Every time you see a light flash, he tells me, you press the buzzer. That's all there is to it. Is that clear? Yes, Isaac. Okay. Let's get your chin firmer in that stirrup. Remember, keep focused on the center of the screen. Otherwise the test is useless. I know, Isaac. Let's get on with it. Okay, I'm starting at the count of three. He counts and I begin to see the lights, mostly near the center at first Buzz. Buzz. Buzz. Erratic intervals, so that you don't just keep buzzing. Dimmer lights out near the periphery. That's the whole point, to check peripheral vision. Light-buzz. Light-buzz.

Then, impossibly, a light appears that is a word. Mona. My hand feels paralyzed, won't buzz. Another light that is a word. Addie. Sweat forms in my underarms. Amid normal lights at which I buzz I see more lights that are names. I don't know whether to buzz or not. Some I do, some I don't. Madeline. Janelle. Ginger. Francesca. Nadine. Gretel. Rosa. Rosalyn. More lights. Plain lights. Buzz, buzz. I think the names of all eleven victims have appeared. Okay, Isaac says, turning off the machine. Now let's do it with the other eye. There's cold sweat on my forehead as it presses against the leather strap. I'll begin now. Light. Light. Rosalyn. Rosa. Gretel . . . In reverse order, but all there. I'm exhausted as Isaac turns off the machine.

When I'm back in the patient's chair, Lacey is studying the charts. Could those names be there? Not possible. But if they are, how do I explain? A sneeze won't do it.

I'm losing it. I need to get a grip for surgery tomorrow. Ballet tonight with Vicky and Maya. Good Chinese food. Maybe that will help.

—What were you doing in there, Dr. Lee?

—What do you mean?

—There's no sign of glaucoma. But there's no sign of anything. You missed bright lights in dead center. But caught dull ones on the edge. You buzzed when there were no lights, many times. As if you were guessing. You missed far more than computes with your normal vision. Were you mocking me?

I reach for her hand to pat it father-like but she draws back as if she does not notice.

—Of course not. I would never do such a thing. I've heard only good things about you.

—What were you doing during the test, then, doctor? Daydreaming?

I'm not sure what to say.

—Probably.

—With all due respect, that does make a mockery of me. And the test, and the whole ophthalmology section.

She's got spunk.

—Let me ask you a question, Dr. Roberts. In three weeks you'll be a full-fledged doc. Doing surgery on your own. How come you've never come to watch me?

—That's a change of subject, Dr. Lee, but I'll tell you. I've been too timid to ask. You're Michael Alton Lee. Rumored for the Nobel Prize this year. Sure thing for the medical services chair, they say. Who am I, a country girl from Oklahoma, to bother you? To expect you to even notice me. You think I wasn't scared to do this exam? I almost threw up when Nurse Chen paged me. Mostly I've been observing Dr. Beecham. Besides, I am learning from you. Lots.

—You didn't seem very timid a moment ago.

—Because your sight is involved. I'll be tough with my patients, if necessary.

I stand, stretch my back. Feeling the horseback riding.

—How could you be learning from me? You've never been in my operating room that I've noticed. And believe me, I would have noticed.

A light pink blush under all that blondness.

—From your disks. Dr. Beecham's schedule is rarely full. When I have free time I borrow your DVDs and study them. You're the master. Your hands are so graceful as you work in the eye.

—Just one moment. Do you have yesterday's disk ?

—Is that not allowed? I had the evening free so I took the disk home. I was watching you perform in bed.

Another blush.

—I didn't say that right.

I want to hug her. I'm becoming a mental polygamist. Nia. Vicky. Now Lacey.

—Did you watch the last operation of the day?

—I'm afraid I fell asleep before the end. No offense, I was very tired. Was the last one something special? Should I borrow the disk again?

—Where is it now?

—I returned it to the shelf this morning.

—Lacey — may I call you that? I'd like you to assist me — in person — the next two days. Do some of the surgeries while I watch.

—Really? That's so exciting!

When your wife is in a coma, every affectionate utterance is welcome.

—But there's one thing, Dr. Lee. Next week you have to take that visual fields test again.

Without daydreaming.

—Whatever you say, Doctor.

Mrs. Newman is waiting. I'm scheduled to replace her scratched cornea next week but she has something in her good eye. It's been there for five days, she says. I check her eye. There's no foreign body in it, but she has a slight cornea condition. Dry eyes, I tell her.

—Dry eyes? I've been *kvetching* to my husband and my friends for a week and now I have to go tell them dry eyes? With all due respect, doctor, can't you do better than that?

—If the eye gets too dry, bits of the cornea lift off their moorings. It feels like a speck in the eye. You want the scientific name for the condition? Punctate epithelial evasion.

—Now you're talking! That's worth my co-pay any time. Say it again.

—Punctate epithelial evasion.

I write down the names of eye drops and eye gel she should use. Both over-the-counter

—Just over-the-counter? No prescription? Well, you know best. Punctate what? Could you write that down, too?

With my seniority, and especially as head of the department, I don't have to see office patients like Mrs. Newman, do routine eye exams. I could just do cataracts all week, like Jack Beecham with glaucomas, or Gene D'Anna and Farley Pike with retinas. But I like the interplay with people. Perhaps because of my early background touring the clinics. Perhaps to keep in touch with real people, as opposed to the black tie mummies at the functions Morgan used to drag me to. Doing only surgeries, with no idea whose eye is under the blade, you might as well twist a wrench on the Ford assembly line.

—How do your eyes get so dry, Mrs. Newman? Do you sit on the beach a lot, winds off the ocean?

—I do the *Times* crossword puzzle there. It takes me all week.

—Maybe you should bring a dictionary. Those drops will take care of it, but remember, sun off the water can be twice as bright. Don't forget your sunglasses.

Since sunlight can be focused to cause various materials to burn, imagine the effect it might have on a retina.

— Scrawled note for *A Brief History of Sight.*

As I escort Mrs. Newman to the door, Lacey Roberts comes bursting in, almost knocks the poor lady over, hurries through the waiting room to the inner suite, holding her smock across her chest. Drops into a chair. Son of a bitch! Son of a goddamn bitch!

—Lacey, what happened?

She sheds her folded smock into her lap. Revealing a rip in her turquoise blouse, part of a white bra showing.

—The old goat tore my blouse! Trying to get at my breasts!

—Jack Beecham? He's a hundred years old.

—He almost didn't make it to a hundred and one. I smashed his face with his camera. He fell like a redwood would, if those things ever fall. I made sure he was okay before I ran out of there.

Camera? I better go check on him. Then you can tell me what happened.

—I'll come with you. The old goat!

—First put on your smock.

Beecham is at his desk, gray suit, slumped over, mostly bald head reflecting ceiling light, hands covering his face. He straightens as we enter. A bruise is already purpling in the wrinkled skin beneath his left eye.

—Get her out of my office! She's a crazy woman!

—Calm down, Dr. Beecham. I want to hear both sides. You first, Dr. Roberts.

Lacey hugs her smock around her.

—I told him I'd be working with you the next two days. He said, I'm not surprised, Dr. Lee grabs all the pretty ones. But listen, do me a favor, he said. He pulled keys from his pants pocket and opens the bottom drawer of his desk. He took out a camera and asked if he could take my picture, for his scrapbook. Sure, why not? I stood by the wall over there and he clicked off several — it was digital — and then he said, Your white smock against the white wall doesn't show up so good. And your blouse is so pretty. Would I remind moving my smock? He was probably right, so I draped my smock over a chair. Ah, nice, he said, clicking a few more. Then he stepped closer and said, Now the rest. The rest of what? Your clothes. Some nude shots. Tasteful. It's for my church group. I'm was totally shocked, of course. Nudes? For his church group?

—Dr. Beecham, I'm surprised at you, I told him. I will not take my clothes off. He came closer. It's very innocent, he said, and he reached for me and cupped my breast. You lecher, I said, and as I tried to move away he grabbed my blouse and tried to tear it off. He's an old man but enough is enough. I was enraged. I wrenched the camera from his hand and smashed it across his face. He fell to his knee. I made sure he was just dazed, nothing worse — I should have just kneed him in the groin, I guess — and I grabbed my smock and got the hell out of there. I'm still shaky from it. And there's something else. In his drawer . . .

—Hold on, Dr. Roberts. One thing at a time.

Beecham, who had been leaning back in his chair, listening raptly, almost enjoying her tale, has brought his hands up to cover his face again. Through his white shirt I can see the outlines of an old-fashioned sleeveless undershirt. His collar button is undone, a dark blue tie no wider than two inches hangs down his chest. Slightly piggish cheeks, overhanging gray eyebrows, which make his eyes appear small, though all human eyeballs are the same size, about an inch in diameter. A double chin that merges turtle-like into his neck.

—Now your side, Dr. Beecham. If this is true, it's sexual harassment. Maybe even assault. You could be fired. You could go to jail.

Beecham clasps his hands on his desk, leans forward calmly. He moves a photograph in a faded beige frame out of his way. Black and white, an elderly woman, probably his wife.

—First of all, it is not harassment. All I asked her to do was let me take her photograph, to which she agreed. When she refused to disrobe, that was the end of it. I did not force her. I'm not her superior, so there was no implied pressure to make her comply.

It's sounding rehearsed, as if he had thought this through, more like a lawyer than a doctor.

—The rest of her story is delusion. I never touched her breast. I never tore her blouse. She's been reading too many of those bodice-rippers my wife reads. She went crazy, grabbed my camera and smacked it across my face. Almost took my eye out. I never saw that side of her before. She's the one guilty of assault.

—And her torn blouse?

—If her blouse is torn she did it herself. After she nearly killed me.

—Why would she do that?

—Ask her.

—Dr. Roberts?

—He's lying, of course. Why would I tear my favorite blouse?

—I'll tell you why.

Beecham leans back, ample belly visible, but points a shaking index finger at Lacey.

—She wants my job, that's why. I'm 74, another year before I have to retire. She's finished with her residency soon. She wants me to get fired, so my spot will be vacant. Figures she'll waltz right in. That's what this whole sham is about.

—If you'll drop the paranoia, Lacey says, the end of my residency will be my last day here. I plan to go into private practice. In my home town. I happen to like Oklahoma. I happen to like Shawnee.

—You started the picture taking, Jack. You told her you wanted nude shots for the church? She couldn't be making that up. What's the church got to do with this?

Neither Lacey nor I interrupt as Dr. Beecham tells his solemn tale:

—When you get old you have to keep up your friendships. Especially if you're a widower, or if your wife is kind of not there, you know? So every Saturday afternoon a bunch of the boys would meet over at Graham Park to shoot the breeze, maybe play cards or checkers, whatever. Six of us if everyone was there, someone not home with the flu or an aching back. They're all retired except me, have plenty of time on their hands. So. A couple Saturdays ago, Manny Rickert shows up at the park carrying a manilla envelope. Have I got show and tell, gentlemen, he says. He looks around to make sure no one else can see and then he starts pulling pictures out of the envelope. Big ones, eight by ten, color, of the most beautiful girls. Naked. Posed very tastefully. Where did you get these? I ask. From the internet, he says. You've got the internet? My grandson is staying with us while his parents are on a cruise. A high school boy. He brought his laptop computer with him. I touch it the other day when he's not there, just out of curiosity. When the screen lights up, there is this gorgeous naked girl posed like that, showing everything. I start pushing some buttons — there are tons of nude pictures on there. Easy to print out. Some are disgusting, young girls performing . . . I won't go into it. . . even a pretty white girl on a big black . . . I won't go into it. But these models posing are so gorgeous, in the woods, on the beach. Be better if they didn't shave their . . . I wonder why they do that, it's not natural. Anyway, I thought I would show you boys, Manny says, give you a cheap thrill. When we finish passing it around — and around again — Sammy Belinski says, can you bring more next week? Maybe, Manny says, but you can all see them on your own computer. I'll tell you the sites. We look from one to the other, 75, 80, 83 years old. None of us has a computer. Who bothered to learn? Here in the office the scribes put in for me whatever needs to be there. Or the secretaries.

I don't know whether to laugh or cry. Is Beecham me in a few years?

—Well, I don't want to be the only dirty old man, Manny says, and then Jake Melcher says, He's right, let's all bring pictures next week. Maybe every week. We can each buy a Playboy, a Hustler, whatever they've got in those adult book stores, you know, and tear a few pages out for every meeting. So we won't have to spend much. And we pass them around. Like a club meeting. What, right here in the park? I ask. People will see us. Kids are playing. We can't do that here. Someone might call the cops. They all agree, but what to do? Then Ike Mahoney says, I know. At the church. We look at him like he's crazy. No, really, over at St. Bede's, they have community meeting rooms. We can see what's available. To look at naked women? We wouldn't tell anyone that. What are we doing then? We're looking at pictures. It's a photography club. Well, we all like that idea. If we can get a room, it will be the St. Bede's Seniors Photography Club. No one under 65 admitted. So Ike talks to Father O'Brien, and he thinks that's a fine idea, a photography club for seniors. He checks the community schedule, and a room is available on Thursday nights. It's small, the priest warns Ike, but that's fine, Ike tells him, we'll just be swapping photos and comparing them, to improve our own work. We don't need a big room, we like a small membership anyway. So everyone can show off their pictures each week. The priest likes the involvement of seniors. Our wives — those that still have them — love it that we'll have a hobby to keep us busy. Also get us out of the house Thursday nights. The room has a lock in the doorknob, it's perfect. So we meet once or twice, with torn pictures from magazines. It feels delicious, like little boys smoking cigarettes in the bathroom.

My wife boasts about my new club to my son, Johnny, he's in real estate, Project One Homes. He thinks hobbies are great for old folks, for when I retire, so out he goes and buys me this camera. A Canon, digital, all the gimmicks. I thank him, and wonder, what the hell am I gonna do with this? Then it comes to me. All these beautiful nurses walking around the hospital. Interns, residents. If I brought in nude pictures of real women each week, I'd be the king of the club. Lacey here is so beautiful, and I've been working with her, so she was to be the first. See, it was all very innocent. Nobody would see them except six old men at the church. Who can hardly get it up any more. What would be the harm? It would be a charitable deed by those who posed. I didn't need my head cracked open by Nurse Lacey here.

—It's Doctor Roberts!

—Yes, of course. I'm from the old school, sometimes I think all the women in white are nurses. That's how it was when I started out. Right, Dr. Lee? Oh, here's one more thing. One night while we were passing pictures around there was a knock on the door. We all froze, said not a word. A key turned in the lock, and the door opened. It was Father O'Brien. We shrunk in our chairs but it was too late to hide the pictures. The priest walks around the table, looking at them. We're so embarrassed. Then he asks if he could join the club. What? I mean . . . but he says he's a man, just as we are, he enjoys looking at pictures, too, if we don't mind. Well, how could we mind? It's his church. So the next week we're all kind of nervous, but we calm down, the priest knows what to expect. He's a little late, but he comes. When it's his turn to show pictures, he reaches into his black jacket and pulls out a small envelope of photos and begins passing them around. The pictures are of boys — young boys — doing things I won't mention. These photos are old, these things do not go on any longer, too many lawsuits, Father O'Brien says, but looking at the old snapshots is rather titillating, don't you think? What can we say? We pass around the pictures of the boys, trying to look interested instead of throwing up.

—The priest is relevant because? I ask.

—To show that everything was on the up and up. I was not going to put Lacey's tits on the Internet or something. I wouldn't know how.

He leans back in his chair. I imagine him lighting up a cigar

—So, how about we do this, Beecham says. I agree not to press charges for getting assaulted with my camera. Dr. Roberts drops her modesty hissy-fit. We forget the whole thing. I'm sure Nurse Chen will pose, I should have asked her first. Chinese charms will be a revelation to the guys.

—Before we do this cozy deal, Lacey says, open your bottom drawer, on the right.

Beecham glares at her, flames burning in his eyes.

—They're for my wife.

—Two thousand Vicodin! I saw them when he took the camera out.

—My wife is a sick woman. She's in pain. The doctors won't believe her. They say she's just addicted to the painkillers. I can't write enough prescriptions.

I jump in, horrified.

—You steal them from the pharmacy?

—I don't steal. I pay for them. A fellow who delivers from the warehouse. Every Wednesday, eight in the morning, I meet him before he turns into Hospital Drive. I pay him half the wholesale price. He needs the extra money for his family, I need the pills for my wife. If the hospital finds a shortage, they blame the trucking company, which blames the wholesaler, which blames the manufacturer.

By the time this is finished, another shipment is being checked in. Same amount. Piddling to everyone. Except my wife. So they start ignoring it.

—As head of ophtho I'm your superior, Dr. Beecham. Harassment I could ignore this one time, if Dr. Roberts agreed. But not detouring drugs. You're taking early retirement. Tomorrow morning I want your resignation on my desk. Effective in two weeks. If it's not there tomorrow, this gets reported to the brass. If they choose to bring in the police, or just fire you, erase your pension, that's their business.

Beecham's face is white. He looks helpless as a broken balloon lying on the asphalt in the rain. With a huge truck approaching.

The rest of the scene is a morality play as he forces himself to look at Lacey.

Beecham: Since we are telling tales, perhaps you should tell Dr. Lee what goes on between you and Dr. Postlethwaite every Tuesday and Thursday in the linen room across from 306.

Lacey blushes red to her blonde roots. They can see the blush in Shawnee. She is not cowed.

Lacey: Sex between consenting adults is still legal.

Dr. Lee: Yes, California is a Democratic state.

Beecham: On company time?

Lacey: During lunch hour.

Beecham: I'm sure that will soothe his wife as she picks up their twins at kindergarten.

Lacey: What? David never told me he was married!

Beecham: He doesn't tell any of them. Why would he? It might undercut his British charm.

Lacey: The bastard! I broke up with him last week. You know why? He tried to set up a camera in the linen room, to photograph us.

Beecham: The old two camera trick. He lets the woman see one, covers it with a towel, as if it isn't his. They let their guard down. Do everything. The other camera is better hidden. At a better angle.

Lacey: I don't believe you!

Beecham: He owes me action prints. For the photography club. That's why I figured you'd pose for me. Instead, I get bashed for it.

Dr. Lee: Enough of this. Dr. Beecham, you'll have your letter of resignation on my desk in the morning. You, Dr. Roberts, will be in the ophtho holding room at 7:30 a.m. sharp. Scrubbed.

—Yes, doctor.

—Well scrubbed.

I can't tell if the shadow in her darkening eyes is hurt or hate.

Chapter Eight: Maya

Ken Chen, or Ken-Chen as they call him, is a strange-looking man, tall for an Oriental, with straight black hair shooting up three inches from his head in all directions. Carefully coifed that way. Tonight he's wearing a stylish gray suit, yellow shirt with white collar, gray tie, polished black shoes. A modern young Oriental businessman on the make. He approaches our table at Mr. and Mrs. Ling's soon after we're seated near the kitchen. From behind a red curtain we can hear the cooks at work. When we arrived we unexpectedly found Chen at another table with three scruffily dressed young men. Coincidence? I don't know. Vicky feels compelled to introduce her brother-in-law as he stands near us. Chen offers his hand to shake. I nod to him but do not stand, do not shake his hand. Impolite. Insulting. I realize after he lowers his hand that that might have been a mistake. Now he knows I know about his threats.

Maya murmurs Hi to her uncle Ken but does not seem happy to see him. Her slim young dancer's body has shriveled in her seat like a fearful puppy. She does not emerge from this posture until an older Chinese woman emerges from behind the kitchen curtain, wiping her veined hands on her apron.

— Grandma!

Maya leaps up and hugs her around the waist. Mrs. Ling kisses the top of her head, sinks to her knees to kiss Maya's face, to hug her.

—Where's grandpa?

—He's cooking, you know that, he'll be out when he can. How was the ballet?

—It was awesome, grandma.

Mrs. Ling closes her eyes for a moment, shakes her head at the slang. Maya is 11, but has made it clear she is going on 12. Vicky introduces me to her mother, I stand and offer Mrs. Ling my hand. Hers is as delicate as her daughter's. When she realizes I'm Vicky's nominal boss she clasps her hands in front of her chest, bows her graying head for a moment. Vicky is smiling through this. It's good to see her smile. I'm glad I have come, have witnessed this familial fondness. My peripheral vision records Ken-Chen watching us from his table, his face showing nothing. His friends, bent over, slurp their food.

—What would you like to eat tonight, Dr. Lee?

I glance at Vicky.

—Just bring stuff, Mrs. Ling, she says.

—Yeah, grandma, just bring stuff, Maya echoes. And tell grandpa I need a hug.

She sounds truly needful, is not just flattering him.

I still feel her small fingers in mine, in the balcony of the theater, after I trade for a seat beside them. Maya is between her mother and me, chattering excitedly before the lights dim, the curtain rises. Have you seen real ballet before, Dr. Lee? Yes, a few times. This is my fourth, she says. I wish they would hurry. Then she's total concentration during the performance, absorbing the story — the skeletons coming alive at midnight and dancing to the music of Saint-Saens. Marie Laveau, their leader, doing an old Cajun dance from the 1800s, seducing and winning handsome and top-hatted Death, who had hoped to remain a happy-go-lucky bachelor. The pale Moon taking it all in, like a scribe of the night. Maya studying the movements of the dancers, both rousing and sublime. She wants to bounce in her seat, I can feel the latent energy, but, ladylike, she doesn't. I glance at her every few minutes. She's sitting on one knee for a higher perch, head never moving. When Death stalks the stage she hungers for safety. Without averting her eyes her hand is groping for mine in the dark. I move it to the armrest. She curls her fingers into mine. We're friends. I'm her protector. I hope Vicky did not overestimate what Maya could deal with, at 11 — going on 12 —given that her father is gone and possibly dead.

I realize only later that not once did I connect the ballet skeletons with my living dead. Thanks to the child.

Subtle spring rolls, bird's nest soup, scallops with rose petals, vegetables in mild garlic sauce. Each dish exquisite as the exquisite Ling girls, Victoria's sisters, younger, twins, gliding among the tables delivering and removing dishes like water nymphs. Waving at Maya each time they pass to or from the kitchen. Too busy to stop and chat. The restaurant is surprisingly quiet, the diners savoring their food. Clearly it is a place you come to eat, not to gossip.

The front door opens, three men walk in, take seats near the front. I try to blink excess water from my eyes. The third man has the same wheat field of black hair. At this distance, in the dim room, he is Ken-Chen's double.

Drinking green tea from a small porcelain mug, I quietly ask Vicky, just above a whisper, who that is.

—Luc Luck, she almost whispers back. He's number two in the Golden Swords. He wants to be number one. The top two Sword leaders always wear their hair like that. It's symbolic of something.

—Of what?

Vicky hesitates, looks at her soup spoon, and at Maya, who is not paying attention. She raises her eyes to me.

—It proclaims that every Silver Bird has done things to them.

—Silver Bird?

—The gang's female auxiliary. Only the two leaders have automatic claims on them. The top leader has more claims than second.

—How do you know all this?

—Ken-Chen himself told me.

Vicky's sisters bring food and beers to Luc Luck and his two companions. I note Luc looking over his shoulder towards the front door, as if he is expecting someone. Closer to us, Ken-Chen unfolds a newspaper, holds it, is either reading the back page or shielding his face from view. On the front page I can see a boxed headline, a photo of the cougar in the jewelry store in downtown Santa Fe. New Mexico. It made the papers here, just as Nia predicted. Not a bad headline: Cat Burglar? I look back at Luc. He's glancing at the door again.

—It's brilliant, the hair styles, I say.

—It's disgusting!

—Not about the girls. But look. Suppose some of the gang are doing whatever they do, and Ken-Chen is arrested. His lawyers ask for a lineup, insist Luc Luck is in it. Or vice versa. The free one has an alibi, he makes sure he's with other people at the time of the crime. What witness could swear which one he saw? The tall hair is all they remember. So he gets off.

—You think?

—My guess is, that's the real reason. That doesn't mean the girls . . .

With a pause in orders, Mr. Ling steps through the curtain. He glances at Ken-Chen's table, turns to us. Maya jumps up, runs into his arms, hugging him, getting more top of the head kisses. Mr. Ling is lean, his hair thin but still black, he could be anywhere from 55 to 75. Vicky stands, holding her red napkin, and kisses her father's cheek. She introduces us.

—A busy night, I note.

Really wanting to ask what in hell Ken-Chen is doing here.

—Always busy, Mr. Ling says. We mostly finished now.

Vicky turns her back to Ken-Chen's table, whispers to her father. He appears surprised, answers back. Vicky resumes her seat, leans across to me, still whispering. Maya goes into the kitchen with her grandfather.

— I asked Mr. Ling what *he* is doing here, she says, nodding towards Ken-Chen. Mr. Ling said, your brother-in-law eats here a lot. Other gangs, too. You don't like them, there's nothing I can do. He pays good American money, he eats wherever he wants. I was so mad, she continues, I felt like telling him about. . .you know. But that would only make things worse. Maybe get Ken barred from the restaurant, but what would that do? Or dad might go to the police. The gang could take revenge on my parents. I don't want to get mom and dad involved.

—Still, it was stomach-churning, eating with that slime ball right there.

—Oh, I'm sorry. You didn't like the food. I should not have praised it so much.

—No, no, Victoria, the food was wonderful. It's just that I'm on edge. Wanting to go tell him off. Wanting to punch his teeth in. He's young, but he doesn't look that strong.

—That's not a good idea. He has a gun under his jacket. Or a knife. Always. That makes him very strong.

Mrs. Ling seats herself in Maya's vacant chair. Vicky and I had passed on dessert — too stuffed — but Maya emerges through the red curtain with a bowl of chocolate ice cream and a spoon. She sits on her grandmother's lap, begins to eat. Spoons some into Mrs. Ling's mouth. Mrs. Ling grins, wipes her lips with a napkin. Her arms are around Maya's waist.

—Maya, you're getting so big. I don't know how much longer I can hold you.

—Sorry, grandma, Maya says, and slips off her lap, sits beside her mother. Just then a commotion erupts as the front door, also hung with a red curtain, opens and two men burst in, pointing weapons.

—Okay, nobody move. Stay where you are and no one gets hurt. Put your hands on the table and keep still. These are AK47s. Anyone moves and you're all dead in thirty seconds. You— pointing at the two waitresses — down on the floor.

This from a slim man wearing a black ski mask, black sweat pants and shirt, black tennis shoes, as he moves up the center aisle toward the kitchen, slowly swinging his rifle from one side of the room to the other. Remaining just inside the front door is another man, dressed exactly the same. He, too, is moving his weapon slowly from side to side like the revolving beam of a lighthouse. There must be twenty diners left, frozen. Nobody moves, but I notice Ken-Chen taking a sip of tea before placing his hands on the table. Mr. Ling comes out from the kitchen, wiping his hands on a towel, to see what the commotion is.

—You — pointing his rifle at Mrs. Ling — Get the money from the register. All the bills. You — he points his rifle at Mr. Ling — you have a safe in the back. Open it and give me the cash.

The hush in the room has a wounded air. Mrs. Ling silently glides behind the counter to the old-fashioned cash register. Mr. Ling disappears behind the curtain. The register pings as Mrs. Ling opens the cash drawer. Maya leans toward her mother and whispers, Mama, what's daddy doing here? Shh, Vicky says, be quiet. Your father's not here. He is, Maya insists, that's daddy in the front, with the gun.

Without moving I let my eyes rove to the man. He's covered head to foot in black, except for eye holes. It could be anyone. I don't know what the girl is thinking. She begins to squirm in her seat.

—I'll show you, she says.

She stands and runs, past the man near us, down the aisle.

—Don't shoot the kid! I shout. Someone else has shouted the same words at the same time. Ken-Chen. He's also used the distraction to slip one hand under his jacket.

—Nobody else move, the leader shouts again.

The man near the entrance has not said a word. Maya rushes up to him.

—Daddy, it's you. How come you don't come home?

If the man's face reacts we cannot see it. He continues to point his rifle at the diners.

—Daddy, it's me, Maya, she says, and hugs him around the waist. The man tries to remain aloof, not notice, like a guard at Buckingham Palace. But he can't do it. The gun wavers. The ski-masked head looks down. Holds that position. Then like a melting snowman he drips to his knees.

—Nobody move, he says, without authority. He sets the AK47 on the floor beside him. He hugs Maya around her shoulders. Kisses the top of her head. Raises the ski mask above his lips, kisses her cheek, clutching her tightly.

The scene has caught everyone's attention. The robber near us is covering the whole restaurant with his automatic. Vicky's mouth has dropped open. Mrs. Ling emerges from behind the register, holds out in a shaking hand a fistful of bills. The robber grabs it.

—What's taking so long back there? he yells.

Mr. Ling is not in sight. The robber looks down the aisle at his buddy.

—Fuck this, he says, the hell with the safe. Let's get out of here.

He rushes down the aisle. His companion lets Maya go, stands, adjusts his mask. Grabs his rifle from the floor and follows his leader out the door.

The diners begin breathing again. Ken-Chen removes his hand from under his jacket. Mr. Ling emerges from behind the curtain, empty-handed. The diners begin applauding. They stand and continue clapping. Maya runs back up the aisle to her mother.

—I told you it was daddy, she says.

Vicky hugs her, her desperate relief apparent, the child a miner rescued from a cave-in, a soldier home from the war.

—What are they clapping for? Maya asks.

—For you, I tell her. You were so brave.

—I wasn't brave. That was my daddy. He wouldn't hurt me.

The applause trickles. Maya sits beside her mother, grabs her spoon, begins to eat her melting ice cream.

—Was that Lenny? I ask.

Vicky shrugs.

—Of course it was, mommy, who else would hug me like that?

—Sweetie, I say, how did you know that was your father? He was all covered up.

—The way he moves. In ballet school they teach us to study movements. His head, his arms, his legs. I knew right away it was him. But why was he robbing grandpa's restaurant?

—I don't know, Vicky says, her words catching, like plastic bags in trees. The main thing is, no one got hurt.

Mr. Ling moves behind Maya, puts his hands on her shoulders as she scoops up more ice cream.

—That's the second time in a month, he says. Never police near when you need them. Sorry you had to be here, Dr. Lee.

—Not a problem.

— If one of those thieves was really Lenny. . . his voice trails off. I'm sorry, Victoria, you know I never trusted that boy.

—I'm all mixed up, Vicky says. Her hands are shielding her cheeks. If that was him . . . Look how he hugged her. Why doesn't he come home?

She spreads the fingers of her left hand in front of her, stares at them.

— I guess I'm still married, she says.

—My ice cream is melted, Grandpa. Could I have a little bit more? Maybe strawberry this time?

—Let's go see what we have.

They disappear behind the curtain like actors at the close of a scene.

I drive home, Vicky in the passenger seat. Maya in the back who normally is quiet, is chattering. She's wound up no doubt by the robbery, her peripatetic father, the ice cream. The clock on the dash shows 11:30. This must be way past her bed time.

—Do you know where I'm going Saturday? she asks. Pause. Guess!

—To see the seals at Monterey?

—Nope. Seen them lots. They're cute.

Not the time to tell her the seals look cute, their eyes like little pools, not because they have pure souls, as some would have it, but because their corneas are flat.

—Actually, I like the zoo better. Because you can see all kinds of critters.

A thought for the evening: Earth as a cosmic zoo, upon which the hundred billion gods rely for entertainment. *Do Not Feed the Humans.*

—Is that where you're going? To the zoo?

—Nope. You want to guess again?

—I think I'm out of guesses. Why don't you just tell me.

—To a *Bat Mitzvah.*

—A Bat Mitzvah? I never would have guessed that.

—Do you know what that is, Dr. Lee?

—As a matter of fact I do. Whose Bat Mitzvah is it?

—My best friend from ballet class. Anna Wu.

—Really? Anna Wu is having a Bat Mitzvah?

—Anna Wu Goldfarb, Vicky explains.

—Any relation to Joel Goldfarb, in coronary?

—His daughter.

—I thought he's a bachelor.

—He is.

—They do that? Adopt a girl to a single man?

—She was very young. Maybe because he's a doctor. All you M.D.s are respectable, right?

—I'll let that pass. Interesting, though.

—Half the Chinese girls in California are being raised by Jewish parents. Haven't you noticed?

—Not really. I haven't paid attention, I guess. How do you feel about that?

—It beats the heck out of drowning us.

An involuntary shudder. I stop at a crossing zone, let people pass in the semi-dark. Half shadows in the foggy glare. Eleven women. All in white.

I press the accelerator, lightly. Maya is quiet, may have fallen asleep. Vicky smiles at something in her head. My thoughts are back in the restaurant. Luc Luck knew the robbery was coming. That's why he kept glancing at the door. Mr. Ling took his time coming from the safe, and never did bring out money. As if he were confident no one would get hurt. If Mr. Ling is more than a kindly restaurant owner, is somehow in league with Luc Luck, why rob his own place? More than that. Why would Ken-Chen, leader of the same gang — who did not seem to know about the robbery in advance — dare to threaten Mr. Ling's daughter and granddaughter, Vicky and Maya, both of whom the old man clearly loves? Turn and turn about, like the pebbles in Molloy's pockets. No way it computes.

All the way home I sense I am being followed. First to Vicky's place, whose location Ken-Chen is well aware of. Then to my own. I have no certainty that this is real, or merely a ghost of my anxieties. They know from my refusal to shake Ken-Chen's hand that Vicky has confided in me — a doctor, an authority figure, most likely, in their street eyes, one station short of the police. Is this to instill fear in me, a warning not to intervene? I don't know what kind of vehicle Ken-Chen drives, or any of his gangbangers. I could not have identified their vehicles in any case. Headlights in the night. I can only hope they belong to strangers.

It's after midnight when I turn the engine off. I hurry into the house, do not want shadow guests behind me. Nia has already gone to bed. Does Mickey, parachuting behind enemy lines, or picking off terrorists in some hot hell hole, or fraternizing with the enemy to obtain information, in danger every minute of being exposed, tortured, slain — his head severed from his neck with a dull saw — does he think about her, fantasize about her, turn his lonely night's pillow into her breast, as often as I do? I doubt it. Mickey has tasted her flesh. Presumably found it mortal. Sweet, delicate, robust, engulfing — yet mortal. He has no need to yearn for a goddess. Does she at all return my feelings? Is she, in her own eyes, less than forbidden?

Gucci. Prada. Dior.
Twisting and turning in a prison of sheets
Arnette. Goat Eyewear. Dirty Dog.
Sunglasses smudged, cracked, broken. Worn at a Devil's rally in my dream. Reflecting rain pelting the neon night. Ken-Chen and Luc Luck are bearing down on me, gorillas in *Donna Karan* shades. Carrying M-16s. I leap into the river, feet crunching broken glass. Broken glass the shattered windshield of a bus. I lift my head above the surface to see where they are. They open fire from behind Nia, who emerges as the Devil. Their bullets are deflected by my *Rayban* wraparounds. They save my eyes. They save my life. I wake up sweating, my head filled with angry fog.

In the morning we leave for work at the same time. Nia relaxed in her cammies, her pony tail. Me facing surgery with apprehension. No more eyeball visitors, please.

—How did the inaugural night shift go? Any good recruits?

—Two winners, surprised to find us open. They took the literature. I'm hoping they'll be back. I'm pretty sure they will.

—Don't count your chickens, Nia.

—We're the United States Marines. We don't enroll chickens.

—You sound like a recruiter.

—And you have to live with me. Sorry about that.

I give her a friendly kiss on her cheek. She slides into her car.

—Nia, don't ever be sorry about that.

Chapter 9: Janelle

—The president wants you in her office ASAP. Also Dr. Roberts.

This from Vicky as soon as I arrive.

—Do you know what it's about?

—I have no idea.

—Is Roberts here yet?

—All scrubbed in the holding room.

—Tell her to remove her scrubs and meet me up there.

Dr. Shannon Kelly is behind her large mahogany table in her wheelchair. Violet suit, white blouse, bit of lace at the neck. Dark blond hair, which in her younger days she used to shake around sexily, cut short now. A bright window behind her makes it hard to see her expression.

—You wanted to see me?

—Yes, doctor.

She does not invite me to sit.

—You and Dr. Roberts were the last ones seen or heard talking to Jack Beecham yesterday. You were arguing. Please tell me what that was about.

I'm puzzled, my mind starts whirling. Why would Shannon — the president — care about that?

—Can you tell me why you want to know?

She lifts a gold pen from her desk, toys with it, clicks it open and shut.

—Jack Beecham murdered his wife last night.

—He what?

—Then he killed himself.

I sink into her maroon leather sofa. It squeals under my weight.

—This is not yet common knowledge. But it will be soon.

She picks up the pen again, but does not click it open. She seems to be making lines on her green blotter, without looking at them, like tic-tac-toe boxes, but the ink point is recessed.

—I can't . . . how did he do it?

She's a good president. Keeps the medical center on an even keel, to use the cliché. A sleek boat plowing through the always rough waters of financial gaps. This may be harder to handle.

—A pistol shot in the head. While she was asleep. Then he turned it on himself. No note, no obvious reason. The question is not how, but why. Did he appear suicidal when you talked, doctor?

— Not at all. He was not happy, but . . .

—Why was he not happy?

—Because I fired him.

I'm frightened by the forthright sound of my own words. They take my breath away. I'm not sure about hers. I see myself being thrown overboard.

—You did what?

The first sign of emotion in her rising voice. As if the WHAT were capitalized. There's no point sounding defensive. Not about this.

—I fired him. I had no choice.

—Beecham was not a great doctor, but he was adequate. He'd be gone in a year. Why the hell did you fire him?

Lacey Roberts knocks on the door, opens it a bit.

—Please wait outside for a moment. Well, Dr. Lee, I'm waiting.

I'm still trying to absorb the information. Murdered his wife? Because of her pain? Then himself? I think back.

—With all due respect, Dr. Kelly, it would not be in the best interest of Coastal Cal to reveal the substance of our conversation. Nor should Dr. Roberts. The public would . . .

—I am not the public, Dr. Lee. I am the president of this hospital. Tell me what happened.

I take a deep breath, ease it out, like a swimmer. Just now, I could use gills.

— Dr. Beecham sexually harassed one of our residents. Assaulted her.

—This being Dr. Roberts?

—Yes.

—In what manner did he harass and assault her?

—He asked her to model for nude photos. Then he grabbed her breast.

—For that you fired him, instead of coming to me? There's not a male doctor in this institution who has not squeezed a nubile tit now and again. Present company not excepted.

—Me? I never . . .

—Don't say never, Michael. I was the tit-ee.

—Oh, Christ! That was so long ago. At a Christmas Party. I was drunk.

—Your wife was back on Long Island, tending to her dying mother, as I recall. You woke up in my bed.

—But nothing happened. I was never unfaithful to Morgan.

—And I'm a Venice Beach virgin. Between times of passing out, Michael, you passed in. Several times. You were rather good, for a sleep-fucker. Nothing happened because six weeks later I had my uterus scraped. It was going to be a girl, I think. I'd already chosen a name. Eva Marie Kelly. Before coming to my senses.

—Shannon — Dr. Kelly — you never . . .

—What good would telling you have done? You had a wife, who would not have welcomed the news. I realized also that a child just then would stifle my career. Attractive up-and-coming young oncologist. I'm quoting *Time Magazine*. That very month.

—You're still attractive.

I embarrass myself by saying that. But it's true.

—Right. So long as I keep my wheels shined and my neck covered.

She moves her wheel chair back from her desk with her arms. Gazes out the third-floor window as she speaks. Gazing into the past. As I am. My daughter would be almost 12 by now.

—But you may keep on being faithful to Morgan, if you wish. Like mind-fucking in reverse. Exactly a year to the day from my abortion, I went skiing in Aspen. To forget what I had done to our child. It was bothering me as the anniversary approached. On a Sunday afternoon, my friend Suki wanted to see the local ballet company, a matinee. They're very good, she says. I've heard that. They tour the country. Even Europe. But they were doing *The Nutcracker*. If I have to sit through that one more time, I'll die. A ballet review in New York years ago actually said it. *We are one Nutcracker closer to death.* My feeling exactly. So Suki watches the Sugar Plum Fairy while ski-bird Shannon tries to knock down a tree. I hate that fucking ballet.

She turns back toward me. The past has passed like the Rose Parade. Leaving no trace.

—That was 12 years ago. Now, tell me again why you fired the horny bastard for copping a feel.

My mind is wheeling with this infidelity of which I have no recall. A daughter lost?

—I'm afraid there was more.

I tell her about the drugs.

—A thousand pills? Shit.

She calls in Dr. Roberts. Lacey tells the same story.

—Are you going to release this stuff to the press? Coastal will look terrible.

—I'm going to think about it. We have to let the staff know now. About his death. If the police come, tell them you can't discuss what transpired. Doctor-doctor confidentiality. It's a personnel matter. Some such bullshit. They won't press it, the murder-suicide verdict was definite. Why he did it is not a police matter. I've notified his children in Ohio, the bodies will be flown there. I suppose we'll have to arrange a solemn, heartfelt memorial. Flowers. Music. Saturday afternoon, I think. And Dr. Roberts, blonde to blonde, keep away from Postlethwaite. He fucks and tells. Not good for your resumé.

Lacey's fair face is apple-red. Shannon seems to realize she was harsh.

—Back in my day we had Lion Tamer Jones. He left, thank God.

—Why Lion Tamer? Lacey asks, chastened, her voice smaller than usual.

—Because every time you saw him approaching, you made sure there was a chair between you.

Lacey grins. As we leave, my face, I sense from cold sweat, is ice white. Do I have to add Jack Beecham to my victims list? We walk together down the long, snot green corridor towards ophtho. Not making eye contact with anyone.

—What was that, Dr. Lee? Victims list? You just said something about a victims list.

—Did I? I was daydreaming aloud. The way I daydreamed though that glaucoma test. Instead of flashing lights, I was seeing names. Women's names. Dead women.

—Dead women? Your victims? You don't lose patients doing cataracts.

—Not patients. Mostly nurses. Is it thirteen now? Does Beecham's wife count, too?

—I don't understand. You're frightening me, Dr. Lee.

I snap out of it.

—Dr. Roberts, are you and I responsible for Beecham's death?

—Lots of people get fired. Most don't kill themselves. Or their wives. He must have been a very troubled man.

We reach the door to ophtho. Suddenly it feels like a sanctuary.

—It makes me wonder, though.

—About the meaning of life?

—About whether the church's dirty picture club is dead.

She tries to suppress a grin, doesn't quite succeed.

—Never underestimate the church.

—Is that the state motto of Oklahoma?

—It could be. I guess I shouldn't have whacked him with the camera. But when he touched my breast, in my mind I became the cow.

—Meaning?

—I come from a rural area. Still — I know this sounds strange — I'm uptight around farm animals. Cows, horses, pigs. I don't know why. One time I was crossing a field, nothing to worry about it, just one cow and one calf in there. I stopped to gaze at a beautiful sunset. Suddenly the cow, who'd been grazing, lifted up her huge head and charged at me. Right at me. I was paralyzed, I thought only bulls did that, I thought I was going to die. The farmer yelled, Move, move, you're between the cow and her calf. So I moved. The cow didn't change direction, didn't come after me. Just loped to her calf and nuzzled it. When Beecham grabbed my tit, some inner circuit closed. I became the cow, grabbed his camera and whacked him. I needed to protect my own.

Running late, I check the day's schedule. Twelve straight cataracts, then a double: cataract and glaucoma in the same eye. Beecham is scheduled to do the glaucoma. Stan Rosen, the other glaucoma man, is on vacation someplace. When the hospital was new, we all did everything. With expansion, the brass felt specialists was the way to go. I haven't done a glaucoma in years. Only when one of my longtime patients insists on me. I tell this to Roberts. She says she did two glaucomas yesterday morning, Dr. Beecham watching. Both went well.

You're on, I tell her.

On a note pad on my desk I scrawl: Glaucoma — what is the root connection with coma?

I'm amazed I never noticed this before. Glaucoma meaning too much pressure in the eye. It can cause pain and blindness. Coma meaning vegetative state. Why do they share the root? Need to research.

—Note for *A Brief History of Sight*

Something else is zooming from the back to the front of my mind, like a guided missile. For 38 years I've been faithful to Morgan. Batting a thousand. Or zero, depending how you look at it. Now Shannon says I screwed her. Drunk as a Yuletide skunk, no memory whatever, but you can't argue with an abortion. Why would she claim after all these years that it was mine, if it was not?

Morgan was not hurt by that infidelity. She certainly could not be hurt now.

I wonder if Shannon in her wheelchair is still capable. An idle, unworthy thought. Or is that empathy? I can't control my own brain these days. Here is Lacey, a gorgeous country lass, returning home soon, sullied by Postlethwaite. She admires me. Perhaps willing. Here is Victoria, a Chinese work of art, delicate as rice paper, tough as a bamboo lance, husband a hood. She's about to divorce him — and likes me. The thought of making love with any of them excites the blood. It also turns Cassandra salamander on her head. Because I would be being unfaithful — not to Morgan, this time, but to Nia. Staff Sergeant Aphrodite Ruiz. Who if I suggested we make love tonight might just as soon shoot me as kiss me.

What we have here is a lack of communication. Thank you, Paul.

The road to madness is bumpy. I jog along it willingly. We can do what we will, but we cannot will what we will.

Patients are backed up in the holding room. Three instead of two. Resting in their beds under light tranquilizer. First up is a big wheel in Silicon Valley. Multimillionaire. I don't have permission to use his real name. Call him Appleseed. Tom Appleseed. Always difficult during exams. Won't look right, left, follow fingers, hates following instructions. With difficult patients I tape their foreheads to the bed, so they can't move around. Vicky's already taped him, the sweetheart.

Apprehensive. First surgery since Mona Drew two days ago. Will another victim appear today? How to react? Anaestho doc puts the oxygen tubes into his nose, deadens his right eye. EKG wires already taped to his chest, under the blue drape.

The valley mogul reminds me of an incident some time ago. The great dot. com bubble was bursting. Striding down a corridor, I hear two residents bitching about the dough they lost. Because of those crooks at Global Crossing, those jerks at JDSU. What rotten luck they'd had. What a terrible fate had befallen them. They certainly deserved better. I peer through the doorway from which this garbage is emanating. The shitheads are bemoaning lost paper profits beside the bed of a woman dying of pancreatic cancer. She is not yet 50. A sunken body that might have been fine and full two months before is barely noticeable beneath the thin blanket. Tubes are taped to every part of her. An emaciated face all eyes. Her large, dying eyes are following the bitching of the two schmucks, back and forth, back and forth, with such astonishment as you sometimes see on faces of the suddenly dead, but rarely on faces of the living. I want to grab them, slam their heads together. Hard. Break their skulls against a wall. See blood run. Perhaps provide the dying woman her final smile. Instead, with ostentation, I copy the names from their badges onto my clipboard, and I leave the room in a rage. My cross to bear: I never reported those idiots. Some carts of shit you don't overturn and stay in the fast lane.

I go to work on Appleseed. Slit the sclera, down under the cornea, into the eye. Apprehensive as never before. Phaco the lens. This is when Mona appeared. Nothing unusual now as it breaks apart. No face. No skull. I begin to scrape and crack. Relax. Lacey at my left, watching. You have consecrated hands, doctor, she says. Vicky at the foot of the bed turns away, hiding a smile.

Done with Appleseed. No problem. I let Lacey do the next. She's good. We alternate through the morning. I begin to hope the return of Mona was isolated, a solitary aberration. But I'm not confident of that. A phrase flits through my head: Beware the glaucoma.

Lunch break. I scrub down, buy a tuna sandwich from the guy in the corridor with the food cart. Chocolate milk in a waxed carton. Vicky is brown-bagging it in the empty holding room, as she does every day. I invite her to join me in my office. We sit on opposite ends of the couch. I can smell her egg salad. She's also got orange juice.

—Thanks for a wonderful dinner last night.

—Also a wonderful robbery, she responds.

—I meant to pay.

—Mr. Ling picked up the check. The robbery was strange, though. Did you notice Luc Luck. He knew it was coming down.

She's an observant young woman.

—Yes, I did. Your little girl is brilliant, though. Spotting her father through his movements.

—He's become gay now. Not flamboyant, but it's there. Maya doesn't know what those movements suggest. They were not noticeable when we were together. But it seems he and Maya played dress up sometimes when I was at work. San Francisco seems to have unleashed the inner Lenny. That's why he doesn't come back. He doesn't want me. He wants to keep his secret up there. Ken-Chen lets him be in the gang so he can pretend he's macho. Get his hands on teenage boys. Only because he and Lenny are brothers.

—You knew this all along?

—I knew none of it. I blamed myself for not being attractive enough.

—You figured it all out last night? Get any sleep?

—Not much.

She looks at her hand, puts down her sandwich, removes her wedding band, drops it into the pocket of her lab coat.

—I guess I'm not married after all. Or won't be, as soon as I file the papers.

—How was Maya this morning?

—No different. Off to school as usual. But she knows what's going on — without knowing she knows.

—One thing makes no sense, though. How could they threaten you and Maya, with Lenny in the gang?

She takes a bite of her sandwich. Unlike me, she is able to eat egg salad without it dribbling into her lap.

—Lenny doesn't know about the threats. He's not in the inner circle. They don't tell him anything, I suspect. Just let him carry a gun. Play at being tough. One thing surprised me, though. When Ken-Chen shouted not to shoot Maya. Maybe he has a heart after all.

—Maybe. Or maybe he was just protecting his hold over you.

—Yes. I thought of that, too.

Last surgery of the afternoon. The cataract-glaucoma double. Are the dead women acting in concert? Will their pattern be the last of the day?

Spooky action at a distance.

That was the aging Einstein's description of quantum mechanics. In which he refused to believe. Until it was proven correct. Still he objected. Becoming, in the eyes of the bright young nerds, a dinosaur. As I am to Nia?

What better description of Mona appearing in Jimmy Doyle's eye than spooky action at a distance?

Nobody understands quantum mechanics, Richard Feynman wrote. He being a leading theorist of quantum mechanics.

Does anybody understand in-loveness? Certainly not someone in love.

Quanta may exist, Einstein relented at last. But insisted the theory is not complete.

In-loveness is spooky action up close.

Shirley in administration has purchased a round trip ticket for me to Albuquerque. After my last surgery tomorrow. I'll spend a weekend away, visit Annabel, as Nia suggested. My nerves are on edge, I should have planned the trip for today, canceled tomorrow's appointments. But that would not have been fair to the patients eager for me to poke them in the eye.

Last patient of the day. Mrs. Thornton has the honor. Elderly.

—You'll do just fine, Mrs. Thornton.

But will the surgeon?

I try to relax. Slice the sclera. Probe deeper into her eye with the instruments. Know she can't feel a thing.

—You'll walk out of here seeing better than you have in years. That's a promise.

Lacey, listening, says Dr. Beecham never talked to his patients.

—Well, I do. Good eye-side manner.

Scrape away at a stubborn nucleus.

—Someone at one of my wife's charity to-do's once asked how I, such a sweet man, can bear to stick pointed metal in people's eyes. I replied, Maybe I'm not as sweet as you think. She smiled.

Lacey, too, smiles.

The lens is turning as I press and probe, trying to break it. It resembles a globe revolving. The entire earth in a single eye. Maybe the entire universe. Who can say it isn't there? That the rest is not illusion? Simple evidence: when you close your eyes it disappears.

Pull apart shattered pieces of lens with tweezers. Earth is covered by water, or so it seems. As in prehistory. Fossils of fish in the desert. In the lower right a dark fossil shape. Human. Hefty black swimmer clinging to the iris, as a child to the edge of a pool. Jesus! My knees weaken again, my throat dries. Desperately need water. Or Scotch. My eyes have become projectors of the past. My patients' eyes the receptors. There's a paper in that. Which I will never write. The hefty shape clarifies. Janelle Williams, New Orleans. The only black victim. My face begins to hurt, the entire right side, jaw to ear. I must have been crunching my teeth while I slept last night. Dislocated mandible.

Addie is angry at you. She gave me a message. How dare you try to replace her with that Nia chick? She's getting her claws out, I can tell you that.

Addie mad at me over Nia? Can the dead be jealous? *Getting her claws out.* I never saw any claws. That's one reason I fell so easily in love. Morgan had claws. Not Addie.

—Did you say something, Dr. Lee?

This from Lacey, watching me.

—Just mumbling to myself. Sometimes I do that in surgery.

Lacey seems satisfied. From Vicky I'm getting a jaundiced eye.

But I'm not just Addie's messenger You know why I'm here, Dr. Lee. You know damn well.

I don't want to hear any more from Janelle. Jab her viciously. She breaks apart. Is swept away in pieces. I clean up minor detritus from the nucleus, remove the cortex — the soft surroundings in the lens. Different people have different textures: fluffy, stringy or sticky. The three stooges of ophthalmology. Mrs. Thornton's is fluffy. Slip the artificial lens under the cornea. *Plastics*, Mr. Robinson advised Dustin. Was it him or someone else at the pool side party? *Here's to you, Mrs. Robinson.* Paul Simon. Second best three-minute evocation of American life I know. Eclipsed only by Dylan. *It's Alright, Ma (I'm Only Bleeding).* The lens fits nicely into place, not too much edging required. I don't seal the slices. Now it's Lacey's turn while I watch and refresh my memory. Mrs. Thornton has glaucoma in the same eye. Too much pressure inside.

—You're doing great, Mrs. Thornton. We're half way home. The cataract is gone. Now Dr. Roberts will get rid of your glaucoma. Stay relaxed, you still won't feel a thing.

The eye's drainage system is clogged. Eye fluid — aqueous humor — builds up. Too much pressure can damage the optic nerve. Reduce vision. Cause blindness if not treated.

Don't confuse this with tears. Tears are not the aqueous humor. Tears are produced by glands outside the eye. Moisten the outer surface of the eyeball.

That's what the textbooks say. We all know different. Tears are produced by the heart.

Lacey is in the eye, through the same incision in the sclera I made a few minutes ago. Replacing the eye's filter system. Drainage system. She has slim fingers for a buxom country girl. Cuts a piece out of Mrs. Thornton's iris, creates a channel into the subconjunctival space. Using the hardest-tipped blade we have. Lacey in the eye with a diamond.

Janelle comes swimming up the channel. Breast stroke amid the excess fluid. Against the tide. She wants her fifteen minutes. Her story is the ironic one. She was killed because she was pretending to be what she was not.

She grew up in New Orleans. After high school she got involved with a trumpet player named Coley in the French Quarter. With cocaine, too, as the night follows the day. When gigs were scarce he put her on the street to support their habit. Moved her up the Mississippi to St. Louis, Chicago, then across to New York. The Route 66 of jazz. One sleep-in stoned-out morning cops raided their East Village pad. Coley pulled a gun, and was shot dead by New York's finest. Janelle got five years in Rikers for possession. I'm not sure how long she was there when she began planning her escape. She faked a heart problem, was moved to the infirmary. Watched the nurses come and go. Selected one who was about her size.

I have to pay attention to Lacey. This is a good refresher course. She cuts away a bit of the sclera, creates a flap door in it that will let the excess fluid escape.

Janelle escaped by calling for the nurse, tricking her into the bathroom, bashing her. Removed the nurse's white uniform and put it on. A reasonable fit. Put on her ID tag as well. Moved through the prison infirmary, looking at charts at the foot of beds, moving toward the door. Out into the bright October sun.

Half an hour later she will be dead. Courtesy of yours truly.

More or less.

I keep her alive in my mind, of course, as I do all of them. Keep their lives moving forward, like Mona in Paris. I will explain it better later, now is not the time.

Aqueous fluid drains through the flap door into the subconjunctival space. From there the veins will drain it away. Lacey closes the incisions with nylon sutures. Good job, I tell her. She nods, leaves the op room. I don't follow her. I pretend to be checking her work, for the benefit of the anaetheseo and the tech. And Vicky. Janelle in the draining eye still has my attention.

So, what are you waiting for, Dr. Lee? How many excuses can you come up with? We need you down here, badly. You've been stalling for years.

She'd enjoyed her half hour of being a fake nurse. At Riker's she'd had to go cold turkey, she's been off drugs ever since. Returned to her family in New Orleans. Read nursing books. Faked her way into a small, desperate clinic and got real nursing experience. With a shortage of nurses everywhere, no one checked her credentials too closely.

You understand what I'm up to here. My psyche cannot bear their sudden deaths — *kaput!* — so I keep them alive. Continue their stories. Their life myths. I imagine what would have happened had they survived. The bedrock of my soul is cracked and fissured with guilt. By keeping their lives going I try to smooth it over. It doesn't always work, not entirely, but since I have not yet gone truly insane perhaps it helps. They are the exact reverse of a coma, in which you are alive but do not have a life.

Back to Janelle. By the time Katrina hits, she's working at NOLA's Charity Hospital.

Yeah, that was a couple years ago. Is it five years already? But people are still suffering from it. If you tread water in sewage, dunk under, walk through shit because that's what your neighborhood has become, an open sewer, you get diseases that last. The guvmint don't give a crap. Plenty doctors and nurses ran from the storm and didn't come back.

I told you at the time, I'm an eye doctor. I'm not qualified to treat other things.

You went to medical school. They must have taught you more than eyes.

That was forty years ago.

The human body change much since then? I been away dead, maybe it has. Besides, we got plenty eye trouble, too. Infections can cause bad stuff to happen to eyes. You know that, doc. Macular generation being one. You could help with that.

Degeneration. I'm sympathetic, Janelle. Really I am. But I've got patients here who depend on me.

Yeah, and you hopin' fo' a big promotion soon.

How do you know that?

And you hopin' to stick it to that pretty chick you livin' with. The dead know stuff. Don't you feel bad for killin' us?

Of course I do. I did penance, working in clinics for five years. Treating the poor, the uninsured

That weren't enough.

I save tons of eyes up here.

And get well paid for it.

Not as much as you might think.

Remember who you talkin' to, doc. I used to trade my body to strangers to get my man his coke.

You didn't have to do that.

Ever have the point of a knife at your throat?

I'll tell you what. I'll think about coming to New Orleans.

You'll think, my butt. You're a fake and a fraud, Michael Alton Lee.

The tech beside me clears his throat, loud. Snaps me back.

—Dr. Roberts did a fine job, I say aloud to the patient.

Lemme tell you 'bout one little girl, Dr. Lee. She six years old. Was a infant when her mama waded through that filthy Katrina water in the Ninth Ward, water to her neck, holdin' the baby above that sewage. Now she goin' blind, be six next month. Docs here don't know what to do. Don't know the problem. You could find it, Doc. I hear you the mose trussworthy, and ain't that a funny one. Y'all come down here and save that little girl's sight. You owes it.

Janelle, listen. I'm sure there are good doctors down there.

Not like you. She be my granddaughter, Dr. Lee.

I'm sorry.

Her name be Addie. After that nice nurse I work wid in New York. You owe me to fix her up. You owe namesake Addie to fix her up. Be your girlfren, no?

She hurls one last barb.

But you don't care nothin' bout us. Don't even play drums for us no more.

I close my eyes. My breath is caught on a nail in my chest. I wave the back of my hand at the others.

—Take Mrs. Thornton to holding. What are you waiting for?

Vicky enters my office without knocking, and sits on the sofa. Gray slacks today.

—She was back, wasn't she?

—Who?

—The woman in the eye, from the other day. Mona, wasn't that her name?

—No, she wasn't back.

—Michael — Dr. Lee — she was, you were off somewhere again.

—Today was a different one.

—A different one? Who was this one?

—I didn't know her. Just her name. Janelle Williams. From New Orleans.

—So why did you see her? Hallucinate her? Imagine her? Whatever it is you were doing in there.

My right hand of its own volition rubs my aching cheek. How to explain?

—I know how they died.

I wonder why I'm telling Vicky this. Tired, very tired.

—So? What does that have to do with you?

—I never told the police.

—Why not?

—It just wasn't . . . feasible. I didn't know the women would die. When they did, my information seemed pointless.

I do not want to lie to Vicky. But partial truths are not really lies. This is not a court of law. That horror I have managed to avoid.

—How long ago was this?

—Vicky, Vicky, Vicky. Almost forty years. I was in medical school.

—And you still have a guilty conscience. You know what that tells me, doctor? It reaffirms what a good man you are. But it's time to let it go, don't you think?

Her words are false of course, but not to her.

—Your weekend out of town should do you good. Enjoy yourself with your niece. I hear Santa Fe is beautiful. Forget about these hallucinations, or whatever they are. Let them go.

Suddenly I understand why they're appearing in the lenses of my patients. They died because of my eyes.

The notion of a guilty conscience is a fallacy. My conscience cannot be guilty. Only I can be guilty. Conscience can be many things: blind, deaf, amused, confused, troubled, uncaring, shrunken, diseased, infected, frightened, comforting — get out the thesaurus. But to be guilty requires action, and the conscience cannot act. It can only judge. It cannot commit a crime. Nor immorality. It wields no knife, no revolver, no cock. It cannot be punished, or put to death. Although it can be a damned nuisance sometimes.

I love Mencken's description of conscience: *The inner voice which warns us that someone might be looking.*

Con science.

The mutability of words is infinite.

So my conscience is not guilty. It is infected, perhaps. Itchy, yes. Tired, certainly. But the guilt is mine. I've whined time and again at dinner parties or in the cafeteria about the abandoning of New Orleans. My favorite American city. Addie and I planned to go there on our honeymoon. Crawfish and jazz and I'll race you to the bed. But what have I done to help? Admit the hypocrisy. I know I won't go. Janelle knows I won't even consider it. Morgan's coma is a good excuse. What if she awakens and I'm not here for her?

Fly to the Big Easy? Try to find that girl with the dying eyes? Addie's namesake? It would be worth a try. Except that she doesn't exist outside my head.

I suppose I could resume playing the drums for them. But I would rather be with Nia in the evenings than alone in a padded garage. How much should you give in to the blackmail of ghosts?

When I read books, certain lines will strike me in relation to the dead. I don't mark up the books, they seem like sacred objects. Which is silly. What's in them, what we transfer to our brain, is what is significant. Still, instead of a defacing mark, I place a two-inch square of stick-it pad, usually yellow, above or below the line I want to remember, perhaps come back to. Although most such pithy bits of wisdom sink into my brain easily, my brain perhaps trained by memorizing for med school exams the names of hundreds of bones. Two hundred in the hand alone. In *Anil's Ghost*, a novel by Michael Ondaatje, for instance, tabbed with a stick-it page, is the line: *A person will walk through a hundred doors to carry out the whims of the dead . . .*

For Janelle, there may in fact be something I can do. Return to my younger days. Work pro bono at a clinic, among the faces of fear and terror. Perhaps

Saturdays, when I'm off. But I need some time for Eyeful. Maybe alternate Saturdays. Perhaps at Mission House, now Mission Hospital, which has a new surgery wing donated by Apple. I could call them when I return from Santa Fe. See if they can use me.

Cut the crud. They can use ten of me.

Janelle knows how to manipulate. Most women do. I'm manipulated rather easily.

As soon as I leave the building my heart defaults to Nia. Love has no erase button.

Worse, it has no rewind.

Does Nia suspect? When dare I tell her? When dare I like Prufrock squeeze the universe into a ball to roll it toward the overwhelming question? Does she then throw her arms around me with reckless glee? Or does she spit in her future father-in-law's face? Do we make passionate love, in her bed, in my bed, on the rug? Or does she pack her undies — I've sneaked a look in her drawer — fold her uniforms and leave? Nothing between is workable. Until now my life has had two acts: Act One: Before Addie's Death. Act Two: After Marrying Morgan. A marriage which like Queen Gertrude's followed hard upon. The first act all games and dreams. The second all eyes and posturing. I assumed it would remain so till I die. (Organs donated. Do they harvest rusting genitalia?) Now Nia presents hope of a blissful Third Act. A self-made paradise on any beach on earth, or in a galaxy of our choosing, eating coconut, drinking mango juice, making endless love while turquoise waves suck enviously at our toes.

A horn honks loudly behind me. The long red light has turned green.

Mona, then Janelle. I can't sit still. I pace about the house. Nia is asleep. My legs carry me to my den. I turn on the overhead light. The Mexican box is exposed, naked. Kneeling beside it, I open the lid. I have not looked through it since the night of Morgan's stroke. The sunglasses that had been in her hand are on top. Then assorted papers, journals, clippings. Dad's revolver is still at the bottom. The clipping that Mona and Janelle are reminding me of is small, just below the sunglasses. It used to be near the bottom, under the gun. Maybe Morgan read it before her mind disappeared.

I lift it out, stand in the center of the room under the ceiling light. That doesn't feel right. I feel too exposed. I switch on my desk lamp, turn off the overhead. Sit. It's the first clipping that appeared back then. My hand trembles as I read it — as I've done once a year for forty years. I'm two weeks early this time. The newsprint seems to be more graying with age than yellowing. From the New York *Daily Mirror*, October 17, 1969. Bulldog edition. Bottom right corner of page 3, as I recall.

BULLETIN
**Twelve Die as Bus
Plunges into River**

> *A bus carrying 11 nurses at the Rikers Island Prison Hospital plunged into the East River late this afternoon, apparently drowning all those aboard. The bus was submerged for more than two hours before a construction crane crew could haul it out of the water. The upper bodies of the nurses could be seen hanging through the open windows. The identities of the nurses and the male driver were not immediately known. More than 100 nurses work the three shifts at the prison hospital, according to corrections officials. At press time police said they had no immediate details on the crash.*

No mention of my name. Or any witnesses. Every year I fear they will be there.

Part Two

Chapter 10: Annabel

Annabel Lee. How could she not be a rebel, with that name hung around her neck since birth like a seaweed wreath? My brother's youngest, 25 years old now, maybe 26. I don't know if Carl and Joan were aware of Poe's lament when they rigged that monicker to a bawling babe. When others pointed it out — I never dared, why make trouble in the family? — Carl would choke a bit and his jowls redden and he'd say of course we did, he's my favorite author, Edward Allan Poe. You can see why I might remain uncertain. Immediately they began calling her Anna — or Ann when she broke a plate or fractured a dog's leg with her tricycle — but her third year in Greenwich High School she asserted herself, became Annabel Lee, make dumb jokes, boys and girls, if you must, it didn't stop UConn from recruiting her. Flaky sixth woman on the Huskies basketball team her junior year, a superb outside shot. Majored in art. Then without waiting to graduate she fled family pressure urging her to switch to business administration. They wanted her to join the Carl Lee real estate firm, as her brothers had. Instead she escaped to Santa Fe to be a weaver. To weave her own destiny, she said.

I'm her favorite uncle (also her only.) Skinny as a twig, splattered with freckles, a mop of red hair like Orphan Annie, she doesn't wear a bra, doesn't need one. Strange to say, we bond. She's living the hand-to-mouth life I used to dream about in my poems. Rents a studio without running water down a rutted dirt road that represents the old Santa Fe, before they gussied up the town. My first stop each visit, before I check into the Hilton, is this studio, where she shows me her latest tapestries. Abstracts in subtle colors. Greens, blacks, blues of the sea. Wry comments on her name. Plywood shelves, spotted with gray paint from a former tenant, are piled high with colorful yarns.

She mentioned on the phone a cat that wanders in at times. She has to squirt it with a water bottle to get it out. It must love the colors, she said, but cats and yarn don't mix. I edge out of my wallet a sly paragraph I'd photocopied from Eckstein. I watch eagerly as Annabel reads:

Your dog sitting quietly at the edge of the universe and looking out sees black and white and shades of gray, nothing else, it is believed. A parrot sees color. A lizard sees color. Bony fishes do.

Crabs do. Turtles do. Rats do not. The cat does not. We have proven this for the cat, we believe, but no cat will commit herself in writing, and it is possible that she cheats during the experiments.

Annabel grins like a comic strip. She's wearing tight blue jeans, a dark green t-shirt that proclaims, across her barely existing and certainly unamplified chest, *I'm A Big Girl.* Can she keep the paragraph? Of course. She says the next time it comes by she will test the cat. Then in a natural but unspoken segue she asks how Aunt Morgan is doing. The segue being that Morgan is phobic about cats, always has been, never found out why. She's doing the same, I tell Annabel. There is rarely much new to report about the comatose. But thank you for asking.

—Hey, I almost forgot, she says. Congratulations!

—For what?

—You're gonna win the Nobel Prize.

—Annabel, where'd you get that? I'm not going to win the Nobel Prize. If I were it would have been years ago.

—No, really, my friend Bobby spends all day reading blogs. One from Sweden said this morning the new dark horse in the Nobels is in neuroscience, Drs. Michael Lee and Max Klonsky of the United States. Bobby calls, isn't that your uncle in California? Damn right it is, I tell him. Whoopee!

Dark horses, I remind her, are called that because they rarely get out of the barn.

—Oh, Uncle Mike, you're never serious with me.

—Count your blessings, I say.

I prepare to leave her place, check into my hotel for a nap. She has a date, she'd said over the phone, but we'll have all day tomorrow. She warns me not to eat a big breakfast, she's taking me somewhere special for lunch. Her grin is mischievous. Her entire lithe body is mischievous.

I try to relax over a steak sandwich and a beer in the hotel bar. The TV is showing baseball, Rockies against Arizona. The sound is very low. A blonde is drinking alone at the bar. Could be a hooker. That's not my style. I cruise down Cerrillos Road to a place I'd passed driving in. Cheeks. A strip joint. Some of them college girls, making ends meet by showing their butts. Hey, I haven't seen a woman's body in two years. I sit at the bar, order a Corona, swivel my seat to watch the stage. A firm young redhead is doing her thing to recorded music. *I Could Have Danced All Night.* A voice from beside me asks, Where you from? I turn. A short, stout woman on the stool is facing not the stripper but the bar. I don't feel like conversation, but she appears to be slightly retarded. I don't want to be rude.

—From California.

—That so? What do you do there?

—I'm an eye doctor.

—Hey, no kidding. That's what I am, too. What a coincidence, us meeting here like this.

Just what I need. A case. Pudgy face, fat thighs visible in the dim light below a short dress. I don't want to leave, I just got here. I don't want to diss her either, as they say nowadays.

—You work in a hospital out there? she asks in a hoarse voice.

The girl on stage is getting interesting. I keep glancing her way as I talk.

—Coastal California Regional Medical Center.

—Interesting. Must be big. My hospital is right down the road. Margie's Doll Hospital. You'd be surprised how many patients we get each day. Mostly it's the eyes that come off. Sometimes an arm or a leg, if a little brother pulled it. But mostly it's the eyes. I'm the eye doctor.

Red snaps off her G-string as she hurries off stage. Natural redhead, to paraphrase Mickey Spillane. *I, the Jury*. Required high school pass-around. Slipped inside Thomas Hardy. The boring one with Eustacia Vye. *Return of the Native*. Now Tess, Tess wasn't bad.

—How do you know my name?

This from my fellow eye doctor.

—I don't.

—You just said it. Tess.

—Really. I didn't know I was speaking out loud. Too many beers, I guess.

—Actually, it's Teresa. But most people call me Tess. Isn't it great, being an eye doctor? Seeing the smiles on those kids when they come to pick up their dolls. Find them all fixed up with a new pair of button eyes. Nothing beats a smile on a child. Isn't that right, Dr. . . .

—Lee.

—Ain't that right Dr. Lee? Hey, I got an idea. Us both being eye doctors and all, how about coming over to my place for a nightcap? If you know what I mean. It's just one street down. Second floor. Over the body piercing shop. We might could make a baby, buy it a doll, and when its eyes come out I can fix the eyes and make her smile. Or you could.

I look at my watch. I can't make out the time in the dim light.

—Sorry, I have to get going. Nice talking with you, Tess.

I head toward the exit as a pretty brunette on stage begins to unzip her sparkling red gown.

—Yeah. Everybody always has to get going, Tess says loudly over the pulsating music.

I slide off the bar stool, push open the heavy door. Step into Van Gogh's starry night.

Next morning my rented Corolla, white, gathers the dust of the earth as it bounces down the road to Annabel's studio. Where she also sleeps. She flings open the door, out she comes, behind another young woman around her age, curvier, black hair — so black it might be dyed, but no, with her tawny skin she must be Indian — a beauty at that — dangling a crash helmet at the end of one arm. The two of them embrace, kiss, long, with tongues and passion. Only when they pull apart does Annabel introduce her favorite Uncle Mike to her good friend Rebecca. Nice to meetcha, the girl says, stunningly built, white tube top, cutoff jeans. She climbs onto a gleaming Harley and roars off, me not knowing what to say. Annabel is weaving her own life. She reads my mind.

— Becky was voted Indian Princess during Fiestas.

And my skinny niece has got her. What is it the women say? You go, girl!

Sopapillas. You've never heard of them unless you've been to New Mexico. Northern New Mexico. I have them every visit. Mostly soft and excellent, sometimes greasy and cracking, over-fried. You tear off a corner of a good one, drop a bit of honey on it, you can have all the goat cheese and caviar and shrimp dishes in all the upscale restaurants in town, I wouldn't trade.

—You haven't had these, Annabel says.

We're driving twenty miles north to an old Spanish town called Española. Or rather she's driving. She insisted on taking her chugging old faded turquoise Ford with its muffler held in place by a coat hanger. She's making a point. She may not be getting rich from her tapestries, rugs, shawls, but she's getting by.

I have no idea what her parents think. They probably don't know about Rebecca. That's just as well. One look at the gorgeous Indian girlfriend and all except Joan would be drooling like me. Nowadays I can't be too sure about Joan, either.

We're seated at a wooden table in El Paragua, surrounded by blue and white Mexican tile. Soft amber lighting. No windows. I tell her a story, to stop from downing too much chips and salsa. I love stories, Annabel says. Her voice clapping hands.

—Once upon a time . . . she grins . . . I might as well start like a fairy tale, because it's a true-life fairy tale. This was in the 1860s, in Brazil. A boy named Santiago was what we'd call a gangbanger today — he led a bunch of streets kids in vandalism, thievery. Even though he came from a good family. He became interested in art, but his father had no use for that. Pop wanted Santiago to become a doctor. One day the boy saw a beam of light from outdoors create an up-side-down image on the wall. He became fascinated as to why this happened. That led him to photography.

I pause as our food arrives.

—The plates are very hot, the waitperson says.

—Anyway, studying photography led him to the human eye — to the retina. He did become a doctor, and the retina, where images are formed, became his preoccupation. Not much was known in those days about how the eye worked. Santiago wanted to find out. He read up on everything that was known. Then he began to experiment with the unknown, with the retinas of animals and fish. The rods and cones in the retina that absorb what we see and start them on their way to the deeper brain for deciphering. I'll skip the science, it gets kind of complicated. But he made exciting, breakthrough discoveries.

I dig into my food.

—This is delicious. So, Annabel, do you have any idea where the story is going? Why I'm telling it to you?

—You're telling me to stop hanging out with losers, to make something of myself. I hope you don't mean I should go into real estate.

—Hey. The story is about me, not you. I hadn't noticed that you hang out with losers. The Indian girl — Rebecca? — seemed very nice. That's the best way to learn about Indian culture. Up close.

I drown the start of a smile in my drink. Annabelle, over her drink, winks.

—I would never tell you what to do, kiddo. Unless you asked my advice. No, the way the story ends is that Santiago — his full name was Santiago Ramón Cajal — Santiago and another guy doing similar work were rewarded in 1906 with the Nobel Prize. The reason I'm telling you is that the work me and Max Klonsky did years ago was important — but in truth, it was an extension of Santiago's work. A breakthrough, but not nearly as original. If I had to guess, that's why we've never won the Nobel. Despite all the talk. And we never will. So. I love having you in my cheering section. But don't be disappointed in a couple weeks — whenever they announce the prizes — that we don't win. I've lived this long without it. I can keep living without it. Okay?

—Okay. But I can still hope .

—I'm hoping as well. Just a little. Nietzsche said, He who has a *why* to live for can bear with almost any *how*.

—You've been reading Nietzsche? I thought he was for us Gen-Ys.

—I've been reading Viktor Frankl. *Man's Search for Meaning*. He quotes the Nietzsche, relates it to life in the Nazi camps, where Frankl was imprisoned. Somehow he survived. He says only those who retained hope survived. Retained hope! While watching themselves turn into living skeletons. It's a good notion for us all. But difficult in practice. We pout over split ends. Curse blisters on our bowling hands. Groan at a flat tire.

—You're still searching for meaning, Uncle Mike? I mean, I am, but I'm only 25. Do you think you'll ever find it?

—I don't know. Looking at Morgan in a coma, I have to wonder. But hey, this is getting heavy. What I really want to know is, what did the cougar want on the plaza?

—You heard about that in California?

—They probably heard of it in Katmandu. Are they selling sculptures of it yet, like Kokopelli? The Cougar of Enchantment?

—It just happened a couple nights ago. By next week they prob'ly will.

I push away from the table, three sopapillas worth of new belly tightening my belt. Not to mention four chicken flautas with sour cream and guacamole. And a frozen strawberry margarita that Nia could bathe in, which Annabel talked me into. It sounded fey but hit the spot, cutting the hots of the chile. What the hell, I'm on vacation.

The margarita is deceptively strong. Before long I'm talking about Addie Judd. I hardly ever talk about her.

—I came close to being like you once, Annabel. A rebel. Before my junior year in medical school I spent a summer at Oxford. I studied literature. I sat on the grassy slopes beside the Thames and wrote bad poetry that I thought was good. So did a girl named Addie. I encountered her there one day. In an instant it was over for any other woman. She was as demure as a fawn, with a figure like a Rodin. We spun fantasies of traveling the world as itinerant poets, ancient troubadours living off the land. Young, foolish dreams. By summer's end we caved. Admitted the world required us to make a living. I went back to med school. She began work as a nurse.

—What happened?

I look down at my plate, empty except for a small patch of chile. I scoop it up with a spoon, swallow a flaming sword. My words come out burned.

—Long time ago. Doesn't matter.

Annabel lays her hand across mine. Rubs the back of my fingers.

— Sounds as if you still love her.

—Maybe I do.

She continues rubbing the back of my hand, offering comfort. Leans over, presses her lips to my thumb. I crave another margarita. But I might drown in it. Instead, I pick up a corner of the remaining sopapilla, hold it, admire it. Looking for Addie in its softness.

—These are incredible. I've never had them so soft and thin, yet also fluffy.

—Tawdry Española, sopapilla capital of the world. Even Calvin Trillin said so.

Gently I remove my hand from under hers. I hear my knuckles crack.

—They were well worth the drive.

Her mischievous grin again.

—That was just lunch. Not the reason I brought you here.

She stops and starts for several blocks, heading south through the center of town in traffic. Bears right to a stone bridge over the Rio Grande, flowing silent sweet and calm between banks of greenery. Not like the angry rapids I've seen boiling up under whitecaps near Taos. The Rio is like life, now sweet, now rough. I could drive to Taos, rent a kayak. Go out alone. Spill into the river over a rushing waterfall that crushes my skull against a web of rocks. No hint of suicide. The life insurance company is satisfied. No scandal from the past. *He leaves behind a wife, Morgan, of Pleasantville, CA, and a son, Marine Captain Michael Alton Lee Jr., address unknown.*

Despite its grand name the storied Rio is a joke compared to the large rivers to the east — the Mississippi, the Hudson, even the East River, unknown if you're not from New York. Stomach acid laden with chile gushes up into my throat like a geyser. Pre-chewed fire. The East River. I close my eyes, fiercely, to make it disappear.

This little trip was supposed to make such connections vanish. Easy to say.

—Where is Mickey stationed these days? Not that I give a crap.

Astonished, hurt, I turn to face her as she drives.

—What did you say?

Her red face is bleaching her freckles. She grips the wheel tighter.

—Sorry, Unc, I was thinking of something else.

She wasn't thinking of something else. I could tell. She meant exactly what she said. But why would she say that about her cousin? *Not that I give a crap!* Why would she be so rude to me? To him? I want to press her on it, but not while she's driving. I let it go, for now.

—We never know where he's stationed. He's doing something dangerous, somewhere.

—Defending this great country of ours.

She says it mildly, her eyes focused ahead on the traffic. The quiet sarcasm is obvious. I let that pass, too. I didn't come to Santa Fe to discuss world affairs.

—You're real proud of him.

As any father would be.

I wonder what Nia is doing right now.

Across the Rio, a few blocks down a wide street, Annabel pulls to the curb beside two dilapidated and abandoned adobe-colored buildings adjacent to a weaving shop that's functioning. Española Valley Fiber Arts Center. That's where I buy my yarn, she says, it's a nonprofit, it helps local women. Beside us is a decrepit two-story building, the bottom half boarded up. The abandoned second story is still proclaiming, in weak and faded letters, Thelma's Beauty Shop. Like an old woman trying to look young. Most of the clientele must be dead by now. Beside the faded beauty shop more dark wood across what once must have been a plate glass window. On the face of the second floor, pale painted words: Johnny's Used. That's all: Johnny's Used. The building has Alzheimer's, can't recall Johnny's Used what. Across the wide street is an equally senile movie theater. The top half of the building whitewashed, two narrow windows peering out, blinded by iron bars. The first level painted dark red. A white marquee, bordered in dull turquoise, moveable letters on each sloping face having a debate. The left side says SET. The right side replies, DOMINGO. They've been shouting those words for years, Annabel tells me. Old geezers no one ever visits, locked in the same argument day after day until eternity.

The surprise is across the street, she says. Beside the abandoned movie house, down a narrow alley narrowed further by prickly weeds, is a shop clearly as old as SET and DOMINGO. A fluorescent light is gleaming inside above a gray head of hair. On the window are the faded words Italian Antiques.

—Doesn't he know he can come out now, the war's over?

Annabel does not respond, but I forgive her. That was not her war. That was four wars ago. Or five.

The door is grimy glass protected by iron bars. A tinkling bell announces us when we enter, as in a country grocer's. Inside is a long, narrow room crowded with glass cases that reach to waist level. We look around. Lying dead in the cases are antique necklaces, bracelets, broaches, earrings. The gray head of the proprietor never turns from whatever he is peering at, perhaps a ledger, through spectacles at his scratched old roll-top desk. As if he is doing watch repair. I have no idea why Annabel brought me here. I couldn't even guess.

We inch our way further into the ancient shop. Jewelry gives way to old writing materials — pens, penholders, glass ink bottles. A single black and white postcard, lying among them, faded to gray, is a photograph of a tall, thin man facing the camera, naked. Between his legs, hanging from his pelvis to below his knees, is a scrotum more than a foot long, and almost as wide. It's grotesque. I take Annabel's hand to hurry her past that case. It's okay, Uncle Mike, she says, I've seen it many times.

I think I'm blushing. She is not.

—I wish my boyfriend Bobby was hung like that.

My face is now glowing with heat. The man in the card is a freak. He looks as if he could hardly walk.

— Just kidding, she says, Bobby does quite well with what he's got.

Bobby? What about the Indian Princess? I dare not ask. I'm not sure if I want to know. We've never talked like this.

We move on. The exhibits in the glass cases have evolved to primitive medical and dental displays: old metal hand-turned drills that make me shudder at the thought of having a tooth drilled with one of those, with no anesthetic except perhaps a swig of brandy; steel scalpels of many lengths; Civil War era prosthetics; optical measuring kits

Suddenly I stop, as if a traffic light has changed. I miss a few breaths before edging forward. It's magnificent. In the last case against the far wall. Eyes. Glass eyes. A hundred antique glass eyes. Staring up at me. Exactly one hundred — I count the inch-square partitions in the flat wooden case. Ten by ten. In each partition a glass eye, like a sadist game of Chinese checkers. A regiment of eyes, lined up in ranks. Eyes like large white marbles, the kind I used to play with as a kid. But life-size — about an inch across. With irises of brown, blue, black, pale green, gray. Most of the whites are clear. Some show thin streaks of bloodshot. The eyes look ready to be popped into the eye sockets of wounded Italian soldiers, if that's where he got these, perfect matches for the living eyes. Or perhaps these already have been used, and popped out when a grenade fell. I've never seen such such a display. Glass eyes rarely are used anymore. Nowadays we insert a ball of plastic into the socket to fill the space, and cover it with an oversized contact lens the shape of the cornea, painted to match the patient's other eye.

The case is amazing, spooky even to me. Wholesale eyes. Eyes by the pound. I tell Annabel.

—I thought you'd enjoy seeing it, she says.

—How did you discover it?

—I buy yarn across the street. Sometimes I wander in here to look around before driving home.

More than seeing it, I know I want to own it. An extraordinary piece of once practical art. Now sculpture. I've always liked the eclectic. Surprisingly, Morgan didn't mind. Our coffee table is shaped like a piano, made from old railroad parts. We picked it up at a flea market. A pair of gold-tapestried easy chairs of slightly different sizes, one taller and narrower than the other, the king's chair and the queen's chair. A bit threadbare, but so are most kings and queens these days.

—That's not for sale.

The graying, bearded proprietor has materialized beside us on mouse feet.

—How much?

—It's not for sale.

—Nothing in the store?

—Everything in the store is for sale. This is not a museum

—So how much?

—But not that.

An interesting sales technique. He probably makes everybody bargain and beg for whatever.

—I look at those eyes every day. They're not for sale. I could sell a hundred cases if I had them. And get out of this rotten city. Toast my aging buns on the Riviera.

I'm one of those retro-obnoxious types who, like some of my long-dead uncles — they grew up before credit cards — carries a fat roll of bills in my pocket. Especially on vacation. On some level I suppose it's in case for some reason I don't want to leave a paper trail. Slowly, with my left hand, I pull the roll from my pocket. With my right I peel off ten bills, fan them on the glass counter like a hand of cards. All C-notes, as they used to say in *film noir*. Hundred dollar bills. A thousand bucks is on the counter. The entire roll, two inches thick held together by a rubber band, are C-notes. The proprietor acts as if he does not notice. Probably I am way underestimating the worth of this case of eyes. I fan five more bills beside the first ten. No reaction. Count out five more and slap them on the glass. Two thousand bucks. He begins to blink. I feel I've hooked him. I drop a single bill on top of the others. Annabel who is standing beside me cuts here eyes to mine. She understands the game at once. Gray hair makes a point of clenching his fists and looking at his fingernails. I speed up the action, drop another bill onto the pile, hesitate only a moment, a third bill, a fourth. We're up to $2400. Gray hair studies the metal ceiling of his shop.

—How much?

—It's not for sale.

Okay, we'll play. Like dealing cards, I drop another bill on the pile, pausing for perhaps a second, then another, then another. $2700. Even the glass eyes beneath the countertop are widening in astonishment. In my mind I set my limit. Annabel is looking from me to the proprietor and back, as at a tennis game. I drop the bills from higher up now, to add drama. The flutter of temptation. Bills are all over the glass. $2,900. I pause. I can see the wavering in his eyes. I drop one more. He clears his throat. Now I see pain in his eyes. His breathing has become rapid, loud.

—Not for sale.

Endgame. I shrug, and stuff the roll of bills into my pocket. His fists at his sides are clenching, unclenching. Casually I lift one of the bills off the counter, and hand it to Annabel. As she takes it she bites her lip. His eyes squint, his face is torment. It reddens in a blotch beneath his scruffy beard. His forehead breaks out in sweat, like a patient before a procedure. I take another bill from the countertop and hand it to my niece. The proprietor is shaking. I reach toward yet another bill. He slams his fist on top of the remaining pile.

—Take it! And get out! And don't come back!

He gathers in his money in a rage, $2,700, stuffs it into his own pocket. He stumbles behind the counter in a daze. Unlocks the display case with a small key. Lifts the box of eyes onto the glass.

—There's tax!

—You won't be paying tax. Not on cash.

But I toss another hundred at him for the tax.

—Only because my wife is in the hospital, he says. We have bills.

An epidemic, sick wives. Now he's called the play, filled me with sadness at my triumph.

—A lid? You have a lid? So they don't fall out?

—The lid broke off years ago. Get out of my shop.

He's beginning to shake with anger.

—Why do you want those?

—I'm an eye doctor. They speak to me.

—You don't see enough eyes at work? Fine. Suit yourself. You know, doctor? I'm no spring chicken, but I just learned something. When the one you love is filled with pain, everything else is off the board. All of a sudden these eyes mean nothing to me. So go. Enjoy them. And do me a favor. Treat them well. Like a pet. Look at them at least once a day.

I want to introduce myself, befriend this man, but after the money game I feel too awkward.

— I hope your wife recovers quickly, I say.

—Thank you, doctor. She won't recover.

Annabel lifts a purple and green shawl from her shoulders and carefully wraps the uncovered box of eyes in it. She holds the display horizontally, as if it were an infant's coffin, or take-out enchiladas, and leads the way from the shop. The tinny bell tinkles. She leans her face into the shawl, faces me with two hundreds between her teeth.

—Take your money, she mumbles through clenched lips.

—It's yours.

She lets the bills drop onto the shawl.

—I can't do that, Uncle Mike. You think I'm still a kid, and those are nickels.

I visualize her tongue kiss with the Indian Princess.

—I know you're not a kid. I'll tell you what. You just sold this shawl. Deal? Nia will love it.

She shakes her head no as we reach her battered car.

—It's not a deal? Why not? You do sell them, don't you? I'm buying it.

—Then you owe me another fifty.

Get three glass eyes;
And, like a scurvy politician, seem

To see the things thou dost not.
>   —King Lear to the Earl of Gloucester, Act IV, Scene 6

The wrapped eyes safely in the trunk, we cross the Rio Grande and head south.

—There's only one way the guy could have screwed me, I say.

—How's that?

—If right now he's opening a carton marked Made in China. Lifting out a case of a hundred more.

—No way. You think?

—Not really. These are authentic. Made in Germany, I'm pretty sure. Where most of them were made since their invention, about 1835. Until after World War Two. Besides, he'd have to be a better actor than De Niro to have pulled that off.

I glance out the window as she merges with traffic on route 84.

—Still, next time you're up here buying yarn, take a peek.

—And if another hundred eyes are there?

—Have one of your loser buddies burn the place down.

—That won't be hard.

I look at her innocent freckled face behind the wheel.

— Hey, who *are* you hanging out with these days? I was only kidding.

—So was I, Unc.

I shake my head. The uppity generation.

—Somebody ought to swat your fanny.

She brakes sharply and swerves to avoid a gold-colored Mazerati that cuts much too close in front of us

—Asshole!

From the trunk we hear what sounds like marbles rolling.

After a silence, Annabel asks, What do you think is wrong with his wife?

—Could be anything. If I had to guess, I'd say cancer. Metastasized.

—Shit. Will you do what he asked, look at the eyes every day?

—Absolutely. And probably think of his wife every time. Not what I'd planned.

—Don't feel guilty, Unc. You gave him a lot of money he probably really needed.

—I could sell the eyes for twice that much tomorrow, I suspect.

—But you won't.

—No. I won't. Maybe they'll be your inheritance.

She starts to say something, stops. Neither of us speaks again during the rest of the ride.

At her studio — her shack — when we open the trunk and remove the woven shawl the partitioned wooden case is half empty. We lean in side by side and gather up the eyes that have rolled around. We almost fill the box. It's like those tests of cognition: fit the round eyes into the square holes. When we're through we've got 99 eyes. One small square is empty. We reach into every cranny. Our hands get filthy. We can't find the missing eye. There are holes in several corners of the trunk. My chest clutches. Did we lose one on the road?

—Those openings go to where the spare tire is supposed to be, Annabel says. Only I never had one. The bottom is stuck, it won't budge, but I'm sure the eye is down there. Bobby is good at stuff like that. I'll get him over here tomorrow. He'll pull the trunk apart, we'll find the eye.

Bobby apparently is good at lots of stuff.

Annabel finds a piece of cardboard, cuts it to fit over the display case. Ties it tight with her thickest yarn, with which she weaves what she calls rasta rugs. In my rental is an attaché case. I keep a fresh shirt and underwear in it for quick trips like this. I toss them in the back of the car. The box of eyes just fits into the attaché case.

Take Annabel to dinner that night at Geronimo. Bobby joins us. He's a nice kid. His rasta hair is an echo of her rugs. He'll take her trunk apart Monday, he says, he's got something to do tomorrow.

Sunday we have brunch alone, me and Annabel. I kiss her cheek, she kisses mine, says I should visit more often. I should. I drive down I-25 to Albuquerque, turn in the rental at the airport. Carrying the 99 eyes in my attaché case, Nia's new shawl and my own few clothes in a Hilton shopping bag. I wonder as I walk what slices of life those eyes have seen. Have some of them been in battle, seen the bodies of Germans or Frenchmen dying in mud and blood in the trenches of the First World War? Or were they fitted into mangled sockets after the peace? Have they seen the breasts of nervous virgins or faking whores in Europe's war-torn towns? They're glass. They haven't seen anything.

The set was complete. This group may never have left the factory. In the realm of sightless eyes they stand abandoned.

What did your eyes do in the war, daddy?

Chapter 11: Laurette

I'm walking through the terminal when my cell phone plays the beginning of Beethoven's Fifth. I pull the phone from my pocket. Recognize the number. Nia.

—Michael? Yessenia.

Her full name. As if this is an official call.

—You'd better come home right away.

—I'm at the airport now. What's happened? Oh, God, Not Mickey!

—Not Mickey. I found a body. While I was out riding. A woman.

—You what?

—I took Eyeful for his Saturday gallop. You know the creek that slashes cross-country? Red Ridge Creek? Eyeful was splashing along when he stopped suddenly, reared up. He nearly threw me. I leaned forward, kept him upright, was lucky he didn't go over. I calmed him down, got off to see what had spooked him. Half in the chamisa by the side of the creek, half in the water, was a body. Human, female. A bullet hole visible in the back of her neck. Not what I expected.

—What do you mean? What were you expecting?

—I'm jumping around here. At the stable, while I was saddling Eyeful, one of the workers handed me a note. In an envelope, not sealed, with your name on it. Just Doctor Lee. It was left under the office door three nights ago, he said. I opened it. Inside, torn from a pad, in a different handwriting — it looked feminine but shaky   it said, I will be here, please come. An arrow pointed to a spot along the creek on a crude map. The only way I found her was by riding the creek.

My heart is throbbing rapidly, wants to fly away, only my ribs are holding it in place.

— My name is on the note? Is it someone we know?

—I don't. But you probably do. She works at the hospital.

—Do you have a name?

—She's a beautiful woman. Dark complected. Haitian, they think. Laurette Dubal.

—Oh, shit! She's a scrub tech in neurology. Why? How?

—I called 911, then the stables. I made sure no one touched her until the police came. They examined her, the neck wound, found a wallet with ID in her jeans. They turned her over to see if the face matched the driver's license. It did.

Then Nia, a trained Marine, hesitated.

— Except her eyes were missing.

—Oh, Christ! Fish? An eagle? Desert rats?

—They won't be sure till the autopsy. They think there are scalpel marks.

—Someone blinded her on purpose?

—There's more. A chain around her ankles so she couldn't run. A wire around her neck, attached to a small glass jar. In the jar was another note. Same handwriting as your name. Four words: A Warning to Vicky. No signature. Do you know what that means? Don't you have a nurse named Vicky?

I sag like a fat man into a chrome and plastic chair. There are lots of Vickies at the hospital. Sometimes it seems as if half the nurses are Vicky. Or Victoria. But the bastards were threatening mine.

—They think she was dead before the eyes were gouged. There was not much blood. The bullet came from a ridge about 200 yards away.

—Two hundred yards, hit in the neck. Wouldn't that take a sharpshooter, like you, or Mickey?

—Not necessarily. The police found half a dozen bullets in the sand, a few at the water's edge. He could have been a lousy shot who got lucky. Unless . . .

—Unless what?

—Unless he was toying with her. Firing shots all around her to terrify her. Before taking her down. Which actually makes more sense. A lousy shot could have just put a pistol to the back of her head.

—Jesus!

— They'll want to talk to you, because of the note.

—I've been in New Mexico for two days.

—That's the problem. You left town. The M.E. — this is just prelim — has her dead for three. Michael, what is this about? They used your name! You were supposed to find her body.

I take out my handkerchief, wipe my forehead, sweating in the air-conditioned waiting terminal. Laurette Dubal. Sweet. Exotic skin. Cheekbones. Maxie will be destroyed.

—Where are you now?

—Still at the scene.

—They let you stay?

—Cops like Marines.

—Especially pretty ones.

—Especially material witnesses. I gave them the note, of course. And Michael? One cop thought it might be a ploy. That you could have left the note at the stables, to point suspicion away from yourself. Then left town. I told them that was nonsense, of course. You had no motive, for one thing. But this guy had it all figured. You both work at the hospital. It could be an office romance gone bad, he said.

—That's crazy.

—I know. I told him you weren't the type for romance.

—What did he say to that?

—He said all men are the type for romance.

—Son of a bitch cop was coming on to you.

—Michael, don't get so angry. Most men do.

—I have to think. How's Eyeful?

—He's favoring his right foreleg. Nothing seems broken, the vet says. I called him out to van her in. He'll know more tomorrow. I don't know what dreams he'll have tonight. He almost stepped on the body. He didn't much want to hang around.

Vicky! A quick, gut-wrenching goodbye. I break the connection, punch up Vicky's cell. No answer. I think of leaving a warning message, hang up instead. She probably hasn't heard yet. If the cops are smart they won't let the warning note get public. It would scare every Vicky in California.

I move toward the boarding area, my mind in an angry fog. Set the attaché case and the Hilton bag on the moving counter. Keys, wallet, watch into the metal bowl. Today's spittoons. I clear through the metal detector without a buzz. The woman behind the X-ray counter, heavyset, black, navy blue uniform, has a three-inch fake pineapple slice on her lapel. My mind is in a hundred places at once.

—Why the pineapple?

—From Homeland Security. They made too many for Hawaii, and thought New Mexico was another country. We should be getting red chiles soon.

Her eyes open wide, as in an old Amos 'n' Andy show. She is mesmerized by my attaché case. She stabs a button, stopping movement on the table. Peers closer at her X-ray screen.

—Ricardo! she yells.

That gets everyone's attention. Her voice is shaky as she questions me, pointing at the case.

—What's in there?

—Eyes. One hundred eyes. Glass.

—What do you want with a hundred glass eyes?

—I'm an ophthalmologist.

—I don't care about your religion. We ain't profilin'. How do I know they're glass?

— Open the case.

—The hell I will.

People are frightened by false eyes. Until they need one.
                              —Note for *A Brief History of Sight*

I reach into the silver bowl to get my wallet, my hospital ID.

—No you don't, Ricardo says, pulling both arms behind my back. Leave it be. And to the woman, ain't no need to yell when you're wearin' that pineapple. Nearly broke my eardrums.

A supervisor appears, gray uniform, pistol in a holster.

—What's the trouble here?

Blond hair cut short, face naturally red, pocked.

—This guy's got a hundred eyes in here.

—Open it, Doris.

—No way, it could be a bomb.

Holster looks me in the eye.

—He wouldn't call all that attention to a bomb.

Though he tells people gathering around to move back. Motions Ricardo to shoo them away. He reaches over, opens the attaché case, pulls off the cardboard cover Annabel had fashioned. Every inch square is filled with a glass eye looking up at him. Except one, which is empty. The empty one is not in the middle. There is no way it could be there. Not even Einstein could get the empty one smack in the middle. There is no smack in the middle.

The holster man counts the length and width of the case. Only 99.

—Where'd you hide the other one? Is this a decoy? Is the hundredth one the bomb? Empty his pockets, pat him down.

Ricardo pats me down, looking for the hundredth eye. This really happened, I swear. Albuquerque International Airport. Excuse me, Sun Port. I felt like I really was on the Amos 'n' Andy Show. But it could have happened anywhere, I suppose. Protecting us from glass eyes at the airports so we won't have to fight them in the streets. Each of these security people's brains contains millions of cells. A hundred-twenty-five million receptors in each retina. Yet they couldn't tell an eye from an Easter egg. I keep telling them, the hundredth eye is in my niece Annabel's car in Santa Fe.

—Get the sheriff up there on the phone! Possible car bomb. Old red Ford with a girl, possible suicide bomber, approach with caution. Don't know the license plate.

—What the hell is there to bomb in Santa Fe? I ask. The Folk Art museum? The Gerald Peters Gallery?

A female guard comes running up, gray uniform pants but a red sweater on top, talks to the holster man with agitation that makes her large breasts bounce. It just came over the Internet, she says. A body was found in California. With the eyes missing. Like, scooped out with a knife. Or a sharpened spoon.

I wince for Laurette. For Maxie.

Nearby a contingent of citizens, perhaps twenty in all, has arrived as a group. Several are carrying small American flags. They move apart and two are carrying the ends of a long banner the size of a bed sheet. The banner says: Welcome Home Jerry. They're standing right outside the security section. Debarking passengers walk down a long corridor and come out this way.

—Okay, that's enough, we're holding up the line here. Get this guy and his eyes into the interview room. So maybe they're not bombs, maybe they're real eyes inside plastic eyes. Is that your hobby, Doctor Frankenstein? You need one more to reach the end? Or are you planning on two hundred?

Not the Amos 'n' Andy Show. The Twilight Zone.

A guy with a video camera is taping the group with the banner. Maybe a friend, maybe one of the local TV stations. Someone asks what they are doing.

—Jerry Jarrett is coming home from Iraq. He's in the National Guard.

A super supervisor in a brown business suit and green tie, maybe the airport security director, joins us in a small room behind an opaque glass door. Holster stands just inside the door, hand on the handle of his pistol. My son will not come home to a welcoming committee at any airport. He'll be debriefed twice overseas before flying home on leave, mostly likely a military flight into the base at San Diego. Be debriefed a third time before he's allowed to leave in civilian clothes. We won't know he's home until he phones from there. Or until he knocks on the door.

—All right, mister surgeon, where did you get these so-called eyes?

—They're not so-called eyes. They're real eyes. Real fake eyes. I bought them yesterday. In Española.

—The glass eye capital of the world? Used to be known for its sopapillas. Low riders. Now glass eyes? You got a receipt?

I reach toward my pocket, then remember. No receipt.

—Why not?

—I paid cash. Twenty-eight hundred dollars. The guy didn't give me a receipt.

—So he could skip out on the tax?.

—I gave him an extra hundred for the tax.

—Also cash, I suppose. Get the name and call that dealer up there, Doris. See if he sold a hundred eyes yesterday.

—He'll deny it. He won't want to be held on tax evasion.

—But you gave him money for the tax. Do you always carry that much cash?

I look in the spittoon, at the rest of my roll. I count the number of airport people in the room. All this while Laurette Dubal lies dead and eyeless in the sand.

My mind fades to a memory from med school. First year. A huge aluminum pot is on the stove in the cafeteria, bubbling over. Someone needs to lower the burner, I say. Right, Lee. Turn it down, see if the corned beef looks done. What the hell do I know of corned beef. I lift off the cover of the pot. Staring up at me from the fatty swirling water is a human head. A human face. Human eyes. The skin of the forehead peeling off. That's med school humor. Somehow I manage not to gag, say instead, Looks more like pastrami to me. Good man, Lee, let's go get some lunch.

I wonder if anyone ever carried a head onto a plane.

—Look. I can't miss my flight. There's six hundred on that roll that I could spare.

Cash means drugs to them. The big shot lifts a brown glass eye, tries to peel it open. It doesn't peel. He holds it up to the light. A third eye peering at his two.

—Maybe only some are filled with drugs, Ricardo says.

They each take eyes, check 'em out. Don't find anything. Hawaii asks how could these be eyes, you can't see nothing through 'em? One by one they put them back. The empty square is still not in the middle. The supervisor idly begins moving them around, trying to get symmetry. The eye of a true artist. A security camera is mounted high in a corner of the room. Ricardo squeezes Hawaii's pineapple.

—You watch your hands, boy, before I flatten you.

The red light on the camera goes dark. Ricardo takes my roll of bills from the silver cuspidor.

—You can spare seven hundred, he says. The security chief will want to see the evidence.

—By all means. Hail to the chief.

The supervisor looks at my driver's license.

—If these eye things were the least bit squishy, *Doctor* Michael Alton Lee, I'd be holding you for California. Don't let me see your face in Albuquerque again. Especially not your eyes.

I place my treasure carefully back into the case, snap it shut, head to the gate for my flight. Jerry has not arrived yet from Iraq. His friends resolutely holding the banner wide. I find it a little much, but sometimes I'm a hypocrite, so I tell them it's a nice thing they're doing for Jerry.

—He left both legs over there, a man says.

After half an hour in the air, resting my own eyes, I glance down at the clouds. They're lined up on parade, like regimental cotton. As in that awful O'Keeffe. Mindless, artless, ugly piece of work. I'm no Clement Greenberg, but if God were always that boring there would be no calla lilies, no cougars, no eyes. No Nia.

I see no sign of heaven above the clouds. No sign of Laurette.

The rest of the flight I'm tucked in with a Scotch on the rocks in a plastic cup provided by a sweet enough gray-haired flight attendant. I miss the leggy clear-stockinged stewardesses of yore. I'm not sexist, just appreciative.

What to do about Vicky? The terrible question circles my cerebellum like a bee around a rose. *I touched a rose that had no thorns, and felt a sting.* The first line of poetry I ever wrote, in high school, after Emily Furst, or Faust, turned me down for a date. I had spent three weeks working up the courage to ask. Later she got knocked up, a sin in those days, but not by me. When the accused father, a teacher, passed a paternity test her parents made her give the baby away. The kid might be famous today, on the tube, or You Tube. Coming next fall, The Fallopian Tube: Inside Lady Gaga, 24-7.

After what the bastards did to Laurette, they would break Maya's legs as if they were swizzle sticks. And then do what to Vicky? The bastards have no trouble running cocaine and heroin. Why do they need painkillers, too? A kindergarten game for the gangbangers. Ring around the hospital. Which is awash in vulnerable nurses, residents, interns, housekeepers. I've got to keep Vicky safe, and the child. And, incidentally, myself. Why was the note left for me? Was it Ken-Chen? By the time we land at San Jose my mind is seeking entry into the drug racket. But I don't know how. They didn't teach us that at Harvard. Maybe they do now. Not to premeds, but maybe to MBAs.

After stowing ninety-nine eyes and a shawl in the trunk of my car, I drive straight to Coastal Regional, take the elevator to third floor, turn left to neurology. The air feels especially moist and medicinal after New Mexico. Pause outside Maxie Klonsky's office. Maybe he knows more than the cops. I knock on the closed door.

—Go away.

I figured he'd be here, would not want to be home with his wife. This is not the time for a family chat.

— Maxie, it's Michael.

—Go away!

The door isn't locked. On his desk is a split model of the brain, highlighting cortex and amygdala, to which we traced the visual pathways in the '70s. Also his computer, journals of neurology, jar of pens, an empty tissue box. Crumpled tissues litter the desk, the floor. Behind his leather chair, the blue afternoon outlines closed Venetian blinds. Maxie is face down on his leather sofa in his usual dungarees, navy long-sleeved T-shirt, red suspenders. His arms are pressed to his head of wooly white hair, as if to block out the universe. I kneel beside him, rest a hand on his shoulder.

—I'm sorry, Max.

His voice is muffled by his arms as he speaks into the sofa.

—I wasn't *shtupping* her, like people think. Like you think. I wasn't a sugar daddy. I loved that girl. That woman. She had class. I wouldn't cheat on my wife for a piece of ass.

—I didn't think Jews cheated at all.

Trying to distract him.

He turns his head, looks at me. A rabbinical expression, though I have no idea what that means. Maybe he's silently calling me a *schmuck*.

—Are you kidding? Abraham and Hagar. David and Bathsheba. It's a Biblical tradition. Besides, being in love isn't cheating. Not when you can't help it.

He's been reading my mind. I back away and slowly, in pain, he turns over, drops his short legs to the beige carpet. His eyes, too, find the floor.

—The fact is, I killed her, Michael. That's what hurts the most. Tomorrow I'll miss her tender body, her sweet affections, her laugh. And next week, and next year. Then maybe I'll get over her, raise her into a fond memory, an angel who gave me a gift. Maybe. Why she wanted me, with my white hair and my bulging belly, I have no idea. Well, maybe I do. I could make her laugh. Growing up in Haiti she didn't get to laugh very much.

—A sense of humor is the best aphrodisiac. But the Prescott Medal didn't hurt your image.

—Laurette was not impressed by medals. Her professor father is being kept in solitary by men with medals.

Images come to me of Haiti in old films. Tonton Macoutes. Killers in dark sunglasses.

—But you're right. At least you'll have a memory. At the end, on our death beds, we don't smile over the joys we passed up because some ancient book said they were wrong. We cherish the joys we savored.

—I've got a memory, all right. And her blood all over my hands. Today and tomorrow and every day for the rest of my life.

—Why do you keep saying that?

He tells me. He needs to spill it. That's one difference between a Jew and a WASP: we WASPs keep it buried inside, let maggots breed in the pores of our projected innocence.

—There's an Oriental deli that Laurette passes every day on her way home from work, he says. She stops in a couple days a week for a few small items: coffee, milk, bread, olives, cheese, maybe a mixed salad. She's not a big eater. So they know her, the clerks, though she does not know — did not know — if they are Chinese, Vietnamese, Korean. What does it matter, they are nice enough, though recently some hangers-on seem to be looking her over. Maybe two weeks ago, one of them follows her out to her car, a Beetle bug. You work at the hospital, he says to her, good guess, he's pointing to the Medical Center parking sticker in her window. She admits it, of course, and he says they need her help. I'll just tell you the basics. They want her to get drugs from the hospital pharmacy a couple of times a week. Painkillers. And all her purchases at the deli will be free. What do you mean get them, she asks? They're in the pharmacy. Locked up, no doubt. You mean I should steal them? I can't do that. I'd lose my job. I'd go to jail. I'm sorry, find somebody else. Unfortunately, they say, you are the chosen one. We know where you live. We know what married doctor comes to see you. We have photographs. We'd hate for this information to become known at the hospital. Or to his wife. But that will happen if you don't cooperate. Another fellow who has been standing nearby in the shadows, listening, slides in closer. Creepy looking. With straight black hair tall as a wheat field. You have beautiful eyes, Laurette Dubal, he says. It would be a shame to lose them because you don't cooperate. They wink at her and return to the deli. Shaking, she manages to drive home. Calls me. She catches me still here, begs me to come over, she needs to talk. I don't like the fear in her voice. I go there and she tells me what happened. She doesn't know what to do. These fellows sounded pretty mean. You have no choice, I tell her, you have to go to the police. Will you come with me? Of course. I drive her across town, to the furthest precinct from her house, in case they're watching the police station. The police say they can't arrest anyone without evidence. The thugs will deny it. It will be just her word against theirs. No DA would prosecute. Now, if she was willing to work with the police . . . So they set it up. A couple of days later the police give her four boxes of pills to deliver, the same brand the hospital uses. They set up surveillance cameras and mikes in a van across the street. She makes the exchange shakily, havarti and black olives and anchovies for morphine and codeine. That's when the fucking cops blow it. She isn't gone ten minutes when they barge in. They've got the exchange on tape, but no, they want the red hot evidence. They bust in with weapons drawn and arrest all three guys there. Possession with intent to sell, intimidation, who knows. They tell Laurette she is safe now. We go out and celebrate. Well, these guys may be shit pebbles to the cops, but they've got connections all over — brothers, cousins, uncles, from San Jose to San Francisco. I took her to the police thinking it was the only thing to do. Now she's dead.

—What else could you have done?

—I know. That's what I keep wondering. And the creepy one with the hair? He wasn't there when the cops moved in. He's still out there.

We sit in silence then, two helpless has-beens having outlived our usefulness. Nobel Prize my ass. But another possible motive for the murder and mutilation of Laurette slithers into my mind like a birthing snake. I do not mention it. Maxie is suffering enough guilt for now.

—What about your wife? Does she know you're here? Did you call her?

—Sophie? She knows I often work late. Even on Sunday. More often than I actually do, if you get my meaning. She knows not to wait up. Wait, why am I talking like this? Sophie left me two weeks ago.

—I didn't know. I'm sorry, Maxie.

—Nobody knows. What's the point? I should get sympathy while I'm sleeping with Laurette? In love with Laurette? Sophie hired a private detective. We've got pictures, she screamed over the phone. I'll see you in court. Since when do neurosurgeons make house calls?

Since when does anyone?

—Did you ever see anyone following you to her house?

—Once I thought, maybe. But it was an Oriental guy. Not who Sophie would hire. I figured it meant nothing. The bastards. I've tried to blame God. *Yahweh* as supreme pimp. It's God who makes old men fall in love with the beautiful young. I'm sixty-four, Michael. I didn't hire Laurette, I didn't assign her here, personnel did that. Human Resources, they call it now. She was some Human. She was some Resource. A woman like that gets under your skin, offers you love, fulfilled desire, how can you resist? Why should you resist? We get one life, why not live it? I didn't ask for her, I didn't seek her, she was given to me like a gift. I'm supposed to turn it down?

I can think of no more to say. Maxie's eyes are welling up. Fear stalks the room like a mountain cat. Is Vicky really next for those bastards? A shudder runs through me. Maxie returns to his loss. As he will for some time.

—I even thought, if my wife, Sophie Podolsky Klonsky, could ride a horse, handle a rifle, hit a target at 200 yards, maybe she killed Laurette. But she was a Brownie, not a Marine. She maybe would have liked to kill her, but she couldn't. The rest of my life I'll be paying for taking Laurette to the cops. I've even been thinking of suicide, Michael. About how to do it. Hanging makes a stinking mess, and you look ridiculous. Eating a gun, like they say, I'm much too chicken. But pills — in the hospital we've got plenty.

—Wasn't Jack Beecham enough? Maxie, you've got people's lives depending on your skills. Children with seizures, with brain tumors. The innocents.

—That's what I told myself, lying here. Also, bullshit makes the flowers grow. How those thoughts play out in the middle of the night, we'll know in the morning.

—What will happen with Laurette?

—The autopsy is tomorrow. Then I'll have to bury her. She has nobody in this country. You're right, Michael. I can't kill myself until after the funeral.

—And the seven days of *shivah*. Isn't that what it's called? When you cover all the mirrors?

—You're right. I have to wait till then.

He doesn't mention the note with my name. Apparently the cops are withholding that.

I'm not too worried about Maxie. The Jews were put on earth for two reasons — to enlighten the universe, and to suffer. Maxie enlightened the world about the visual pathway. Now he'll suffer with fortitude. Self-slaughter is not contained in kosher blood. Suicide is a pagan ritual. At the moment we Christians pull the trigger, or plunge in the dagger, or dangle from the rope, or leap from the bridge into the icy waters, at that moment we make pagans of ourselves. Pagan meaning not the absence of belief, but the presence of the beast. Which in other circumstances can be admirable. Sometimes I think it's the beast, on a tight leash, that allows me to slice up other peoples' eyes. As for those who choose to exit like a radish, like my mother — I have no opinion. For years I hated her for abandoning us in favor of barbiturates. Till I learned the real reason.

We cannot control our thoughts. That is a given. The worst of them leap from the dungeon of our unconscious across a single synaptic gap faster than the speed of light — the only thing even old Albert would have conceded is faster than the speed of light. This being the case, can a thought in its virgin birth be as terrible, as terrifying, as an act that has consequences?

I'm stalling. Here is the fact. Or factoid. When I answered my phone at the airport in Albuquerque, and realized it was Nia calling, I blurted: *Oh my God! Not Mickey!* But in the nanoseconds that followed those words, in the merest fractal of time, part of me hoped — or thought it hoped — I choke on these words — that it was about Mickey. A hero, to be sure, fallen in battle, coming home in a flag-covered coffin. I pictured Nia and I falling into one another's arms, weeping, comforting each other. A perfectly natural, unpremeditated act. Holding each other tight in mutual grief. Pressing chest to breast and lips to hair to offer solace. Falling tears mingling. All natural acts.

Such a powerful love.

Such a beloved son.

This despicable thought passed in no time at all. In the absence of time, a mere hiccup of the mind. No one wants their child to die. Do I despise myself for it? Of course I do. In the real world, if a hand grenade were about to explode at Mickey's feet, I would dive on it to save him. Without a moment's thought. If a bullet were headed his way I would step in front of him, like a mortal Superman. I would die in his place easily. So from where did that shiv of a notion come? It is unthinkable — yet it passed through my mind like a razor blade. Are we all capable, in the time it takes a church bell to chime one chime, to be mental assassins? The self-evident premise is that we cannot control our thoughts. Who then should I blame?

Do you see it now? Have I made it clear — how close to madness I am slipping under Nia's earthy pull? Her casual yet apocalyptic sexuality?

Chapter 11: Sophie

The autopsy on Laurette was completed Monday afternoon. Maxie scheduled a burial service for noon Tuesday, so her friends from the hospital could attend during lunch hour. The cause of death was as expected — a rifle bullet high in the back, fired from afar at a downward angle. It severed her spinal chord, lodged in her heart. Death was instantaneous. Her eyes were gouged out after death, with pocket knife or other sharp object. The optic nerves severed. Eyeballs not found at the scene.

One surprise. Laurette was six weeks pregnant. Maxie had not known. It was possible Laurette had not yet known. News of the fetus fed Maxie's pride. At 64 he would have had a love child. He reveled in the concept. But it made his mourning twice as hard.

Monday is a day of office visits. Some patients mention the murder. It has been reported by all the media. Vicky and I hardly talk. We convey our pain with our eyes. We suppress our fears. I don't think she knows about the note.

I cancel surgeries set for Tuesday and take a personal day to be with Maxie. Stan Rosen, back from vacation, will pick up a few. The rest will understand the postponement — a death in the hospital family.

I pick up Maxie in late morning, me in a blue suit, Maxie in dark brown. With ties. The day is obscenely bright to tired eyes. We don dark sunglasses. Maxie looks ten years older, a bad trick of his slumping posture. I doubt he slept much, I know I didn't. We drive to the funeral parlor. Laurette's remains already are there, in a plain pine coffin, nailed shut. That's Jewish tradition. Maxie knows Laurette's father is in prison in Haiti, her mother dead of cancer, sisters and brothers scattered about the island. He has no names, addresses, will get word to them later, some way. First things first. Jewish law requires interment as soon as possible. Laurette will be laid to rest in B'nai Hashem Cemetery, in one of two adjacent plots Maxie purchased more than twenty years ago. Reserved, he assumed at the time, for himself and Sophie. The funeral home, though carpeted and silent, smells oddly like the hospital. Apparently the same disinfectant is used for disease and death.

We ride together in a black limousine that follows close behind the hearse. More of a cultural than religious Jew, feeling solidarity with Jews everywhere and with the State of Israel, but ignoring ancient rabbinical law, Maxie nonetheless knows the rabbi of a reform temple near Palo Alto, from attendance at High Holiday services. Rachel Weitz. She used to be a psychologist, Maxie says. She has agreed to perform a brief graveside service. We find her already near the grave after the hearse and the black limousine curl up a narrow blacktop road amid a thousand tombstones, amid planted palms waving in a soft breeze, to the highest point on the grounds. I catch momentary glances at the names on the monuments: Hirschfeld, Cohen, Bobkoff, Janowitz, Stern. We alight, stretch legs, look around. The southern tip of the bay is visible beyond the mostly gray stones, which are set in grassy squares or rectangles separated by foot-high pipe dividers. The sails of small boats gleam distantly in the sun. Life goes on.

—The view is wonderful, I tell Maxie, inanely.

—If you're alive. It's the most desirable part of the cemetery. That's why I bought early.

Funeral home attendants in gray uniforms open the rear of the hearse, set the coffin on the grass beside a newly dug grave. A black hole that forbids, yet beckons. Beside it is a sizable mound of earth, soon to be returned to the ground, minus the mass of the coffin. They slip mesh ropes under the wood, which will enable them to lower the coffin into the grave carefully when the time comes. A cardboard box of black yarmulkes is beside the mound. The box is marked Charmin Extra Soft. I turn it around so the brand does not face the rows of empty folding chairs where the mourners will sit. We each slip a yarmulke on, pressing them to sweaty heads against the mild whispering breeze. Rabbi Weitz approaches, removes small black gloves, offers her right hand to Maxie. She is wearing a black suit cut to the knee, a white silk blouse, dark stockings, low-heeled black shoes. A close-fitting black hat, its veil pulled off her face. On her ring finger is a slim gold band, in her hand a black prayer book. Her ankles are nicely turned. She's what Hawthorne or Hardy might have described as comely — especially if she were the wife of a pinch-nosed or pince-nezzed preacher. In her case, Maxie informed me on the ride over, she's married to a former wide receiver on the Raiders. Maxie introduces us, we shake hands. She's surely the comeliest rabbi in all of California. Tongue-tied, I can think of nothing to say that is not about football. I move away in case they want to talk.

Cars are beginning to roll noisily into a gravel parking area below the rise, the somber occupants climbing a flagstone path up the short grassy hill. I recognize many from the hospital, but don't know all the names. One brightly hued figure coming around a bend, as if stepping into an operetta, starts my heart pulsating. Nia, in her dress blues with red trouser stripes, jacket with brass buttons and red trim, wide white belt, white cap she rarely wears to the recruiting office, dark hair tucked under it.

—What are you doing here? I ask after we hug politely.

— Having found Laurette, I felt . . .

Her words trail off. She looks about, stares out at the bay.

—Coming from an island, she says, I imagine Laurette would have liked this view.

People begin to occupy the twenty or so folding metal chairs set up in rows facing the gaping hole. Most are in civilian clothes, some are wearing pale green hospital smocks. Others stand at the rear. Among these, a red-faced man in a dark gray suit motions to me discreetly. I recognize Captain Doyle, little Jimmy's father, as I approach.

—Are you here on duty, Captain? To see if the killer appears at the funeral?

—Something like that. But I want to tell you, doctor, I had no knowledge of the sting that led to her death. I wouldn't condone such stupidity. You don't deal with gangs like that. I hope those responsible will be punished. Please convey my sympathy and apologies to the hus . . .

—Dr. Klonsky. I will. But aren't the state police handling this? She was found in a state park.

—They've asked for our help. We're both short on manpower. By orders from the top, the drug sting motive is being kept under wraps. So we don't just look for Oriental perps.

—But that's who . . .

A black limousine bypasses the parking entrance and stops at the bottom of the hill. A chauffeur jumps out, opens the rear door facing us and helps President Kelly out of the car, She stands, supporting herself on a wooden cane, begins to climb the incline slowly. The chauffeur walks beside her holding a folded wheel chair. At the top of the rise she sits in the chair, the cane across her lap, and he wheels her the rest of the way. She signals him to stop at the rear of the gathering. I approach her out of courtesy. I'm not sure what to call her after her recent revelation. She co-opts a decision.

—What a terrible thing, she says.

—Yes.

—I hope they don't come in threes. The center will seem cursed.

One could argue that Beecham's wife already makes three, but I let it be.

—I didn't see you Saturday, Michael, at the memorial for Dr. Beecham. I couldn't decide if that was courage or cowardice.

—I was in New Mexico.

—A convenient coincidence, then.

I'm not sure why she is bugging me. I choose to ignore it, she's the president.

—I like your cane.

It's dark wood, wavy in the shape of a snake, including a head. As in the Caduceus.

—Do you think it's too phallic?

—Not with those sharp fangs.

—Yes, I see your point.

The rabbi's feminine but firm voice asking everyone to please be seated ends the conversation. I take a seat beside Maxie in the front row. Nia sits beside me. I squeeze her blue cloth knee, strictly in fatherly fashion. If my hand remains an instant longer than it should, the first tiny signal, she pretends not to notice.

Rachel Weitz is standing beside the open grave, facing the mourners.

—Since the service is short, she says, I shall conduct it in both Hebrew and English.

She opens her prayer book to a page marked with a black ribbon, and intones several passages in Hebrew, glancing at the page, then at us, then at the page again. I feel rather than see the tears that Maxie is refusing to let fall. The first prayer concluded, the rabbi lowers her book.

—We are gathered here on this otherwise beautiful day, she begins, looking out at us, making eye contact with one after another, to pay our final respects to . . .

—A whore! A damn *shiksa* whore — may she burn in Hell!

We mourners gasp as one, turn as one to see where this obscene interruption, this verbal desecration, is coming from. Or I should say all but one of us turn. Maxie Klonsky buries his face deep in his hands, lets the tears flow at last. Maxie alone among us knows the voice.

It's a stout woman, bulging in all the wrong places, places for which many women her age go to the gym or ride a bicycle in order not to bulge. Rolls of fat are stuffed into a squat pink dress covered with mammoth red roses, which appears to have been chosen in direct proportion to its inappropriateness for the occasion, all topped by an outlandish matching hat. She careens like a tug among icebergs from the rear to the front, mourners leaning away from her bustling perfumed hulk to let her pass.

—Ah, there he is! King Klonsky, hiding his face in his hands. Ashamed, Max? You should be ashamed. Some cheap shiksa slut, you want to put her in my grave just because she made of your wilting circumcised *putz* a lollypop?

Maxie, hoping I think to minimize the scene, lowers his hands.

— It's not your grave, they're both in my name, he says softly,

—It figures! The great Nobel loser Klonsky needs two graves for himself. One for his flabby body, the other for his flabby mind.

—You can have the other one, Sophie. Is this scene necessary?

—Sure, I'll sleep for eternity beside your imported whore, while you move on to the next one. Trojan wives, they call them, because old men need to wear rubbers again.

She is definitely tipsy. I begin to rise, to put an end to this, but Nia pats my knee, says better let her do it, it could get physical. She stands and moves toward Maxie's wife.

—Ah, you brought the army for protection. She's cute, this one. Is this your new lay, Klonsky? The other not yet buried and you've got a new snatch lined up? And there's your best friend, Michael Lee, in his Hollywood sunglasses. Or is this one yours, Michael? A little touchy feely while your wife is in Tacoma? Wait till she comes home, I'll let her know, you can be sure of that.

Sophie steps back as Nia approaches wearing her best sympathetic expression. I glance over my shoulder at Captain Doyle. He's watching but has not moved. Freedom of speech, I guess, unless there's an assault. But it could be disturbing the peace. I suppose cemetery security should be handling it. None are in sight.

—And you, Mrs. Klonsky says, turning. A lady rabbi. Burying a slut in an old woman's grave. That's what we Jews have come to — women wise-men. But listen, don't feel bad, Maxie, it's not your fault. It's God's fault.

Nia is about to take Mrs. Klonsky by the arm and pull her away when the rabbi discreetly motions her not to. She mouths the words, Let her talk.

—Sure it's God's fault. All of you know that. He hates women. Spread your legs and get knocked up, and for nine months you're carrying a baby in your belly, and another year nursing it with your swollen breasts till they hurt like coconuts.

She has to be drunk. How else could anyone do this?

—Then a few more years taking care of the stinking little one. Meanwhile the proud father can screw his way to Heaven. This one, that one, the other one. Get them all pregnant if he wants, make more babies for the Good Lord to torture with life. That's what the Catholics want. Or else just wear those Trojans and bonk away. So it's not Klonsky's fault, he was made this way, all men except queers are made this way. Except it is Max's fault, because King Kong Klonsky is God himself. He struts around the house like God, and God can do whatever he wants, including putting this whore in my grave.

I flash back to a discussion Nia and I had on this very subject a month ago. She'd made eggplant parmesan — makes the best in the world — and as we devoured it with Chianti she said there was one reason she was concerned about marrying Mickey: because he was two years older than her.

—What's wrong with that? I asked.

—In twenty years, when my skin is wrinkled and my breasts have gone south, he'll leave me for someone younger, prettier. If I married a man a good bit older than me, that wouldn't be a problem. I could still compete. I'd feel more secure.

—Do a lot of young women feel this way?

—I don't know. But they ought to think about it. If they don't, they're in denial.

—I can't imagine anyone leaving you.

She was not referring to me. I knew that. Still, I mined what nuggets of fool's gold I could from her words. Pyrite fantasies. Better than none. Not because of her sentiments. Because of her casual reference to her breasts. Is she willfully turning me on?

Nia can't stand drunken Sophie any more. She grabs her arm.

—I understand where you're coming from, Mrs. Klonsky, but . . .

—You know where I'm coming from? I haven't come since 1988. June the 6th it was, D-Day, the last time Klonsky made me come. I got too old for him, I guess. Too fat. But men don't get too old to slip it into the honey pot. Now they've got these pills to help. Hard-ons in a bottle. As for you, Dr. Lee, I hope your wife is fucking every stinking wetback in Tacoma.

The mourners are both shocked and mesmerized. Nia begins to tug Sophie away, but the heavyset woman wrenches free and shuffles toward the grave. I have a vision of her jumping in, like Laertes. She'd break a leg, or a hip, and the earth would shake. Instead she plops herself down at the edge of the grave, legs hanging in. The instant is frozen. Everyone waiting to see what will happen. Maxie, beyond mortified, drags his beaten body toward his wife.

—Look, Sophie.

He reaches down for her.

—Look, nothing, she says, and slides off the side of the grave, down into it, out of sight.

— Now, she shouts, her head unseen, just this disembodied voice, now you can bury your whore in my grave! Over my dead body!

Apparently she's flattened herself onto the dirt. The mourners are standing to see what they can see. The president's chauffeur is wheeling Shannon Kelly slowly downhill, away from the tragicomic scene. Rabbi Weitz urges us to sit, says she will continue with the service. Comely, she's also brave. She intones another Hebrew prayer while Sophie Klonsky reclines out of sight.

Cemetery security arrives at last, two men in gray uniforms, flashlights on their belts, walkie-talkies. Summoned by someone's cell. Rachel nods toward the grave. They slide down in. Nia kneels beside the edge and they hand the woman up to her straining arms head first. The flowered dress hikes above the top of her rolled half-stockings. Nia taking deep breaths grabs her under the arms and drags her gently across the grass. Captain Doyle at last decides to act. He approaches and cuffs Sophie's arms behind her back with twists of plastic, material of many uses. Right, Dustin? She's rolling on the ground as he tells her she's under arrest for disturbing the peace. Another man in civilian clothes comes forward, apparently an undercover cop. Together they stand her up, half drag her toward the parking area. Captain Doyle calls to me. When I reach him he hands me a disk from a camera the other cop is holding.

—I don't see any suspects here, he says, but Sergeant Wilkes caught all the excitement. You might want to dispose of it before it shows up on the Internet.

At the top of the incline the gravediggers are lowering the coffin into the grave. When the pine box containing the remains of Laurette Dubal touches bottom they pull the ropes out from under. Rachel Weitz nods to Maxie. He regains his composure at least momentarily, reaches down, takes a handful of dirt from the large pile beside the grave, tosses it onto the coffin., where it splatters like heavy rain. Echoes like a death row gate clanging shut. The rabbi looks about. A few other men follow, toss handfuls onto the box. Ashes to ashes. Laurette Dubal, 33 years old, will never be seen again.

—Thank you for coming, the rabbi tells the mourners. You may leave now, I know many of you have to get back to work at the hospital. Or you may remain as long as you like, and contemplate the fate that awaits us all. Or, perhaps — is she looking at Maxie or at me? — contemplate such truths as reside in Mrs. Klonsky's overwrought words, God's way of testing, perhaps, whether older men can place their moral instincts above their animal ones.

Oy, vey. The comely rabbi has scored for women on a Hail Mary.

From below we hear an engine revving. Sophie Klonsky, heir to Schopenhauer, is being removed from the scene in an unmarked police car.

A wistful thought skitters across my mind like a silverfish: is it kosher to invite a comely rabbi to lunch? Innocently, of course. To ask her advice about Nia? I must confess to someone. Cassandra salamander is devouring my guts.

—What do you mean, heir to Schopenhauer?

We're drinking Scotch in my den after the funeral, Maxie and I. Seated in the maroon armchairs. Nia has gone to work.

—I'm sure Sophie hasn't read Schopenhauer, Maxie. However, he presents human sexuality exactly the way she did. The only difference is, he was a misogynist. He believed women should be happy with their situation. Let their husbands support them and the babies while screwing any other women they want. Marriage is stupid, he argues, because it imposes monogamy on man, who is not a monogamous beast, and cannot be happy trying to be one. On that part of course, he and Sophie — and most of American womankind — disagree.

—First of all, Maxie responds, the guy was an anti-Semite. I know you don't buy into that, but he was.

—That's true.

—Secondly, Sophie probably did read him. She majored in philosophy.

—Really?

—It was a way to attract university men, who presumably would make a lot of money. Like me. She was a lot slimmer then. But she's a smart woman. How else could we have stayed together? The problem was, with our first kid she fell in love with motherhood. She had three more, and each time, her uterus replaced her brain for thinking functions. When each kid finished high school, they bailed to colleges in the east. You know all this stuff. When I said four was enough, her innate smarts shriveled altogether. She descended from philosophy down through the book club ranks. Then to crocheting in front of soap operas while munching chocolate kisses. The only kind of kisses in our house for years. Ultimately she hit rock bottom: *American Idol, Dancing With the Stars*. I couldn't take it anymore. But today's performance was a new low. The wisdom of the whining soaps, not Schopenhauer. She really freaked over Laurette. Move out of the house at her age? Just because I need a little fun? It wasn't taking anything away from her. But most women don't see it that way. She probably started drinking more. Today was not Sophie. But tell me something, Michael. What's with you and Schopenhauer? The last few days you're spouting him all the time. A new discovery?

—On the contrary. It goes back to when I was eight years old.

—When your mother died?

—It was Schopenhauer who killed her.

—Hold on, I need to take a piss. Pour me another drink. Laurette hurts like hell. Then tell me what you're talking about.

A minute later I hear a throttled shriek. Christ! What the fuck is that? The shriek is Maxie's, coming from my office. I hurry back there. He's standing three feet from the display box with the 99 eyes, which sits atop my Mexican trunk. He appears afraid to go closer.

—In the dim light that thing scared the hell out of me. It could give someone a heart attack.

He is breathing heavily. Asthmatic.

—They're glass.

—I see that now. But Jesus, after yesterday . . .

— What happened yesterday?

—I went to the morgue to identify Laurette. Before the autopsy.

—They didn't trust the driver's license?

—I had to see for myself. I wanted to see for myself. To say goodbye. When they pulled the sheet off her face, I wretched. Luckily I hadn't eaten anything. Her eyes. Nobody warned me that they had taken her eyes.

—Oh, Maxie!

—I fell on her, hugged her one last time, to keep from fainting. I wept. You know something, Michael? There's nothing deader than a corpse without eyes. That's what these marbles brought back to me. Especially with one missing.

I tell him I'm sorry.

—It's not your fault. I'm a doctor, I operate on brains. Glass eyes shouldn't freak me.

—They freaked Nia. I left the display on the kitchen table Sunday night. Without thinking. She was asleep. She told me that the next morning she nearly gagged. She wanted to throw them at me while I slept, one eye at a time. I think she was exaggerating, but I'd planned to keep them on display in the living room, a conversation piece, and she banished them to my office. Like a wife.

—She's right. I don't keep jars of pickled brains at home.

We've just returned to the den for another drink when there's a knocking on the front door, then a pounding, a cry of open up, I know you're in there!

—Oh, Jesus, it's her. Is the door locked? I don't want to see her now.

—The door's locked. I'll close the drapes.

Outside, Sophie is standing on the mown grass, peering in through the Venetian blinds.

—Not now, Sophie.

—I know he's here, she says, as I draw the drapes. I do the same in the den, the bedroom, Nia's room. Where there's a white spread, bed military precision made. Teddy Bear in a Marine dress uniform between the two pillows. I never noticed that before.

—Listen, Max, she says, loud. I'm sober now, can you hear me? A jail cell for a couple of hours will do that. I wasn't dressed for it. Too much pink, the hookers said. Listen, Max, I want to apologize for my performance at the funeral. That was a terrible thing to do. And say I'm sorry for your loss. Well, maybe not, to be honest. But nobody should be murdered. Even so, you didn't need to put her in our grave, Max. That much maybe you'll agree. It's okay, now that I've thought about it. We'll find other graves for us, far away from her. I want to come home, Max. Not today, not tomorrow, you need time, I know. But then I want to come home. In a week, maybe two, when you've forgotten her. We'll talk, you'll say you're sorry, we'll make the kids happy, we'll spend our old age together, like we always planned. Remember that couple we saw one time in a cafeteria in Denver? So old, they were so annoyed with each other. But still they were practically feeding one another. That would be us some day, we said. You remember? We can be together, Max. Listen I'm staying at Mamie's, if you want to talk. If not, I'll call you soon. Next week. Maybe tomorrow.

Breathless silence as she apparently departs. The closed drapes are like a theater curtain. The silence between acts? Punch and Judy, by Euripides. *Love makes time pass. Time makes the love pass.*

—I guess I could change the locks, Maxie murmurs.

—Don't think about that now. You'll have plenty of time to decide.

—You're right. I don't want to think about Sophie. How can I forgive her for that scene?

—You know what's always amazed me? How often she visits Morgan. They were never friends.

—A *yenta* and a broomstick. No offense, Michael. There was too much of a divide between them. Emotionally opposite sides of the Grand Canyon. But Morgan's stroke gave Sophie the perfect audience. She talks and no one interrupts. She talks and no one disagrees. But the orderlies hear. They gossip. They made me a laughing stock behind my back. That's partly what drove me to Laurette. Then the pity turned to envy quick enough.

—Laurette loved you, Maxie. That was clear whenever you were together.

—Paunch and all. It was a miracle.

He dabs at his eyes with a handkerchief. The light in the room is fading. I think of turning on a lamp, decide not to. We sit in the gray of our twilight years. Tomorrow I will catch up to Maxie, become 64. *Will you still want me . . . ?* How far in the future that seemed when *Sergeant Pepper* first arrived.

—Tomorrow I'll go to her grave and cover it with flowers, Maxie says. Lots of flowers. I'll sit beside her and talk. Apologize for Sophie's behavior. But that's tomorrow. Right now I want to get drunk as a skunk. And hear how Arthur Schopenhauer killed your mother.

Chapter 12: Kate

We are all connected, through our mothers, to only a handful of women living tens of thousands of years ago. . . The past is within us all.

—Bryan Sykes
The Seven Daughters of Eve
—Note for *A Brief History of Sight.*

I keep talking. To keep his mind off Laurette for a while.

—Okay, it wasn't just Schopenhauer. The U.S. government aided and assisted.

—This I can believe.

—My mother's name was Katherine. Katherine Lee. Born Katherine Neilson. Aunt Kate or cousin Kate to the relatives. Katie to my father. Mom to me and Chuck. She was a high school English teacher, and loved to read. She took me to the library every two weeks to get kid books, and made sure I read them. With dad away in Korea, she'd cook supper for me and Chuck, then slap a piece of fatty roast beef onto a roll for herself — with mustard or horse radish if she was feeling indulgent — and sit at the formica kitchen table with a cup of coffee, a pack of Camels and a book from the lending library down the street. John Hersey, I remember, *Rebecca*, by whomever wrote that. Best sellers, but they were good books in those days. Daphne Du Maurier wrote it. Mom loved to dance, and when Dad was home they'd go eat lobster or steak — the restaurants were his choice — and then go dancing. Or to a Broadway show. Those she picked. *Show Boat*, I remember her loving, and *The Voice of the Turtle*. And *Streetcar*. When Dad was away, which was most of the time, her best friends were the characters in books. In our small living room was an old mahogany bookcase about three feet wide, with wooden claw legs. The books on those shelves fascinated me more then the newer ones, perhaps because they were there before I was born. Most had no dust jackets. John Dos Passos, Upton Sinclair, Sinclair Lewis — *Babbit*, I remember and *Main Street* and *The Great Gatsby* — no Hemingway that I can recall. Right in the middle, the thickest book, just said, in black letters on tan, *Schopenhauer*. I remember asking if that was the name of the book or the author. Both, she said. One day when she wasn't home I took it from the shelf. I blew dust off the top. The binding was coming unglued in places, pages were dog-eared and brittle, things had been underlined — some a long time ago, I could tell from the faded ink, others more recently. Mom had been through the wars with that book. At seven or eight I didn't understand a word, of course. But I still have it. One of two things of hers I've kept all these years. And the memories. A few weeks after dad went down, she was depressed as hell, but she took me and Chuck from Yonkers all the way to the Polo Grounds, to let us see our beloved Giants versus the Phillies, Willie Mays versus Richie Ashburn, who was my favorite non-Giant. Him and Musial. Mom was reading a book on the train. But when the game started she watched every minute of it, even two extra innings, which must have driven her nuts. Because the whole time she would rather have been reading her book. But she knew that would have been sacrilege. Respecting our sacred game took precedence. For six months she would be our father like that. Then she took the pills.

I stand, go into my office. From a top shelf I take down the Schopenhauer in its special plastic wrapper, and remove it carefully.

—I'll read you just a couple of passages. All were underlined or marked in the margins by Mom. Well, this first idea I believed before I read it in here.

If children were brought into the world by an act of pure reason alone, would the human race continue to exist? Would not a man rather have so much sympathy with the coming generation as to spare it the burden of existence? Or at any rate not take it upon himself to impose that burden upon it in cold blood.

—What do you mean you always believed that? You didn't want any kids?

—Life is too painful. Me and Addie never talked of kids. Were going to make the world a two-person Paradise. Morgan didn't want kids, either. Then after we're married for nine years she gets pregnant. An accident, she says. Miraculously, she was a great mother. Too strict with the boy, I thought sometimes, but look how he turned out.

—You're saying you didn't want Mickey?

—Not at first.

—Interesting.

Maxie lifts his Scotch, drains half of it.

—I'm drunk, he says, I better not say anything else.

—What's interesting? Out with it.

—Just that you resented Mickey's being born. Now you're after his girl.

—Thank you Dr. Freud. That's nonsense. What makes you think I'm after Nia?

—Every time I see you together, your eyes are devouring her.

Alcohol heartburn swims up-gullet like a salmon. Is it that obvious?

—Back to my mother. Schopenhauer's got a whole essay here in which he defends suicide. Where many religions and cultures make it a crime, he says it is heroic. Here's a few lines she marked. He's speaking of religious leaders:

They tell us that suicide is the greatest piece of cowardice; that only a madman could be guilty of it; and other insipidities of the same kind; or else they make the nonsensical remark that suicide is wrong; *when it is quite obvious that there is nothing in the world to which every man has a more unassailable title than to his own life and person.*

—A bit later on he quotes Pliny:

Life is not so desirable a thing as to be protracted at any cost. . . . The chief of all remedies for a troubled mind is the feeling that among the blessings which Nature gives to man, there is none greater than an opportune death; and the best of it is that every one can avail himself of it. . . Not even to God are all things possible; for he could not compass his own death, if he willed to die, and yet in all the miseries of our earthly life, this is the best of his gifts to man.

—Here's Schopenhauer again. I'll stop after this:

It will generally be found that, as soon as the terrors of life reach the point at which they outweigh the terrors of death, a man will put an end to his life. But the terrors of death offer considerable resistance.

—Hamlet said the same thing better. *What things we know not of.*

—True, but my mom didn't mark up Hamlet.

—I can see where this book could have influenced her.

—It was the only book of philosophy on the shelf.

—But her terrors — what were they? Loneliness at the loss of your father? From your description she sounds like a stronger woman than that.

—She'd had a hysterectomy, but the cancer supposedly had been arrested. Loneliness is what they told us, why she took the pills. For ten years we believed that. We hated her for it. At least I did. Because what about me and Chuck? Didn't we count? Didn't we offset her loneliness? It wasn't until ten years later that we learned the truth.

—You mentioned the government.

I lay the Schopenhauer carefully on an end table, and hold up the bottle of Scotch, which is almost empty. Maxie shakes his head no.

—It was the week I graduated from high school. Chuck graduated from Rutgers the same week. The Winslows said they were making a party — just for the four of us. A homemade chocolate cake, and something special. We asked if our friends could come. Not this time, Clara said. Which seemed very strange. After dinner, we blew out candles on a cake. Dan entered the kitchen carrying an old cardboard box. This has been in the basement closet, way in the back, under a plastic wrap, for ten years, he said. Your mother left it with us, sealed. She felt that at the time, you both were too young to understand. She said the day Michael graduated from high school would be a good time to give it to you. In all honesty, we know what's in here. But she swore us to silence. Whether it was right of her to keep this from you for so long, neither of us is sure. But we promised her.

—You mean, you knew she was going to kill herself?

—She asked us, first, if we would take you boys in when she died. We couldn't have children of our own. We said we would.

—Why didn't you stop her! Charles half shouted.

—How could we? Clara said quietly. Without having her locked away in some asylum? She was the sanest woman we knew. She had her reasons. That's what's in the box.

Charles began ripping the yellowed tape off the top.

—Take it easy, I said, don't hurt what's inside.

A faded envelope on top of a pile of papers was marked Medical Records. We raced through them. The hysterectomy was there, but nothing more about cancer. Something about depression. Then came property records. The small house in Yonkers — mom and dad owned it. After her death, the Winslows sold it. They divided the money into thirds. One third in trust for me at age 25, one third for Chuck, the last third for the Winslows, to go towards our upkeep.

—Those were her instructions, Dan said. We carried them out to the letter.

—There's still nothing about why she died, I said. Why was she so lonely? She had you folks. She had other friends — the teachers at school.

—Keep going, Dan said.

The candles on the cake had blackened wicks. Chocolate, my favorite. I was hungry for cake but far more hungry for answers.

The next manila envelope had a return address in the upper left corner. It was thicker than the others. Chuck and I sat beside each other to read the sheets, slowly. They were to Mom from some Congressional committee. Others from some lawyer representing her. Letters going both ways. It turned out that in the late thirties, Mom was part of a group trying to organize the teachers into a union. She attended a bunch of meetings.

—Not the Communist thing! Maxie says.

—They interviewed her. They told her she had been a Communist in the thirties. She denied it. They had pictures showing her at those meetings. She was just trying to organize a union, she said. So they switched tactics. If this was all so innocent, please identify for them anyone else she knew who was at that meeting. Anyone in these pictures. Mom was horrified. Whatever the government was up to, she was not about to snitch on her friends. Ultimately she took the Fifth Amendment. They threatened her with prison. She didn't break. They threatened to take away her teaching license. She didn't budge.

—Joe McCarthy and that gang, that's why she took the pills?

—Wait, Maxie. There was another envelope. Smaller. With a single sheet of typed paper in it. The signature was a blurred scrawl, illegible. That one I have on my shelf. Be right back.

I go to my office. From the top shelf I take down an 8 by 11 sheet of paper preserved under laminate. I return to Maxie, and remain standing as I read aloud:

Dear Mrs. Lee.

It has come to our attention that you have refused to answer questions to help your government root out the Communist menace in this country. That is your legal right, if you are willing to pay the consequences.

Since the last time we questioned you, however, some new facts have come to our attention, which may convince you to change your position. Therefore we feel it appropriate to inform you of them at this time.

Previously it has been reported, and so recorded, that your husband, Marine Captain Thomas A. Lee, is missing in action, since his plane went down in the Yellow Sea. However, we now have witnesses who tell a much different story. They maintain that although Captain Lee did drop his aircraft to a lower altitude, he then righted it and flew safely past North Korea. As his craft plunged into the sea, according to these witnesses, who are prepared to testify under oath, Captain Lee parachuted to safety in Mainland Communist China. In other words, Captain Lee is not really Missing in Action, but is in fact a turncoat. A coward who abandoned his own troops and joined forces with the enemy, no doubt betraying some of America's best-kept secrets.

At the moment, these new facts are closely held by this committee. But should you continue to protect your friends and fellow teachers against prosecution for their un-American activities, there would be no reason for this new information about your husband to remain secret any longer. It will, as it must in a free society like ours, be reported to the press and through them to the public. Any effect this might have on your life in the future — and on the lives of your two fine sons being labeled the children of a turncoat — cannot, of course, be our major concern.

If you care to meet again with the committee, perhaps to revise your testimony in light of this new information, you may contact us at the usual number.

Should you show this letter to the press and claim it is a threat, we shall deny its authenticity. At the same time, we will bring forward the above information about Captain Lee.

Looking forward to your change of heart, I remain,

—Then comes an illegible scrawled signature, and the scrawled name of the House un-American Activities Committee.

Finished reading aloud, I sink into my chair, exhausted from revisiting the past.

—That's when your mother killed herself?

—Four days later. In June, 1952. Her death was for me and Chuck. To save us from the false, trumped up disgrace of a turncoat father. Which could have ruined our lives. It would have, in those days. Maybe no college. No med school. A lifetime blacklist.

—Sons of bitches! When you found that out — you were about 18? — you stopped hating her? And perhaps all women. I'm sorry, Michael, Freud again.

—When I found that out, I started hating the government. I was in a bomb-throwing mood. But at what? At whom? I guess I did stop fearing girls, women, fearing emotional commitment, risking being abandoned, as my mother had abandoned us. Maybe there was a residue — why I couldn't return Morgan's love. Perhaps I still couldn't trust. Then Addie Judd appeared — overseas. I'll say *interesting* before you do. I was cured. I fell hopelessly in love. The future was at our feet.

—Then Addie died.

—Yes. Then Addie died.

Lest he ask how, I'm sober enough to short-circuit the question with another quotation.

—Some Frenchman — I can never remember his name — once wrote: *Chance is perhaps the pseudonym of God when he does not wish to sign his work.*

The heavy, textured silence of cogitation follows. I pull open the drapes to let in the late afternoon light, which is filled with white motes drifting aimlessly. Maxie and I identify.

—Chinaman's chance, Maxie says.

His voice is slurred slightly from the booze.

—What?

—The Chinese gang killed Laurette. The way it was done, she didn't have a Chinaman's chance. I heard that expression constantly as a kid in Pittsburgh. We knew what it meant, but not why. Not where it came from.

I'm not sure of the origin. I doubt it still applies, though, with China taking over the world economy. *Progress is our most important product.* Ronald Reagan for General Motors. Now it would be for Beijing.

A knock on the door. Maxie cringes. Not Sophie again! I peer through the blinds.

—Relax, it's not her. It's a van from the funeral home.

—I wonder what they want. It's all paid for. Death on a Credit Card.

A good name for a book. I open the door. A young man is holding a paper sack.

—This is for a Max Klonsky. If there was no answer there, they said, bring it here. It was supposed to go in a coffin, they said. We found it outside the funeral home this morning. But someone screwed up, it never got to the right person. They said to get your signature, but I ain't got no pen or paper.

He glances about the house from the doorstep, says, *It looks like we can trust ya.*

He hands me the sack. It feels like there is a glass jar inside. I hear liquid sloshing. Suddenly I know what it must be. Jesus, Maxie doesn't need this now. But the bag has his name scrawled on it. He's a grown man, I can't protect him.

I fail to tip the kid. Is there etiquette for this sort of thing?

Maxie's eyes are half closed with exhaustion.

—This came for you.

—What is it?

Outside, the van is pulling away.

—Prepare yourself, Maxie. It won't be easy.

He tries to widen his heavy lids, reaches out from his chair.

— Give it already!

I hand him the bag. He pulls the small jar from it. It takes him a moment to focus.

—Oh, Jesus! Oh fucking God in Heaven! Oh, shit!

He rolls into a fetal position in the soft chair. Cradles the jar to his chest. Begins to blubber, can't hold back, tears pouring down. Laurette's dark eyes float in the jar, the jar he's clutching to his heart.

He doesn't want any drug beyond Scotch. Any tranquilizer. I offered Xanax earlier. He said Laurette deserves that he feel all the pain, not dull it with chemistry. I guide him to sleep on my bed.

Captain Doyle comes by soon after I call the precinct.

—Maxie's prints are on the jar, I tell him. But there might be others. The person who put the eyes in the jar.

Doyle agrees, takes with him the jar of water with Laurette's eyes floating in it, bobbing eyes turning this way and that, as if trying to discover where they belong. Where they are going.

Maxie is snoring lightly. I want to wait up for the fingerprint results. I go to the computer, Silicon Valley's answer to sex. I Google Chinaman's Chance. The phrase apparently originated during the building of the railroad in the west. Chinese workers were paid less than whites, but had to do the most dangerous jobs. Like blasting with dynamite. That's not quite an explanation for what it means. It's been shortened through the years from Chinaman's Chance in Hell. But the origin is no clearer.

Laurette's murder, I think, had to do with more than running drugs. With more than the three gang jerks arrested. Choosing her to steal drugs made no sense at all. It's too late now, I'll check my hunch in the morning.

I put up coffee to brew. Hours pass. Maxie is still asleep. Or passed out. Captain Doyle calls back.

—We got a few clear sets, probably Klonsky's, as you said. We'll take his tomorrow. A few other partials that we ran through the system. We got a hit.

—You did?

My heartbeat accelerating.

—Don't get excited, doctor. The guy's got no real record. No violence. One arrest, for soliciting. He copped a plea, paid a fine, that was it. The prints might not mean anything.

—Do you have a name?

—Yeah, it's here somewhere. Come to think of it, this guy could be related to the killing. Sounds Chinese. His name is Chen.

—Kenneth Chen? The bastard! You nailed him, Captain.

—No, that's not right. Not Kenneth. Lenny. Lenny Chen.

—That can't be.

—You know him?

—Not really. I know of him. From what I've heard, he couldn't hurt a fruit fly in heat.

I don't know what to make of Lenny Chen's prints on the jar of eyes.

—Captain, do you have full computer access at the station?

—No, doctor, we prefer smoke signals.

—Okay, one point for you.

—I'm serious. Since 9/11 the feds have mandated almost all their money to terrorism. There's not much left over for police work. At the same time, the DOJ estimates we've got 15,000 Asian gang members in California alone. Vietnamese, Laotian, Cambodian even more than Chinese. That said, what is it you need?

—I didn't realize there were near that many. I'd like to call you tomorrow with another name to check. A girl. About 16, I think.

— No girl gouged those eyes.

— I didn't say she did

—It's a good thing we're looking Asian. A new report came in the other day. Says Los Angeles alone has a hundred thousand gangs. A hundred thousand! Mostly Mexican and South American, of course. Guys get deported, spin glamorous tales of gang life, come back with a couple of new recruits. One guy was deported 23 times. International street gangs are the new Mafia. Especially in the drug trade.

—Let's hope they don't hook up with Al-Qaida. But if they wipe out America, who will they sell drugs to?

I hang up. A hundred thousand gangs in L.A. Like 800 billion suns.

Impatient, antsy, I keep looking at my watch. There's no reason to. Medical Records been closed for hours. I hear Maxie stirring, ambling to the bathroom, washing his face. I imagine dry tears flowing down the drain. Virtual grief. I'd had too much drink myself, so I call a taxi to take him home. He says he's not going home, Sophie might be there. He's going to Laurette's. He needs to look over her possessions, figure out what to do with them. Which is bullshit, that can wait, he concedes. He wants to sleep in her bed. One more time. Amid the aroma of her sheets. Her things. She may be in her grave, but he's not ready to cut her out of his life. Not yet.

Chapter 13: Ginger

Valentino. Jalapenos Sol. Nike.

The dream takes place in a bar near Columbia called The West End. It's packed with students, as it usually was in life. All are wearing sunglasses, skimpy bathing suits, hiking boots, though beyond the windows it is night, headlights and tail lights of yellow cabs shooting by in both directions. In a corner brown leatherette booth sit Martin Luther King Jr. and Meyer Lansky, the gangster, drinking beer, nibbling not pretzels or peanuts but ginger snaps.

Ellen Tracy. Bottey Veneta. iZon.

Dr. King pulls an unmarked manila envelope from his lap. Bulging slightly in the middle. Silently he pushes it to Lansky across the table upon which the two beers sit, half drained, and the open box of cookies. I thought you might want these, King says. Lansky nods, moves the envelope out of sight beneath the table to the seat beside him. As if he knows what's inside without looking. This apparently is the first time they have met. They talk. Bones. Diseases. The hikers in sunglasses pay no attention to these celebrities in their midst, even when Dr. King picks up a ginger snap and fits it into his eye, like a monocle.

Maui Jim. Bucci. Daggers.

I wake with a throbbing hangover from too much Scotch. I seek meaning in my dream, if any. With me, dreamed initials often matter, for some reason. They're often a good starting point. As in Meyer Lansky. A criminal who got away with it. M. L. *Mike Lee?*

Martin Luther King. The good guy. *Max Lubitch Klonsky?*

Jew and non-Jew are reversed, but it's a dream, not a memory. They talk of bones and diseases. They must represent us. We were both med students. It's a thinly disguised replay of what really happened. With dream alterations. In real life we met for the exchange at the Riviera, on Seventh Avenue down in the Village. The Riv. Closer to where Maxie lived. So why the West End in the dream? Because the bus went off the west end of the island! The only place they would have died that day. Also, in life this exchange was not the first meeting of Maxie and me, it was the second. We'd met for the first time — the beginning of our long friendship — a week earlier. On Rikers Island.

Hikers. Rikers?

Why dream this now? No doubt because the victims are coming back and I don't know what to do about it.

I'm lying in bed, in no hurry to face the morning — it's Wednesday, no surgeries. I turn onto my side, press my throbbing headache into a cool part of the pillow, my right arm underneath it for support. I pretend the pillow is Nia's breast. At night that often cures insomnia.

The ginger snaps puzzle me the most. Instead of the peanuts in bowls at the West End. Is someone supposed to be gay? It doesn't fit. A ginger snap in the Reverend's eye. Me looking at it. Unless — Virginia Soto. Who went by Ginger. Who wanted to be a nun before she became a nurse. Is my unconscious hinting that Ginger will be next?

At times I write down my dreams . But never my sexual fantasies. Nia's bedroom is fifteen feet from mine. I'd surely get arrested, in this Christian nation of ours, by the erotic thought police.

There's been a new element in the fantasies this week. Our intimacies are being watched, from every angle, high and low, by 99 lascivious eyes. The effect is explosive.

I don't hear Nia come home.

Morning. I complete my ablutions, don a light robe. Nia's door is open, her bed already made. I look out the kitchen window. Her car, the red Volvo convertible, is gone, though this is her late day as well. The dear girl has brewed extra coffee, anticipating my hangover. What a wife Mickey will be getting. I pour a cup, add milk, carry it to the breakfast nook. There's a small package on my side of the table. On top a folded note on her off-white stationary. The writing is almost calligraphy, which she practices during slow days at the recruitment office. She's never idle.

Dear Michael,

> *I couldn't find an appropriate card for you. This will have to do.*
> *Happy Birthday.*
> *Love,*
> *Nia*

She remembered my birthday! Amazing. I almost forgot it. The gift is in dark blue wrapping paper from one of the closets.

Love, Nia. Not just her name. Not fondly, or affectionately. Don't read anything into it, I warn myself, but my chest is giddy. *Love, Nia.*

I tear open the wrapping. It's a book, trade paperback, a new copy but not a new book. It came out a few years ago, they made a hit move of it. I haven't read the book or seen the movie, but I always wanted to. Cormac McCarthy. *No Country for Old Men.* The cover looks dim and foreboding. I flip through the pages. McCarthy appears to have returned to the old, icily simple style I enjoyed before he became famous. *Child of God.* A crazy old hillbilly coot who rapes corpses. The title ironic. Then McCarthy turned faux-Faulkner. *All the Pretty Horses,* the rest of his border trilogy. He became famous but he lost me. This one looks good, however.

So why have I suddenly become depressed? My eyes heavy, salamander spinning a web, like a spider, in my gut. I always believed the half-life of happiness was four hours. This morning it's four minutes.

The title. This came out — I check the copyright page — in 2005. Why did Nia choose it now? She could have selected a new hardback, the price wouldn't hurt her. But it's not that it's paperback that matters, it's the thought that counts, right? *Love, Nia.* So why this book? *No Country for Old Men.* To send me a message? To her I am an old man. And no country? She knows Hamlet is my inner alter-ego. Approaching Ophelia, he wants to put his head in her lap. She demurs. *Did you think I meant country matters?* Nia's subtle refusal, before I've even asked: Her country is not for old men.

Her car pulls into the driveway. Should I talk about this? No, just thank her for the gift.

She enters through the kitchen door, singing, finds me at the table. Shorts, tennis shoes, Marines T-shirt, sweat circles around her armpits, hair in a pony tail. I ask if she had a good run. She nods, approaches, leans over, kisses me lightly on the top of my head.

—Happy Birthday, Michael!

As if everything is fine.

—Thanks for the book, it looks good.

—I hope so. I got it in the mall. They have employee recommendations posted. Five of the seven recommended this. Maybe because the movie just came out in DVD.

My depression, which has a mind of its own, which comes and goes as it pleases, can't decide whether it's free to move on.

—That's how you picked it?

—Is something wrong with that?

I stand, put my arms around her — careful, I'm sweaty, she says — and kiss her cheek.

— Thanks for remembering. That was very thoughtful. I'm sure I'll enjoy it.

—I hope so.

She excuses herself to shower.

—One thing I've been meaning to ask you. Those two guys who showed up your first night at work. Did they ever come back?

—One did, and signed up. Another signed Friday. I'm hoping for more as word gets around. The corps is so depleted since Iraq, every body counts. Let me rephrase that. Every recruit is important.

I nod, wave her off to get clean. Lucky Dial. Lucky sweat. I sip cool coffee, inhale the brief holding of her. Begin humming the Beatles. They've been in my head for days. The same old tune. *Will you still want me . . .* I place the coffee in the microwave. Thirty seconds will warm it. I punch in 64.

Feelin' groovy.

I get down to the business of the morning. Get the medical records department on the phone. About a month ago, I tell Mollie. Maybe six weeks. No, I don't know her name, that's what I need. A girl about 17. A bullet in her brain. Dr. Klonsky operating.

—You have no record of her being admitted? Well, there wouldn't be. She was brought to ER almost brain dead, died during surgery. You're right, Mollie, I should have told you that in the first place. I'll hold . . . That sounds right, 16. Susan Fong. An address listed? Okay. No insurance, the family never paid. Thanks Mollie. I appreciate it.

I catch Captain Doyle at the precinct, sipping coffee, like me.

—I need you to run something through your smoke signals, Captain. On the Dubal murder. Do you by any chance have gang rosters in your computers? Yeah, I imagine they wouldn't be complete. Only those who've been arrested? Okay. Susan Fong, 16, of Santa Clara. You remember the case? Mid August.

—Loitering in a gang roust in July.

— Does it say what gang?

—Silver Broads? A police joke, right? Silver Birds. *Hadassah* of the Golden Swords? You're well-versed in ethnics for an Irishman, captain. Does the computer connect her with any one guy?

— She could have been the main squeeze of the gang leader, Kenneth Chen.

I listen as he recalls the case to me.

—That's what happened? He saw a rival gang member pointing a rifle at him from across the street as he drove by, and he ducked, let his girl take it in the head? A great leader. I'd follow him anywhere. Here's the thing, Captain. Max Klonsky told me about that girl after she died. He said she was nearly dead when they brought her in to ER. He warned the family not to get its hopes up, the chances were only one in twenty she'd survive an operation. But if he didn't operate she'd be dead in an hour. He gave it a try. He was real shaken when he lost her. He says to me the next day, when I remind him of the odds, he says, That's what they pay me for, the twenty to one shots. What I'm thinking, Captain, is maybe Ken Chen killed Laurette Dubal for revenge. He blamed Klonsky for her death instead of himself, the coward. At least in front of his gang. That would explain the rifle shot from afar, instead of a pistol to her head. Eye for an eye, isn't that the mantra of all gangs? His girlfriend gets killed, he kills Klonsky's lady.

—There's no military record, he didn't learn to shoot there.

—Maybe he never learned to shoot. He just kept firing until he got lucky. That's why the ankle chains. He made her a sitting duck. The drug stuff never made sense, it could have been a cover, to spread suspicion. If he just kills her, it points right at him. The arrest of his three honchos with the drugs puts pressure on him to take revenge for the whole gang.

—That's all speculation, doctor.

—Sure it's only speculation. You need proof? You're the police, not me. But that's enough to make him a prime suspect, isn't it? A person of interest, excuse me. You'll pick him up? If you can find him. I guess that would be necessary.

I hang up. The state police want city cops to question me about the Dubal killing. Because of my name on the note. The Captain said to consider myself questioned, we'll fill in the blanks later, his donut is getting stale.

Hadassah?

I sip my coffee. It's luke warm again. The thing is, what to tell Maxie. He feels so guilty about taking Laurette to the cops. Would this make it better, or worse? That Ken-Chen would have killed her anyway, blaming him for Susan Fong. The bastards. I need to ponder, see what Nia thinks, she's good about people. Or Vicky.

Damn! What to do about Vicky? Without delivering a ton of pills, is she next?

I should call Maxie, see how he's holding up. But he might be still asleep at Laurette's, hung over. Given how my head wants to burst, his must be giving birth. I leave him be. I don't have the number there anyway. When he wants to talk he'll call me.

I take the book of sonnets from my complete Shakespeare set as I leave. I stop in room 103. Morgan's eyes are closed, her breathing regular. Call it sleep? I'm not sure. She's asleep in another world. If there is another world in there.

I ask her how she's doing. Sit on the hospital chair beside her. I'm going to read you some poetry today, how's that? Her eyelids do not flutter. I close my eyes and are wrenched by her pain, though Maxie says she's not in pain. Her false imprisonment, then. I no longer cry, though I would if I could.

I turn to Sonnet 138. When I came across it recently it knocked me out. I would not read it to Morgan if she could hear. Even Shakespeare knew the problem, the subject being Nia and me — I hope, some day soon.

Reading aloud, best rendition I can muster. The new meaning of rendition: torture in a far away place. Okay. Sonnet Number 38:

> *When my love swears that she is made of truth,*
> *I do believe her, though I know she lies,*
> *That she might think me some untutor'd youth,*
> *Unlearned in the world's false subtleties.*
> *Thus vainly thinking that she thinks me young,*
> *Although she knows my days are past the best,*
> *Simply I credit her false-speaking tongue:*
> *On both sides thus is simple truth suppress'd.*
> *But wherefore says she not she is unjust?*
> *And wherefore say not I that I am old?*
> *O, love's best habit is in seeming trust,*
> *And age in love loves not to have years told:*
> *Therefore I lie with her and she with me,*
> *And in our faults by lies we flatter'd be.*

—Do you get it, Morgan? The old English can be difficult. It's like a little play. I am old and Nia is young. She says she never lies — and tells me I am not old. I know she is lying, but I choose to believe her, since she says she never lies. I don't tell her I am old, so she trusts that I am not. Even though she knows the truth. The key line: *And age in love loves not to have years told.* Of course, today being my birthday, Nia is very cognizant that I'm old. But can we fake it? Here's typical Bard: *Therefore I lie with her and she with me.* The pun the sonnet is building to. By lying to each other, we lie with each other. Sex — or love — is triumphant. Which is what they both want. *Love's best habit is in seeming trust.* The old boy says so much in one line.

—Is that what you offered me, Morgan, only seeming trust? Did you have lovers I knew nothing of?

I never thought of that before.

I peer at her eyes. They're open but offer no response. A small smile steals across her lips. An illusion, of course, to further madden me.

Think back. Who could it have been? I have no idea.

A flash of white light explodes momentarily in my eyes, my brain. *An accident,* she'd said. Is Mickey even mine?

Mrs. Newman is ready in surgery. Fuch's Dystrophy — bad endothelial cells — caused corneal edema, requiring a corneal transplant. From a donor. A cadaver. Aka penetrating keratoplasty. The aneseo guy has injected her with retrobulbar, a combination of lidocaine and marcaine, because this surgery takes longer than a cataract, the eye needs to be deadened for an hour. Her head is taped across her forehead to the table so if she falls asleep, then wakes up not knowing where she is, and jerks up, she won't pierce her eye. Many docs only tape patients they feel might not hold still. I tape them all. Why take chances?

Some patients ask to be put totally out during the procedure. That's not necessary. Eye deadening medication takes care of it. We don't let them tell us what to do. Instead we reassure them. Tell them full anesthesia could cause other problems, with this they won't even know what we did. And they don't. Lots of time in the holding room afterward they'll ask, So when are you gonna start?

I'm about to insert the circular blade in Mrs. Newman's eye when she speaks through her fear.

—Dr. Lee, are you sure you've got the right kind of cornea?

—Absolutely. It's been measured several times, it's perfect for you.

—Measuring I trust you, that's your job. I mean, you know, the *right kind.*

She has me puzzled. I insert the circular blade, am about to twist it, cut out her cornea. Delicate stuff. Suddenly I understand what she means. I hold off what I'm doing.

—Mrs. Newman, are you referring to a Jewish cornea?

—Shhh, not so loud. I wouldn't want to offend anyone. But you understand me, that's why I like you.

What to tell her? I've never been asked anything like that before. I'm stumped. But silly inspiration wings its way into the windowless operating room like a drunken dove.

—All corneas are Jewish, Mrs. Newman. None of them has a foreskin.

— I'm serious.

—I'm afraid the eye bank doesn't distinguish from whom the corneas come. They're harvested in the emergency room — mostly from young people, maybe 17 to 25. Just the corneas, the rest of the eye is useless for transplanting. The cornea is put in a nutrient broth to keep it fresh, put on ice in a styrofoam cooler, like they're going on a picnic. Off to the eye-bank they go. The nearest is in Santa Clara. When we schedule surgery, we call and they send one over. Yours probably arrived here yesterday.

Talking to keep her mind occupied. One thing I never tell patients, harvesting from corpses is not done by doctors or nurses, or even techs. Volunteers from the Lion's Club or the Elks can go to the ER and cut on the dead. Sever the optic nerve and the muscles that hold the eyeball in place, remove the cornea. It saves money, but it's not an image most patients would want to carry around. Joe Roto-Rooter or Sam Six-Pack supplying their new part.

I *shush* Mrs. Newman to remain quiet. Press the blade in, twist it. The cutting complete, I lift out the circular button in front of the lens that is the cornea. Set it aside in a dish. It will go to pathology lab for tests. Anything we remove from a person goes to the lab. A precaution.

The scrub tech hands me the dish with the replacement. A different scrub, experienced in corneas. Annie something. Heavyset Irish woman with a round face like a blushing oatmeal cookie. Been here for years, knows her stuff. The new cornea will be slightly larger than the old — say 8.5 millimeters to 8, give a margin of safety. A silence while Annie hands me the harvested cornea allows Mrs. Newman to speak.

—You mean I could even be getting — how shall I put it, the proper word has changed so much during my life. *Schvartze*, my father said. Colored, Negro, Black, African-American. I could be getting a cornea from one of them? See the world through their eye?

— Human corneas are all the same, I assure her, there's nothing to worry about. As I told you last week, they just help the lens focus the image on the retina. Interpreting what you see is in your brain.

—So this new part of me could be from a big black man. Or woman, is that right?

—Correct. No difference.

—You know something? It might be interesting. Seeing the world through their eye. I might have plenty to tell the mahjong ladies.

—Okay, you need to keep quiet now. Talking moves your head, your eye. We can't have that while I stitch.

I lean forward, set the cadaver cornea in place. I never use the word cadaver, of course. Say donor cornea — like a contribution to the temple building fund. Say harvested — like wheat in a Van Gogh. I need to stitch all around it. Interrupted sutures, as on the face of a clock, 12, 6, 3, 9. Then fill the spaces between. The nylon is 10-0. Forceps to tie a knot with. Scissors to cut the nylon. Forceps to bury the knot. Annie knows the drill. I'm about to begin at 12 when I pause. Corneas are clear but in the new one for Mrs. Newman something is gleaming — not a face but a goddamn silver cross.

What the fuck? Where did that come from?

A glimmer of understanding. A stage set for Ginger Soto.

What would Mrs. Newman think if I told her she's got a crucifix in her eye? Well, take it out, she might say. Like a cinder. Or she might jump down from the table, the tape breaking her neck as she twists. Or she might be okay with it, since Jesus is nowhere in sight. I turn my head and cough into my mask to avoid questions about the delay. Also to hide my grin at the irony.

I recognize the cross specifically. In miniature, it's the huge ungainly aluminum cross that towers over the landscape in desolate Groom, Texas, population about 12. Surrounded by sculptures of the twelve stations of the cross. Right off Interstate 40, we used to see it driving to Dallas to visit Morgan's sister, who married an oil man. My dream interpretation was correct, at the bottom of the cross is a motel maid who can only be Ginger Soto. Breaking the pattern, showing up in the first surgery of the day instead of the last. Rebellion in the ranks?

I keep control. Ginger not a threat as long as I concentrate. I begin the sutures. Infinitesimally small for large fingers like mine. That's why I usually avoid corneal cuts. Nylon suture at 12, at 6. At 3. This would be so much easier for Lacey with her slim fingers.

Inter faeces et urinam nascimur. St. Augustine could never have imagined that his most quoted axiom, centuries later, would be that one: *Between shit and piss are we born.* The quotation always reminds me of Amarillo, and vice versa. Ginger Soto was born there. The shit is at Wildorado, 10 or 15 miles west of the city, depending where in sprawling Amarillo you measure from. That giant slaughterhouse, whose pungent perfumes you never forget if you once drive by. Hundreds, maybe thousands of cows standing about — they don't have room to mill — perhaps hearing the bleating of their cow friends or their sisters and brothers whose throats are being cut in the nearby building — perhaps knowing they are next, shitting a storm about it. Who wouldn't? Driving by, if you forget to roll your windows up tight as you pass you carry the smell in your car all the way to the Big Texan restaurant at the far end of Amarillo. Eat a 72 ounce steak in an hour and it's free. For what better cause can a cow give its life?

Ginger's dad, Frank Soto, worked at the slaughterhouse. Came home every evening stinking — his clothes, his lunch pail, his hair, every part of him stinking. A hot shower in an outhouse was the first order of business before Elsie Soto, Ginger's mom, would allow him into the doublewide. When she was old enough it became Ginger's job to scrub his lunch box and wash his clothes. She tried to hold her breath the whole time, and wondered how such a foul place as Wildorado could exist when about 30 miles up the Interstate east of Amarillo was the huge silver cross at Groom, donated by some millionaire, billed as the largest cross in the Western Hemisphere. By referring to this particular construction as piss I in no way mean to denigrate the crucifix as a powerful symbol to hundreds of million of people. I merely object to its enormous incarnation alongside a federal highway as (to borrow from Tom Robbins) another roadside attraction. Ginger, however, thought it the most beautiful thing on earth. On Sundays Elsie would drive Ginger to the cross and they would pray together at its base — pray for Frank to get another job, or for the shit of doomed cows, sold by the ton as fertilizer, to take on the aroma of roses.

A slaughterhouse can also be called an abattoir. Far more refined. Feces would tickle the nostrils like Chanel. Or a French style boutique, in which a sales person resembling Lacey Roberts demonstrates to lip-licking husbands the latest silk lingerie from Paris. For their teen mistresses. The Wildorado Abattoir, on the other hand, is a prehistoric beast, with razor-sharp tusks, which roamed North Texas during the Cambrian era.

Fourth definition for abattoir: A *pissoir* for French clergy.

Which leads us to Ginger Soto's embracing a nunnery.

Nylon stitch into 3. Begin filling in with tighter stitches around the edges of the cornea-clock. Long story short, Ginger, decked to her neck in crosses, became a nun. Was told the local order thrived on helping people. Was ordered to study nursing. Which she did. Was sent off to serve those who needed her skills most, men and women locked in cages for their sins. There's always a shortage of prison hospital nurses. Ginger wound up working, and working well, in the prison ward at Rikers Island, New York. Three years later she was on the bus that plunged into the river, killing all on board.

I place a round of new stitches between the others. They will keep the cornea attached for months, till they can be safely removed, leaving the cadaver cornea in place, whether it's Jewish or Schvartze or Saudi royalty.

A zoom effect occurs in Mrs. Newman's eye. Across a narrow road at the bottom of the giant cross is a small motel. After drowning, Ginger has gone home to Texas, is working as a maid at The Crossroads. She changes and washes sheets and pillow cases, scrubs toilets and sinks. She does not mind, because she is washing the sheets and pillow cases and toilets of pilgrims, who arrive in buses from all over the South. From each room when she is finished vacuuming she peers out the window at the great edifice, knowing she is one day closer to her goal, which is to become the Keeper of the Cross. Near the base of the monument is a small gift shop selling postcards, small replicas of the cross, all manner of religious symbols, to the passing parade. The shop is run by a gray-haired woman named Betsy George. She's been there for years, is bound to die or retire soon. Ginger has been promised by her multiple angels, once even by God himself, who perched on the crossbar disguised as a bluebird, that when Betsy George retires or dies, she, Ginger Soto, clearly qualified, as a former nun, will achieve her goal in life and become Keeper of the Cross.

I lean closer to the eye. The small sutures are more difficult as the circumference becomes crowded as a rush-hour bus. Ginger, mop and pail in hand, stands in front of The Crossroads, peering up at the most beautiful thing she has ever seen, the millionaire's tourist cross. Turning, she looks at me. I wait expectantly. She says nothing. I knew she would not. When she went to work at The Crossroads, in her life after the river, she took a vow of silence. She would not speak, she vowed, until she attained her dream. This does not stop her from waving to me gaily, as if killing her was the best thing I've done.

Hey, Doc Lee, how's it going?

Startled by her voice, I accidentally snap a suture.

—Cheap nylon!

I take another piece.

Ginger, you're talking. Does that mean you got the job?

It sure doesn't look like it with her mop and pail.

Did Betsy George finally retire?

Nope, she's stubborn that way. But she's dying. Tomorrow afternoon.

How do you know that?

I'm going to kill her.

I snap another stitch. Sweating. Glad I'm not a resident being judged.

—Damn it! We need better materials in here. Vicky, make a note of that.

I don't think she does. She knows I'm playing to the others.

What do you mean you're going to kill her?

Nervous now. Don't want to snap another.

I pray every day at the stations of the cross. For all the dead women. But mostly for Addie Judd. I also pray for you. How long do good people have to wait before they get what they want, doc? I've been a nun, a nurse, scrubbed toilets for worshippers. It's time, don't you think?

Some good people never get what they want.

Well, I decided you have to go after it. Make it happen. So tomorrow I'm gonna poison her tea. I bring her tea every day at four. I'm using rat poison. With lots of orange to hide the taste. She likes orange tea. I talked with Jesus, he said it was okay.

Are you sure it was Jesus you talked to, not Satan in disguise?

Are you kidding? Satan wouldn't come near this place.

What if you get caught? The Texas Rangers are pretty good, I hear. There would be lots of evidence against you. Where you got the rat poison. You bringing her the tea. You being the one who benefits from her death.

Do you really think the Texas Rangers are more powerful than Jesus?

Not many people get away with killing, I say. Knowing the opposite is true.

You seem to have done okay.

A sharp spasm strikes my back. I try to complete the sutures without looking at her.

Addie will be visiting you soon.

Then she is gone.

—I'm almost finished, just a few more stitches, Mrs. Newman. You're doing great. Making my job real easy.

I take deep breaths before I finish. All the madness that's swirling around me like autumn leaves, inside and outside my skull, hit me with a rush. A crisis in every direction. Nia. Maxie. Vicky.

—Take you time, Bro', I ain got to hurry, Mrs. Newman says, I ain goin' nowhere 'cep back to da hood. Shoot some one-eyed craps. Score some mothafuckin one-eyed horse. Maybe a street ho' or two.

The four of us — the tech, the anestho, Vicky, myself — all bite our lips, hard, to keep laughter from erupting. Not because Mrs. Newman captured the intonation of a black street kid — she didn't — but because she did the black patois with a Yiddish accent. I can hear her tutor angels applauding: Jack Benny, Groucho Marx, George Burns, Fred Allen. I recall her telling me that she worked in Hollywood when she was young. Did cartoon voice-overs. Once, when she filled in for Daisy Duck, she began ad-libbing with a Yiddish take, plenty filthy. It cracked up Huey, Dewey and Louie. It couldn't be released, of course, but the piece of film, stashed in a Disney vault somewhere, is said to be priceless.

—Yo', Doc, how long afore I kin shoot some one-eye hoops?

Corneal replacement often takes an hour. I wrapped this up in 48 minutes, despite Ginger. Vicky and I each sip from a bottle of water during the resulting break. Vicky looks tired, her face drawn, her skin tighter than usual over her cheekbones.

—Dr. Lee, can I ask you a favor?

—Of course. Anything.

—It's real short notice. Could you come to my place for dinner tomorrow night?

—That's not a favor, that's an honor.

—Mrs. Ling asked me to ask you.

—Oh? She's not trying to . . .

—She knows you're married. She knows I'm married. This is about Ken-Chen. He'll be there as well.

—He'll be there? What is this, an antisocial evening? I don't understand.

Thinking: not if the cops find him first, and some evidence.

—When they killed Laurette I got really frightened. I couldn't sleep. I sat up all night watching Maya breathe. And I decided I had to tell my parents about the threats. I didn't want to at first, but we're a family. They're smart, maybe they would have an idea. Mr. Ling listened in silence. I could see the anger building in his face. A tic started in one eye. When I was through, he looked at Mrs. Ling, and said they would think about it. Last night Mrs. Ling called me. She said there would be a dinner at my house Friday night. Eight o'clock. They would bring the food. She said I must call Ken-Chen and invite him. She gave me the number. They know him from the restaurant, as you saw. I should tell him he could bring my husband, too. Maya will be at her friend's house. It's a family peace talk, I guess, though Mrs. Ling did not say that. She said I should ask you to come as well. They know I told you about the threats.

—What did Ken-Chen say?

—He asked if I would have the drugs. I didn't know how to answer. I said maybe, it depends. He was suspicious, he said there better not be any funny business, you saw what happened to that other bitch after she went to the cops. I said I know, how could I pull funny business after that?

—I don't know what to make of this. I'm the only one who's not family.

—I work with you, to them that's family. Will you come?

—Of course. I don't know what help I'll be. But I know the food will be good. What about the restaurant?

—They're closing early. A family matter. Thank you, doctor. Oh, yes, they asked you to bring something.

That surprised me. They run a well-stocked restaurant.

— Beer? Wine?

—Something you've never brought to a dinner party before. The other night, when Mrs. Ling and I were talking on the phone, I told them about your new eye collection. Last night she asked if you could bring to dinner two eyes. Brown.

—Why would they want those?

—To play a trick on Ken-Chen.

That did not sound good. Like tempting the devil.

—He doesn't seem to have much sense of humor. What if he takes it wrong? But I guess your folks know what they're doing. At least now I understand why I was invited. Because of my beautiful eyes.

Vicky punches me lightly on my arm.

—Now you know how women feel.

I'm not sure whether to smile or nod. She's so damn quick.

—Also, if I may say so, you did a great job with the cornea just now. Even though you had a visitor.

—Ginger Soto. From Texas. Was it that obvious?

—Only to me. The others didn't notice a thing. But doctor, this one, too, you saw killed? And didn't report it? That's very strange.

—Some day I'll tell you the whole story, Vicky. Trust me.

—Like that T-shirt that's in all the store windows? *Trust Me, I'm a Doctor.*

—Exactly. I need to get one of those.

Somewhere in one of the books in my crowded library a stick-it note marks a seminal sentence. I don't remember which book — I think it's an E.M. Forster — but the sentence has informed my life. It reads: *It is a pity that Man cannot be at the same time impressive and truthful.*

—One reminder, Vicky says. Tomorrow you've got a glaucoma. It's one of Dr. Beecham's patients. Dr. Roberts can't assist, she'll be in Oklahoma for her sister's wedding .

—I forgot about that. I'll brush up tonight. It's like riding a bicycle, as they say.

—I know the saying. I used to ride all over Chinatown as a child. Last week I got on Maya's bike. I didn't get five feet before I toppled.

—Thanks for the encouragement, Victoria.

—That's what nurses are for.
Before I can think of a comeback she is gone.

Chapter 14: Mrs. Ling

Friday morning. I'm uneasy about this so-called dinner party at Vicky's. Me and Victoria and the two elderly Lings alone with Ken-Chen? And them planning a trick on Chen? It doesn't feel right.

I lift the eye display off my Mexican chest. I take two brown eyes, slip them into a plastic sandwich bag. set it beside my coffee. Reaching to the bottom of the trunk, I pull out my father's pistol. It feels rough, rusty to the touch, though no rust is visible. I take it to the kitchen to examine it. I have no idea if it's loaded or not. Nia — it's her late morning — joins me there in sweats, asks what the gun is about. My father's, I tell her. She takes it from me, cracks it open.

—It's not loaded. I just wanted to make sure. Do you know anything about guns, Michael?

—Not a thing.

—Have you ever fired this?

—Never.

She's looking at it closely, sniffing the barrel, turning it over in her hands, releasing what I figure is the safety catch, pointing it at the floor, cocking the trigger. Pulling it. Click.

—It feels like it hasn't been fired in fifty years. Or oiled, either.

—That's about right. It's just a remembrance of my dad. I used to think I'd learn to shoot, but I never got around to it.

—What's it doing out now?

I tell her about the dinner party, my uneasiness about Ken-Chen, that he may have killed Laurette.

—Shit! So why go?

—I can't leave Vicky and the old folks alone with him. He's already invited. They expect me to be there.

—Perhaps I could come as your date. With a revolver that works.

—It's at eight o'clock. You work until nine.

—For this I could close early.

—I would love for you to be my date (how nice that sounds) but I don't know what's going on. I can't get you involved. I'm probably overreacting, the Lings wouldn't put their daughter in danger.

—Whatever you say. But don't take the revolver. If you pull it on someone who's really armed, you're dead. God, those eyes.

— My contribution to dinner, apparently.

—You couldn't find a nice Chinese beer? Michael, do you ever get invited to normal dinner parties?

—That's an oxymoron. They're all neurotic. But the fact is no, not since Morgan's stroke. I'm the extra man. If they also invite a single woman, it looks like they're trying to fix us up behind Morgan's inert body. If it's me alone, her coma hangs over the roast beef like rancid fat. The truth is, my favorite dinner party is eating here alone with you. I don't have to work to be funny. Or amusing, as the hostesses prefer.

—But you are amusing. Funny. I could listen to your stories forever.

—You bring it out in me.

Forever! Are we veering too close to something? Perhaps.

Change of subject.

—Just handling the revolver gave me itchy fingers, Nia says. I haven't fired my rifle in months. I think I may go to the shooting range in Santa Clara and fire off some rounds before work. Get the old feeling back.

—I'd like to come with you. Let you show me how good you really are. As you said a few days ago. But I've got surgery in half an hour.

I could listen to your stories forever.

How could anyone misinterpret that?

Forever.

Palpitating breaths. The time is getting ripe. A green banana gently yellowing toward the moment. How does the banana know to do that? It was not taught by its mother, or by an uncle behind the barn. Determinism — a clear example. It's written in banana genes. It can will itself to turn yellow, but it cannot will itself to become a peach.

Two hours of perfection exist in the life of a banana, those hours when the taste is clean as vanilla and there is resistance to the teeth, the palate. After that it devolves rapidly. First, subtle too-softness, hours later hints at disgusting yellow mush. Followed by the long sad slide into brown. Knowing the perfect moment is essential, in fruit as in sex.

When I was a kid the Winslows took *Life Magazine,* as they put it. So did much of America. One issue featured a photo of old graves uncovered somewhere. The long dead bodies suggested to me overripe brown bananas. Half a century later the synaptic connection lingers. Memory consists of two spider webs in the brain. Call them A and B. In web A we consciously store pleasant memories, wrap them in spider silk, to be taken out, unwrapped, experienced whenever we please. The first good kiss, for instance. Or Willie Mays making his iconic catch. Over web B we have no control. Here are stored like a spider's undigested flies or wasps the memories we would sooner forget: the model airplane I was making from balsa wood and glue when the priest knocked on the door to tell us my father had gone down in the Yellow Sea; the taped cardboard box marked Dole Pineapple in which my mother stored her own obituary; most vivid of all, the yellow bus levitating straight up out of the river in the claws of the construction crane, water pouring off the roof in a torrent, water pouring out the open windows, water dripping off the hair and faces and dangling arms of the five nurses visible from the shore side, where I stood, shivering in wet clothing. Addie in the middle. Web B holds this one fast, has painted my retina with it at least once a day since it occurred.

I wish Nia a good day as she disappears down the hall. She has not mentioned Mickey in some time. I wonder if that means anything. I select a beige sport jacket, one with large side pockets, slip the two brown eyes into the left — they clank, billiards for sadists — drop the pistol's weight into the handier right. At a crucial moment it might give someone pause. I can always decide later to leave it in my desk.

Even without bullets the gun creates an oddly light-hearted feeling. As if I'm going off to war. I lose sense of who I am. Am I really living this passion? It's the same feeling as after the red car struck. A broken pelvis? Fractured vertebrae? Not me. Not hardly. The hurt is gone. Was it ever there? But pain from rejected love cuts deeper, lasts longer, leeches away sanity. Ulcerates self-control. Sets the very soul to trembling. Ergo my cowardice with Nia. A *no* will not be acceptable.

As I drive, apprehension about Ken-Chen fades into the marijuana high of a Hollywood set. Tonight could be a Coen Brothers production. The first thing I do in the ophtho suite is detour to the retina wing. One operating room is in use by Dr. Pike, but the other is not. I select an MVR blade. It's about eight inches long, has a solid handle. The point of the blade shaped like an arrowhead. It's razor edged. I slip it carefully into my inside pocket. It has more possibilities as a weapon than anything we use in cataracts.

The day at the hospital was uneventful. No hallucinations, no mirages. I wondered several times if Ginger in Texas would actually kill the old lady. I don't think she has it in her, she's no Raskolnikov. After the final surgery I checked my cell phone and found a voice mail from Annabel in Santa Fe. That was unusual, I don't think she's ever called before. I hope everything's okay.

It's not. When I call her back she says she found the 100th eye, it was in the spare tire well just as she thought. Bobby came over on Monday like he said and pried it off. Then her voice wavers and she's crying. Annabel, what is it? She says she's sorry, but the crying becomes sobs. Annabel, what's wrong? Oh, uncle Mike, she says, I'm so miserable I want to die. What is it, tell me? She says Rebecca, her Indian girl friend, and Bobby, her boyfriend, both broke up with her, and took up with each other. What Bobby had to do last Sunday was see Rebecca. Monday when he came to unjam the trunk he brought Rebecca along and they were holding hands, looked as if they had slept in their clothes. They certainly had slept together, were making goo-goo eyes. Her words. After he found the lost eye they both said see ya around, just like that, and left holding hands and smooching.

She's afraid to go into town for fear of seeing them together. It hurts so much she's thought about killing herself.

—Annabel, don't think like that. I know what you're going through, believe me, but people survive that. It takes time. Maybe you should get away from there for a while. Listen, I've got an idea. I'll send you a plane ticket, you can come out and stay with me and Nia for a while. There's plenty of room, and the sofa in the den opens into a bed.

She's gotten control of her sobs but still is teary.

—Uncle Mike, that's why I was calling. I had the same idea. I don't know where else to go. If I could come out there I could bring you the missing eye, not risk mailing it. It's a beautiful gray-green, like the sea. I can just see the post office crushing it. But Unc? I don't want to fly. If I drive it's cheaper, I can see the landscape across the whole southwest, take pictures for my weaving. It might help me concentrate on my work. I might even meet new people in campgrounds. I can't believe they did that to me. It's too cruel.

—Annabel, if you have that much confidence in your car — you'll have to drive across the Mojave desert, that's four hours of nothing but heat and sand — make sure you have enough water. To drink and for the car. And buy a spare tire. Put it on your credit card if you have to — do you have a credit card? — and I'll pay for it. I'd love to have you visit for a while. You can stay as long as you want. You'll like Nia — she loved your shawl, by the way. Maybe she'll make a Marine out of you.

—Not likely, Annabel says, which is the understatement of the year.

—You haven't been out here, have you, since that time your folks went to Europe and you spent the summer with us. What was that, about eight years ago?

—Ten, Annabel says.

I expect her to reminisce, say something nice about that summer, but she says nothing, the *ten* sounding curt, if one word can be curt. After seconds of unnatural silence I get pompous.

—Listen, no more of those suicidal thoughts. I know that's easy to say, but you're young — think of all the tapestries you have inside you. And don't worry, the right guy for you — or the right girl — will come along when the time is right.

Only inserting *or the right girl* saves the vapidity of my Polonius speech, recaptures the mellowness we share. Followed by sincere goodbyes and see you soons.

Punching off, I make a mental note to give Nia the scarf. It's hidden in my closet, I wanted to wrap it. With everything that's going on, I forgot.

Vicky goes straight home to help Mrs. Ling prepare dinner. I catch up on paperwork, get coffee in the cafeteria, sit alone, thinking, to kill time. Wearing my beige jacket, which still has the unloaded gun in the right outer pocket, the MVR blade in the inner. Apparently without any conscious thought I've made the decision to take them with me. I hope dinner with Ken-Chen is as Vicky supposes, a family peace gathering, and neither weapon, as I now wrongly conceive of the retina blade, will leave my pocket. By the free association that is so much of my thought process — perhaps of everyone's — my mind drifts to a passage in a novel I read in 1971. I know it was that year because I was an intern at Stanford. As an intern you barely get time to sleep, let alone read. This was the only novel I read that year. It took me three months. It's called *The Book of Daniel*. By E. L. Doctorow. Of Long Island. I've read most of what he's written since, and still think *Daniel* is his masterwork. I needed to read it back then, even splurged for a hardback, when I heard what it was — a fictional projection of the Rosenbergs. Executed as Communist spies in the early fifties — during the same Red Scare that killed my mother. Also, the novel was narrated by one of their sons. How could I not grab it up? Oddly, what's remained of the book in my consciousness ever since — why the blade in my pocket dredged up the memory — is not the politics, but a scene from a movie that the narrator describes. A man is sharpening a straight razor. A woman, half-naked, sits in an upright chair. The man approaches the woman, spreads her eyelids wide as they will go. He begins to bring the razor down toward her eyeball. It's one of the most horrible things most of us can imagine, a razor slicing across our eye. The camera cuts to the night sky outside a window, where we see a full moon. A knifelike cloud slices across it — a symbolic representation of what the blade is doing to the woman. The audience has just relaxed, relieved that the portrayal of the mutilation was only symbolic, when the camera moves back inside the room, and shows in close-up the razor slicing into the woman's eye.

My interning that year, beginning to cut into eyes for real, no doubt heightened my fascination. The scene suggests why everyone is given a light tranquilizer in the holding room. Why should they believe that once we squirt tetravisc or lidocaine jelly into their eye, they won't feel a thing? Trust me, I'm a doctor?

I ponder who is more the trickster here: the filmmakers who conceived the scene — Buñuel and Dali — or Doctorow for inserting it in his book. Raising the question of what is more terrifying, depicting an awful action or letting it be imagined

And what of the screams? In the film would we hear these screams as the cloud crossed the moon — in which case isn't the symbolism much too heavy handed, even absurd — or only later, when we see the actual eyeball being cut?

Doctorow. Doctor Ow?

My peripheral vision picks up a wheelchair coming toward me. Shannon Kelly, Madame President, a paper coffee cup balanced on her folding tray. Neat gray suit, white blouse with lace at the collar, clear stockings, legs still good at what, 45? She was the youngest hospital president in the country when she took over eight years ago. She always looks fresh and crisp, even late in the day.

—Are you waiting for someone, or may I join you?

I motion her to join me at the table. Company is welcome.

—I'm just killing time until a strange dinner party.

—Strange how?

—I'm having dinner with the man who may have killed Laurette Dubal.

—That sounds cozy.

I tell her the story. Ken-Chen, what I know and what the police know about his involvement. Or what we surmise.

—This dinner party — will the police show up as uninvited guests?

—No. Max Klonsky took Laurette to the police. Look what happened.

—So you're not going to do anything?

—I'm going to see how it plays out.

—Michael, he could kill again. At the dinner.

—So could the police, barging in. Someone is planning something. I'm not sure who. I just hope they know what they're doing.

—I suppose I shouldn't ask if that's a gun in your pocket or if you still like me. It's not quite in the right place. You did have a crush on me ten years ago, you know. I know, because it was mutual.

—I really was out of it that night. From mixing too many drinks. I have no memory of it. That's not an insult, by the way.

—I'm not insulted. We scored a bulls-eye.

—I'm sorry if I hurt you — the pregnancy.

—It was the tree that hurt me — trying to ski around both sides at once.

Diversion achieved. I ask how her meeting went with Dr. Roberts.

—Very well. I'm glad she's gone back to Oklahoma for some wedding. She'll realize what she'd be doing, giving up Beecham's slot to work in the sticks. I think she's leaning towards giving us a year. You know how that works. A year becomes ten in a flash. I just hope she's as good as you and the other docs say. And that she learns to keep her knees together.

—Is that now a condition of employment?

—I mean at the hospital. It can cause personnel problems. Off campus she can screw sea lions, I couldn't care less.

—Interesting image.

—Inbreeding of the staff can get messy. If we're not careful.

The cafeteria is filling up with nurses and orderlies coming down to eat and visitors investing in a cheap tasty meal after doing their duty with relatives or friends. One fellow I know of, a prominent lawyer, drives half way across town almost every day to eat lunch here. Not because it's inexpensive and good, he insists, but because it keeps him in touch with his mortality. An odd assertion by most anyone else, but this fellow's bombastic closing arguments in court, I'm told, sound as if he believes he's immortal. Thunderbolts of wisdom from on high. A ring of empty tables remains around us, however. The staffers don't want to intrude on the president, or don't want to feel constrained while cutting up. The visitors are made uncomfortable by the woman in the wheelchair. There but for the grace. The truth is, I share the feeling, doctor or not. Do Shannon's sexual intimations sound too aggressive, coming from a wheelchair? To me they do. Would Nia, in a wheelchair, still be Nia? I think not. Whereas Morgan, in a wheelchair, would still be Morgan. Perhaps because it would be several rungs up from her coma. Mostly because her stately upright bearing never hinted at the erotic.

None of this is meant to demean the handicapped. It's just one guilt-ridden opinion. One spine-challenged lovely most likely could prove me wrong. Shannon certainly could.

—I'm glad we ran into each other, Madame President, but I have to run.

I wince at using the unfortunate verb. Twice.

—Can I help you get anywhere?

—I'm quite self-sufficient, Dr. Lee. As you may have noticed through the years.

—Of course.

As I stand she locks on my wrist with manicured fingers. Not unpleasantly.

—Michael, I've heard that people would die for Mrs. Ling's cooking. You don't have to prove it. You wouldn't want us to win the Nobel posthumously.

A nail is digging into my wrist bone.

—Not you, too. My niece in Santa Fe told me last week that a friend reads a Swedish blog, and it mentioned me and Maxie as a new dark horse. Some source. A rumor from the North Pole. Santa Claus died years ago Shannon. Along with God, Freud and Wonder Woman. Leaving us humans to fend for ourselves.

—I don't read blogs. I hate the word, it sounds like crap that clogs toilets. From what I hear, much of it is. But my friend Lourdes, who manages a hotel in Vegas, called this morning. She said in the past three days the odds on you guys winning had dropped from 100 to 1 to 20 to 1. An hour later she called back and said you were 18 to one.

—Vegas is taking bets on the Nobels?

—Bookies in Europe do. Vegas is always seeking class. Or so it tells itself. Imagine some blue-haired lady playing nickel slots, her husband wanders off, when he returns she asks where he's been. Oh, I placed a few bucks on a Nobel Prize. In neuroscience. Erudition comes to Excaliber.

—Exactly. It's nonsense, Shannon. The Nobels are closely kept secrets. They don't even announce very far ahead which days the prizes will be awarded. You know that.

—But neuroscience is all the rage right now. Eighty percent of the applicants we get for internships or residencies list it as their long term goal. How the brain controls the body. Med schools all over are building new wings to accommodate the field. You and Klonsky were pioneers, in the dark ages. Today big names are building on your work.

—If you interpret the field loosely. So what do you think the Nobel Committee is up to? Like the Baseball Hall of Fame opening itself up to the Negro Leagues?

—Your analogy, not mine.

—Okay, to an Old Timer's Committee.

—It's always been my impression that the Nobel jurors *are* an old timer's committee.

She's still holding my wrist. I don't mind.

—Schopenhauer says the way to avoid disappointments in life is to not have any hopes.

—A truism. But what a way to live that would be. At the risk of offending, I just ordered a case of Champagne. Two of you from the same hospital? Ours! If it doesn't happen, we can drink it at the Christmas party.

Was that a subtle wink?

I disengage my wrist, gently. With a surprising splash of regret. Moving away, I offer a small wave of goodbye, and follow the corridor around the building, past two nursing stations, to 103. A quick unplanned visit to Morgan. She's asleep — how I tend to think of it — as always. President Kelly sends you her best, I tell her. And stare into her expressionless face. Lean over, kiss her forehead. A nurse tending to her roommate, noticing, smiles a small smile. Sweet but troubled is her instant reading of me.

Nestled in the brain's medial temporal lobe is an inch-long, almond-shaped, almond-colored organ called the amygdala. From the Greek word for almond. This is the home of sweaty palms, palpitating heart, the desire to get the hell away from where you are. The home sweet home of all our fears. Maxie and I came across it many times during our work on visual pathways. Neural connections often led there. When the eyes, or any other organs, send a message that we ought to be afraid, it's the amygdala that bangs the drums. Some alerts go directly to the terror almond, others are routed first through the cortex. But nervousness, apprehension, anxiety, terror, panic, phobias, all keep apartments in the amygdala. It's not a village for the neurotic, as it might sound. The purpose of fear, in evolutionary terms, is preservation of the species. If a tiger gets loose in the zoo, as one did in San Francisco the other day, the amygdala shouts: move, feets.

My own amygdala is puttering along about half speed as I drive up the road toward Vicky's house, toward a pleasant Chinese dinner with a killer. I'm not terrified — but uneasy would be sugarcoating it. I find myself hoping they've got plenty of booze, will serve it early and often. It's not green tea I'm craving.

Vicky's place is in a perfect location for a secret conclave, if that's what this is. A few years back a developer from San Diego bought and cleared five acres of woodland, bulldozed a dirt road to the property, planned to erect ten three-bedroom houses. He had just finished the model home when the housing boom went bust, and he was indicted on some construction scam down south. He lost his money, couldn't make payments, the bank took over the property. With lucky timing Vicky acquired the model home cheap. Meanwhile, the cleared land is greening with brush, and the road remains barely passable. The only intrusion on total silence is bird song.

With the sun sinking into my dark glasses I turn onto the road of dirt and weeds. It's rather late for a dinner party. Perhaps the Lings catered to a late lunch crowd before heading here. Or perhaps darkness itself was a requirement.

When the single lane road was plowed two years ago, rows of trees were left on either side. Now their boughs are mingling overhead, forming a living green canopy, like you might expect on the road to Versailles. Enough of the fading sunlight speckles through the canopy to make me keep my sunglasses on. I pass an old-model forest green car parked off the road, no lights, and spot three shadows in it. I'm guessing it's Ken-Chen and two of his gangbangers, watching to see who goes by. But I can't be sure. I meant to arrive early to get a drink and give up the two glass eyes for whatever they're intended — hoping they don't get damaged. I pull my car up beside Vicky's house. Only hers is visible. The Lings, if they already are here, have parked out of sight. I turn off the engine, the headlights. My hands awkwardly finger the empty revolver, the MVR blade. I don't really expect to die tonight, but I find myself recalling Voltaire: *We shall leave this world as foolish and as wicked as we found it on our arrival.* In other words, it's no big deal if I do.

Vicky greets me at the door, takes both my hands in both of hers, just for a moment. I can see no one else. A palette of Chinese cooking aromas fills the house. She thanks me for coming, takes me to the kitchen where Mrs. Ling wearing a red apron over a gray blouse and slacks, has oil buzzing in several woks, assorted vegetables sliced on cutting boards. We nod, she wipes her hand on her apron, but it's too oily to shake hands, she says. She recalls meeting me at the restaurant. I get a tour of the house from Vicky — kitchen painted yellow with red decor, most of the rooms white with framed reproductions on the walls. Renoir, Van Gogh, Chagall, Chinese masters with whom I am not familiar. Maya's room is pink, crowded with stuffed animals, hung with ballet posters. Amid all the color a poster of Plisetskaya in black and white dominates. The next door is closed, Vicky's bedroom I assume. She does not open it.

She offers me a drink, has no Scotch, just beer and wine. I make points with a Chinese beer. It's cold and crisp. A knock on the door and in walks Lenny Chen, her husband, clearly familiar with the place. He asks for Maya. She's at Annie Wu's for the night, Vicky says. He settles for club soda. Has a subtly gay aura with a nervous edge. Thinning hair at maybe 30. He glances back at the door, I sense he's as nervous about this dinner as I am. Another knock, Vicky opens the door, Ken-Chen is standing there. He turns and nods to his two buddies, they step out of the porch light into the darkening night. Apparently they are his backups, who were not invited. He waves them across the road, perhaps so they don't overhear talk, and steps into the living room from a slight entryway, shoots his cuffs like a Chinese George Raft, if I have the right guy. A bear hug for his brother, another, unwelcome, for his sister-in-law. He reaches out his hand to shake with me. Unlike in the restaurant I offer my hand. He takes it — then twists it sharply behind my back.

—What the . . .

—No weapons, tall doctor! That's what they told me. What's in your pocket?

—Easy there, it's not loaded. It's an antique. Nobody told me no weapons.

—I never thought you had one, Vicky says. I'm sorry.

Ken-Chen motions to his brother. He approaches me, lifts the pistol out of my pocket, cracks it open. Affirms that it's empty.

—Where's the bullets? Ken-Chen demands.

—I have no bullets.

He lets me go, examines the gun himself, tosses it onto a sofa, shaking his head. My shoulder hurts like hell from his twist.

—That was dumb, doc. A stunt like that could get you killed. Quick.

Nia's words almost exactly.

The tension diminishes. Vicky gives Ken a beer. She knows his favorite, Bud Light. We adjourn to the dining room. The table is set only for four. We sit, and Mrs. Ling emerges from the kitchen, nods to the Chen brothers, sets small cups of steaming soup in front of us. We begin to sip with porcelain spoons, which are white with blue filigrees. The soup is very hot.

—Hey, how about that tiger escaping in the zoo, Lenny Chen says, to start a conversation.

Ken-Chen shoots him a hateful look. Lenny says no more. I wonder what that was about.

—They discovered the wall was only 12 feet high, not 15 like they thought, Vicky puts in. That's still quite a jump. It's terrible that a boy got killed.

—Dumb Mex kid probably was taunting her, Ken-Chen says. It's terrible the cops massacred the tiger. Tatiana. A beautiful animal.

—What else could the cops do, it was coming right at them, I say.

—They knew it was an Asian tiger. Otherwise they use a stun gun.

I choose not to argue with him. My shoulder still smarting.

—You like the zoo? I ask pleasantly. Maybe vapidly. He's not a kid, he's in his 30s. With obvious leadership qualities, to put it politely. I think of Laurette Dubal. Of Maxie holed up with his pain. Ken looks at me, frowning, suspicious. Finally accepts that it's an innocent question.

—Not really.

The soup has cooled some, we begin to eat. We hear a slight noise, perhaps from Vicky's bedroom. Mr. Ling enters the dining room, dressed in his black cooking clothes, a white apron, slippers. He nods at Ken-Chen.

—You didn't tell me your parents would be here, Ken says to Vicky. As if he's offended. He seems congenitally offended.

—At a dinner party? You've tasted my cooking.

Ken-Chen laughs. He says she's right, the fucking Chinese tiger could cook better.

Mr. Ling asks Lenny to please get the door. There has been no knock, no doorbell. Puzzlement on our faces. Lenny does as he is told. In single file six men enter the hallway and then the dining room. All are wearing dark suits, white shirts, ties. All are Asian, perhaps all Chinese, I can't be sure.

—What the hell is this? Who are these guys? Ken-Chen asks, twisting in his chair, taking them all in. Where are my compadres?

—Your compadres are temporarily indisposed, Mr. Ling says. Or is it permanently? I'm not really sure.

He looks toward the new men as if for an answer. None of them speaks.

They're mostly in their early thirties to mid forties, I would guess. One is older. Mrs. Ling returns from the kitchen, sets a small covered dish on a sideboard, clears the soup bowls, paying no attention to the newcomers, acting as if nothing unusual is going on. The six all stand against the walls, arms folded across their chests.

—Damn you, Vicky, you lied to me, Ken-Chen says. You said a dinner party.

—Don't call my daughter a liar, Mr. Ling says, gently. It is a dinner party. These men, all friends of mine, were invited. Mrs. Ling has even created a new dish for the occasion. You will have the honor of being the first to sample it.

I have no idea what is going on, nor why I am here, the only white person in the room.

—But perhaps, Mr. Ling continues, our guests should introduces themselves first. No names are needed, gentlemen,, just your affiliations, please.

They look from one to the other. The man at the far left begins, and they go around the room in order: Black Dragon. King Cobra. Wah Ching. Wo Hop To. Natoma Boys. Asian Westside Crips. Ken-Chen's head follows their words like a carnival ride about to stop. Or about to start. Mr. Ling explains.

—These honorable gentlemen are heads of triads. Or second in charge. Or war chief. Not all Chinese. One Vietnam. One Korea. One Cambodia. All here for same reason. Want peace. Tranquility. Do not want street gangs to hurt civilians. Bad publicity. Police come around. Not good for triad business. Golden Swords act stupid. Want into drug trade. Don't ask nicely. Don't know how to do it. Killing innocent people not the way. Especially women. Ken-Chen here is leader of Golden Swords. We believe he pull trigger on hospital woman. Or decide who pull trigger. For private grudge against hospital surgeon Klonsky. This be nonsense, Ken-Chen let girlfren' take bullet, then blame the doctor. You should read your Confucius, Ken-Chen. That wise man say: *Before you embark on a journey of revenge, dig two graves.* This tribunal is here to judge and sentence Ken-Chen. For two crimes. Arranging the public murder of woman Laurette Dubal. Also, threatening torture and death to family of triad member.

Ken-Chen looks around wildly, as if for help. He's not shooting cuffs any more. Then replies.

—The killing of the Dubal woman was a private matter. It's not the concern of other gangs. Or triads. I never have threatened the family of a triad member.

Mr. Ling, thin and ageless in his apron, face lean, dark eyes narrow, continues to play the part not of a host but a prosecutor.

—It has come to our attention that Lenny Chen, my son-in-law, was forced to cut out the eyes of Ms. Dubal, under threat of death.

—That was just initiation. Lenny became part of the Swords without one, because he is my brother. Other gang members, mainly number two Luc Luck, complained that this violated gang rules. He was right. Therefore, we needed an initiation. The woman was already dead, it was not so terrible. She felt no pain. And there were no other threats.

—My daughter, Victoria Chen, will speak now.

Vicky stands, repeats the threats that Ken-Chen made to her about Maya and herself if she did not deliver drugs. Right down to the Ichiro model baseball bat. Ken-Chen leans back in his chair, a show of relaxation.

—I never said those things seriously. Victoria is hungry for my body. She is taking revenge because I refused to sleep with my brother's wife. If I did say those words, it was a joke.

—Dr. Lee, can you confirm any of this?

I did not realize I was here to be a witness. I affirm that Vicky told me exactly those things.

—Did it sound like a joke to her? Mr. Ling asks.

—Absolutely not. She was crying in my office. She was terrified. Mostly for her daughter.

—Did she go to the police?

—No. She spoke to me because she had to tell someone. But she warned me, no police. She said she had not even told her parents, so as not to worry them. She was trying to figure out how to get the drugs they wanted, as far as I know. After that I have no knowledge.

—After Laurette was killed, Vicky says, I had to tell my parents. I was so scared for Maya. Mr. and Mrs. Ling have always been wise, given me good advice. I thought maybe they could help. The truth is, until tonight I did not know my father knew any of these gentlemen. As for you, Ken-Chen, brother-in-law, I spit on your body.

—I don't believe this, Ken-Chen says, hotly, but slow on the uptake. Threatening people is how gangs exist. This whole charge is nonsense. Nobody was hurt. Nobody threatened families of gangs.

Mr. Ling does not smile. He merely puts his hands together in front of him, in a gesture of respect, and bows from the waist.

—Victoria Chen, born Victoria Ling, is my daughter.

—I know that, but . . .

Dawn finally breaks over the face of Ken-Chen.

—You? That can't be. Police eat lunch in your restaurant. The Golden Swords robbed you with automatic rifles the other night. Without my knowledge. It was small potatoes, I didn't care. If I knew you had . . .

—Arranged it? With your friend Luc Luck. Through intermediaries, of course. My son-in-law knew nothing. Robberies are good cover for me, should police ever suspect.

Ken-Chen begins to stand. The nearest triad leader pushes his shoulders back into the chair. He looks at the other men again.

—This is a joke, right? Some kind of initiation for me? A step up into a triad? Mr. Ling is a cook, not a crook. Not boss of all bosses, like with the Italians. We talk in his restaurant sometimes. About dumplings, not gangs.

No one says a word.

—Gentlemen, have you heard enough? Mr. Ling asks.

The six jurors nod.

—Very well. You may now vote.

In turn, from left to right, each of the men in the dark suits says, Guilty.

—The decision is unanimous. Now you may discuss suitable punishment.

Mrs. Ling,, who has been watching from the kitchen doorway, approaches Mr. Ling, whispers something.

—Ah, yes. Mrs. Ling reminds me that we have not yet offered Ken-Chen the new delicacy we promised. Mrs. Ling?

She lifts a covered chafing dish from the sideboard, sets it in front of Ken-Chen. He keeps his hands beside him under the table. He does not want to lift off the cover. Who knows what he suspects.

—Mrs. Ling, will you do the honors? her husband says.

She speaks aloud for the first time since the tribunal began, as she lifts the cover off, allowing steam to rise.

—A new invented dish. Garlic sauce with cashew and brown eyes.

The eyes of Laurette Dubal appear to be looking up at Ken-Chen from the sauce. He turns away, begins to retch. Nothing comes out. The eyes are the glass ones, of course.

—Mr. Ken-Chen does not appear hungry, Mr. Ling says. Will you do the honors, Victoria? Dr. Lee?

I'm not sure what he means, until Vicky lifts an eye out of the broth with her fingers and pops it into her mouth. I follow suit. Ken-Chen bolts for the bathroom.

—Frighten with false fire, Mr. Ling says. Is all right, gentlemen, no way out from there.

The garlic sauce with cashew flavoring is exquisite as I swirl the eye in my mouth. Some triad leaders look queasy themselves. Mrs. Ling approaches me with a bowl of water. I remove the eye from my mouth and drop it in. Vicky does the same.

—None worse for wear, Mrs. Ling says.

When the triad men realize what has transpired, they laugh, nod, speak in Chinese, good joke, fun game, or the equivalent.

Ken-Chen returns to the room wiping his mouth, looking about for a route of escape. Seeing none, he takes his seat. The men begin to discuss his punishment. The first man says his eyes should be cut out, as was done to the murdered woman, and they should be seared in a wok and he be made to eat them, or face death. The second man says it would be better to remove only one eye, so he can see his other eye frying in the wok, see what he must eat. Then his second can be removed. Ken is looking green. I find myself almost pitying the bastard. The third man, the eldest, says all this is childish. Two bullets in his head, while he kneels, execution style — call it putting eyes in the back of his head if you want.

Vicky asks for permission to speak. She says that since she brought the complaint, she would rather not see Ken-Chen killed. She is a nurse and opposes killing of any kind. Could he not be taken to the border, she asks — Nevada, Arizona, Mexico — be made to cross over, warned not to set foot in California again, under pain of torture and death.

— Very kind of you, Mrs. Chen, the elder says, considering how he threatened you and your child. But that idea would not send much warning to other gangs. We must prevent our women and children and grandchildren from being threatened. He must be dealt with severely. He must be left in Polk Park, in the same spot where the Dubal woman was found. In this way the press, and the street gangs, will understand that the execution of Ken-Chen is to atone for the murder of Miss Dubal. Also with a note, warning against the threatening of gang families, or even worse will be done to the offenders. We might also burn into his skin the symbols of all the triads represented here, to make clear this was a group decision. The dragon, the three dots, the hot quarter and so forth.

How long he has been contemplating his move I do not know, but at that instant Ken-Chen stands quickly, leaps behind my chair like a karate expert, grabs my neck from behind in a choke hold, and with the other hand presses a knife blade, which must have been in his own jacket pocket — or in his shoe when he went to the bathroom — against my neck. He pulls me to an off-balance standing position. I feel a trickle of blood on my neck, like a shaving cut.

—I'm going out the door, Ken-Chen warns them, his mouth beside my ear. One move to stop me and the doctor gets his throat cut. I won't be afraid to die, since you're planning to kill me anyway.

Perhaps I actually will die here this night, this moment. Seek the Voltaire wisdom for comfort but my mind is muddled. Happy to discover that I truly am not afraid to die. It's the pain of the knife slashing across my throat that terrorizes.

All movement has stopped. Utter silence. No scary post-production music. Ken-Chen nudges me forward a step with his body, the knife raw at my throat. None of the men moves to interfere. I am grateful. They would rather lose him here than cause my death. He presses me forward another step, his body pushing into me from behind. The men remain still, silent. What will he do with me outside? How long will I be his hostage? Are his supposed bodyguards still alive? If not, will I become his instant revenge?

One more step. We are four steps from the door. I see a flickering in the eyes of the elder. Something is about to happen.

Crack!

An explosion behind my head. I think I've been shot. Ken-Chen's knife falls away from me. A second shot. The arm around my neck goes limp. Chen begins to scream, curse, staggers away, tries to grasp each shoulder with his opposite hand, can't do it. Both arms are hanging limp. I duck from him, turn as he does. Mrs. Ling, not three feet away, is returning a small pistol to the pocket of her apron.

—Goddamn bitch, Ken says, bending forward in pain.

Two of the triad men come forward, grab his arms.

—That hurts, you bastards!

—With your permission, Ken-Chen, Mrs. Ling says, the two bullets could have gone into your skull. However, I bow to the tribunal to inflict its own punishment. Now if you gentlemen would kindly remove him from my daughter's house, before he drips blood on the rug, I should be very pleased.

Ken-Chen, both shoulders possibly destroyed, has slipped into a galaxy of pain beyond speech. Mrs. Ling returns to the kitchen. Each of the triad men in turn steps forward and shakes hands with Mr. Ling.

—Dinner as promised, tomorrow at my restaurant, he says. Seven o'clock. Wives and girlfriends welcome . . . But not both together.

Barks of laughter amid the waning terror.

Vicky dips her cloth napkin into the bowl of water on the table that holds the two glass eyes, and presses the cloth to the slight but burning cut on my neck.

—I'm so sorry, Doctor Lee. So sorry. I never should have asked you to come.

Mr. Ling approaches, shakes my hand.

—I, too, am sorry, doctor. Please do not hold your wound against my daughter. I made her invite you. Under tribunal rules, we need an impartial witness.

Lenny Chen is standing in the open door, watching the tribunal lead his bleeding brother to a waiting van. Several engines start up. Mr. Ling calls Lenny in.

—My son, you are no longer safe with the Golden Swords. No longer safe in California. You must move from here. Chicago. New York. Chinatowns always need men. All kinds men live there. You and Victoria will first arrange for your divorce, of course. We will make sure at times you get to see your daughter.

—First I have to warn you, Lenny says. Ken-Chen is an evil person. He deserves whatever he gets. But Luc Luck, the second in charge, is worse. He's crazy. Out of his mind crazy. He admires what the Arab terrorists do. He will plan something big to avenge Ken-Chen, even though they hate each other. To impress the rest of the gang. To become solid as the new number one.

Mr. Ling, nodding, puts a hand on his son-in-law's shoulder.

—Thank you for telling me this. The triads are already aware. We do not interfere with street gangs, unless it becomes necessary, such as tonight. We will deal with whatever comes.

I hold the wet cloth at my throat. Vicky has been waiting to speak.

—Mr. Ling, my dear father, you astonish me. All my life I never knew. How did you conceal that you know men like this? That you are triad boss of bosses?

He puts his arm around his daughter's shoulder, kisses her forehead.

—Victoria, first I must make sure you understand. Triads are not like street gangs. We don't fight. We don't rob. We don't kill. We are businessmen. Big business. Imports. People have wants, needs, we fill them. The government calls us illegal. The government is not very smart. If they make our products legal, availability spreads. Demand drops. Drugs become not so cool anymore. They put us out of business. But they don't do that. Never will. So that is not our concern. Now, you ask how I conceal that I am boss of bosses. That is easy. Because it not be true.

—But we just saw. . .

—It be hard, Victoria, for Chinese men, Cambodian, others, tough triad men, to be led by a woman. They would lose face. So I pretend to be boss. And they pretend.

He turns and looks toward the kitchen.

—Mrs. Ling, are you almost ready? We still have dumplings to make for tomorrow.

Chapter 15: Rachel

After the Lings had left, Victoria fed Lenny and I a marvelous dinner. It was hard to believe it had been prepared by Al Capone. We ate in silence interrupted mostly by small talk, such as Lenny wondering to which city he should move. None of us wanted to discuss what we had witnessed. What was there to say? My reaction to what might have been a near-death experience seemed dulled, as if by a dose of tetravisc. Vicky felt sick over the sentencing of Ken-Chen. She hated him but did not want his fate of torture and death on her hands. After several bites of mu shu pork she excused herself to her bedroom. She did not return. Lenny and I continued eating in silence, as if stuffing ourselves with relief. I was still alive and except for a slight soreness on the skin of my throat, reasonably well. Lenny's banishment to a city far removed seemed to free him from the trap that was the Golden Swords. Mr. Ling — or Mrs. Ling — or the two together — did seem to posses, as Vicky had intimated, a rare wisdom.

Never fond of lychee nuts — they taste like soap to me —I skipped dessert. I didn't want to intrude on Victoria and whatever thoughts she was wrestling with on her bed, about Ken-Chen's eyes or her newfound knowledge of her parents. I shook hands with Lenny, confident I would never see him again, took my father's revolver, my glass eyes and my leave.

The ride home is like a trip down the barrel of one of Fletch's telescopes. The further I get from Vicky's house, the larger what occurred there appears. My death rises in front of me like a full moon. When Mrs. Ling shot Ken-Chen through the shoulder, he might easily have pulled the blade of his knife through my vocal chords, instead of dropping it. If her hand shook and her shot was slightly off, he most likely would have. If she did not have the gun and he had gotten to the door he might easily have killed me before running off into the woods. With these thoughts my right knee begins to tremble, as it had not done during the action itself, my pressure on the gas pedal becomes erratic. I pull into the slow lane and ride that way all the way home.

The flirtation with death is not the cause of my weekend anxiety, however.

On the kitchen table is a note from Nia reminding me that she is spending the weekend in San Diego, visiting her folks. I had forgotten that. Depression begins to creep in like internal fog. I had been looking forward to describing the evening to her. Need to tell someone. I return the revolver to its place, the eyes to theirs. Too late to call Maxie? I've called him three days at home, always get the recorded message, the old one spoken by Sophie. Makes me think he's still staying in Laurette's place, from fear of Sophie's further wrath or from refusal to surrender his love to the grave. Her number, if she even has — or had — a land line, is not listed. Messages to his cell phone have gone unreturned. No doubt he did not carry it to the funeral — why would he? — and it lies on his desk at his home, lifeless as his heart.

Too keyed up to go to sleep, I pour a short Scotch. In Nia's absence my mind wanders to the conversations with Shannon Kelly in recent days. That bygone Christmas. Our apparent lovemaking, hidden to me till now, no doubt by a combination of denial and the mix of beer, wine, Scotch, vodka, whatever else people had brought to drink. Which I consumed at the party with a sense of of freedom, however fleeting, with Morgan gone east and a holiday weekend ahead. Shannon's abortion, unknown to me. My child! Her accident. Her confession just this afternoon of a crush on me back then. Mutual, she said — was that another denial on my part rather than just a drunken screw? It's not surprising, she was quite the intelligent up and coming stunner, as *Time* had said. I turn to my bookshelves. Amid medical and eye books, where Morgan would never have occasion to look, is one called *The Object Stares Back: on the nature of seeing*, by James Elkins. He was, perhaps still is, not a doctor but an art instructor in Chicago. The book a gift from Shannon a few days after Christmas that year. It had just been published. I pull it from the shelf, gaze at its cover of a pair of eyes peering closely at a butterfly. Sit in a wing chair, open the book, read Shannon's inscription: *For Michael, who stares back. Remember me. Shannon.*

Two pairs of words are the saddest in the language: *If only,* and *Remember me.* The inscription is uncanny, as if somehow she knew right then that I would not remember. Remember her — when? When Morgan and I divorced? Which every few years seemed a good idea, but never happened. I turn the pages. Shannon had either read or flipped through the book before wrapping it. Had underlined a sentence here and there in red ink. I browse among them. On the very first page, perhaps what first caught her eye:

Seeing is like hunting and like dreaming, and even like falling in love. It is entangled in the passions — jealousy, violence, possessiveness: and it is soaked in affect — in pleasure and displeasure, and in pain.

A few pages later, also underlined: *My eyes can understand only desire and possession. Anything else is meaningless and therefore invisible. I cannot look at anything — any object, any person —without the shadow of the thought of possessing that thing. Those appetites don't just accompany looking: they are looking itself.*

That's not exactly the retinal detachments and macular degenerations they taught in med school.

Was Shannon in love with me then — or at least in lust — and me too married to notice? Or too afraid to leave Morgan to notice — Morgan with her knowledge of my guilt?

I remember how Shannon looked back then, long blond hair pulled in a ponytail as she bent over her microscopes in the oncology lab or spoke with the most terrified of patients, telling them their tumors had metastasized into the lymph nodes, giving them six months to live. After hours, letting her straight hair down to bob freely on her back as she strode in colorful blouse and seasonal slacks and low heels that nonetheless clicked on the hard floors of the corridors, her strides and her eyes exuding determination. A young, talented doctor on the upward move. Who underlined for me these sentences, and others. Now, with crushed vertebrae that confine her to a wheelchair most of the time, her hair clipped just below her ears, organizational responsibilities of the hospital almost visible like water buckets on her shoulders, do these sentiments — does that stunning young woman — still dwell inside her, a garden perennial clinging to life in winter, waiting for another spring?

How many books has she inscribed for other men since her accident?

I return the volume to the high shelf, and smile at a color photograph in a gold frame two shelves below, Nia smiling into the camera in her dress blues, white cap. Nia who should be back here Sunday night or Monday. My eyes don't register until a moment later Mickey standing beside her, dressed as spiffily. Then behind them, the nose of a jet fighter. It's your point, Mr. Elkins.

The night is mostly sleepless until I take a Valium and get four hours. And awake into a world of nameless anxiety. Is Ken-Chen dead? How is Vicky doing ? Nia's door is open, her bed made, Marine Teddy Bear in place. Right, she's away for the weekend. I knew that. My blood seems to be vibrating in my veins. Anxiety is worse than pain for me, it always has been. This is the worst I can recall since Addie drowned. It can get so bad I want to die. I prescribe for myself a ride on Eyeful. Down a cup of coffee, not hungry, grab a dog-eared, underlined paperback of Schopenhauer, maybe I can find comfort in him. Shove it into the back pocket of my corduroys, drive on out to Destiny, as I've already begun to call Polk Park. I might have taken my birthday present from Nia, but fiction I can only read at night. I'm not sure why.

I let the horse wander for a while, then pull her up. She's heading for the stream. First I think it might be interesting to see where Laurette was found. Then I realize Ken-Chen's body, eyeless or not, might be there already, and I don't want to be the one to find it. It could raise too many questions. I guide Eyeful toward the wooded hills of Blue Oak and Gray Pine, find a tree to sit under, lean my back against. Loop the reins around a limb. A cougar is watching from a distant ridge. The same one I saw with Nia? Who knows, there are hundreds in the park. Mostly they leave humans alone, living on everything from bighorn sheep to lizards and even cockroaches. But once in a while they attack a small child, or someone who makes the mistake of playing dead. Cougars have killed six humans here in fifteen years, I've read. The thing to do if one approaches is look it in the eye, stand tall, maybe throw rocks. Probably it will slink away, like a cat, which it is. Don't run, that could trigger its hunting instinct. The Elkins fellow is right again — in this vast landscape of part rocky ridges and part hills of lush trees what I focus on is the cougar. It stares back. Until in a minute or so, as if with a shrug , it disappears behind the ridge, out of sight.

I unclip my cell phone. It's Saturday, but I've got Captain Doyle's cell number. He answers while throwing a football around with little Jimmy. I tell him he can call off his search for Ken-Chen, the triads are taking care of it. I offer no details — nothing of the scene at Vicky's. He says my sources are interesting, which I concede. I also tell him Lenny Chen, whose prints are on the jar of eyes, is heading out of state, and will never return. There may have been other accomplices, but that's police business, that's all I know and all I want to know. One more thing,I tell him: in a day or two he might want to check the site in Polk Park where Laurette Dubal was found. It's just an educated guess, I say, and let it go.

I realize that while talking with the captain I paid no attention to my anxiety. As soon as I hang up it returns. What this hints at is frightening. My anxiety apparently is not about the killings. I flip through the Schopenhauer at random, looking for answers among things I have marked before. The first one I come across is telling:

After sixty . . . the strongest impulse — the love of women's society — has little or no effect; it is the sexless condition of old age which lays the foundation of a certain self-sufficiency, and that gradually absorbs all desire for others' company.

He's certainly wrong there, unless I'm a freak — and I know I'm not. Maxie is one example. Beecham and those in his photo club are others. Schopenhauer wrote a hundred years ago. Perhaps seventy or eighty is the new sixty.

I flip pages, seeking further comments about love and passion. And find the following:

The old man is genial and cheerful because, after long lying in the bonds of passion, he can now move about in freedom. Maybe. But then follows the killer comment: *Still, it should not be forgotten that, when this passion is extinguished, the true kernel of life is gone, and nothing remains but the hollow shell.*

A fucking bulls-eye! That's exactly how I will feel if I do not win Nia. A hollow shell, with no reason to live. Under the sighing tree, beside my grass-nibbling horse, I tremble. My brain throbs. The true source of my anxiety has been stripped naked. Today is the first day, since she moved in months ago, that I will not see her, morning, evening or both. Tomorrow will be another. And already I'm shaking inwardly. Going through withdrawal like an addict huddled trembling on a prison cot. She has become a drug to me.

I fear I need to confess this addiction. The mere thought induces its own anxiety. Is there, somewhere nearby, a Damn Fool's Anonymous?

Living with Nia has become Dickensian. It is the best of times, it is the worst of times.

Driving home, I realize I have not yet volunteered at the Mission Hospital. I've filled a small medicine bag in my trunk with lidocaine, Tetrovisc and a few of the other necessary tranquilizers and painkillers they sometimes run short of; no need to take surgical instruments, they usually have enough of those. Maybe next week I'll call or e-mail Mission, set up a schedule. It's more important right now that I find a confessor.

I can't call the rabbi today, it's her *shabbus*. I grill a steak for dinner, then leave it half uneaten. Butler gets a rare treat. Sunday at noon I call. She's just finished teaching a Hebrew School class.

—Yes, Dr. Klonsky is right. I used to be a psychologist. I don't practice anymore, but if what you need to discuss is important, shopping for a new pair of boots can wait. My husband won't mind, he's watching the Raiders on TV. He won't even notice I'm not there until the game is over. But lunch would not be appropriate. I'll wait for you in my office. Beside Beth Israel Temple, Fremont and Fourth.

It's not hard to find. She's got facing armchairs across from a simple desk. Degrees on the wall in plain black frames that suggest Hobby Lobby. A calendar from a Kosher deli. The blue and white flag of Israel.

—I want you to know I'm not crazy, rabbi, I begin, taking a seat after we shake hands.

—An interesting way to start, Dr. Lee. Has anyone accused you of being crazy?

—No, but you might well think that after you hear my story. Two stories, actually.

—Well, choose one, and try me.

—These are things I've never told anyone on the planet, as the youngsters say. I appreciate your meeting with me, but in all honesty I'd feel more comfortable if you'd tell me a little about yourself. So I know to whom I'm confessing. As a psychologist you would not do that, but in your present role . . .

—An ambiguous one. Very well. Rabbi Rachel Weitz, up close and personal. I was brought up in Beverly Hills, in a Conservative Jewish family. That's half way between Orthodox and Reformed, if you know anything about Jewry. I went to USC, majored in psychology, minored in comparative religion. I did pretty well. In my third year, the dean of students called me in. He said they've got a football player who is of all-American caliber, but he's not doing well in two of his classes. Psychology and math. They don't ask professors to go easy on athletes, he said, that's frowned upon, though done all the time at some institutions. But they would like to provide him with a tutor, which is perfectly acceptable. We have a tutor fund that's open to any student. Coach Rigby has asked me to find a tutor for this young man. The computer selected you as our top choice.

—I told the dean that all I know about football would fit on home plate. He replied that Jason doesn't need tutoring in football. A fine young man, I'd like him. We'd just meet in study hall a few times a week. Anyway, the extra money was good, so I called Jason and arranged to meet for coffee first. See if we got along. He showed up ten minutes late, tall and good looking. I told him right away he would have to be on time or it was no go. That put his ego in place, and we got along just fine. He worked hard, got his grades up to gentlemen Cs, made second team all-American at wide receiver. Jason Schroeder. When the tutoring stopped the dating began — I had forbid it at first. In the summer we started living together. When the time came he was drafted in the second round by the Raiders, and I got my masters in psychology. I hung out my shingle, was doing well, liked the work, was out at the stadium for every home game, watched the rest on TV. After a year we got married. For five years things went fine. Jason was a pro bowl wide receiver three times. Until one Sunday, during a home game against Kansas City. Late in the fourth quarter Jason caught a pass that was under thrown. He got hit high and low. Somehow he held onto the ball, but once he hit the turf he didn't move. I was terrified. The trainers and the coach ran out there. Clearly he was unconscious, there was no way to know how bad he was hurt. I hurried down to the field and tried to get to him, but some assistant coach said I could not go out there, he didn't care who I was. I feinted left and ran right, as Jason had taught me to do in case of muggers. I pushed through his teammates and watched as he was strapped onto a stretcher. I rode with him in the ambulance, stayed at the hospital for six days, praying for his recovery. Several vertebrae were damaged. They knew he would never play ball again. The question was would he walk again. Would he ever regain consciousness? Then, on the seventh day — I don't mean to sound Biblical — he opened his eyes, and moved his fingers, his toes. He was back with us — more and more every day. Now, don't misunderstand me, I never for a moment thought that God had made him well in answer to my prayers. No way. My notion of God is not someone who cares that much about our daily woes. But what I realized was how much my praying had helped *me*. Helped me get through this terribly anxious time. I gave it a lot of thought while Jace was recovering, doing physical therapy. I always wanted to help people, and I wasn't sure how much I was really helping in psychology sessions. Becoming a rabbi suddenly loomed as a way to reach more people. Maybe I'm the crazy one, to get back to your opening, but it's working for me. Jason coaches football and track at Fremont High. The kids are in awe of a former Raider, and he's great with them. We're planning to start our own any day now — that's a secret my mother would love to know. Anyway — I don't know why I got so wound up. As a shrink or as a rabbi you don't get to talk about yourself very much. But there you have it — The Rachel Weitz Story. I doubt a movie version would appeal to Angelina Jolie. So — if you want to leave now, Dr. Lee, feel free. If not, let's hear what you want to talk about.

She drank from a water bottle on her desk, and offered me one from a half refrigerator I had not noticed. I was even more enchanted with Rachel Weitz now than I had been at the funeral. I began with Nia. I told her the whole shameful, passionate story.

—I guess that makes me an animal, given what you said at the funeral the other day.

—We're all animals, Dr. Lee. I shouldn't have lashed out like that. But I was feeling for that poor woman.

—Because she's Jewish?

—Because she's hurting so. It's a fear many women have these days, being discarded when they get older. I'm 34, and already I wonder how old I'll be when Jason leaves me for someone younger. I've had women confess to me that they want to marry someone fifteen or twenty years older than themselves, to avoid losing out to younger competition later on. As for your infatuation, no one would call you crazy for that. For one thing, you did not leave your wife. But given her condition, and the certainty that your psyche craves affection, by living in the same house with this beautiful, intelligent young woman it seems only natural that you would become infatuated. Many men would. If not most.

—Madly in love. Not just infatuated.

—Whatever word you want to use. What I did not hear you say is whether the woman, Nia, returns your feelings.

—I don't know.

—Why not?

—I haven't told her how I feel. I haven't asked.

The rabbi, nodding, sips from her water.

—You presented two serious moral problems you're dealing with, Dr. Lee. It seems to me you need more information before worrying about morality. If Nia does not share your feelings, the moral problems vanish. Adultery would not be an issue. Betraying your son would not be an issue.

—She must feel the way I do. These things she says. *I'll show you how good I am.*

—That was in the context of shooting a rifle, correct? It could have been all she meant. Perfectly innocent. All the examples you cited could be innocent. Isn't it time to find out?

—If she rejects me, I no longer have a reason to live out my life. That's how desperately I want to be with her. Like I said, its crazy. I didn't ask for this, it just happened.

—Dr. Lee, if this turns out to be all your fantasy, a one-way emotion — which is quite possible — then it would not be a rejection of you. You're married. She's practically engaged to your son. Even aside from the age difference, getting involved with you may never have crossed her mind. If that's the case, it might destroy your fantasy, but it's not a rejection. People survive divorces, broken love affairs, the death of spouses. Even the death of children. You do that by keeping busy — with work, with friends, all sorts of ways. Look at Dr. Klonsky — what he has to accept. How is he doing, by the way?

—I don't know. He's not returning my phone calls.

She looks at her watch, a small gold thing that she wears facing inward. Usually that offends me, as a sign of selfishness or self-importance. But somehow not with Rachel.

—Have I overstayed my welcome?

—No, the Raiders game will last another hour. You said you had two problems. Why don't we move on to the second one.

I glance at the calendar on the wall. Buying time. The September picture is showing. The Wailing Wall in Jerusalem. Old men with gray beards, dressed in black. Rachel follows my eyes, gets up from her chair, turns a page on the calendar, to October. A few days late. Haifa, by the sea. She sits again, smoothing her skirt.

—Do you think there will ever be peace over there? I ask.

—Several synagogues organized a fact-finding trip last spring. I went. We met with Palestinians as well as Israelis. The hatred on both sides goes way beyond words. There won't be peace in my lifetime. Maybe not in God's.

She turns up the cuffs on her long-sleeved turquoise blouse. She has slim wrists. Painfully, I imagine numbers on them.

—But we're not here to solve the world's problems, Dr. Lee. Just to help a bit with yours, if we can. Perhaps you should tell me your second concern.

—They may be related, I'm not sure.

I take a deep breath. How to begin?

—This is the really crazy part.

I tell her about the beginning — dating Morgan, leaving for a summer in England.

—Morgan told me to be sure and come back with a British accent, so she could pretend she was making love to Lawrence Harvey. Her favorite actor. It may have been intended as a joke, but I brooded over the remark for days. I was none too secure back then.

I tell her about meeting Addie, falling in love for the first time, our blissful though semi-pure affair that eventful summer of 1969. It was our lover's moon yet men went walking on it one weekend in July. A great triumph for science and engineering and America. That same weekend Mary Jo Kopechne drowned at Chappaquiddick, in Ted Kennedy's car. A personal tragedy for two families, a political disaster for the country. Ted would never become president, with all that might have meant. We Harvard men, more than others, perhaps, were feeling, what next? With life so fragile, me deciding to break the engagement with Morgan in favor of Addie.

—That's when I killed eleven women.

She looks at me, her gaze steady, trying not to appear shocked. My mouth dry, I drink from my own water. And wish it was vodka. Rachel uncrosses her legs, crosses them the other way. Her stockings are clear. A purple skirt. Not dressed in black, she is more than comely. She says nothing, waits for me to explain. Leans back in her chair. Which seems to draw me forward on a string. Encourages me to confess to her what I have not revealed for forty years, though it has rarely left my mind.

—The women I killed are still alive. The past two weeks I've been seeing them — in the eyes of my patients, during surgery. That part's dangerous.

She says nothing. She will not help. Finally she suggests I begin from the beginning. I take another deep breath.

—Addie was flying home from England the day before me. I saw her off at the airport, kissed her gently. Told her I loved her, wanted to marry her some day — probably after I graduated, so I could make a living. She said she would think about long term commitments later. She had two conditions before we got more serious. The first was that we had to keep our relationship a secret — from everyone — until after I broke off with Morgan. Our summer romance had been great, she said, but what if that was all it was? And she did not want to appear to be stealing someone else's fiancé — not to anyone, most of all not to herself. I needed to decide about Morgan separately from her, she said. For that reason, she wanted us to spend time apart back in New York before we saw each other. To make sure what we were feeling was real. I asked her how long, a day? A week? You're funny, Michael, she said, but I'm serious. At least a month. I'll be busy settling in as a nurse. You'll be back in school. During that time we won't see each other, or talk on the phone. No contact at all. Then, when we do get together, if we still feel the same, we'll be sure it's not the Thames or The Tower of London that mesmerized us, it's each other. A whole month? I asked. Well, if that's what you want, I'll try to stand it, I said. That would be, what, October 12th? I know! Addie said. Let's make a date. You can take me to dinner on my birthday. But wait a minute, I said, isn't your birthday October 16th? That's more than a month. Sorry, a month and four days, but my birthday feels right. Maybe we'll do something special to celebrate, she says slyly, squeezing my hand. You've got a deal, I said. What choice did I have but to agree? From what I'd heard of summer romances, there was a certain sense to it. We hugged, kissed, long and firm. Then she was off to the boarding area. I stood there for an hour until I saw her plane take off safely into the British clouds. I spent the next month counting the days.

    I continue on to my breakup dinner with Morgan when there is a thud against the outside wall. Then another. I look at the rabbi quizzically. Another thud.

    —I'm usually gone by one o'clock on Sundays. The boys play ball against the bricks. I can shoo them away if it's disturbing you.

    It is, but I can tell by Rachel's intonation that she would hate to break up their game. You rarely see a few kids playing together around here, spontaneous, on their own.

    —It's not a problem, I said (thud — pause — thud) and entered the essence of my story, as if entering a dream. The scene so vivid I am living it again. Ball against the wall syncopating with the uneven beating of my heart as I let it all pour out like a river.

    —Addie worked in a prison hospital on Rikers Island, in the East River. In New York City. On the 16th, in late afternoon, I drove out to pick her up. Until three years before that you had to take a ferry, but in 1966 they opened a bridge. Just one parking lot, though, on the south end of the large island. Buses carried staff and visitors along the edge of the island to their cars. Addie got off at four, I was going to hold her, hug her, take her to a great restaurant. Now we could be openly together. Make love for the first time. You can imagine how my heart was pounding. I knew for sure we were for real.

    —The day was cloudy, rain had been forecast. I left my sunglasses in my car, which I rarely do, but in your breast pocket they can get in the way when you hug. I was a few minutes early. As I walked along the river the sun came out, unexpectedly. Bright, slanting through the gaps between Manhattan's skyscrapers, made doubly bright reflecting off the water. My eyes can't take much sun, that's been a problem since I was a kid. I've always needed sunglasses. Addie thought they looked cool, actually. I came upon a yellow bus — one of those half-sizes, like for special ed kids or something. The doors of the bus were open. I saw something glinting on the dashboard. I looked closer and guess what — it was a pair of sunglasses. Clearly they belonged to the bus driver, but the bus was empty, just standing there. I tried them on and they fit. I could relax the squint in my eyes. I walked nonchalantly to the building where Addie worked. No one was around on the grassy fields. It's a prison island, after all, with about eight different prison buildings. I think now there are ten. Anyway, I pocketed the sunglasses as I entered the building, asked the receptionist if the four o'clock shift had left yet. The woman said they were in a staff meeting in the administration building down the road. It's about half a mile, she said. I thanked her, went outside, donned the sunglasses. The bus was gone. Damn, it might be picking them up at the other building. I started to jog along the road in that direction. But med school doesn't leave you much time for exercise, a pickup game of basketball on an occasional Saturday morning, that was all. After perhaps a quarter of a mile I was winded. I slowed to a walk —and saw the bus rolling along the road up ahead, beyond the administration building. I tried running after it, to catch up with it, but there was no way. It rounded a curve and was heading to the staff parking lot. I'd have to call her from the mainland, I figured — this was 1969, remember, way before cell phones. Suddenly I heard screaming up ahead, around a bend. Like kids on a rollercoaster as it begins its descent. I tried for a second wind, began trotting and came upon a knot of people looking at the water, yelling, crying. I asked a guy what the hell had happened. A bus carrying nurses had gone off the road, bumped down the rocky crags and into the water, he said. This is out in the middle of the river, don't forget. It had submerged in seconds, and nobody was doing anything except yelling for help. I didn't know what to do. I yanked off my shoes, dropped my jacket onto the grass, quickly picked my way among rocks and broken glass to the highest rock I could find. And dove in. Held my breath, kicked my way deep. I had been on the swim team at Harvard, was comfortable under water. But I was never a deep sea diver. I frog-legged my way down, down. The water was greasy, oily from ships. I kept going down, frantic with adrenaline, till I touched something solid, metallic. The top of the bus. I grabbed the edge and pulled myself down further. All the windows of the bus were open. Hanging through each window was a nurse in white. I looked franticly for Addie. Out of breath, I could not help but let myself rise to the surface. A few gulps of air and I kicked down under again. Pulled myself around the bus, window by window. I found Addie, hanging out the middle window. I tried to lift her out. But she was lifeless. All of them. All of them were already dead. Another nurse hung further out the window so I tried to get her out. She was wedged in. My lungs were exploding, I needed air again. Came up, gasping. Thought of trying one more time but my whole body ached, felt frozen. There was no point. I swam to shore, waded out of the water. More people had gathered while I was under. They applauded my effort. One of them asked if I had seen anything. They're all dead, I told them. Nurses, doctors, whose friends used that bus, stared at the black water and cried, hugging one another. We received word that a construction crane was on the island, at the far end, where a new prison building was going up. It was on the way,

I pause, my mouth dry. Drink from the water bottle. I think I had been looking out a window while I spoke. I was far from the rabbi's office, deep in the past. I focus on the rabbi now. A fist is pressed to her lips. Pools of tears glisten in her eyes. She starts to speak, stops, decides to go ahead.

—Dr. Lee, I don't see how you get from this terrible accident to murder. You did all you could to save them.

—Let me finish. It won't take long. A light breeze had come up. I was soaked, and shivering. I put my shoes back on, and my jacket. My hands in my pockets, shoulders hunched. Clouds had covered the sun again. My eyes were stinging from the filthy water. The fellow I had spoken to before, he was about my age, came over and said, nice try. He was also a med student, NYU. Volunteering at Rikers. I gave no more thought to the sunglasses, which had fallen from my pocket. I don't know how long it took for the crane to get there, then to back and fill to find the right position near the edge of the river, drop its huge claws into the water, feel about like a robot. When the claws found the bus the workers in the cab kept pushing and pulling all sort of levers to get a hold on it. The crowd had grown, but not too much. The prisoners of course were in their cells. Most doctors and nurses had to stay with their patients. A fellow came running down the road yelling. The Mets Won! The Mets Won! He stumbled to a stop when he realized no one was paying attention. This was the day in 1969 that the Amazing Mets, the Miracle Mets, as they were called, came from ninth place the year before to win the World Series. One of the biggest stories of the year in New York. One of the biggest sports stories ever. New Yorkers still remember what they were doing, like with JFK. Then with a rustling roar the bus began rising out of the river like a huge yellow cadaver. Rising from the dead. With the dead. Water poured off the top of the bus and down the sides. From the shore where we were, each window was hung with an arm in a wet white sleeve, a lolling head hanging on a white shoulder. Faces and hair getting soaked further, an added insult, from the waterfall cascading off the top of the bus. Higher and higher the bus rose in the jaws of the crane as we stared, mesmerized. Till the black tires were clear of the water and the crane slowly swung the bus over the craggy rocks onto the road.

—My God, how awful, the rabbi said when I paused. She had found a tissue in her pocket, was dabbing at her eyes.

—The police had arrived by then, were moving us back from the scene. That's all I remember. Not a day or night has gone by in forty years when I have not closed my eyes at least once and seen the yellow bus hanging over the water, dripping onto the dead nurses who hung out the windows like wilted bouquets of dead white carnations. Five on the side I saw, including Addie. Turned out there were six more on the other side.

—And the driver?

—He was dead as well. A gray-haired old man. The odd thing is, this should have been a huge story in the newspapers. But there was also a big anti-Vietnam peace march in Washington that day, more than a million people. Not just hippies and students. For the first time the middle class had poured out from all over the country to protest the war. It was a major event. And in New York the Miracle Mets were an even bigger story. There was no Internet back then. The newspaper pages were filled with stories, pictures of the march, the game, the celebrations. I didn't have a TV, not while in med school. I wouldn't have watched the celebrating anyway. The time of the bus crash was too late for the the early editions. Just one tiny bulletin made it into the *New York Mirror*. Somehow I got back to my apartment. I have no recollection how. I started to drink. Addie was dead, that was all that mattered. I had seen her, touched her lifeless hand for the last time before I drifted up to breathe. I had plenty of booze on hand, was working on finishing it all. Late at night I needed to talk to someone. But who? The whole town was out celebrating the Mets, every bar in every part of the city. Me and Addie would have been out there as well, probably at Mr. Laff's, where some of the ballplayers hung out. In my drunken state I called Morgan, of all people, and asked if she could come by and bring more booze. She showed up with a large paper bag filled with clinking bottles. I loved her for that. Also the *Daily Mirror* with that little bulletin on the crash. I stayed smashed for a week, throwing up regularly. Not eating. Not leaving my apartment. Took my phone off the hook, didn't want to hear from anyone. Morgan came by every evening after work to keep me company. To talk. To take my mind off things. Addie and I had been saving our first lovemaking for that night. But the only night that came was eternal night.

Pausing, I gulp water. The tennis ball is still thudding against the wall. I had not noticed it while I talked. Recollected.
—I'm so sorry, Rachel said.
—There's just a bit more to tell. But it's crucial. The first speculation was that the driver, who was 65 or 70, I forget, had suffered a heart attack at the wheel. Or a stroke. Lost control of the bus and it plunged off the dirt road onto the steep rocky incline toward the river, flipped, a large projecting rock crashed through the windshield, shattering it as the bus rolled down into the river. The eleven women clearly had drowned, autopsies were hardly necessary. But when they opened up the driver they found no sign of a heart attack, no sign of a stroke. Instead, his eyes were all cut up by the broken windshield. For days it was a puzzle. Someone remembered that the sun had broken out strong just before the crash, and would have been slanting right into the driver's eyes. For this reason the old man — I don't recall his name — always wore sunglasses when he drove. Nurses who rode with him on other routes or other shifts told this to the police. But the police found no sign of sunglasses on his body or on the bus. They could have floated out of the bus under water. Divers were sent down briefly, but it was hopeless, with the currents and all the rest. The official theory became that because it had been a cloudy day, with rain forecast, the driver had forgotten his sunglasses. Just as he made a turn on the road, the last sharp turn before the parking lot, the sun blinded him, he lost control and the fatal accident occurred.
—Accident, Dr. Lee. That's the first time you used that word. It was an accident.

—Which would not have happened if I hadn't stolen his sunglasses. Borrowed them. I would have given them back. By then eleven women were dead.

—And the driver.

—Yes. I don't know what happened after that. What was to know? I had never met Addie's parents, was in no mood to crash a funeral and watch her laid under the earth. I could not have taken that. So I drank and drank and missed a week of school. Which was a stupid thing to do. When I finally came out of it, thanks to Morgan getting some food into me from time to time, I went to the dean and explained. Said my girlfriend, the love of my life, had been killed. Told him frankly I had been drunk for a week. He said that under the circumstances, if I made up the work I had missed and two exams, they would overlook it. But I had to buckle down, drinking for any reason would no longer be an excuse. I did as he said, buckled down. Good thing, because it was only all that work that kept me sane. That and Morgan. There were times when I really wanted to die. When word came in the spring that my application to intern at Stanford had been accepted, we got engaged for the second time, Morgan and me. We married a year later, right after graduation. Before I could screw it up again.

—That's a tragic story, Dr. Lee. May I call you Michael? Have you ever considered that you've put much too much guilt on yourself? What happened was awful, but it was not murder.

—Have you heard of felony murder, rabbi? You could be sitting in a car on the street, the getaway car during a robbery, and if someone is killed during the holdup you're guilty of murder, even though you were waiting outside.

—Yes, but borrowing sunglasses — even stealing them — is hardly a felony.

—It depends how much they cost. You're right, it was probably a misdemeanor. I think they'd have to be worth over $300 to be a felony. I haven't looked into that in a long time. Laws change. But the moral responsibility is the same. My theft, their deaths. Plenty of deserved guilt. Taking those sunglasses killed those women. Only two people know the whole story. Morgan, and Max Klonsky, whom you know from the funeral. The fellow who said a kind word at the Rikers scene turned out to be him. He'd been doing volunteer intern work at the hospital. He called me some time later, said he would like to get together. We met in a bar. He gave me a manila envelope. In it were the fatal sunglasses. He'd noticed me taking them from the bus, seen them fall from my jacket pocket as I dove into the water. He picked them up, for no particular reason, he said, just thought it was a good idea. When the investigation wound up focused on the sunglasses, he considered going to the police. But the women had been dead for a month by then. He'd seen me try to save them. Why destroy my life as well? So, quietly, he gave them back to me. That's how our friendship began, on Rikers Island. But his actions indicated he clearly thought I was guilty. Neither of us has mentioned what happened since. Not once. Instead we wound up working together. What I haven't told you yet is that I have kept the nurses alive — even though they are dead.

She tries hard to remain expressionless.

—Without alcohol I could not cope with my guilt — except by bringing them back to life. Imagining what they would be doing had I not killed them. Let their lives continue. So I've got Mona Drew off in Paris making it as a singer. Janelle Williams in her nursing smock in New Orleans, still mad about the lack of help after Katrina. Ginger Soto back in Texas, cleaning motel rooms, hoping her God will deliver her to something better. I saw no harm in doing that, if it helped me to cope.

The rabbi begins writing on a pad.

—This is fascinating. doctor. Do you mind if I take notes? Just for myself, of course. Everything here is confidential. I try to keep up with psychology trends, and I don't recall anything like this in the literature.

—No, that's fine. The thing is, in the past two weeks they've been showing up unbidden. In the eyes of my patients. As I repair cataracts, replace corneas. This is new. And dangerous. I could blind someone if my hand slips. When I try to imagine why now, what do they want, what comes to my mind is not them, but Nia. Mona even told me they were upset because my love for Nia was crowding them out of my brain. Now that, I admit, is borderline nuts. But I suppose they could be related.

The rabbi has her hand under her chin, listening intently. She drops her hand, stretches her arm as if it has tightened on her.

—Let's take a break, she says. Rest room time. I'll call Jason and tell him I'll be late. I'd like to give you a few observations. If that's okay with you.

—Absolutely. I guess that's why I'm here.

When we reunite in her office she asks if I'm hungry. I say I am, sort of. She says she is starving, there's a good kosher deli on the next block, I can buy her lunch as payment for her time. I remind her she'd said a few hours ago that having lunch together would be unacceptable. That was before we knew each other, she replies. And before she got hungry.

It's a traditional kosher deli, sights and smells I remember from New York. Salamis hanging from the ceiling. Sides of roast beef behind the glass counter, corned beef floating in fatty water. Oil for fries bubbling. Formica tables, chrome chairs, leatherette booths. A classic faded sign on the wall, from World War II, I believe: *Send a Salami to a Boy in the Army.* From a dark red booth we both order pastrami sandwiches, Dr. Brown's cream soda. And a knish to share. The order is written on a pad by a clean-cut young man, who looks like a college kid making spending money of a Sunday afternoon.

—Whatever happened to those great old Jewish waiters? I ask Rachel. Those ancient ones who used to tell you what to eat, snarl and mutter if you didn't listen, never wrote down an order, remembered everything.

—I suppose they all died out.

—Somebody ought to have cloned them.

—Hebrew National tried, she says. But all they kept getting were female rabbis. So they gave up.

I grin. It sounds like something Vicky might say. The same dry sense of humor crossing disparate cultures. The waiter sets down two cold cream sodas. I ignore the glass, take a swig from the bottle. Rachel is not too much a rabbi, or a lady, to do the same. She looks around, it's 3 o'clock, half way between lunch and dinner. The place is nearly empty, no one will overhear us.

—I heard a good Jewish joke the other day, I tell her. A waiter serves a Jewish couple in a restaurant. He comes back a few minutes later, and asks them, Is anything all right?

Rachel grins, but quickly gets down to business.

—I'm not a psychologist anymore, she says, but I still love the subject. I keep up with the literature, as I was saying. Some neuroscientists are beginning to believe we might have a gene for morality. Some stronger than others, like any other gene. What happened to those nurses was terrible, but for you to see yourself as a murderer for forty years suggests an extremely strong morality gene. Perhaps too strong. Which fits in with being faithful to a not very satisfying marriage. And your concern that with your wife in a coma, a sexual adventure still would be wrong.

—That fits in with both my parents. My father enlisted in the Marines during Korea, when he was well past draft age. My mother killed herself during the McCarthy years, rather than give up the names of friends.

—Of course, morality is not always clear cut. One could argue that leaving two orphans is worse than snitching on friends.

Feeling a flare of anger, I try to keep calm, speak softly. Old memories are surfacing like the bubbles in the cream soda.

—It was more complicated than that. She made provision for us. And saved dad's reputation.

The sandwiches arrive. Half a kosher pickle beside each. I remember how pungent they are. I recall Speedy Alka Seltzer in his tablet cap. He saved me from many a sleepless night. *Plop plop, fizz fizz.* They don't write songs like that anymore.

—I'm sorry, Rachel says. I had no business saying that. I didn't mean to cast aspersions on your mother. I didn't mean that I believe that — just that some people might. Perhaps the lesson for me is we ought to stick to the issues at hand.

I nod, bite into my sandwich. The rabbi does the same. Grease runs down my fingers. Good pastrami. I cut the knish in half and we indulge. The college kid waiter doesn't come by to kibbitz. Maybe he'll learn.

—The notion of a gene for morality is fascinating, though. It would go a long way toward establishing determinism as a universal truth. You'd be out of a job, of course. No more rabbis, priests, ministers. No more Muslims, Hindus, Buddhists. We'll never have a peaceful world with all these conflicting certainties. But if all faiths came to understand that our actions are predetermined by genetic history, there would be no point in fighting anymore. No more suicide bombers. No more wars. The world could be truly united, realizing we're all in the same genetic prison. Why not help each other, make sure everyone has enough food, truly understand we are all brothers and sisters, not under one God or other but in the evolution of history?

—You sound a bit like the theme song at Disneyland, Dr. Lee. *We Are the World*. No offense, it's a nice vision. But half of this country hasn't accepted plain old evolution yet. Genetic morality without God will be a hard sell, even if they find the gene.

—But what a start that could make.

—Do you think any religion would give itself up to science?

—The observances could be kept. Ceremonies. Pageants. Symbols. As long as everyone realizes these are just theatrical events. Which is what they are.

—My ceremony is stronger than your pageant! Take that!

—Jesus, and I thought I was cynical.

Rachel sets down the uneaten part of her sandwich. I finish mine.

—I'm just teasing, she says. From what I've heard today, I don't think you're cynical. You're a dreamer. Who's been badly disillusioned several times. And if I may say so, perhaps not so much a determinist as you pretend. If all our actions are predetermined, how can you beat yourself up for forty years over borrowing a pair of sunglasses? Wouldn't a determinist say the fact of those sunglasses falling into your path was determined five thousand years ago, in Africa or the Orient or somewhere? By a butterfly beating its wings or something. But let's change the subject. I have some thoughts about your dead women. Some questions.

I drain the last of my soda. She does the same with hers.

—First question. Your stories that keep these dead women alive, so to speak. To lessen your sense of guilt. You didn't mention Addie, the love of your life back then.

—There's no way I could keep her life story going.

—Why not?

—Because her life would have been spent with me. Loving each other. Living together. Marrying. Body pressed against body every night. There is no other life I could give her. But she is not in my bed, I'm not that crazy. Give her a future with other lovers? No way. I'm better off with her dead than imagining her with someone else.

The rabbi upends her bottle, seeking the last drop. The college boy comes by and takes the empties.

—More cream soda?

We both hesitate.

—Come on, live a little!

The boy has possibilities. We both smile, nod.

—Two cream sodas, coming up. But rabbi, don't let him get you drunk. You know those *goyim* and their drinking.

—I won't, James Reilly. My mother, may she rest in peace, will thank you for the warning.

College boy hurries off, a slight awed smile creasing his face. Awed at himself?

—James Reilly in a kosher deli?

—Maybe your One World starts here.

—We should write down the date. Genesis Two. In the beginning was cream soda.

—Okay, enough. Now listen, this could be revealing. All afternoon you've referred to killing eleven women. What about the driver?

—He was a man.

—I realize that. Didn't he also drown?

—Of course.

—Yet you don't feel guilt about him.

—He was old. He'd lived his life. And he was at least partly responsible for his own death. The nurses were not. If the sun blinded him for a moment, why didn't he hit the brakes? Slow to a roll? He didn't have to go over the rocks and into the river.

—But you still feel responsible for murdering the women. Because you borrowed — okay stole — a pair of sunglasses.

James Reilly pops the top on two Dr Brown's, sets them in front of us, with fresh napkins. Lingers for a moment, finds no clever remark, moves away. Rachel waits until he's gone.

—About your method of keeping the women alive in your psyche. That's fascinating. I don't recall reading about that precise manifestation, except for the psychos who keep decaying bodies around. But that's different. Now these women are coming back visibly, interrupting your surgeries. Mona, you said, told you they are upset because of Nia. That your head is too full of her. That you're not paying enough attention to them. I think she may be right. That your two problems are connected.

—Appearing in the eyes of my patients is not only a hostile act, it's dangerous to my patients — and therefore dangerous to me. My reputation. My career. That's scant thanks for keeping them alive.

—Let me try a theory on you. I can understand how you continue the lives of the nurses in a fantasy world, and still live in the real world. Novelists do it all the time. Half the time their minds are off in space, or on the ocean, or in a lovely actress's bed — wherever the fictitious scene is set — while at the same time they're driving a cab to pay the rent, or teaching Composition 101 in junior college. Nathan Zuckerman could want to marry Anne Frank, but Philip Roth couldn't. So no, you're not crazy in your ability to do that. Often the fictional world can be more rewarding than the real one. As when we're engrossed in a good book, or a good movie. We know the characters are not real — yet they also are real, for us, for a time. The famous suspension of disbelief. It gives us a brief respite from the truths of our lives, of our future deaths. I suspect that's why we're a species of storytellers, going back thousands of years. But it's interesting that you leave out the driver — the old man. Your mother committed suicide. She might have been perfectly justified. I'm not going back there. But you had to miss her terribly. That was an unavoidable side effect. Then you fell for Addie Judd, and your emotional world was made whole again. Not that she was a mother figure, but you were starved for affection, and she provided it, with maybe some erotic touching thrown in. Apparently in an exciting way that Morgan Albright was not capable of. When Addie died, it was a double blow. You married Morgan for whatever reasons — companionship, money — don't wince, I'm not accusing you,

Jason made millions in the NFL. You were seeking that lost affection, perhaps. But you've suggested you did not find it there, even before her coma. So keeping the nurses alive in your fantasies may not have been about assuaging your guilt. Not entirely. You spoke to them, and they to you. They were all young, in their 20s and 30s. Many of them pretty, that's how we conceive of young nurses. Your talks were friendly. Rewarding. Perhaps that's why — or at least part of why — you've kept them alive. They were beings you cherished. Who satisfied your need for affection. So the fact that you are so infatuated with Nia could suggest you don't need the dead nurses anymore. You are in love with Nia, so the nurses are hurt, rebelling. Maybe by appearing in the eyes of your patients they are making the big break. Getting you angry at them. In other words, maybe your subconscious, where their second lives are coming from, is preparing you to jettison them. Mona blamed Nia in so many words.

—You make it sound like I'm one of those schizophrenics with 12 personalities.

—Not at all. You're still Dr. Michael Lee when you converse with them. When you string out their lives. You know the difference between the living and the dead. But it's possible that you love them a little for the comfort you get from them. That could be another reason why the old driver stays dead. His affection you didn't want.

She sips from the new bottle of soda, dabs at her lips with a napkin.

—Does any of this make sense?

My mouth is parched. I drink a long drink. My mouth still is parched.

—Much of it does. But this is still, I think, mostly about guilt. Can you imagine what it feels like, killing eleven people? Having to live with that?

—I can only imagine eight.

Instantly I am hurt, surprised, angry. My pants sticking to the leatherette, I don't want to move, don't want to appear to be squirming.

—Rabbi, this is not a joke.

—Of course not, doctor. I suppose I need to explain. The fact is, I omitted part of my autobiography earlier. When I gave up psychology to become a rabbi, I needed to do something that would stop me from feeling like a fraud. Something to earn my Jewish stripes, so to speak. I went to Israel, and enlisted in the Israeli army. Jason was not happy, but he knew whom he had married. The Intifada had begun. Arab terrorists had become suicide bombers, blowing up buses filled with women and children. Blowing up market places. Mossad located a school in a refugee camp that was specifically for training them. We received orders to blow it up. We rode into the camp in tanks. At the offending school, a mud hut, I threw two hand grenades. When the dust settled, eight potential suicide bombers —all women — were dead, their bodies shattered, pieces scattered about. Plus their male teacher. No one had told us the bomber recruits were female. So I have eight women on my conscience. Like you, I don't count the man. He was teaching them to kill us.

—That was different than my nurses. That was war.

— It was also different in another way. My intention was to kill.

—This never troubled you?

—It always troubles me. The Israeli leaders told us these girls got what they deserved — that the Palestinians admitted the girls and young women had volunteered to become martyrs, to kill Jews. They would have died anyway when they detonated their belt bombs, and taken hundreds of innocent people with them. What troubles me was that either side could have been lying. Maybe these young women had not volunteered at all. Maybe they had been conscripted. Forced into martyrdom. But I never tried to give them a second life. No need. Faulkner improved on Shakespeare on that one: *The past is never dead. It's not even past.* That's another reason there will never be peace over there. Both sides have such long memories. But as you say, it was war. It troubles me, but I don't feel guilty. Stepping into the heart of the Intifada made me a better rabbi. More confident, more legitimate, in my own eyes.

Her story stunned me. I did not know how to respond. The deli was filling up with elderly Jews coming for dinner at five o'clock. We had been talking a long time.

—My problems seem foolish after that. We better wrap this up.

—Don't feel foolish. I shouldn't have spoken about Israel. I purposely left it out of my personal history earlier so you would not feel this way. I rarely speak of it to anyone, for that reason. Each of our psyches is a world all its own. Each is important. Know Thyself. That's our most important task on earth. Between these two crises, at work and at home, you may be groping toward self-knowledge.

—Just one selfish thought, then. If the dead nurses leave — if my psyche lets them go, would be a saner way to put it — and Nia and I become lovers, that would be my dream come true. But if Nia turns me down, and your affection theory is correct, it will be more devastating than ever. Lonelier than ever, not having my nurses to fall back on.

—We don't know about any of that. What Nia will do, what the nurses will do, what you will do. Bring them back in some other form? We don't know. Even if it's predetermined, we can't know. The only thing certain is that you'll learn from it. You'll find out what you have to do to survive. From every experience, however painful, we learn something. A gospel in which everyone should believe.

—That's rabbi talk, Rachel.

—I'm sorry. What you see is what you get.

—Whatever happens, I'll still know I killed them.

— Maybe they're getting ready to leave so you won't kill them again.

She looks at her watch, reaches for her purse on the seat beside her. Black leather, small gold clasp. Everything about her is modest but impeccable. I pull the check towards me.

—Thanks for the pastrami. I have to get going, before Jason thinks you did get me drunk.

—Thank you for the therapy. I'm not even Jewish, let alone in your congregation. That was very kind.

—You carry enough guilt for a *minyan,* doctor. That's ten Jewish men. So you're an honorary member of the tribe.

When I offer to walk her to her car, she says it isn't necessary. We shake hands. Hers is warm, feminine, firm. The last place I would look for a hand grenade. Right or wrong, the rabbi is hypnotic. She's going to try getting pregnant, she'd said. Her husband is a lucky man. Even if his back hurts. Even if the Raiders lost.

After she leaves I order a beer, sit there musing on what she said. My mind goes back to Long Island, January, 1970. Winter break. The nurses have been dead three months. The police have never connected me to the missing sunglasses. I decide it is safe to visit Addie's grave.

The cemetery is in one of those little Long Island towns you never heard of unless you grew up there. The sky is winter gray, the air chilly, a nasty wind is blowing. In the passenger seat instead of my beloved Addie are a dozen pink roses. I find the cemetery with the aid of a map, and ask at the visitor gate where I can find the grave of Addie Judd. A short, bald man is in the booth.

—Judd, Addie, he mumbles as he turns the pages of a thick, worn ledger. Here it is. Terrible tragedy that was, if I remember correctly. Corner of Jefferson and Third.

The blacktop roads in the cemetery are narrow. Two cars could barely pass. They are numbered in one direction, names of dead presidents crossing them. Washington, Adams, Jefferson. I park in the road, gather my roses, walk to Third. It's a corner plot, eight Judds buried there, going back to the 1800s. Names, dates, Biblical verses on the stones. In the far corner a grave so newly dug the rolled turf on top is still green in midwinter. Light snow begins to fall as I cross to read her stone. The far corner location presumably leaves room for parents, maybe her grandparents. The stone is a polished gray granite. Etched into it are her name and dates:

Addie Lynn Judd

October 16, 1946

October 16, 1969

There is no biblical verse carved into the stone. Only, centered beneath the dates, a single word:

WHY?

I stood there, crying, as the wind whipped harder and sleet began to slap my face. I knelt, and with the pink roses I spelled out on the still-green grass the same brief question:

WHY?

Not long after I leave, I know, the wind and sleet will steal my roses.

Never will I return to her grave to provide an answer. I do not know the answer.

Part Three

Chapter 16: Sweet Marie

Was there a landscape where their abandoned thoughts could arrange to meet, without their knowing about it?

—Henning Mankell
The White Lioness

I'm engrossed in a Swedish mystery. Nia had finished it, recommended it, before leaving for the weekend. I sense her scent on the pages. Or her soap. On weekends she reads in the tub, in a bubble bath. The plot has just moved from Sweden to South Africa, from the murder of an innocent woman to an international conspiracy,

My mind drifts. A thought occurs that has never occurred before. For forty years I have kept alive the dead, ten dead women, all except Addie. I've imagined their lives for them, before death and after death. For most, of course, I knew nothing about their lives before the day they drowned, I had to invent those even as I invented their afterlives. But in the more than two years since Morgan's fall, since her departure into a coma as into an ocean liner sailing away from the pier with no one waving goodbye, I never once tried to bring her back, to relive our life together, let alone wonder where she was living now inside her head. There were thirty-six years before her fall, and in a sense there had been no difference between then and now. I try to recall what we had done with our lives together. I can think of nothing beyond dozens of charity balls whose committees she was on, me standing in a tuxedo leaning against the wall, drink in hand, Scotch and soda or vodka and tonic depending on the season. Thirty-six years of balls and I can hardly recall a real conversation that took place at any of them. There was plenty of talking, men or women approaching to make small talk, yet I can remember none that was memorable. We must have gone on vacations, Morgan always planning them, the social director of our marriage, cruises to no place, mostly, which were charity balls on the water. With shuffleboard. Men much older than I would win. Knock me out of the box to score. That's been my life away from work and reading — escaping into books, escaping into eyes. The early days of intimacy became fewer and fewer, as did our words. It was the secret of what I had done that linked me to her like ankle chains. Sometimes I think I can resurrect a life for her as she lies in her coma, even as I have done for my victims. I have tried, to no effect.

A brain in a coma can be largely inactive, but I cannot imagine it being totally empty. What, for instance, is the constantly expanding universe expanding into? I wonder if the last thought a person has before collapsing remains vivid in there, like words frozen on a screen. Is this what is writ large in Morgan's cortex, this final silent thought: *If only I had reached the gun?*

Whatever her motive, the gun was, however, empty.

I try to get back to Kurt Wallander and the Mankell mystery, but am too distracted by thoughts of a life lived blind to passion. I set the book aside, slip into the stereo Bach's *Goldberg Variations*. I bought a new record, I used to say, arriving home. Morgan with that irritating smirk would point out that they are not records anymore, dear, why do you insist on living in the past? Perhaps because Addie is in the past, I would think — can someone be waiting for you in the past? — but of course I would not say it. The underlying music of our marriage: unspoken thoughts. If Prufrock measured out his life in coffee spoons, ours at least contained a progression, from mono to stereo, from records to tapes to CDs to DVDs. I read somewhere that in the music business they're still called records. I'm cutting a new record, a singer will say. It made me happy to hear that, a small vindication. Anyway, Beethoven and Mozart are music's Tolstoy and Dostoevsky — I love them both — but when my mind needs to clarify I often turn to Bach. I can't articulate why. Morgan believed it had to do with how Bach died.

The exact facts of his death are elusive. My file in alphabetized folders, for possible use in *A Brief History of Sight*, is in the den. Most gems I found on the Internet. I pull out the Bach folder, glance through the entries. Like so many things on line they must be read through an invisible question mark. For example:

Bach became increasingly blind, and the celebrated British ophthalmologist John Taylor operated on him while visiting Leipzig in 1750. Bach died on 28 July, 1750 at the age of 65. A contemporary newspaper reported the cause of death was "from the unhappy consequences of the very unsuccessful eye operation."

By 1740, Bach's eyesight was failing. Two cataract operations resulted in his complete blindness. He died of a stroke on July 28, 1750. Legend has it that he woke up that morning able to see for the first time in months — but died later in the day.

John Taylor was born in England the son of an apothecary in 1703, studied medicine and specialized in ophthalmology. He rose to be eye doctor to King George II and became a shameless self-promoter. During a visit to Leipzig in 1749, Taylor operated on Bach's ailing eyes. When the first operation failed, he tried a second one. After those operations, Bach's blindness was total and his health failed. He died less than a year later. Taylor had probably killed him. You'd think that Handel, a surgeon's son, would've known better. But in 1751 he too submitted to Taylor's knife, and he too came out none the better for the surgery. Taylor went blind before his own death in 1772.

From the Internet's so-called facts you choose what to believe. As in life. Morgan's reasoning about me and Bach was that I felt kinship not with his music, but with him as the victim of another murderous ophthalmologist. I did not argue the point.

Mercifully the phone rings. I expect it's Nia assuring me she is safe, just delayed. It's Maxie. Immediately I'm as warmed by his voice as I am chilled by recalling his circumstance. I lower the volume on Bach.

—Where the hell are you, Maxie? I've been calling you all week.

—Right now I'm at Miami airport, waiting out a delay. The past four days I've been in Haiti. I couldn't stand the thought that I had betrayed Laurette. I had to do something to make up for it. There was one thing that just might do it. I flew down there with ten grand cash in my pocket. It's a beautiful country, where I had the feeling you could be killed for no reason at any minute by men in sunglasses, real or imagined. A thousand dollars American spread around got me past the guards at the Ministry of Justice. Two thousand got me in to see the Minister. I pointed out to him that the only crime ever committed by Claude Dubal, Laurette's father, was to speak against the government. Well, the seriousness of that crime grew and grew until another two thousand American convinced the minister that Claude Dubal had indeed been imprisoned long enough. He made some calls and I was at the prison when Laurette's father emerged, blinking into a sun he may not have seen for years. I introduced myself, and took him to a cafe. I explained what Laurette had meant to me, told him that she was dead — a pointless killing by an American gang. I took the remaining five grand from my pocket and quietly slipped it to him. To keep, and to spread around the Dubal family as he saw fit. He thanked me, in a daze at being released from prison after nine years, at the news of the death of his daughter, at his sudden fortune. I couldn't tell which. Probably all of it. He invited me to dinner but I did not want to spoil the day by saying too much, talking too much. Instead I let him take me to the thatched village where she was born. Where she grew up. A village waiting for the next hurricane. I sailed back to Miami but on the pool of tears in his eyes. Now I'm stuck here by bad weather in New York. Go figure.

I wait for him to finish. Love makes poets of us all.

As does death.

—That's a wonderful thing you've done, Maxie. Did it help? With Laurette?

—It helped diminish the guilt. I feel she can now more nearly rest in peace. Her father's freedom is the treasure she wanted most. I don't worry much about an afterlife, but I hope that from up there somewhere, Laurette saw, Laurette knows. As for me, the loneliness, the loss of love, it did not help much. But I am coming home stronger. Ready to get back to work. Perhaps that is my gift from her father.

His flight is announced, he begs off. Never have I admired Maxie more.

Or hated myself more, by contrast.

—One more thing, Maxie says.

No, I want to shout into the phone. The conversation has reached its end. Let the curtain fall. But he keeps on talking.

—You have to read the new Philip Roth. It's called *Exit Ghost*. I read it on the plane.

—Why must I read this book?

I'm trying not to sound annoyed.

—It's about an *alta cocker* like us, even older, he's 71. He falls madly in lust with a gorgeous 30-year-old. Married, yet. He's totally infatuated. Even though he's had prostate trouble and can't get it up any more.

—So?

I pretend to ignore the relevance to any real person, living or dead.

—So, when Roth writes about something, that makes it okay.

—Is that a Jewish axiom, Maxie, or just yours?

—You remember 1969? *Portnoy's Complaint?* Everybody was reading it. It made masturbation a conversation piece. More than that. An extreme sport.

—I remember 1969, I say. Drily.

Maxie doesn't catch my pain. I play along.

—Too bad Portnoy isn't coming out today. TV could make it a reality show.

He chokes, over an airport drink or two, I realize. I click off before he can respond.

Where the hell was I? Someplace important, I think.

Busy hating myself.

I slip the Book Review section from today's *New York Times*, which out of a lifetime of habit I still have delivered every Sunday. J. M. Coetzee, the South African Nobel Prize winner, also has a new novel out. Like Roth's, it is also about an old man who falls for a young woman. This is not exactly headline news, so why are two such eminent writers dealing with it in what may be their last books — the desire for young love, with their potency and their pricks already in the grave? Is Maxie right? Is cosmic change in the air? Is the animal instinct in the aging male about to be not only acknowledged, but accepted? Those two writers are known for taking political and social and literary risks. For breaking new ground. Will the unwritten rules now change? Dare I renew my wavering hope that Nia will be mine? Or did someone lace the writers' fat-free milk with aphrodisiacs?

Guidance. I need guidance beyond the rabbi's. What would Methuselah do?

Dear old *Alma Mater.* Another item in the *Times* is about Harvard — the medical school. Seems a student there has been exposed as a man who spent seven years in prison for murder, then changed his name. Applying at Harvard, he passed the exams, aced the interview, was admitted much like the other students, and was doing well. Apparently no one asked how he'd spent the past seven years. Now a battle is raging about whether a murderer should be allowed to become a doctor. There is no school policy on that. Some students claim that since the killer was outed, his presence makes them nervous. His supporters argue that he has already paid his debt to society.

Were I on the board that will decide whether to expel him, I don't know how I would vote. Maybe I'm not objective. I might have to recuse myself. My prediction: they will find some technicality upon which to get rid of him. Great minds can always find a technicality.

It's a fine example of an acute observation by my mentor Schopenhauer: *If I maintain my silence about my secret it is my prisoner. If I let it slip from my tongue, I am its prisoner.*

Which is not to say the killer let it slip. On the question of how his past was revealed the *Times* is silent.

I have not had time to digest Rachel's interpretation of my women. I've avoided considering it. If she is correct, if I have been keeping the nurses alive to assuage not my guilt but my need for affection, the tragedy of my life could have an intriguing title: *A Harem of the Dead.*

A paperback original. I would prefer, like most literate minds, to have lived a hardback life.

Telling the rabbi my secrets was a conscious act. They did not slip from my tongue. But is there a difference? Am I now their prisoner? Am I the rabbi's prisoner?

Only, I suppose, were she to violate my trust. Which means she does have power over me, should she choose to use it.

Von Zipper . . . Black Flys . . . Intellitec
A peacock is walking on my lawn. I am watching through the window in the den. The peacock begins to strut, spreads its feathers in a huge, colorful fan, mostly blues and greens, patterned with large white peacock eyes. On each feathery eye is a pair of sunglasses.

Arnette . . . Carrera Sport . . . Daggers
A woman dressed in black, like a nun, comes up the walk. Approaches the peacock. She is holding a wooden pointer, of the kind used to point at the blackboard in school. I believe it is the rabbi. Holding the pointer in her right hand, she begins to swing it at the peacock. Methodically she is knocking the sunglasses off every peacock eye.

Reptile . . . Lure-Eyes . . . SEXX Vision
Another woman comes traipsing across the grass, dancing, like one of the three graces on speed. Freed from imprisonment in marble. Hair piled high, figure nude, well-shaped. Nia or Addie, neither of whose naked flesh I have seen. Perhaps a combination of both. Grabs the pointer from the rabbi, holds it above her head, is about to jab it hard, like a dagger, into one of the peacock eyes. Just before it pierces the feathered eye I wake, shivering. A single refrain shuddering in my brain: *cock eyes cock eyes cock eyes*

In the morning Nia's door still is open, her bed still made, she has not returned yet from San Diego. There's no reason to hang around with the Teddy Bear. I arrive at the office early, nobody is in ophtho, it's gloomy and silent as a waiting room peopled by ghosts. I can squeeze in a visit to Morgan. I walk through the quiet corridors just coming to life. In the country, cocks would be crowing about now. I pass though the oncology ward, the doors to the rooms of most patients still closed, all except one, where I can see a woman asleep with her mouth wide open, as if she is screaming silently, a tube entering her body at the base of her throat. I move down the cardiac ward, where signs outside most doors are marked Telemetry — their heart action being monitored with machines. Down the ICU ward — Intensive Care — where each patient has his or her own nurse. I nod to Vidya, a friendly redhead who once told me she loves the grueling job because of the satisfaction of seeing people brought in nearly dead walk out a few weeks or a few months later under their own power, and resume their lives. The pressure is so intense in the ICU that sometimes when she gets home late at night she tries to open her front door with her ID card. I wave to Julie Macy, a phlebitis tech. A friend of Laurette Dubal, she had been at the funeral. She's been drawing blood for twenty years, and with fair skin and an auburn pony tail still looks 21. A sweet young female vampire? There are hundreds of workers in the hospital, most of whom I never get to know beyond a nod or smile in passing — recognizing a fellow employee in scrubs of pale blue or pale green or lavender or white, scrubs provided free by the hospital, colors not denoting rank or position, as patients and visitors tend to assume, but the color preference of the wearer. Some workers disdain them because they look too much like pajamas, wear instead just the scrub bottoms with their own blouses, or just the scrub tops with their own slacks or jeans. Only us docs stand out in white lab coats, and housekeeping crews all in maroon scrubs, perhaps to mask dried blood. I pass signs beside patient doors marked *Name Alert* because the two patients in the room have similar or even the very same names. Gallegos. Smith. Liu. You'd think the administration would avoid this, avoid risking fatal errors dispensing meds to the wrong patients. They do try, but when beds are scarce, as they usually are, sometimes there is no choice. I'm noticing details this morning that I ignore every day.

A crowd is blocking the doorway to Morgan's room. Another old woman has died. This is a new patient since last I was here, a teenage girl in the bed, wan and peaked as a corpse. The bed is surrounded by two young docs I vaguely recognize, two nurses and an aide. The girl, maybe 16, is hooked to an IV and oxygen. Dark hair, thin face. Her arms on her blanket look emaciated.

—You're Mike Lee, the diagnostician, one of the docs says.

I can't recall his name, his ID badge has flipped inward.

—Ophthalmology.

—Yes, I know. But your rep is solving hard cases out of the blue.

—Ah. That stems from a couple of lucky guesses years ago.

I thought that legend had faded into history, like the arrow heads that dotted the hospital grounds before the multiple expansions, the donor-named wings.

—Do you have a minute to venture a lucky a guess here?

I glance across the room. Morgan in her coma isn't going anywhere.

—What's the problem?

—Millicent here has hardly been eating for months. Lost 25 pounds, and she started at a hundred. Says she's hungry but food makes her gag. Arm and leg muscles atrophied. Pain all over, stabbing cramps in the abdomen. We've scanned every organ in her body — and I mean every one — all of them are healthy. Blood tests for every disease in the book. Millicent is a perfectly healthy girl. But is so weak she can hardly move.

I look at the girl, see pain and stoicism in her large brown beseeching eyes.

—You've looked for ALS? Pancreatic cancer? Parasites? Lupus? Mold?

We've tested for everything. She's as healthy as you and I. Except that she's dying.

I move closer to the starving girl. She reminds me of what Anne Frank must have looked like in the camps. The real Anne Frank, not Roth's. A crazy thought whispers in my brain. You never know, it can't hurt to ask.

—Millicent, I'm Dr. Lee. Tell me, has some voice been telling you not to eat?

Her large eyes widen in her narrowed face as she looks at me. Her thin arms begin to shiver. Without a word she has given her answer. I wade in as into an icy stream. Risking frostbite.

—You know, Millicent, lots of people hear voices. Quite normal people. I hear voices myself sometimes.

I can feel the eyes of the docs and the nurses on me. Skeptic city. They assume I am lying to comfort the child. Fair enough.

—You do?

—Sure. More than one. There's Mona, Janelle, Ginger. Others. Who talks to you?

—My mama.

—Your mama tells you not to eat?

She nods her head slightly on the pillow. She has no strength for further affirmation. Or is still testing the waters.

—Does your mama tell you why you shouldn't eat?

Her hoarse, weak voice seems to trickle with static over a telephone wire battered loose by a passing storm.

—So I can . . . die . . . and join her . . . in Heaven. So she can . .. hold me again . .. like she did . . . when I was little. So we can be . . . together again.

The docs, nurses, aides are shaking their heads, in wonder or disapproval. Millicent only has eyes for me.

—If you die, how do you know you'll go to Heaven? Not everyone does, you know.

—They don't?

—If you die on purpose, it's called suicide.

—I know that. My boyfriend Mitchell did it last year, with a gun. Right in his family's living room. So they could see his blood. See how much he hated them.

—Is Mitchell also telling you not to eat?

Eyes riveted on mine, squinting.

—How do you know that?

—We doctors know things. Many people think God doesn't like suicide. That if you do this you won't get into Heaven.

—So why is mama telling me not to eat?

—I would guess because she loves you very much. She wants you to be with her again. But she is too impatient. If you live your full life, a normal life, as a good person, some day your time to go to Heaven will arrive. Then you can hug your mom all you want. But both of you have to be patient. Till God decides the time has come. Does that make sense?

—I think so.

—Maybe you should start eating again. If your mom objects, you can set her straight. You're smart enough to do that, I can tell.

The beseeching seems to have left her eyes. Her face has relaxed. She who does not eat food is digesting my words.

—Before you stopped eating, Millicent, what was your favorite food?

She comes back from wherever her head was.

—Strawberry ice cream.

I look at the nurses, the aide.

—I would think the cafeteria might have some of that. Don't you?

The aide says it is not open yet. I suggest she might find someone who can open it. Doctor's orders. We stand motionless around the bed while the aide disappears. It seems an hour but is only minutes when the she returns with a scoop of strawberry ice cream in a plastic cup.

—No cone? Millicent asks.

—Later, a nurse named Amy says. Later we can bring you as many cones as you want.

Other nurse raises Millicent's bed into a nearly sitting position. She takes the cup and a plastic spoon. Hesitantly she tastes a bit of the ice cream. Then another. Soon begins to devour it in chunks.

The entire room seems to exhale.

—I also like chocolate, Millicent says.

The others, speechless, are looking at me.

—Sorry I don't have a silver bullet to leave behind.

I cross the room to Morgan's bed before Millicent thinks to ask how she will be able to hug her mama and her boyfriend if they are in different places. Sitting on a chair, I face my wife, my back to the others. I sense them reluctantly at first then eagerly drifting away. To be messengers of the miracle through the wards. My eyes are moist, my chest heavy. Which of the eleven drowned does saving Millicent make up for?

The ophtho secretary, Diane, has called in sick. Victoria has become the communicator. There's a phone message on the machine from Nia. Not to worry, she got a late start from San Diego, she's going directly to work, has potential recruits to interview. She may crash at home this afternoon. Also a message from

Annabel. She's driving across the desert at night when it's cool, arriving today, will go straight to the house to crash. She remembers where I left the key. Not to worry.

Vicky asks if I saw the newspaper, where they found the body of Ken-Chen. The same place Laurette was found. Somehow I am not surprised. She is glad they didn't torture him, didn't take out his eyes. Just gave him two new eyes in the back of his head.

—You sound like a gangster's daughter.

—I'm quoting Mrs. Ling, she says. And did you hear about the theft at the San Francisco zoo? It was on the radio as I was driving in. Three men with ski masks and guns drove a small van in through the delivery gate early this morning, before the zoo opened. The van was marked animal control. It parked near the cougar compound, lowered a ramp from the back of the van, a guy held a pistol on a zoo attendant and forced him to open the compound gate. A chunk of fresh meat and the promise of freedom lured one cougar onto the ramp. His name is Zorro. A larger chunk attracted him inside the van. They slammed the gated rear doors behind him, inserted a huge padlock, and drove off with the cougar. A police spokesperson said they had no idea why anyone would steal a wild animal. The only clue came from the zoo attendant, who said the robbers spoke a foreign language. It sounded like Chinese, he said. The police confirmed that an animal control van had been stolen from the city lot on Sunday.

—You sound concerned, I tell her.

—I'm thinking of Luc Luck. How Lenny said he was crazy. To take over the gang, he'd have to do something bigger than Ken-Chen ever did. To show revenge for the killing of Ken.

—With a cougar? How?

—I have no idea, Vicky said.

It's a nicely routine day at the hospital. I stop at Barnes & Noble on the way home and pick up the new Roth that Maxie had recommended. At the house I find Nia's convertible parked as usual in the two-car driveway. A battered turquoise Ford with New Mexico plates is on the street. The tag says *Land of Enchantment*. A perfect omen, with my two favorite women inside. I enter quietly so's not to wake them. Butler does not come running up wagging his tail, as he usually does. Down the hallway Nia's door is open. Still in her camouflage fatigues — she's managed to pull off her boots — she's sprawled on her bed, on her left side, one arm slung over her head, breathing evenly, deep asleep. Beside her on the queen-sized bed, in old jeans and a man's loose shirt, barefoot, Annabel is also asleep, also on her left side, spoons position, her right arm resting on Nia's hip. On the lower end of the bed, half keeping their feet warm, Butler is snoring softly. He opens a baleful eye when he sees me glancing in, but doesn't move. He likes being just where he is.

In my den something is different about the case of glass eyes. The tense empty slot in the not-quite-center has been filled. It feels peaceful, as if my world has come together. Perhaps it is the presence of Annabel, my favorite portion of family. I sit in the den by a window, a glass of club soda at hand, and open *Exit Ghost*. No sidekick Scotch, tomorrow is a surgery day. The Roth is in large type, and moves quickly. The old guy, Roth's alter ego Nathan Zuckerman, 71, as Maxie said, is smitten with a luscious 30-year-old, who is married. I take a break, light the oven, preheat. Back to the book. There are any number of observations I could identify with, but one makes my skin shiver. I'm not sure why, perhaps it is just the original simile. I mark it with a yellow stick-it paper.

Looking at her provided a visual jolt — I allowed her into my eyes the way a sword swallower swallows a sword.

The man is a genius with fertile yet disturbing imagery.

The sweet smell of pepperoni tickles their noses.

—Mmmm, pizza, Annabel calls out.

—Pizza! Nia echoes.

They burst into the kitchen together, barefoot, jostling, rubbing their eyes, like children. They see the empty box on the counter,

—Yuck, frozen, Annabel says, not the most gracious of guests. Is there a place to get a real one? I mean, this is a celebration. My return here after ten years!

—It's two miles, Nia responds. I'm driving.

—I'm buying, Annabel retorts.

—The hell with that, Nia says.

She grabs her wallet and they start toward the door in their socks.

—Wait a minute, I forgot something, Annabel says, and dances back to me and throws her arms around me in a powerful hug. I love you, Uncle Mike. Thanks for inviting me.

Nia saunters over more slowly.

—I guess I forget that much too often, she says, and puts her arms around me, not quite as fiercely. Thank you for letting me stay here all this time.

I wait for her to echo I love you. Something else comes out.

—Until Mickey gets back.

They fly out the door together. I watch them through the window springing like teens into Nia's slick red convertible. I'm amazed at how close they seem to have become so quickly, with the difference in their ages. Then I realize that Nia is 27 and Annabel 25. No difference at all. It's just in their manners and mannerisms — Nia the mature Marine recruiter, Annabel the Santa Fe flake. Nia an almost engaged woman, Annabel still searching for herself. I wonder if one will influence the other. So far Annabel seems ahead on points.

I always have felt twenty years younger around Nia. Somebody screwed up my birth certificate. As I watch this new playfulness, another ten years drops away. I want to roar with life.

I use the time while they are gone to open the sofa in the den into a bed, already made.

They return still bouncy, laughing, carrying a large supreme pizza and a bottle of chianti. We toast the evening, toast friendship. Me drinking Dr. Pepper.

—That's a lousy job — no offense, uncle Mike — when you can't drink a glass of wine at night.

—Only three nights a week. Sometimes you have to sacrifice.

—I suppose. But not on this trip, Annabel says, raising her glass.

I'm not sure if she is genuinely happy or is nicely covering the pain of her lost lovers. The black boy. The Indian Princess.

—On this trip, anything goes, Nia echoes, and clinks Annabel's glass.

No matter the censure encrusted on the retinas of others. My unexpressed love for Nia is sonnets made flesh. Dare I call it Shakespearean? It is poetry that bleeds.

If I am a Fool, then Fate has made me so. How old was Don Quixote when he longed, even lusted, for Dulcinea? Do we laugh at him?

I suppose we do. But kindly. With understanding.

Twisted words form in my eyes beneath the clouded surface of sleep: *Beware of fools bearing swords*. Till a ringing phone wakes me, and I drown.

The digital clock glows 2:13.

—Dr. Lee?

The sleepiest kind of a yes.

—This is Jada, triage nurse at the ER.

— I am not on call, nurse. As a department head I'm never on call.

—Sorry, doctor. We've got a bad one. We don't know who in ophtho to bring in.

—Who's on the call list? How long have you been with us?

—The schedule shows Dr. Beecham.

—Oh, fuck. Excuse me, Jada. My fault, I'll come in myself.

—Thank you, Dr. Lee. We might have had to call you anyway. You've never seen one like this before. A young Marine. Dr. Klonsky is already on his way.

She hangs up before I can ask for details. It's the right thing to do, not the time for chatter. I scramble into yesterday's clothes, hurry out quietly so as not to disturb the girls. The young ladies. Going 90 on the deserted freeway I make it in four minutes instead of seven. A young Marine? Can't be! Mickey is ten thousand miles a way. Iraq, Afghanistan, Palestine, Korea — somewhere in no-man's-land. He would not be home on leave without calling right away. If not me, then Nia. I screech up to the emergency entrance, yank on the hand brake, leave the keys, the car running, so security can move it out of the way. Maxie's car is parked in front of me. There must have been a highway pileup if they need a neurosurgeon. I scrub down quickly. Jada, a pert redhead, points me to surgery room two. *You've never ever seen one like this before*. She doesn't know me. In forty years I've seen everything.

But it turns out she's right. Nothing like this before. Ever.

In the center of the operating room is not one gurney but two, side by side. One is occupied by the patient, covered to his neck in light blue drape. On the gurney beside him is a length of thick iron chain, coiled on the white sheet like a dark snake. Each link in the chain is two inches long. The metal of the links is at least a quarter inch thick, perhaps more. Where the chain unfolds from its coils it crosses the slight space between the two gurneys and continues on toward the patient's head. The Marine. At the end of the chain is an old anchor from a boat or sailing ship. The left half of the anchor is visible beside his head. The right half disappears into the young man's skull, behind his ear. The point emerges from the socket of his eye, which is not an eye any more. I have removed maybe half a dozen fish hooks from eyes through the years, clipped off the hooked, flanged part, pulled out the straight part, saved the eye. But this is a whale in comparison. Moby-Dick in a goldfish bowl.

A string of epithets emerges from my lips. Nobody notices. Nobody cares. ER techs and nurses are keeping close watch on his IV tubes, his drug level, his vital signs. He's lucky to have any. Maxie in brown scrubs is bending close to the head, checking the angle of entry. I ask if the lad can live. Maxie say it depends on if it went into his brain, and if the brain is bleeding.

I look closer at the eye. The globe is busted, that's the only word for it. He won't see through that again. We'll have to remove it, replace it with an artifice.

—Looks like you're up first, I say to Max.

—The techs have a saw, Max says, but if the anchor has passed through his brain the vibrations alone could kill him. The fire department is rushing here with bolt cutters. We'll clip off the outer sections on both sides. Then go in and check the damage.

Two uniformed cops are standing out of the way behind the ER techs. They seem unsure whether to stay or leave or wait outside.

—Can you guys tell me how this thing happened?

A police sergeant takes on the narrative.

—There's a sailors' bar down on the waterfront, called Ahab's. We know the place, it can get pretty rough sometimes. Not a place you'd want to go alone. We get a call at least once a month. The decor is a bunch of sailing anchors. Pretty old, some rusted, some cleaned up. The walls are fake paneling over plaster board, but the hanging anchors are secured pretty good, into the stud beams. A couple hours ago this young Marine — the sergeant looks at his pad — name of Billy Dove, according to his dog tags — he gets into a fight with three soldiers. Some witnesses say they're arguing about Eye-raq, and who can't fight for beans. Others claim the Marine has his arms around a bar girl named Irene and one of the soldiers says she has quite a rack, too bad it's pointing south. Whatever. All half drunk and spoiling for action. Punches start flying. Billy Dove takes a left to the stomach, a straight right to the jaw as he's buckling forward, staggers back, maybe half conscious, grabs at the wall for support as he goes down. This here anchor comes down after him, ripped from the wall. You're looking at the result. The bartender calls 911, some of the patrons stay and watch, fascinated, others scram. The fire department and your techs did the rest.

I shake my head. Operating lights are glinting off the anchor, hinting at what might be words scratched into the forged iron. I lean closer. Words definitely were scratched into it long ago, perhaps with a carpenter's nail. I can make out in uneven letters, SWEET M. The rest is inside Billy Dove's head. Except for an E near the other end, the part poking out from his eye.

—Any idea what that says?

—Sweet Marie

The sergeant flips a page on his pad.

—They've got these little brass name plates on the walls by the anchors. What ship it came from. This one's marked Sweet Marie. New Bedford, Mass. 1851.

The boy lying there under full anesthetic reminds me of my son. Of the thought that has haunted me ever since the moment in Albuquerque when Nia called and I feared it was bad news about Mickey, but not bad news, half welcome news that he was dead, that Nia was free. This execrable moment that I tried to excuse on the ground that you cannot control your thoughts, which still is fact, but which, remembered, has made me wonder every day since then what kind of lousy human being I am. You can't control your thoughts, but how do you excuse them? You can only vilify yourself, and still they are there like ineradicable brown stains deep in the toilet bowl of your soul. I would like to save this young Marine to make up for that obscenity about Mickey, but even if his brain survives, if Maxie keeps him alive, there is nothing I can do about his eye. I'll have to remove it, leave Billy Dove half blind. From now on part of his face will always be a fake.

Shrapnel in Baghdad?

No, Sweet Marie near San Francisco Bay.

I wish Vicky were here to assist, enucleation being a rarity to the ER nurses. I hate to wake her, with Maya at home, but I think: if this Marine were Mickey, I would want the best. I'm about to ask the triage nurse to call her, then realize she's on my cell phone. I punch her name. After four rings she answers, groggy. But she's a trooper, says she'll be there as soon as she can. I tell her not to rush too much, Maxie will be working on this kid for at least an hour. Will you drop Maya at Mrs. Ling's? I'd rather bring her along, Vicky says, wrap her in a blanket, put her to sleep in an empty room. Or on a gurney nearby. I've done that before. Great, I tell her, but one thing. Do not bring Maya into surgery. Under no circumstances.

I do not want her seeing this boy with an anchor in his head. She might never recover.

Vicky understands, clicks off. Maxie is moving the boy's eye at different angles alongside the anchor, peering one way, then the other,

—The kid may be lucky. The angle inside the skull is shallow. The metal might have missed the arteries, missed the brain. Though the pressure could still have him bleeding.

A fireman in black hurries in with the bolt cutter, shiny steel with red handles. Maxie lines up the cutting edge as close to the boy's ear as he can without risking further damage. He's about to squeeze when the fireman, who in his long-sleeved T-shirt looks as if he lifts weights ten times a day, offers to cut it instead.

—One quick clip if you can, without jolting it, Maxie says.

We're all crowded around the gurney now to watch this. The EMT like a black-clad Superman squeezes the cutter, meets resistance, gathers his strength, squeezes again, his face red. The freed partial anchor tugs its chain with a clatter from the adjacent gurney to the floor. The sound is like a huge shutter, like a warehouse door opening for business, 6 a.m. by the docks.

I point to the sharp anchor emerging from the busted globe of the eye. The fireman clips off the point. There's not much more he can do. Maxie leans close, examining both edges.

—There's no way to pull it out, he says. That could really mess him up. I have to go in and check the damages.

The Marine's hair is already skull-tight. With the help of the ER nurses Maxie carefully cuts a flap into the bone behind the boy's ear. He begins lifting out the rest of Sweet Marie, with a quick glance at me. The eye's a goner, don't worry about that, I tell him.

With aching deliberation Maxie removes the piece of anchor. We fear brain matter will come out with it but see none. Just a bit of blood. A nurse blots it away with a folded towel. Maxie closely examines what he sees.

—The brain wasn't penetrated. This is one lucky Marine.

If you need to have an anchor in your head.

He orders an MRI of the brain to see if there is internal bleeding. Techs role his gurney down the corridor to radiation. Vicky arrives, another nurse has found an empty room down the corridor for Maya to sleep in. Back from radiation, the Marine's luck is persisting. No sign of internal bleeding in the brain. Maxie puts a temporary flap on the skull patch, in case something else shows up. Then it's my turn. Removing the punctured eye — the enucleation — will take an hour.

I go to it. With Vicky assisting, I sever the eyeball from what's left of the optic nerve, and bind the nerve ending. I drop the lopsided eyeball into a tin of water. It's shredded, like fish bait. I'm careful not to damage the muscles around it.

Then I see her. Not Gretel Reinhardt, whom I had half expected, the way you half expect a distant headache to half arrive, are not sure if you need Tylenol yet. Gretel's was the death I regretted most after Addie. Her mother Marta had been a gypsy child in Nazi occupied Poland, in a collection camp for German gypsies, who would later be sent to Auschwitz to be gassed. She was one of a dozen gypsy kids Leni Riefenstahl, Hitler's filmmaker, recruited to play extras in her film *Tiefland*. Riefenstahl swore till her dying day — she lived past 100 — that no harm came to the children. This was not the case. Records later showed that most had been killed in the camps. But Gretel's mother Marta somehow was still alive when the war ended. As a young adult she made her way to the States. Married, had a child, named her Gretel, who grew up to become a nurse, to help others. Was working at Rikers Island. Stepped onto the fatal bus. It was her body that was protruding through a window the most, I think, the one I thought I might rescue. It didn't happen. After Addie, my horror has always focused most on Gretel, whose mother escaped the Nazis so her daughter could be killed by me. But no, this is not Gretel, she was a gypsy, as I said, with olive skin and black hair. This girl, about thirteen years old, has fair skin and blond braids tied with white ribbons. She's wearing an old-fashioned dress, a petticoat, I guess, which drapes to her ankles, a white ribbon at her waist. Nineteenth century attire. She's skipping along what appears to be a wooden pier, waves lapping at the stanchion. Gray sea birds are squawking overhead. I know at once who she is. Not possible, yet I know. She's wheeling one of those large hoops kids used to push along with a stick. She grabs the hoop, pauses beside the prow of a wooden boat. In the prow is carved a likeness of this girl. Beside it in blue paint are two words, the name of the vessel: *Sweet Marie*.

I can't know how this is happening. The girl must have lived around 1850. What did the brass plaque in the bar say? *New Bedford Mass, 1851*. Why is she hiding in an eye tucked in the socket of a living U.S. Marine?

I turn away and she disappears. Return to my work. I can't leave an empty socket. I fill the space with an hydroxyappetite ball. It's porous, so the blood vessels will grow into it. I tie the muscles of the eye around the ball it to hold it in place. Pull the conjectiva around it also. Lots of stitches.

She's prancing on the hydroxyappetite now, is sweet Marie. Running along the pier, clouds in a blue sky above her. Stops beside a much taller ship, with sails being unfurled by seamen. Shades her eyes from the sun, appears to be looking for someone on the deck. Sees a seaman in a dark blue cap. Waves to him. The seaman with a broad smile waves back. He begins hauling up with another sailor the huge anchor of this larger ship, muscles straining beneath thick wool sweaters. The anchor passes the name of this ship. It's the great whaler *Pequod*. A weather-beaten man with a dark beard, hobbling on a wooden leg, dressed all in black, approaches the girl. He pulls lightly at one of her braids, as if ringing a bell, as if for luck. Leans over and kisses her forehead. Then he climbs briskly up a gangplank like a vigorous whole man. As soon as he's aboard, the first seaman hauls up the plank. The whaler is held to the pier only by ropes. The scene is a mirage of questions, all in the hydroxyappetite ball, as if it belongs to a fortune teller. Is the one-legged man Captain Ahab, boarding the Pequod? Is Marie his daughter? His niece? The daughter of a seaman on the ship? None of whom, except one who calls himself Ishmael, will return to tell the tale? As thick ropes from the dock are tossed on board and the *Pequod* bobs and lifts away from the pier, only *Sweet Marie* remains tied up. The child herself has disappeared.

Is the failed poet imagining a Deep See Saga?

I focus back on the enucleation. Insert a spacer between the conjectiva and the eyelid, so later, when the Marine has healed some, they can insert a scleral shell — what looks like a large contact lens that covers the front of the ball. Painted to make it a match of his real eye. In the old days, until after the Second World War, they would use the kind of glass eyes I have at home. But those were heavy, prone to popping out. Which is not as funny as sadistic movie clowns have made it seem. Curved plastic lenses are a definite improvement, in appearance, stability and weight, if not in symbolism. Scariest eye scene ever in a film? Worse than the Buñuel? Carl took me when I was a kid. A French film, *Diabolique*. A guy drowned in a bathtub. His wife, suitably horrified, finds him. The dead man in the film reaches into the blank white of his rolled-back eye. He begins to edge it out with his fingernail. Fake enucleation. I won't say what happens next, but I was terrified all the way home that night. I can still visualize the scene after fifty years, without even closing my eyes. Did my psyche latch onto that scene, make me become an ophtho to overcome my terror? To face my fear? Long before JFK was shot and soft coed lips brushed my cheek? Decisions and revisions that a moment can reverse — but can it, in important matters? Can we choose what we will? What made you, Mr. Elliot, an anti-Semite? Did you read too much Schopenhauer in your youth?

I tape a pressure pack on Billy Dove's eye so the socket tissue won't swell too much. He'll be needing painkillers for a while. The odd thing is, when he wakes up, his sight will be the same, except for depth perception. Eyes are part of evolution's back-up system. Like with kidneys, we can live with only one. Another reason for doing an enucleation: the wounded eye, if left in place, can in effect begin to attack the healthy eye. Nature calls this sympathetic inflammation.

I slump into a chair against the wall as the techs roll the boy out of the ER into an empty room the triage nurse found. It's in the cancer ward, but no matter. Billy Dove. Could his great, great grandfather, someone, way back then, have been a whaling man? Or a fishing boat captain, who named his rig after his little girl? And what happened to *Sweet Marie,* that its anchor from New Bedford wound up across the continent in a bar on San Francisco Bay. And what of the girl? She was not one of the nurses from the bus. Why did I see her? What complaint or information was she trying to convey?

There is a strange feeling in the ER. It is suddenly large and hollow as a stadium. A tech is straining to lift the heavy chain and broken anchor from the floor. Maxie and Vicky, only ten feet from me, are breathing, perspiring, but seem distant, as if we have no genuine friendships, as if we are colleagues, no more. I realize we have shut down our feelings for one another to concentrate on the patient. Now that Dove and his gurney are gone, the mood eases, humanizes. My shoulders are tight`from concentration. Vicky notices, moves behind my chair, massages them. Maxie, exhausted, plops — that is the only word for him — into a chair beside me, glances at Vicky's working hands, raises an eyebrow without raising an eyebrow. Vicky is too tired to think of what looks appropriate. Me too tired to care. Her hands feel much too good.

—Lucky Marine, Maxie says again. How's your son doing? Heard from him lately?

—Not for months. I think he should be recalled any day now. Where he can phone or e-mail. Though knowing Mickey, he might just appear unannounced. He likes to surprise.

—I hate that, Vicky says. It's just a power trip over others.

Maxie glances away. I notice the rim of red around his eyes. Like paint that won't wash off. The mark of Laurette, whom he will never see again.

The ER clock shows 6. I have my first surgery at 7:30. No point going home. I have to grit my loins— that's not right — and get through the day. Maxie's first appointment is at 9, he says he's going up to nap on the sofa in his office. The best part about his dungarees, they look slept in anyway. Vicky's checked on Maya several times, the child is asleep. She decides to ask Aunt Gloria to pick up Maya at 7 and get her ready for school. She sits where Maxie had been, finally allowing her own exhaustion to show. Both of us are weighed down by Billy Dove and the anchor in his head. Not something you want to see very often.

—Who was it this time? Can you talk about this one?

I'm startled at how aware she has become of my eyeball visions.

—This one I can talk about. It has nothing to do with me. Strange.

I tell her about the girl in the petticoat, the one-legged captain, the two sailing boats.

—It's as if you took *Sweet Marie* and started a story. A sequel to *Moby-Dick*. You should have been a writer.

—I wanted to, long ago. As a doctor, or most anything else, you're doing what anyone can do, if they get the training. As a writer, what you produce is original. It could be lousy, but it's yours. But that's an egotistical way to choose your life's work. So here I am. Cataracts to enucleations — three gurneys, no waiting. Dr. Michael Lee at your service.

—You help people. Writers don't. But it's odd how your stories appear in other people's eyes.

—That I haven't figured out yet. Especially this Sweet Marie, someone I never saw, never knew existed. Yet I really saw her, an actual physical presence.

The double doors to the ER slowly swing open wide, as they do when any doc or tech or someone else with an ID card swipes it through a reader on the wall. They don't open fast enough for a security guard in black with gold trim, pistol in a holster on his belt, who bursts in like a wayward storm, asks who's in charge. I glance around. No one else here has rank.

—What is it, corporal?

—Trouble. A wild animal is loose in the hospital.

—What?

— A mountain lion. Cougar. One of them big cats. He's roaming the first floor.

—How the hell? Never mind. Did you call animal control?

—On the way. Police SWAT team, too.

—Tell security to stay calm. Not stir up the critter. I'll have all personnel take cover behind closed doors, with patients if possible. Animal control will bring it down with a tranquilizer dart.

—It may not be that simple, doc. Wired around the critter's neck — sort of positioned in front of its chest — is a metal canister. It looks like a homemade bomb. When I saw that I holstered my pistol. If it's really a bomb, a misplaced shot could bring half the hospital down.

Chapter 17: Nia

—Jesus!

I stand in the middle of the ER, Vicky and the corporal beside me, and summon Jada, the triage nurse. Other ER docs and techs hover close.

—Should I alert President Kelly? Jada asks.

—Not yet. What could she do from home?

My heart rate is soaring. I have to keep calm. Be logical.

—Okay. Right now we're the control room. The cat can't get in here without swiping a card. First: we have to assume the bomb is real. It could be Crackerjacks but we can't assume that. Second: we have to alert the staff, without freaking the patients. The stairway doors are heavy, and close by themselves. The cougar is probably confined to the first floor. Jada, does that mic have a cord?

She goes to her desk, brings me a cordless microphone. Pushes a button on the side. I blow into it, get feedback.

—Attention, all personnel. This is Dr. Michael Lee speaking. We have a small situation developing that I want to alert you about. Please listen carefully. The situation is confined to the first floor. All employees on the second and third floors are to remain there. That includes everyone — nurses, doctors, housekeeping. No exceptions. Go about your normal business. If your shift is over, stay where you are until further notice.

—Good word — situation — Jada says.

—Those of you on the first floor. Make sure the doors to all patient rooms are closed. Stay in the rooms with any patients who need reassurance. Or go to the secure areas behind the nursing stations. We have an animal prowling the first floor corridors. A cougar. It may not be dangerous. But it could be. So take all precautions to keep out of its path.

My face perspiring. I think what to do next.

—The bomb, the corporal says.

—No point mentioning a bomb. That would terrify everyone. Did you see a fuse?

—No, sir.

—What about a timer? A clock?

—Not that I saw. But I wasn't close for long before it headed down a corridor. It could be the kind of bomb that killed our guys in Iraq. Explodes on impact.

— Shit, I don't want anyone shooting at it. Listen, corporal. Go out there to your commander. Carefully. Tell him not to let the SWAT team, or animal control, into the building.

—How can we stop them? We're just private guards.

—This is private property. Your commander has to tell them that. This is private property, and the security firm has things under control. If the police and animal control would wait outside until they are needed, that would help us. He can play up the danger of the bomb. Actually, he can let the bomb squad in. But only in here, back door to ER. They might have some ideas. You got that?

—I don't know if the captain will agree.

—Tell him it's President Kelly's orders. His job is on the line.

—Yessir.

The corporal peers both ways through the windows of the ER doors. He swipes his card and the wide doors yawn. Instinctively I pick an MVR blade off a table as we crowd behind the doors until they swing closed as if they are bored. I have to laugh at myself. What would this six-inch blade with its six-inch handle do against a leaping cougar? I drop it into the pocket of my lab coat.

—Flat feet, I mutter. In the Marines I'd have learned to command.

Vicky, beside me, hears.

—You're doing great, doctor.

—But now what? How the hell did the creature get in here?

—Luc Luck is my guess. Lenny said he's crazy. This has to be him. When a cougar got stolen from the zoo I thought of him.

—But why bomb the hospital?

—These gangs live for revenge. It's their only purpose in life. They tell themselves it's honor, but it's sick. When Ken-Chen's girl friend died in ER, he blamed Dr. Klonsky, right? Got even by killing. Laurette. The triad took revenge, killed Ken to stop the killing. But Luc got a different message. He couldn't go after the triads — that would mean torture and death — but he needed to do something big to take over the Golden Swords. He read about that Santa Fe cougar thing. Saw how the tiger escaped last week. A sick plot forms in his head. The Golden Swords steal Zorro — that's the cougar's name — and set him loose in here.

—Why now? He couldn't know you and I would be here at 6 this morning.

— It's shift change. Security coming and going. Half the nurses, housekeeping, leaving. I bet they drove up in a stolen ambulance. Opened the back doors in the confusion. Let Zorro loose. If there's a bomb, and Luc gets us too, it's a bonus he'll laugh about.

—I think the bomb is real. Without the bomb it's just a stupid prank. Luc is showing the Swords how tough he is, to be their leader. From what I've heard, he's a killer, not a joker. Some believe he set up Ken-Chen to be killed by a rival gang, the night Ken's girlfriend took the hit.

A figure blots out the light in the ER door. The corporal is back. He swipes his magic card, the doors yawn open again.

—Captain Johnson is not happy. He made me say it in front of witnesses. That this is your orders. Or Dr. Kelly's.

—I don't give a damn if he's happy. Is he doing what I said?

—He stopped the first squad car. They were not happy either, just standing around.

—They shouldn't be standing around. Have the police — have your captain suggest to the police — that they cordon off the hospital. At least a block in every direction. Nobody comes through. In case the bomb goes off.

He hesitates.

—With all respect sir, when the SWAT team arrives they'll run right over us.

—Tell them . . . Shit!

I reach for the cell phone in my side pocket.

—Tell them a Marine sharpshooter is on the way!

—Really? Yes, sir.

He peers through the door glass again to make sure no cougar is waiting outside. Swipes his card and scoots through. I hit the phone button for home.

The clock shows 6:15. I should have thought of this sooner. One ring, two, three. An interminable wait. Five, six, don't give me a message machine, please, not now!

Some day I'll show you how really good I am.

—Hello?

—Nia?

—It's Taylor Swift.

—Annabel. Where's Nia?

—In the shower.

—Listen, Annabel. We have a crisis at the hospital. I need Nia here. Fast. Tell her to grab her rifle, make sure it's loaded, and get down here. Tell her don't let anyone stop her. You got that?

—Roger.

—Okay. Go get her.

—The water just stopped. You want to talk to her?

—No, just get her down here.

—Can you tell me . . .?

—Later, kiddo.

I click off. Perspiring all over. I should have thought of Nia ten minutes ago.

Breathing deep, I try to remember what I read about cougars at Polk Park. I pick up the hand mic, flip it on.

—This is Dr. Lee again. Everyone is keeping calm. That's great. Now here's some advice. The animal at large is a cougar. In the wild, they are afraid of humans, and wouldn't bother you. They would run in the opposite direction. They're allowed to roam free in the larger state parks. They keep away from people.

—Because they have plenty of other prey, Vicky whispers.

No point mentioning that.

—We suspect this one was stolen from the zoo. So he might be used to people. He might be friendly. But don't try to find out. First thing. If you see him lumbering toward you, don't play dead. If he's hungry, that will interest him. That's why all the patient doors should be closed. He can't open them, they latch shut. Second thing. If you see him, don't run. That might set off his natural instinct to chase. The best thing to do if the cougar somehow confronts you is stare him in the eyes. Yell at him. Wave your arms, make a noisy scene. Chances are he'll back off and lose interest in you. Now, none of this should happen. You should all be in secure areas. But if a patient is buzzing for a nurse — well, we can't neglect our patients, the problem could be serious. But be careful if you enter the corridors.

I can think of nothing more to say. I switch off the mic, set it down.

—What do we do now? one of the techs asks. You're assuming, doctor, that the explosives, if that's what's in there, would be set off by a bullet. But what if there's a timing device?

—The bomb squad could disarm that, another tech says.

—But how do they get close enough, without stirring up the beast? It's a standoff. Crazy, but well planned.

I turn to the others.

—Listen, folks. The bomb squad will want to evacuate the hospital. Obviously we can't do that, with 600 patients, most of them bedridden, connected to IVs or oxygen. But there's no reason for you to stay in here, in case a bomb goes off. You can leave now, out the back door into the parking lot.

—If a bomb goes off, Jada points out, you'll need all the medical personnel you can get.

—Not dead ones. You'll be safer outside, then can come back in. But Jada, stay here in case I need help with the mic.

—I'm not going anywhere.

The others look at one another, some shrug, begin to file out the back.

—We'll be right outside till it's over, an ER docs says.

There's nothing to do but wait. I imagine Nia rushing in here in nothing but her rifle and her underwear. *I dreamed I shot a cougar in my Maidenform bra.*

—Maya!

Vicky gives me a look half tortured, half determined.

—I have to go get her.

She moves toward the doors.

—Hold on, Vicky.

I grab her arm.

—Maya's asleep. Her door is closed, right? That's the safest place for her. The cougar can't open doors without pushing down on the lever. It can't do that.

—They teach rats and mice to do that.

—But not animals in the zoo. They just toss a hunk of raw meat into their cage. Maya is safest where she is.

— What if the bomb explodes? I have to go get her. Take her away from the building.

I have no answer for that. Vicky is about to swipe her ID through the card reader.

—Check the corridor first!

She looks at me with annoyance, presses her face to the window in the double doors. With a huge roar the head of the beast appears in the window as it leaps against the ER door.

Vicky staggers back.

—My God. I almost got one of us killed.

—You almost got yourself killed.

She's shaking. I fold my arms around her. She twists to look up at me.

—You don't seem worried about the bomb. You think it's a fake? What are you waiting for?

—A Marine sergeant. Nia Ruiz.

—What's she got to do with this?

—She told me once she can shoot a cougar in the eye from hundreds of yards. I'm betting she wasn't exaggerating.

—And if she was?

—Then we'll know real quick if the bomb is real.

—Michael, that's terrible.

—I don't have a better idea. Do you?

Floor collapsing, patients falling, tubes twisted, the dead, the injured, I see it clearly and it's all my fault, all my fault. Why is it my fault? Because I was there when they took Ken-Chen away. Because somehow I'm in charge.

I check the clock. Eight minutes gone.

The bomb squad rushes in through the ER door. Three of them in dark blue, one carrying a small wire cage in which to carry a bomb they are removing. It seems to be lined with velvet on the bottom. They rush toward the doors, can't push them apart.

—How the hell do you open these things?

—Do you know where the bomb is?

—In the hospital, they said. First floor.

—Look through the door.

He does. The cougar again leaps against it, mouth, teeth filling the window space.

—Holy shit! That's the bomb, around his neck? How are we supposed to disarm that without killing the beast first. Or tranquilizing it? Depending on what they used, any trauma could set it off. Who the hell would want to bomb a hospital? They're nuts, or they're terrorists.

— Does the bomb look real to you?

—Hard to say. The cougar looks real. And hungry. But we can't let him keep us trapped. Is there anything in here I can throw.

He looks around.

—How about that pail over there?

—Whatever you need.

The officer moves to the abandoned gurney, lifts the half-full pail of water from the floor. Moves back toward the door, hurls the pail. Powerful crash. Water splashes all over, including the thick glass window. He peers through.

—The cat is taking off down the corridor. They don't like being thrown at. You ever encounter one in the desert, throw rocks at it.

His nose is pressed beside something stuck on the glass as he peers down the hallway. He moves his head, then leaps back.

—What the fuck's on the window?

—Billy Dove's enucleated eye.

—Enuc . . . never mind. It looks like somebody shit an oyster. Open the damn door. We'll go after it.

—And do what when it turns on you? Please wait, officer. The Marines are on the way.

—I wish.

Bright white explosion, orange fireballs, falling walls, beds, gurneys, wheelchairs, oxygen tanks, scales, vital signs machines, dialysis, whole nursing stations. Computers, patients screaming, patients too old or cancerous to scream, surgery preps, cardiac arrests, recovery room, CCU, ICU, newly sutured skin ripped apart in free fall. Patients strangling in their oxygen tubes. Piles of smoking rubble. Movement under fallen boards. Reach in, movement stops. Rip boards off a broken child. One-legged now. Bloody stump. Maya.

I shut my eyes tight, too tight for scenes of the apocalypse. Why did I call Vicky in? If anything happens to that child, suicide will not be good enough.

The rear door bursts open, Nia in cammies and combat boots rushes in, carrying her rifle with fixed bayonet. Her wet hair in a pony tail is darkening the back of her shirt. Quickly I explain the situation. She needs to kill the cougar with one shot. There's a possible bomb around his neck, so she needs a clean head shot.

—Remember what you said on horseback? I ask.

—Which eye?

—I picked the left.

We manage a grin at the memory. Escaping from the terrible present.

—You take me too literally, Michael. You've got too much faith in me. But let's go. Where the hell is he?

—This floor. Somewhere in the corridors. They bend and bend again at right angles, around the nursing stations, into the different wards.

She adjusts her scope by aiming out the back door. Tightens the bayonet.

—Where did you get that?

—From under my pillow. I meet a lot of creeps at the mall.

—But you're going to shoot, right?

—From as far away as I can. And pray the bomb isn't real.

—Okay. I'll be right behind you.

—What for?

—To watch your rear at the intersections. Point out hidden niches. There won't be any danger for me.

—Not unless I miss.

—You won't miss.

Vicky has curled up on a gurney, in fetal position, holding her stomach, which must be killing her with fear for Maya. I peer through the door. Nothing. Swipe my ID card. The doors open. In a moment we're in the corridor. It smells like the zoo already. Impossible — till I see a large puddle of pee on the floor. Perhaps from when the bucket hit the door.

Nia is moving in a half crouch, her rifle across her chest, like stalking an enemy in a jungle. I'm right behind her, looking around. The ER waiting room is empty at this hour. A break for us. Out into the central corridor. It splits, one direction radiation and surgery, the other patient rooms. No cougar visible the length of either. I decide to check the patient rooms first, and motion Nia in that direction. Past the declining numbers, every door shut. Nurses or aides peering out through the narrow glass windows of some. A nursing station is empty, Nia leaps swiftly behind it, makes sure the beast is not crouching there. A fork leads to ICU. I nod in that direction. Patient doors are closed, the nursing station abandoned, nurses, one to a customer here, must be in with their charges. Back to the main corridor. I notice dawn light emerging from the very last room.

—Shit. They left the last door open. Someone chickened out. Or maybe saw the beast and fled.

Room 103. Morgan's room.

What if the beast is in with her? She's helpless in her coma. Spent her life phobic about cats. Thousands of bucks to shrinks didn't help.

Nia sprints that way before I can hold her back. Slows outside the room, crouches, bayonet in front of her. She's about to enter the room when the beast comes out, lopes away down the hall, coming right at me. Me with an eye blade in my pocket. I hold my breath. I don't stir. About fifty feet before it reaches me it turns down a fork towards registration. Nia comes jogging up.

—Did you look in Morgan's room?

—I saw the cougar coming toward you. I've got to get him, assess any wounded later. He went that way. Where does that lead?

—He'll have to come straight back at us, or pass the ER and come down the patients' bloc again.

—Did he ignore you because he just devoured someone?

—I don't know. He could be just getting impatient, frustrated, trying to find a way out.

—Maybe I should call ER, have them open front and back doors and get the hell out of the way. Let him find his way out. There are cops out there. and the bomb would be less of a danger outside.

I grab my phone to raise Jada. Too late. He's coming toward us from the far end of the corridor.

—Here's my shot, Nia says.

She swings herself onto a vacant gurney, kneels on one knee, aims her rifle.

—I'll get a downward angle over the bomb. Okay, two more doors. . . Shit!

The door the cougar is about to pass pushes open. A child is entering the corridor. Maya.

—Fuckit. The kid ruined my shot. I couldn't take a chance.

The cougar has heard us, seen us. Maybe he smells gunpowder, who knows how they think. As if in a frenzy he accelerates from a lope to a full-speed charge. I duck behind the nurse's station. He's coming right at Nia. Why doesn't she shoot? Did she freeze? Too late now, he's almost on her. She waits on the gurney on her left knee, I see her back leg tensing for the impact. The careening beast leaps at her, flying. She steadies herself, the cougar is in midair, she jabs the bayonet into his face — his eye. With a terrible pained roar he's hanging there, front paws on the gurney, swiping at the bayonet. Nia pressing and twisting with all her strength to make sure the blade penetrates his brain. After an hour that is only seconds the wild howl stops. Slowly, Nia climbs down from the gurney, lets the impaled beast down slowly, gently, onto the floor, so as not to disturb the bomb. Jams the blade in deeper, to make sure he's dead.

For a moment I'm stunned. When I return to my senses I call the ER on my cell, tell Jada to get the bomb squad down here, fast. Across from room 124.

Nia is carefully removing the bayonet from his eye socket as I kneel beside her.

—Damn! she says.

—What's wrong?

—You wanted the left eye.

What a woman! I hug her from the side. She peers closely at the bomb.

—Is it real?

—Depends what it's filled with, I guess.

My cheek feels wet. I touch it gingerly. Blood. Where the hell did that come from, I was five feet from the leaping beast? I look at Nia, startled.

—Your face is pouring blood. Get down to ER.

—Just a scratch, no problem. He caught me with a claw as I nailed him.

—That's more than a scratch.

—Couple of stitches, no big deal.

A whole lot of stitches. Scar tissue. That beautiful face. The *Mona Lisa* slashed by vandals. Desecration of *The Birth of Venus*. I feel woozy, can't stand, lean on the gurney. I should be rushing her to ER but I do nothing. My legs are nailed to the floor. I don't even think about taking action. Why did I get her involved? The swat team could have handled it. Or animal control. It's their job, not hers. What have I done to her?

The bomb squad guys lope up, kneel by the beast. Carefully they cut the wire around it's neck, place the bomb in the rectangular cage, the size of a shoe box. I come out of my guilty stupor.

—Is it real?

—We'll know when we detonate it.

—Where will you do that?

—Don't want to cross the city with this thing. Don't know what might trigger it. There's a big excavation site down the road. Two blocks long and very deep. Be a safe spot, if it blows.

—It's surrounded by chain link. For the new cancer center.

He stands, gingerly holding the cage with the bomb

—I'll have the swat team shoot at it from a distance. See if anything salutes.

He bends in front of Nia.

—Do you know you're bleeding?

—It's just a scratch, she says.

Her blood has begun to puddle on the floor.

Several nurses and aides have seen everything, through a narrow window in a supply room, through windows in the doors of patients' rooms across the corridor. Feeling safe now, they open the doors, remain at a respectful distance from Nia, who is still kneeling by the cougar, breathing heavily, winner of a championship fight. Spontaneously they begin to applaud. Nia does not seem to hear.

Vicky comes running up, holding Maya's hand. She stops a few feet from the animal. I hug the child. I feel my body trembling with what might have been.

—Thank God you're all right.

—The tiger ran right past me, Maya says, half shaking, half proud.

—You jumped back just in time.

I rub her head, hug Vicky. Nia is still kneeling, rifle at her side. Pieces of greenish cougar eye hanging on the end of the bayonet, like boiled okra.

—You're Nia, Vicky says. I'm taking you to the emergency room. Get the docs to sew up your face.

—It's just a scratch.

—That's an order, Vicky says.

I help Nia up. Try to take her rifle but she says she'll keep it with her. Vicky, with one hand holding Maya's, takes Nia's with the other, begins to lead them down the corridor, back toward the ER. Nia is walking unsteadily. Vicky in white, Nia in desert camouflage, Maya in purple pajamas. I watch from the back as they walk. The image burns deep into my brain. It seems religious, in a way.

The animal control guys move in carrying a large cage and a dolly. They drag and shove the dead cougar into the cage, strain to lift it onto the dolly. Seeing the vacant eye socket, one of them notes that it was one hell of a shot.

Morgan! I forgot about Morgan. I hurry toward 103, slow down outside the door, hesitant. I don't want to see her torn body, maybe missing limbs, maybe missing her face. I steel myself, step into the room. Morgan is on her side, breathing as usual, slowly, eyes open but no sight there. Still in her coma. Unharmed. An old woman in the other bed is also alive, asleep, unharmed. For whatever reason, the beast had no interest in them. Thank God.

—Are you okay?

Morgan does not answer. I lean over, press my lips to her cool forehead.

Walk back towards the ER. Jada over the intercom is telling the staff, the entire medical center, that the crisis has passed. They can go back to work, or home, or whatever their schedule calls for. When I get there, I thank her with a handshake, then a hug. ER personnel are streaming back into the room from the parking lot. I ask Jada where Victoria is.

—She turned her little girl over to an aunt. She's in ophtho, preparing for surgery.

That would be me. I check my watch. Still plenty of time.

—And Nia Ruiz? The Marine?

—The docs are working on her face. Triage One.

I step out the back door to breathe fresh air. The interrupted change of shift is resuming, cars pulling out, cars pulling in, workers standing in huddles discussing what occurred. Rumors no doubt flying about like bats. The first sharp rays of the morning sun lighting up the day. I unwrinkle my shoulder blades, take a deep breath. It's been ages since we removed an anchor and an eye from the skull of Billy Dove. About two hours ago.

Suddenly a terrific BOOM shatters the morning. Followed by a huge plume of earth shooting hundreds of feet into the air two blocks downwind, blocking the borning sun. I watch in silence, mouth parched, as the distant earth takes its time returning to the ground from whence it came. As if each small clod is borne on a tiny parachute.

I am not the praying type. Not even prayers of thanks. What comes to mind is a bumper sticker I saw the other day. Tan on black, on the rear of a Jeep. *American by Birth, a Marine by the Grace of God.*

I step back inside. My eyes trying to adjust to the lesser light, I shut them and see the devastation, half the building gone, bodies and parts of bodies everywhere, arms, legs, heads, dead patients, mostly old half naked and broken in their backless hospital gowns, twisted young stocky bodies in the maroon scrubs of housekeeping, pale green scrubs like stylized pools of water in the wreckage, clipboards with patient medical records lost forever. Dizzily I open my eyes. The ER is still there — and the bodies and parts of bodies, entire beds and gurneys and nurses are shooting high up into the air like the dirt in the excavation. Which is the reality? Blink, press water from my eyes. Docs and nurses and techs in the ER are giving me thumbs up. I can only nod numbly. Great job, doc! they are saying. I nod my thanks. I realize that deep down I never truly believed it was a real bomb that could do real damage.

Nia's face is cut to pieces. I will only love her more.

She's on a gurney, awake, as they wait for a strong local anesthetic to kick in. A nurse is cleaning her wounds of any crap from the cougar's claw. A nurse's aide is lining up swaged atraumatic needles. Pre-attached to treated silk thread of different lengths. These thin needles don't need eyes, they make for a more compact stitch. Nurses don't have to waste time threading them. The stitches might be easy to remove in a week. In ophtho, like in most internal work, we use thread that dissolves on it's own. You can't go back into eyes to get the sutures out.

—How bad is it, doctor?

Jim Holloway, a bright young ER surgeon, brown hair under a scrub cap, sanitary mask over his nose and mouth, is waiting for the nurse to finish sterilizing the wounds.

—She took a real ripping. Half way through to her cheek lining. I'm looking at 25 stitches, maybe more. Number seven thread. A damn pretty face to bear the Mark of Zorro — he's pleased with his out of place joke — until she can get plastic surgery. One lucky Marine, though.

—How do you figure that?

—The claw strikes an inch higher, she could have lost an eye.

Lying still in her cammies — they must be bloody — draped in maroon, eyes closed, Nia has been listening. Squinting under the surgery lamps she flicks irises toward me without raising her head.

—That blast we just heard. Was that what we think it was?

I'm not scrubbed, I can't go any closer. The jagged rip down her cheek is raw and red. Instruments of repair gleam on a tray nearby.

—That was the sound of six hundred people gasping, who might be dead if it were not for you.

She doesn't nod. Doesn't respond. Her expression does not change.

—Ready for you now, doctor, the nurse says.

I leave Triage One. Step into the corridor, out into a blast of dusty air. Into the devastation.

Patients have been let back in. I manage to pulverize four cataracts without my hands shaking. We take a break. On the way to my office I grab a housekeeper, ask her to do me a favor, get us two chocolate milks and two cheese Danish from the cafeteria. I hand her a ten. This would be on me, doctor, she says, except that my child is sick. I understand. Buy something for yourself as well.

She thanks me and hurries off. I collapse onto my chair, Vicky onto the sofa. We're both too spent to speak. The sky outside the window is bluing but my ears hear the portent of a hurricane sweeping toward the open door of the office. In rolls President Kelly — Shannon — in her power chair and her power mode.

—Why the hell didn't you call me at home, Dr. Lee?

I'm too weary for this stuff.

—Do you have a rifle? A bayonet?

—You'd be surprised.

But it's a fake, her voice softens quickly.

—That's some young lady your son has found himself.

Lacey Roberts comes in behind her. Her mass of big blond hair has been cut off, the color is nearer her natural light brown, barely reaches her shoulders. Sex pot to serious doc after three days at home in Oklahoma. The housekeeping woman enters carrying a tray. Shannon grabs one of the Danish, unwraps it partially, takes a bite before tossing the rest onto my desk. Vicky corrals the other and the milks, and hands one to me.

—Pardon my French, Shannon says, but you two look like cougar shit. You're off duty as of now. Take the rest of the day off. Then take the rest of the week off.

Sleep. Rest. Wallow in your laurels. Dr. Roberts here has joined our ophtho staff. She'll take over your schedule this week. She'll work with Dr. Beecham's nurse.

Shannon Kelly as angel of mercy. A new side of her.

—And doctor, thank you for what you did. I'm still freaked at the thought of what might have been had the bomb gone off in here. Afraid I might dream of it for awhile. Like I used to dream of a tree coming at my face. I heard that for an appetizer you removed a ship's anchor from a Marine's eye. That I would like to have seen.

—Me and Vicky. And Maxie Klonsky, of course.

—Speaking of whom, yesterday's odds from Vegas had you and Max down to six to one for the Nobel. With the British books, you're four to one. It would be so great for the hospital.

— I wish you wouldn't give in to false hopes, Madame President. It's not going to happen, you know that. We're history.

—I'm not a religious person, Dr. Lee. I place my faith in bookmakers. They give you better odds than God. Now go, the two of you. I don't want to see your faces until next week. And be careful as you leave, the pavement is crawling with media. You'd think something happened here.

I nod, rub my eyes, my cheeks. I'm too tired to stand. Media here? For a non-event?

Trying to fool myself. Sometimes almost does count.

—And Michael?

—What?

—Next time, call me.

She's resting in the recovery room. The gash on the right side of her face flows like a raw red river from just below her eye in a quarter moon to her chin. Glows like a stream by moonlight with antibacterial ointment. It's criss-crossed every few millimeters with ominous black X's. No bandaging. It's left open to the air to begin the healing. The stitches should be pulled in a week. I inhale sharply, to conceal my initial shock. Says she'd like to go home, perhaps I should drive, she's still a bit woozy. She knows I'm off duty, President Kelly came by to thank her. She swings her legs off the bed, winces. Didn't they give you painkillers? I didn't take them, she says. I warn her about the media outside. She says she can handle them.

—You want a towel to cover your cheek?

—Why would I want to do that?

Her expression is genuinely curious.

We leave through the back door of the ER, me still wearing my lab coat. She'd left her car right there, half in the street and half on the curb. A handful of reporters, photographers, television cameramen are joined by more media mob flowing around the corner like the Missouri joining the Mississippi. Still cameras are clicking, video tape rolling, look here, Sergeant, can you look over here, will you wave for the cameras, how about a thumbs-up sign? She ignores all of them, waits stoically.

—You've got two minutes for questions, I tell them, holding up my hand. One at a time.

They've been shouting questions already like a quiver of arrows flying at her. She waits until we understand just one.

—How does it feel to be a hero?

—I'm not a hero. I was just doing my job.

—You're a Marine recruiter, isn't that right?

—I'm a Marine. We're trained to protect people. Any Marine would have done the same.

—Witnesses say a little girl ran into the corridor just as you were about to shoot the cougar. That's why you had to use your bayonet, and got your face clawed. How do you feel about that?

—There was no little girl in the way.

—Witnesses said . . .

—No witnesses were inside my head. I would have preferred to shoot, but the cougar's head was bobbing as he charged. I was afraid I might miss and hit the bomb. The bayonet was safer.

—Not for you.

—For everyone in the hospital.

—That's a nasty looking wound. Does it hurt?

—Only when I laugh. I guess I won't be doing that for awhile.

—Okay, one more question, I say. The sergeant has to rest.

—You're a beautiful woman, sergeant. How long before you can get plastic surgery?

—I'm not planning on plastic surgery.

—You're not? With a face like yours?

—Plastic surgery is a lie. I believe in truth.

—We understand your boyfriend is also a Marine. What will he think about that?

—You'll have to ask him. Now if you'll let me pass . . .

But they don't of course, they keep the cameras rolling, shouting more questions about the little girl. Until a voice from the rear of the pack shouts over the hubbub.

—It's all a lie. It's all bullshit.

A few near the rear turn to look at the thin young woman who is shouting.

—There was no cougar at all.

—-Who are you?

I open her car door and Nia slides into the passenger seat. Her keys are in the ignition. The girl in the rear is drawing the media away.

—What do you mean there was no cougar? Who are you?

—I'm a volunteer in the hospital. I saw everything. My name is Annabel.

—Annabel what?

—Annabel Lee.

—Why do you say there was no cougar? A dozen witnesses saw it. Animal control carried out the body.

—It's a government cover-up. Just like Roswell.

—So what mauled the sergeant's face?

—It was a huge monster. Like in a Japanese film. You know, Godzilla? That's what it was. Maybe from Communist Cuba. Maybe a mutant. When he was stalking the halls, his head almost touched the ceiling.

Mumbling and grumbling and the shutting off of cameras and murmurings of *fucking kook* among the ladies and gentlemen of the press as they turn and rush back toward us. I gun the engine, release the brake. We bounce off the curb and speed away.

—Shit! Nia says.

—What's wrong?

—It really does hurt when I laugh. I've got to warn Annabel about that.

I swing around a corner onto a lonely back road, where I can lose them if they try to follow.

—I love her, Michael, and I only just met her. She has an adorable soul.

Me nodding as I take a sharp turn with both hands on the wheel.

—Which makes her very vulnerable.

I park at the end of our block, wait to see if they show at the house. Docs don't list home addresses in the book. Neither do Marines. For ten minutes no one appears. I glide down the block, into the driveway, turn off the engine. Like the medical center, the house is still standing. I had not been certain. The first hint of Post Traumatic Stress Syndrome?

—You'll be all over TV, I warn Nia.

—Only if I turn it on. Do you think they'll show Annabel? That's what I'd love to see.

—She made them look like asses. I don't think they have the guts.

—Maybe it'll be posted on You-Tube.

I open the front door. Suddenly depressed.

—That's your generation, Sergeant. Not mine.

What will it be like for her to go through life knowing she has saved perhaps hundreds of lives? As opposed to my having taken eleven. The chasm is Biblical — like living on opposite sides of the Dead Sea. Yet still I want to couple with her. I see no reason for a bayoneted cougar to interfere. It was I who summoned her and her rifle. I have to keep reminding myself, It was I who took the responsibility. Had she not answered, left early, slipped in the shower that morning — but she was there, she did what she did.

Does this at last absolve me for the dead eleven?

Not really.

Captain Doyle calls that afternoon, excited as a robin earth-dancing at the first worm of spring.

—I thought you'd want to know what went down, doctor. We've got them all.

—All?

—All of the Golden Swords.

With jaunty Irish enthusiasm he relates what was happening while the fate of Coastal Regional and all those in it was still not known. While Zorro the suicide-bombing cougar was still prowling the corridors and Nia was tightening the screws on her bayonet. From a faint wistfulness in his tone I know he wishes he'd been there himself. A tale he could tell his grand kids twenty years from now. Probably by then he will have been there.

—It seems a couple of cops patrolling the perimeter blocks spotted an animal control truck parked on the street. They stopped to investigate, peered through the window without touching anything. They phoned in the plate, we confirm this was the vehicle stolen from a repair yard a few days before. They look around, up the block are a bunch of young males horsing around, watching the hospital from afar. Cruise that way, exit the patrol car. One of the men, tall with tall hair, begins moving away, then breaks into a run. Our men yell for him to halt, he keeps running, one of the cops fires a warning shot in the air. The guy pulls a pistol from his wind breaker, whirls and fires. Misses and keeps running. Officers hit him in the shoulder, the back of the knee. He collapses in the street. They approach and kick his weapon away. Cuff him behind his back. The others, all Orientals, some juvenile, stand about, place their hands on top of their heads when ordered to do so. Pat-downs produce only a couple of knives. What are you fellas doing here, why didn't you leave the neighborhood while you could? We wanted to see the hospital blow. All quick to implicate the wounded man, Luc Luck, as the brains behind the plot. Which was probably true, if you call that brains. They were not shy about giving up the details. All are members of Golden Swords. Fifteen in the gang. The mother of one works in the hospital cafeteria. The sister of another is a radiologist. So why did they go along with this? Luc called a meeting. Everyone in favor of the bombing was to raise their hand. Go against Luc and you're in big trouble, he's probably the next leader of the gang.

—So all fifteen members voted to do this?

— Bingo, doctor, conspiracy against every one. If they cop a plea a few might get no jail time, just long probation, with the proviso that if they break the law again, even if they run a red light, they can go away for five or ten.

Proviso? From a homicide cop?

—What about Luc Luck? What happened to him?

—Oh, I left him hanging, didn't I. The officers called for an ambulance, medics curtailed the bleeding, took him to the nearest emergency room for the bullets to be removed. That would be Coastal Regional, two blocks away. He says don't take me there, that place is going to blow. I don't want to die. The cops and medics find this amusing, By the time they get to the ER the cougar is dead, but no one tells Luc that. Not for hours. They use local anesthetics to keep him conscious. By the time they were done he was a blathering idiot. They put him in the behavioral health ward, rotating a pair of cops on guard outside his room. It could have been a ploy to plead insanity, but the medics think it was genuine terror. We've got six hundred counts of attempted murder. Enough evidence, enough witnesses, to put him away for life. Even if they move the trial to Beijing.

—Your guys did great, Captain.

—So did you and your beautiful friend, I hear.

A few hours later, a florist delivery van pulls up outside. I open the door and a kid is hiding behind a floral bouquet the size of an elephant.

—Delivery for Sergeant Ruiz, he says.

So many different kinds of blossoms I couldn't name half of them. I help him — guide him — into the living room, ease the huge glass vase onto the rug. Empty, it could sleep four. I tip him appropriately, hope he goes back to work instead of to a bar. He doesn't know who it's from, says there's a card. I summon the girls from Nia's room, where they've been listening to music. A disc from a hot young Santa Fe band, *Lydian Gray*. A wonderful sound, a cross between the Beatles and Kurt Weil, if that makes sense. The four musicians are aged 15 to 17, Annabel says.

—Holy shit!

When Annabel sees the bouquet.

— I think you've got an admirer. She glances at Nia.

—Could Mickey have sent me that from the desert somewhere?

—If he's got a credit card. Annabel again, and if he's lonely enough.

Her eyes sparkling, Nia begins looking for the card. It takes a good five minutes to find it among all the flowers and foliage. But her face falls.

—It's not from Mickey.

—Then who spent for something like that? It must have cost a fortune.

She reads the handwritten card, hands it to me. Blue ball-point ink, skipping in places. I read it aloud, for Annabel's benefit.

Dear Miss Sergeant Nia. Mr. and Mrs. Ling thank you for your courage action Tuesday morning. Prevent many bad thing from happening. You be guest at our restaurant free all rest of life. Also feed Dr. Lee. Hope you like flower. Mr. and Mrs. Ling.

Nia is hiding her disappointment well.

—This is so nice. I've heard of their restaurant but I've never even been there. Why would they do this?

—Vicki and little Maya, who dragged you to the emergency room, are their daughter and granddaughter. Plus, the Lings are, let us say, prominent in the community. Imagine the vicious talk in this town if a Chinese gang had blown up the hospital.

Nia nods, circles the vast bouquet. Circumnavigates would be a better word.

—What the heck should I do with this?

—I know what I would do if they were mine, Annabel says.

—What?

—Take them out of the vase one by one, toss them all over your bed, and make mad, passionate love on them.

—With who?

Annabel and I choke down our offers without putting voice to them.

A parade from the hospital steps and the handicapped ramp through downtown to City Hall will take place Saturday. Nia at first refused. She was not

Miss America, she would not show herself off like some freak. President Kelly quietly called San Diego, convinced top brass what great publicity this would be for Marine recruiting. The brass called Nia, told her she would ride the main float in the parade, in her dress blues, saluting frequently.

—But . . .

—That's an order.

The brass suggested she might put on heavy make-up that day to lessen the starkness of her wound.

—So you don't scare the children.

Nia hurled the phone onto the sofa as she told him to fuck off in seventeen languages. Including sign language.

—I didn't know you were ambidextrous, Annabel said.

She took leave time to have a few days of privacy before the parade. Annabel cooked soft food so she would not have to chew very much. When I could I sneaked unnoticed looks at her wound. It was true, I was being honest with myself. I loved her no less for her imperfection.

—Were you serious, what you told the press the other day?

We were eating an instant oatmeal breakfast Wednesday morning. With dried cranberries for those of us who could chew without pain.

—Serious about what?

—Not wanting plastic surgery.

—Of course.

—Why is that?

—I thought maybe you would understand, Michael. I've finally seen combat. I've got my war wound. It makes me feel better about myself. Why should I hide it?

—No reason. To me you're as beautiful as ever. But like that reporter asked, I wonder what Mickey will think.

—If he can't handle this, he won't be handling me. Do you think his love is that shallow?

—There's no way for me to judge. We've never been close, you know that. I certainly hope he's not that shallow. He'd be an idiot to let you go.

Annabel is looking from one of us to the other, silently. Holding her spoon in her hand, her oatmeal half eaten. I have no idea what she is thinking. I wouldn't find out until later.

—Tomorrow is supposed to be real hot, she says after awhile. Let's go camping in the mountains.

Nia agrees at once. They'll take her car, buy food and beer on their way out of town in the morning.

—Lots and lots of beer, Annabel says.

I lunch with Maxie in a small Mexican place downtown. Do not mention Laurette. What more is there to say? But she is a presence at the table, eating silently.

—Have you heard any more from Sophie?
—I've been screening my calls. Avoiding her.
—How long can you do that?
—How long can I live?
He wipes his lips with a napkin.
— Someone saw her coming out of a movie the other night. With an older gentleman, who was wearing a yarmulke.
—And you felt?
—Thrilled.
—To love, I say, lifting my beer.
—I also felt sick.
Maxie looks away for an instant.
—I'm sorry, Maxie. That was a dumb thing to say.
—It's okay. Life goes on. I want some ice cream. Sometimes it helps.
I buy a chocolate cone next door. He surprises me by choosing strawberry.
—What happened to the chocolate maven?
—This one's for Laurette, he says.
We cross the street into Graham Park, lick our cones on a bench in the noon shade of a large blue oak. Not far away at a wooden picnic table five older men are cackling at muttered remarks while passing around a magazine. It can't be anyone else. The St. Bede's Seniors Photography Club lives on.

Having finished *Exit Ghost*, on the way home I stop at the library and pick up the Coetzee book, and spend the afternoon reading in the quiet house. Butler whimpers occasionally for the absent girls.

The Coetzee is more intellectual, more political than the Roth, but the central old man's quiet lust for his young secretary, though understated, runs as a constant structural counterpoint to the sometimes difficult ideas. There is no point slapping a stick-it note in a library book, so I copy one sentence onto a pad: *For an old man, after all, what is there left in the world but wicked thoughts?*

Can I prove it isn't true? Will Nia give me new life in the flower-strewn glory of her bed?

Or is such desire alone a wicked thought?

The half life of happiness, for me, is four hours. Perhaps this is genetic, determined in seratonin's opium dens. For Nia I would guess about twelve. Why else would I so often hear her three-in-the-morning not-quite-whimpering?

I know something is wrong when the convertible pulls into the driveway in midmorning instead of late afternoon. It's confirmed by their manner as they haul in their sleeping bags, leftover food, beer, paper plates, charcoal, with barely audible murmured hellos. As if they are returning from a funeral.
—What's wrong?
—We're fine, Nia replies.
Which does not precisely answer my question. I hadn't asked if they had slept in poison ivy.

—You guys left here yesterday fluttery as butterflies. You come home today like moldy pork chops. Something happened.

—We're just tired, Nia says.

She's still stunning, despite her stitches. Long tanned legs emerging from blue denim shorts. The new Joan of Arc of California Coastal.

—We couldn't sleep. I was afraid a cougar might pounce. I didn't have my rifle, I must have left it in the Emergency Room. I'm not used to sleeping outside. The insect sounds. The animal sounds.

Way too many excuses.

—You camped twice during the summer. You never complained about sleeping. You're not being truthful with me.

—She's tired, Uncle Mike. Why not back off for now?

—What about me? You think I don't worry about you? You girls are family. I'm entitled to know what's going on.

—Okay, Michael. I'm going to tell you what's going on. Then I'm going to sleep. I won't answer any questions. I won't explain anything until after the parade tomorrow. I have to be Marine Barbie on a fucking float. Smile through my wound. I won't discuss it until that's over with. Okay?

—What choice do I have?

— None. I made a decision in the park last night. It's not going to make you happy.

—What was the decision?

—I'm breaking up with Mickey.

For a moment the kitchen spins, the table levitates. Should I laugh, should I cry, should I just hide and watch, as, according to Lacey Roberts, they say in Oklahoma?

—You're what?

—I'm going to break off with him as soon as I can.

She seems in complete control. No tears. Like the Terry Clark cut she plays so often: *No Fear.* One night she danced around the living room for me to that song, using a tablecloth as Salomé's last veil. With her clothes on, of course. She'd been out drinking margaritas. One too few.

—Why are you breaking it off? Did you hear from him? What did he say?

—I sleep now, explanations tomorrow. That was the deal. I'll see you guys later.

She disappears into her room and closes the door till it clicks. I hear her hurl herself onto her bed. A gasp of pain as she hits the pillow. From her wounded face or from her heart? I cannot tell.

Annabel has been standing quietly, as if trying to disintegrate into the atoms of which she is composed. Her long fingers are laced in front of her to keep her nerves from showing.

—Tell me what happened.

She shakes her head almost imperceptibly. Puts a six-pack of beer in the refrigerator. Pulls one out, pops the top, drains a mess of carbohydrates. Her lean body can afford it.

—Don't be in a hurry to hear, Unc. There's time enough to get upset.

She moves off into the den. I don't know what to make of this. Nameless fear fills my belly. Cassandra salamander smiling smugly. But the bomb in the hospital was not a metaphor. I still see that tall earth falling, hundreds of patients, nurses, docs falling with it. Even the kid who had Sweet Marie in his head. Chicken Little has taken up residence within me.

She's not going to marry Mickey! She's going to break it off as soon as she can! Morgan still lives, but that is minor under the circumstances. I can pitch my woo at her without being an ogre!

It does not escape me that she and Annabel might have become lovers high up in their cammie sleeping bags, or naked under the autumn stars. But if that transpired they should have returned happy as cunnilingualed clams. It could have happened anyway, an experiment for Nia, led on by a needy Annabel, but they aren't acting as if true love was born in Destiny Park.

It's not yet noon but I pull one of the beers from the fridge, sip it, slowly. I can't imagine what went on up there. I think: Mickey will be devastated. But I never was much concerned about that in the context of Nia and me. I try to calm my nerves. She will tell me tomorrow. Will that open the door for her and me? Will I ask the overwhelming question? Do I dare to eat a peach? Will I wear my trousers rolled?

It's going to be a long night. Tomorrow I have to stand on the hospital float behind Shannon, in case her chair begins to roll. Pure nonsense, but she's the boss.

Half way through my beer I hear an unusual clink coming from the den. Another, another. A sound I've never heard before. I sidle in. Annabel in her cutoff jeans, sitting cross-legged on the thick white rug, is surrounded by glass eyes. The segmented wooden case is flat on the sofa-bed, empty. One by one she is choosing an eye from the rug and flipping it with thumb and forefinger into the air. Trying to land it in the case, like in a carnival game, cage an eye, win a Teddy Bear. The partitions are too small, the eyes keep bouncing off.

—Is that a new game? What do you call it?

—I'm not sure yet. Maybe *Chinese Eyes*. Maybe *Annabel Is a Lowlife Piece of Shit*.

—Uh, oh. When I was a kid in Yonkers there was a game like that. Called Jimmy Hoffa's Eyes. Only they used real eyes.

She is not in a laughing mood. She does not even tell me I'm gross. I kneel behind her, place my hands on her shoulders. Her muscles are pregnant with tension. I begin to knead them, gently.

—Want to talk about it?

Reaching beside her she picks up a handful of eyes in one hand, seems about to hurl them hard across the room. Maybe break a window, a mirror. Glass on glass. She stops herself with a sigh, places the eyes one by one back on the rug. She's wearing a yellow tee shirt that says, *I'm Important.* A fresh tear darkens on her breast.

—I can't talk about it now, she says.

A full moon — a great round bauble as I close the bedroom drapes. I can't fall asleep, didn't expect to. Nia came out for food, took it back to her room, closed the door. Not a word to anyone. As if walking within a plastic bubble all her own. Now I hear soft sobbing, sandpaper on my heart. I want to go in and hold her, whatever happened. But I must respect her privacy. Fate has taken charge. The only way, short of his death, that Mickey could be out of the picture, that the forbidden path to Nia's love could have been cleared for me.

A salamander is nibbling my entrails. I don't know if salamanders have teeth. This one does.

Maui Jim . . . Smiths . . . Acles sunglasses . . .
The hospital is exploding, leaving a vacancy in the sky. I put on sunglasses against the glare.
Luxottica . . . Oliver Peoples . . . Provider . . .
Nia, Vicky, Maya are drifting high above the debris, like winged angels. They wave to me but I do not see.
Wiley X . . . SEXX VISION . . . Survival Optix . . .
A female rabbi angrily rips the sunglasses from my eyes. I am blinded by the light.

In her dress blues and white dress cap in her red convertible with the top down, and with her wounded beauty, Nia is the image of America. If she cried all night it does not show, though a hint of her inner pain has dulled her eyes. Annabel in jeans and tee shirt climbs into the back, lets me sit up front. I'm wearing my usual blue oxford button-down, bland chinos, loafers and my white lab coat for the hospital theme. While putting on the coat I stuck my hands in the pockets, a habit at work, and pricked my finger on the MVR blade I had put there to fight the cougar in case Nia missed. Good thinking, Dr. Lee. I leave the blade for safekeeping among Morgan's assorted skin lotions in her medicine cabinet above the doublewide bathroom sink.

At the hospital the streets are cordoned off except for one lane left open for ambulances or those with Saturday appointments. The parking lot is a carnival of noise and color, someone arranging marching bands and floats in the order they will appear, handing out large numbers, black on white board, starting to get the bands in position. A Marine color guard will lead the parade, followed by a Marine marching band bussed up from San Diego. A fire department ambulance, police on horseback, a high school band, park rangers on horseback, several dot.com floats — the companies called the mayor and talked their way in. Another high school band, a Coast Guard float, a Marine Drill team, the local Miss Teen America contestant, a middle-school band, more dot.coms. A hospital float carrying a member of each department — nurses, ER, aides, housekeeping, security, oncology, radiation, neurology, the works — Lacey Roberts doing the honors for ophtho, probably wishing she had kept her golden locks another week. Smiles and hugs all around as the participants climb aboard floats decorated with masses of flowers, there having been no time to get any fancier, bare floats hauled out of city storage where they are kept for the parades on Memorial Day, Fourth of July, whatever. Then the heart of the matter. A civic float on which the mayor will ride along with the city council. Behind that the one everyone will be waiting to cheer — the Marine and Medical Center hero, Staff Sergeant Yessenia Ruiz. Followed by another hospital float, featuring the top brass, with President Shannon Kelly in her wheelchair at the front, me behind it for safety reasons, which hardly seems necessary. Another high school band bringing up the rear, trailed by sanitation department trucks and workers who will be cleaning up confetti and horse droppings, so the street can be reopened to traffic as soon as possible and the parade will leave no trace.

—It's ludicrous, all this for me, Nia says as we sit in her convertible, waiting for her float to clear the morass.

—It's not for you, sweetie. No, let me rephrase that. It's not only for you. It's for themselves. For the hundreds in the parade and for the thousands who'll be lining the curbs, waving, clapping. Imagine what a disaster it would have been for this town, the whole region, if the bomb had taken the hospital down. Everyone would have known someone who was maimed, or killed. The whole town would have been in stress syndrome. This is a way for them to let out their undigested fears of what might have been. I don't know whose idea it was, but it was a great idea.

—It was mine, of course.

Shannon Kelly has rolled up beside the car.

—It was still a great idea, I respond.

—And great publicity for the hospital. It will wrap music and flags into the bandages and operating tables in which we mostly exist in the public mind. Make us more popular.

—Sure. People will start breaking their necks to get in.

That's Annabel from the backseat. Shannon frowns, as if wondering who the hell this impertinent urchin is. She peers for a closer look.

—I know you. You're the Godzilla girl. I saw you all over TV. That was a perfect way to break the tension.

—Annabel the clown, that's me.

The accidentally escaping bitterness in her voice is palpable. Is it something old or something new? Whatever the hell happened in the park the other night? Did she come on to Nia and Nia turn her down?

—Even with the parade, Shannon says, I'm betting behavioral health will be swamped for months. Aftershocks of the catastrophe that didn't happen. Speaking of betting, Michael, Vegas is down to three to one for you and Klonsky.

—For the Nobel Prize? Holy crap, Uncle Mike. You'll be famous. You'll be rich.

—Yes, but will I be happy?

Annabel leans forward in the backseat, stretches her long arms around my chest, kisses the top of my head.

—I think you're ready for Santa Fe, she says.

—I appreciate the optimism, ladies, but the human visual system has over a billion neurons. Me and Maxie barely made a dent. It was the dark ages compared to today. Now they operate on the brains of flies and count the neurons. A hundred thousand in a fly's visual system. Something to think about the next time you swat.

Through the badinage Nia stares out the windshield at masses of movement and color. Saying nothing. Is she seeing again with all those neurons the cougar coming at her? Or is it something else, something worse?

Flags. Cheers. Applause. The essence of a small-town parade. People are waving from the sidewalks or on second story balconies. Hoards of children. Police on motorcycles are racing up and back. Showing off for the teenagers. On our float, Madam President makes sure the wheels on her chair are locked. The rest of the hospital board is arrayed behind her.

—What's this about, Shannon? You didn't need me here for safety.

—I like your company. Is that so terrible? Actually, I wanted to make sure you'd be here. There's something in my little speech that will interest you.

With Nia being honored, I wouldn't have missed it for anything.

She's on the float in front of us, surrounded by low banks of flowers. Standing tall, maintaining a perfect salute for blocks at a time. Breaking it off to wave at the crowds, then returning to Attention. Sometimes the floats have to halt so the various marching bands don't crowd one another, don't muddle each other's tunes. People in the crowd crane their necks to see what's coming next. During one stop Nia spots something, spins off the float, rushes to the side of the street. She's recognized Vicky and Maya, waving. She hugs them both, is shaking hands with two old folks behind them. Mr. and Mrs. Ling. She kisses them each on the cheek. Then hugs them, all together. The parade starts to move. She hurries back to her float, puts one hand on it and vaults aboard. To new cheers.

Finally we reach City Hall, two whitewashed stories with a sloping red Mexican roof. A moveable stage has been set up in front, portable steps brought up for the dignitaries. A ramp for Shannon's chair. The mayor, a short, bald fellow, takes Nia's hand, leads her onto the podium. A police officer wheels Shannon up. She waves for me to join her. I shake my head but she insists. What the hell.

The crowd from the street has flowed in and around the stage like an incoming tide. A helicopter overhead is shooting video. Another chopper lands in the parking lot behind the city center. Things stall until a man is escorted out of City Hall onto the platform. It's a surprise appearance by the governor, who is up for re-election. He's a shoo-in to win. Doing things like this, dropping in unexpectedly at civic events, is one reason why.

I'm a few feet from Nia on her wounded side. Surreptitiously, I study her stitches while the mayor talks, the governor talks, the crowd applauds. She's got her dress hat under her arm, her dark hair in a ponytail. Her torn skin seems to be holding together nicely, the sutures should come out Monday. There is whispering on the podium.

—I thought I was here to introduce the hero of the day, Staff Sergeant Yessenia Ruiz, the governor says. But I'm told the plan has changed. The sergeant will be introduced by Col. Russell Mack of the Marine Base in San Diego. Colonel?

From the crowd in front of the podium a handsome middle-aged Marine out of Hollywood casting, a George Clooney type, vaults among us, takes the microphone in one hand.

—The sun is getting warm, so I won't take but a moment of your time. I have two jobs here on this wonderful occasion. The second, if you'll bear with me, is to introduce Staff Sergeant Ruiz. The first is this.

He reaches into his pocket and removes a small leather box, as for a bracelet or a watch.

—All of us at the Marine Base in San Diego quickly heard about the actions of Sgt. Ruiz at the California Coastal Regional Medical Center last Monday. At first through the press, I imagine. After the details were verified, the Marine brass in Washington was informed. Researchers went to work, but could find no precedent for what you are about to witness. It was decided to proceed anyway. Sergeant, if you will step forward, please.

I can't imagine what the hell this is about. It's clear Nia can't either as she moves beside the Colonel.

—Staff Sergeant Yessenia Ruiz, it is my honor to present to you, for courageous action above and beyond the call of duty, in the name of the countless civilians you saved from death or injury, a citation that has never before in our history been awarded outside of a combat situation: The United States Marines Medal of Valor.

Her faces flushes around her sutures as the colonel opens the leather box, pulls out a black and gold hexagonal medal on a gold chain, hands the empty box to the nonplussed governor, steps behind Nia — I lift her pony tail for him — and affixes the medal around her neck. It gleams against her dress blues, reflecting the sun out into the crowd, which has begun cheering wildly, shouting Nia, Nia, Nia, making this half-Mexican young lady from San Diego their own. She fingers the medal that rests a few inches below her jaw, steps to the mike as the shouting grows even louder. Nia indulges them with waves — the Marine Barbie she does not want to be — until finally they quiet down to let her speak. Just before she starts, President Kelly whispers something to the mayor, who nods.

—Ladies and gentleman, and all you wonderful kids, Nia begins, I want to thank you so much for this wonderful parade, which I do not at all deserve.

Shouts of Yes Yes Yes and Nia Nia Nia. She waits for quiet again.

—I also want to thank Colonel Mack — she turns toward him — and everyone in the Marine Corps whom he represents — for this unbelievable honor. Knowing what my brother and sister Marines are facing in combat every day, in Iraq and Afghanistan and other dangerous places, it is definitely not deserved.

—Yes, Yes, Yes from the crowd.

—Though I will admit that the San Jose Mall, where I work in the recruiting office, can get pretty rowdy at times.

Laughter and cheers. She ought to be in politics.

—The truth is, I had prepared a few remarks to make here today. But this medal has driven them from my mind. So I will just say thank you again to all of you. *Semper Fidelis*. God bless America.

She turns from the mic amid another crescendo of Nia Nia Nia. The mayor holds up his hands for silence but there is no silence it seems for a hundred miles. He lowers his arms in surrender.

—That's it, he says, though very few can hear. Thank you all for coming on this great occasion. Drive home safely.

Nia is kneeling at the front of the podium, signing autographs, mainly for kids. To free both hands she has slapped her white dress hat on her head. It is delightfully askew. I look a question at President Kelly, who is guiding her chair towards me.

—I thought you were supposed to speak, Shannon.

She nods, shrugs. Squeezes my hand, much to my surprise.

—My news will keep, she says. Sergeant Ruiz is a tough act to follow.

Chapter 18: Michael

Nia had been too nervous to eat breakfast before the parade. All hungry now, we walk to a cafe two blocks from City Hall. Other diners wave and smile when they see her but are polite enough to let us eat undisturbed. The Saturday special, quiche and salad, for all of us. Annabel asks if Nia's speech really was knocked from her mind by the medal.

—Not literally. But I couldn't say what I was planning to. I've been doing a lot of thinking the last few days. God or Fate let me save a lot of people this one time, but the nurses devote every day of their lives to that. I love the Marines. But it may be time to do something else. I might go to nursing school, maybe in San Diego, so I can spend more time with my parents. Or else in Santa Clara. When I get my degree in two years, I'd come back to Coastal and see if they'll give me a job.

—How could they not? You were going to say that in your speech?

My plate is turning like an old LP. Quiche-salad-quiche-salad-quiche . . .

—I know, it's personal, but what was I supposed to talk about? Cougars? Gangs? The medal — she fingers it at her neck — shut my mouth. It didn't change my mind, necessarily, but it shut my mouth about leaving the Marines.

—How would Mickey feel? I ask.

Stupidly, perhaps, but they have yet to clue me in on what is happening.

—The Marines are the main thing you two have in common, you said once. Your team. I guess you have a separate identity now. Between your wound and the Medal. I hope you can absorb them deep inside. In your gut. In your soul. Absorb the confidence you exude.

—Mickey doesn't matter any more. I promised to tell you why after the parade. But not here, we need privacy.

She turns to Annabel.

—Would up in the park be all right with you?

—It won't be a problem, Annabel says.

We take her protesting car, which she'd wisely parked behind City Hall. Out the highway, into what the signs still call Polk Park. The paved road becomes narrow dirt that twists and climbs into the hills among clusters of blue oaks. Disturbed lizards flee in all directions, like the speculations in my brain. I have no idea where we are going, or why.

—This is as close as we can get, Annabel says. The same place we went camping.

Nia is still in her dress blues, me in my lab coat. Annabel in shredded jeans is the only one who looks sane among the trees, the bushes, the distant rocky ridges. Me and Nia are refugees from a Terry Gilliam film. Or a Peter O'Toole.

We walk down a winding dirt path, Annabel trailing behind. I wait for her to catch up, but she has stopped moving. She is sitting on her haunches. We move back toward her. She is crying.

—Annabel, what's wrong?

She shakes her head side to side, almost wildly, as if she would snap her neck. I kneel beside her, grab her shoulders to stop her. The tears are rolling down like dripping faucets. She sniffles, her whole body beginning to shudder.

—I didn't know what to do, she says.

—About what?

Nia, too, is kneeling beside her, dress blue knees in the dirt.

—Do you believe things happen for a reason? Annabel asks through sniffles, small sobs.

—What kind of things?

—Everything. Why I'm out here.

—You needed to get away from Santa Fe. For your own reasons.

—But why here?

—Because your uncle Mike is here.

—And because Nia is, Annabel says, wiping her nose with her thumb.

—You didn't know that.

She takes Nia's hand.

—That's my point. I think some angel or destiny brought me out here to meet Nia. To tell her. That was so hard yesterday. Now it's even harder to tell you, Uncle Mike. But you can't hear it from Nia. It has to come from me.

—Tell me what?

—You don't want to know.

—Annabel, if you're carrying some burden, some secret, you need to let it out. The wrong kind of secret can drive you crazy. Believe me, I know.

She's sniffling in her sobs now. Still squatting. The muscles of the young. Nia gives her a blue handkerchief.

—It's been driving me crazy. Ever since I got here. But you'll hate me if I tell you.

I touch her gently under the chin.

—Annabel, we're all adults here. We love each other. We won't hold anything against you.

She wipes her eyes with the blue hankie, then her nose. Her voice is tremulous when she unburdens herself.

—Uncle Mike, remember the summer I spent out here with you guys?

—Sure. Six or seven years ago.

—It was ten years ago. I was fifteen then. Only half a summer, actually. I left at the beginning of August,

—I remember. You got homesick. We flew you back to Connecticut.

—Yeah. Well, Mickey took me up here one day that summer.

—I knew he had a special place somewhere up here, but he never told me or Morgan where. He said it was his secret hideaway.

—It was very secret.

She starts to shudder again, holds the handkerchief to her eyes, as if hiding.

—He used to take high school girls up here.

A loud sob.

— And rape them.

My knees tremble. Nia sits quietly on the red dirt. I can't see her expression.

—Why would he tell you that? I ask. That's nothing to joke about. He was 19 that summer, finished with his first year of college.

—He didn't tell me. He wasn't joking.

She hesitates, finds a stone beside her in the dirt, turns away, hurls it over the nearby precipice.

—He raped me.

My niece always had a wild imagination.

—No offense, Annabel, but that's hard to believe. Mickey isn't like that.

I'm wondering in a panic how well I know him.

—No offense? You think I would make up something like that? You think I would cry about it? You want to hear the gory details?

I don't know what to say. Annabel is a kidder. But rape? Nia's eyes are cast down. She has heard this before. Yesterday. And believed it.

—I wasn't homesick that summer. I had to get away. I was 15. A virgin. Until that afternoon. A nice little healthy hike, he'd said.

She pulls her hair back off her right temple.

—You see this little scar.

—I remember. You fell while you guys were hiking.

—I didn't fall. He shoved me into a boulder when I refused to do what he wanted. I hit my head. He made me undress. Do stuff I had never done before. Crying the whole time. He picked up a large rock, held it near my face, said he would bash my brains in if I told anyone. While he was inside me he was choking me. To make his point.

The world is closing in. The East River rising over my head. I can hardly breathe. I cannot see. I am drowning in a river of saliva. Semen. Hymen blood.

—I saw those two little eyes he's got down there.

Eyes? I love my niece but she has problems. Mickey is a good-looking kid. Maybe this is fantasy, what a 15-year-old feeling her hormones wanted to happen.

Nia looks up from her perch. Takes off her dress cap, shields her eyes from the sun.

—Did you ever see Mickey's penis?

—When he was a baby, of course. Changing diapers.

—You probably couldn't see them back then. Mickey has two little freckles on the left side. Close together, small. They're not really visible — except when he's extended, and you're getting a close-up look.

—What's that to do with anything?

—I was as skeptical as you, Nia says. I was gonna marry this guy. Until Annabel described them to me.

Those two little eyes he's got down there.

Somehow I manage to stand, shakily, stumble to the nearest tree like a drunk who needs to piss. The earth acts as if it's spinning like a globe. I hug the tree to keep from falling into a blue abyss.

—Do you want more proof?

I follow Annabel fifty feet to a tall blue oak. My shoes slip and slide as if I'm walking on ice. Beneath the ice, giant pirañas wait. With rapacious eyes.

—You see this tree here? When he was done with me, he took out his knife and carved a notch. His Tree of Desire, he called it. Two recent notches were already there. He pointed at one and said, In the mouth. He pointed to the other and said, Up the butt. That was ten years ago, and you can still see the indentations in the bark. Look, now there are five, all almost covered over. He was a busy fucker.

Maybe the others were consensual I think, but clearly Annabel isn't making this up. It could be the root of her sexual confusion. She hates and fears men sexually because of the psychological scars from this violent first time. She turns to women for solace, relief, like the Indian princess. But basically straight. I walk back, legs shaky as on my first day in medical school. Nia is hugging her knees, tears in her eyes, as if the blue space below the nearby precipice were a lake of sorrows.

—Nia, you know Mickey. Could he do something like that? He was a B student. A ballplayer. The only good thing me and Morgan collaborated on.

—Are you still suggesting Annabel is making this up? Now? Ten years later?

There was no way to answer, only to concede, evade. Our dinner in Monterey to celebrate his becoming a Marine. The smugness he could not contain. He was raping young girls and getting away with it.

— Ten years in the Marines could have cleansed him of this garbage.

—What will cleanse Annabel? You're saying forgive and forget? Apply an emotional statute of limitations? I love the Marines. I love being one, as you know. I loved it that he was so good they put him in Recon.

Idly she touches the Medal of Valor under her chin. As if she is Catholic and the medal a crucifix.

—Did you read about those five female Marines in Iraq a few months ago? They stopped drinking water after four in the afternoon, in hundred degree heat, so they would not have to go to the latrine during the night. Because when they walked to the latrine in the dark they were getting raped — by their brother Marines! Instead, they died of dehydration, all five of them. To me that was the most sickening story of the war. And it hardly got any attention. Three paragraphs in the newspaper, and I never heard of any investigation.

—That's awful, Nia. But you're not accusing Mickey. He's off on his own somewhere.

—I'm not accusing him of anything. It would be hard for me to believe he's like that now. But it's hard for you to believe he was like that then. You expect me to marry him after learning this? What if he's horny and I'm not in the mood? Dueling bayonets? I'll just have to get over him. Maybe I am already. I figure he could have found some way to make contact the past two months. Maybe he's raping Arab girls in their burqas. How could I ever trust him?

Quiche rises in my gut. Wants out. I fight hard not to vomit.

—Annabel, why did you tell this to Nia now?

—I never met Nia till this trip. You know that. I didn't know she was going to marry Mickey, until she started talking about him. About what a great guy he is. How hard it is to be apart for so long. I love Nia, we get along great. For a long time the other night I lay in my sleeping bag and looked at the stars, and debated the harm it might do. I didn't want to hurt her. But I finally I decided I had to tell her. You have to go into marriage with your eyes open. Maybe it was wrong, I'm still not sure.

—You did right by me, Nia says.

I fold my head into my hands. My breathing seems to have stopped, I feel I'm about to black out. I force myself to take deep breaths. This was the boy Morgan did such a great job of raising. Stop that, I can't blame her. I was much too busy cutting eyes.

—No other girl accused him back then, I say.

—They were probably ashamed, like I was. Like most women still are. And afraid. When Mickey with a knife or a rock in his hand says he'll kill you, he's kind of convincing.

My eyes are reddening. I can feel it, as if color were pain.

—Maybe it would be better if he never came home. If an enemy sniper gets him.

Says I, who killed eleven.

Neither of the women murmurs a dissent.

I embrace Annabel, tell her how sorry I am. That she did the right thing by warning Nia. I embrace Nia, apologize to her as well. Embrace them together as in a family hug. My only family. A family in grief. A family bereaved.

Then I break away, hurry behind a large red boulder, fall to my knees, as if in supplication. I vomit spinach quiche.

Sunday I don't get dressed, I stay in my pajamas and robe, leave the bedroom only twice, once to fix a cheese sandwich with mustard, and get a beer. Nia remains in the privacy of hers. Annabel visits back and forth, hugging, trying to offer comfort. The original victim trying to lift the pall from the house. Without success. Nia is free of Mickey. Perhaps is available. I do not think so that Sunday. I have lost a son, not gained a lover.

Monday morning Annabel putters off for Santa Fe in her jalopy — what is the origin of that odd word? — the trek up the dirt roads having rendered it into critical condition, by the sound of the engine. She's got a cheap mechanic at home, assuming she makes it home. She leaves amid heartfelt hugs and kisses, many promises to keep in touch. Promises are so often made to be broken, like those of a politician, but I think not these. We all need each other.

—One thing, Uncle Mike. I don't know if you noticed, but one of your eyes is missing again. I couldn't find it after my game the other day. It's in the den somewhere. I promise.

—Don't worry about it. Just drive safely. I'm sure I'll find it.

When in fact I'm not sure at all.

Monday afternoon Nia has her stitches removed by Dr. Holloway. She drops in to ophtho, amid hallway applause, to show off her new face. It's less garish without the line of black cross-stitches that for some reason reminded me of the KKK. Holloway did a good job, the scar in that beautiful face though long is tight, slim, neat, like a dueling wound. It can't decide if it wants to be red or white. Probably it will wind up pink. Yessenia Ruiz, the fifth musketeer. She asks if I want to have lunch. I tell her I'm not hungry.

—You have to eat, Michael!

I haven't eaten but two bites in two days. Mickey's rapes are stuffed in my chest and my esophagus like rags soaked in gasoline. That's a serious symptom of something, turning down lunch with Nia.

Monday, late afternoon. Day is done. I'm about to leave when Maxie comes waltzing in. Not waltzing, *schlepping.* Got a few minutes? he asks. Of course. We sit. Maxie without preliminaries assaults me with more terrible news. He has prostate cancer.

—Fuck. When did you find out?

—Last week.

—Bad?

—Enough so they want to operate pretty soon. I've been studying the different surgeries, which ones don't leave you leaking. It's hard to say. I'm leaning toward the implantation of radioactive seeds. They all leave you impotent. My sex life is finished, Michael. At 64. Gone like Laurette. They all have the same estimated survival time. Five years.

—Jesus, Max.

—I didn't want to burden you. But I have no one else to lean on.

We stand, hug each other for a long time. Buddies. Forty years.

Mist clouds my eyes behind my sunglasses as I drive home in the right-hand lane, cars speeding by the damned slowpoke. Two of them give me the finger.

At bedtime, in the den, I tell Nia about Maxie. She hugs me in sympathy. I hold her tight. I will drown if I let go. I hold on to the hug as if it's a living thing. It is filling the emptiness inside me, at least for the moment.

Now?

Now I should press the question. Find out once and for all. She is wearing a tank top and shorts. They are reeling me in like a fish on a line.

—When you cry during the night, I ask, has that been about Mickey?

—Lately. I've been sensing something is wrong, without knowing what. This is the longest he hasn't made contact. But Annabel's confession blew me away. As if I knew it was coming. It made me want to scream. I did, over and over, out there in the park when we were camping. Annabel held me in her arms like a child while I wept. Almost the whole night.

My lips are pressed to her forehead. Her perspiration. I want to lick it off.

—Before that. When the midnight tears were not about Mickey.

We separate. She squeezes my hand.

—In the dark of night, there is always something to cry about. We both know that, you and I.

I rub the underside of her wrist, gently, with my thumb.

—In your dress blues, people see a model of confidence. Now the Medal of Valor. People don't really know one another.

The moment of decision has arrived unexpectedly, like an express train on an abandoned track, broken down shacks on all sides, hillbillies who marry their cousins on gray porches smoking pipes, watching for something to gossip about. I lean forward. I kiss Nia lightly on the lips.

In my fantasies she returns my kiss, throws her arms around my neck. Our kiss becomes hungry, a tiny biting of lips. Knees grind centers of gravity. Tongues flick impatient wet entreaties.

—*I love you Michael. I was committed to Mickey, but I've come to love you more. That's one reason I cry in the night.*

My fantasy for weeks, complete with shameless engorging.

But that is not what happens. She does not play her role. Instead she steps back, picks a glass eye out of the display, studies it.

—I'll help you find the missing one, she says.

My answer is the absence of an answer. Defeat by default. The rags in my throat sink to my stomach, churn into sour butter. I want to cry, tears thick as lava, hot. I battle for self respect, I can't let them boil out. I am Hemingway's Old Man, and she is The Sea.

—We need to talk, Nia. Can we do that now?

—Sure.

I sit on the sofa, she joins me there, at the farthest end. One bare leg is pulled up under her. The other is stretched full length in my direction.

—I love you, Nia. I think you know that. More than Mickey ever could. More than anyone ever could. I thought my passionate years were over long ago. But you've brought them back. You've given me visions of a third act to my life. I was hoping you feel the same about me. Some of the things you've said encouraged me. Gave me hope.

Her face looks pained.

—What things I've said?

—Let's play doctor. Some day I'll show you how good I am. Others. They didn't mean anything, I kept telling myself — but maybe they did. Always my soaring feelings for you overwhelmed logic.

She does not reach out to comfort me. Of this I am acutely aware. As if I have been slapped. She keeps her distance on the sofa.

—Oh, Michael, I'm so sorry. I never meant to encourage you in that way. That's just the way I talk. With Mickey being my boyfriend, it never occurred to me what you were feeling.

—And with Morgan still alive, it would not be right.

—That, too. We do have much in common, Michael. It's respect for what you do that has me wanting to be a nurse. Since I've been here we've gotten to know each other's souls.

—And I'm more than twice your age.

—You're arguing against yourself, Michael. That's no way to proposition me.

—I know. I've run your lines through my mind so many times I know them all. I can say them now because there is no chance. Is there?

—I'm sorry, Michael. Really sorry. I think of you as family. I love you in that way. But not in a romantic way. That's something you feel or you don't. I just don't. Seeing your pain, I wish I could. But I can't.

—Maybe it wasn't your words. Maybe it's your pheromones.

—I can't help those. Whatever they are.

—I'm not a womanizer, Nia. I think you know that by now. In all the years with Morgan I've never been with anyone else. Never wanted to. This is not about lust. There's an incredible physical attraction, I don't deny that, you're so damn beautiful — we have the greatest times of my life in my fantasies — I guess I should thank you for those — but this is way beyond that. This is deep, edge of the world love. I want to share your life, as long as Fate lets me. Support you in anything you want to do. Just you being here with me makes me young, alive, happy — and also despairing that you don't feel the same. If you want a child, I'm sure that still is possible. I can't guarantee I'd be around for the bratty teenage years. But even a guy your age couldn't guarantee that.

She says nothing. Then repeats the truth I do not want to accept.

—I don't know what more to say. Except that I'm sorry.

Torment becomes me, I become torment. My body feels twisted, like those leafless trees on the Monterey Peninsula, in sight of the sighing sea, but unable to move closer. Ridiculed by barking seals. This anguish in my chest cannot last, I tell myself. Knowing it will, perhaps as long as I live. I sit there silently. Afraid she will decide to move out. Knowing I will never get over her until she does. If then. My inner fear has been realized, the flip side of my passion. Without Nia there is nothing to live for. Prostate, blocked arteries, kidney, liver, pancreas, stroke like Morgan's. All the fun stuff of getting old. Can you die of a broken heart? At my age? It would be one for the record books.

The fates are cruel only to be kind? I think not. The fates are cruel only to be cruel.

There is no point prolonging this session. I will try to treat it with humor, if I can.

—I'll let you go to bed now. You're returning to work tomorrow, right?

She nods, stands. I get up too, I want to hold her one more time. She looks at me, does not want to encourage me. She hands me the glass eye she is still holding, so that her arm comes between us.

—If you change your mind, you know where to find me.

She smiles. I blink. Something is wrong. In her eyes, in both her eyes, I see a red outline. A face, drawn in red ink. Blood ink. I step closer. Nia stiffens, afraid I will embrace her. I don't. I merely stare at her eyes. The red lines have created the face of a woman. I cannot read the expression on the face. But who it belongs to is clear. It is the face of Addie Judd. It is Addie as I knew her, except that in the sockets where her eyes should be there are no eyes.

If you have experienced what we metaphorically call a broken heart, it need not be recorded in words. Just double the pain if you know it will be your life's last passion. If you have never experienced a broken heart, consider yourself lucky. Or dead.

There are no adequate words with which to record it. A ripple of anguish washes across my chest, a breeze-blown flag is planted in the arctic ice of my soul. (See what I mean? Country music says it better.) I want, need, to hold Nia so badly my chest is reaching out for her with arms of its own. But she has gone to bed, in her own room. Tears are forming. I begin to turn off the lamps. In the den, as I deny the light of the desk lamp like a priest snuffing a candle, I remove another glass eye from the display. Clinking together in my palm the two offer a sense of solidity. They add firmness to my identity, as if to say there is life still to be lived. But who ever put faith in a glass eye? I sit on the edge of my bed in the dark like a sleeping tern on a wooden post at the water's edge on a moonless night. Tears become muted sobs. I muffle them with a pillow so Nia will not hear. The most anguished ones break free.

For an old man, after all, what is there left in the world but wicked thoughts?

Which are hardly reason enough to live.

Glass eyes turning and turning in my closed hand. Rubbing against each other, squeaking, clicking. Bogart with steel balls in *The Caine Mutiny*.

Bogart always had steel balls.

Thoughts of taking charge tame the agony blowing through my chest, through the opening little remarked on in medical diagrams: the aperture of despair.

I allowed her into my eyes the way a sword swallower swallows a sword.

The small glass globes are clinking in my hand. How would it be to not have eyes? To not have to see the dead nurses? To ease my conscience by inflicting punishment, which I have evaded for forty years. Not have to look at Morgan in her bed of the living dead. Nor to look at Mickey when he returns. To lose the painful anguish caused by Nia's face, skin, ever-hidden breasts, untouchable sex. I place the glass eyes under my pillow, which in my nightly fantasies so often serves as Nia's chest. Excited by apprehension, I slip quietly out to my car, open the trunk, bring in the medical bag. I find my way to the bathroom, open Morgan's side. The MRS blade is visible in the half-light of the moon filtering through the clouded window. I take them with me back to the bed. I find a glass eye, hold the point of the blade next to it. Not one star is shining. All have been snuffed out. All of them hidden by astronomic sunglasses. I touch my finger lightly to the blade, the point shaped like an arrow head, edges sharp as a witch's wit. Gauge the Tetravisc in its syringe. How much pain do I want to inflict? How much pain is deserved?

Somehow I fall asleep, amid eagerness for morning to come. I awaken in my clothing to the sound of the shower running. Painkiller and blade on the bed beside me. I imagine Nia raising her arms to wash her hair, naked except for the Medal of Valor around her neck. Droplets of water kissing every part of her. I twist my face into the pillow, bite the corner against a wave of anguish that drills between my ribs. I am too educated, too sophisticated, too old, to carry on like this, you say. Only if you have never been there.

I pick up the Tetravisc, look at the blade.

I allowed her into my eyes the way the sword swallower . . .

Swinging my legs off the bed, I engage the blade by its wooden handle. It fits my hand perfectly, as it is meant to do. I recall sheet music far back in the sepia hues of childhood, at the Winslows. The title in serif type above the giddy, drunken notes. *Drink to Me Only With Thine Eyes.*

A perfect motto for Nia.

The water in the shower stops. She will be drying herself.

I hear the door opening. Bare feet padding down the hall. Now is the time — now or never. The near destruction of the hospital has not yet absorbed. The return of my murdered nurses is not yet over. My son the rapist, not accepted. Maxie's cancer, indisputable. Rejection by Nia, the most painful cut of all. They will put these together. They will put a name to it. Post Romantic Stress Disorder. The diagnosis will not matter.

A man can do as he wills, but not will as he wills.

Blindness by Schopenhauer.

The door to her room closes. I wait two counts, step over there, push the door open, the blade in my hand at my side, where she cannot see it.

—Michael!

She secures the bath towel tighter over her chest.

—What are you doing in here?

—Sit, Nia. Relax. I'm not going to rape you. I am not my son.

—Whatever it is, can't it wait until I'm dressed?

She sits on the edge of the bed. I think of a bayonet under her pillow. It can't be there, she left it with her rifle in the ER. The techs were going to autoclave the blade for her. Lock it up securely. She hasn't retrieved it yet.

I sit beside her. Addie is redlined in her eyes. Addie blind.

—Would you look down for a second? I ask.

As if I am about to snap her picture.

Left eye or right? It doesn't matter. I breathe deeply. I raise the blade in my right hand. There is no stopping now. With a sudden thrust I jab the point deep into the right eye. Fluids and blood splatter across her face, and mine. Nia screams, shrieks, wails. Michael, what are you doing?

I raise the blade again. She grabs my wrist to stop me, the damp bath towel falls into her lap. I let her encircle my wrist an instant while my remaining eye absorbs for the first and last time the sweet mellow sighing of her breasts. Then I wrench my hand forward, Nia still struggling to hold it back. I jab the point of the blade toward my seeing eye. She is screaming, shrieking, as if a loyal dog has been run over in the street. That is all I ever was to her. A loyal dog. I lie back across the bed. She stops screaming, needs to do something. What? My world has become dark, peaceful. There will be no more visitations from the graves in the eyes of patients. No looking at my son again. No desperate agony over Nia's unseen shapes, for they are not visible now. I hear her scruffle for her cell phone, punch three buttons.

—I need an ambulance. Nine Blue Oak Lane. Hurry!

— Have you gone crazy, Michael? Is it because of me? Jesus have mercy!

How long will the painkiller last?

I hear her hopping on one foot into her underwear. Pay attention to sounds, it's a new ball game. Dressing, most likely in cammies, she has to work today. With the Tetravisc, I feel no pain at all. Not yet. Just the pleasure of taking action at last. Nia's downcast face the final image on my right retina. On my left, the sweet meat of her nipples. The slaughtered rabbit, the guillotined criminal, both retained after death their final images. Perhaps I will as well.

They will have to enucleate. Take my retinas with the rest. But the images are still in the brain, they passed through the visual pathway in which Maxie and I pioneered, they will be subject to recall, like the face of your first love. The photo album of memory. Will I be able to see them without retinas? I will find out. A sacrifice for science, you might say.

Double enucleation. It sounds gruesome. But think of Hiroshima and Nagasaki. My act of contrition is not so terrible after all.

What will it matter? I have been blind all my life.

I sense the ride in the ambulance, the rush into the Emergency Room.

—Dr. Lee! What the hell happened?

Lacey Roberts. Her Oklahoma accent unmistakable.

Nia, who followed the ambulance in her car, to the defense.

—With a cold spell coming, he wanted to light the heater. The pilot light has been off all summer, but there must have been a leak, gas accumulated in the cabinet. He bent in with a flame to light the pilot, and Boom!

—An interesting story. There are no burns on his face, his hair is not singed, or his beard. He still has eyebrows. His eyes appear pierced by a sharp instrument. I don't do PR, Sergeant Ruiz, tell it to the president.

I'm lying on the gurney in the privacy of darkness.

—The EMTs said they only treated you for possible shock. Why aren't you screaming in pain, doctor?

—Tetravisc.

—My God! You planned this! You did it to yourself! My brilliant mentor has gone crazy! I don't believe it.

—Do you know your Gilbert and Sullivan, Dr. Roberts? Let the punishment fit the crime.

—What crime?

—That's a long story. The Tetravisc is wearing off. Please proceed, if you don't mind.

—Put him under. You understand I probably can't save your eyes?

—That was the idea.

Anetheseo cups my nose. I get woozy. I hear a gasping sound, a muted cry, after light footsteps enter the room. Vicky?

Darkness soon delivers drugged silence.

—Michael Alton Lee! Are you awake behind those things? What the fuck did you do? Why did you go nuts on me?

—Good morning to you, too, Shannon. If it's still morning.

—You can't tell, can you? You'll never be able to tell.

—I'll be able to tell when the birds begin to sing.

—Jesus. You're playing Hamlet. Is this real madness or feigned madness?

—I hear breathing. Aren't you afraid your shouting will wake my roommate?

—Not a problem. It's your wife.

—Man and woman sharing a room?

—It's allowed if they're married. Never mind that. What the hell happened? Sergeant Ruiz says you were lighting a pilot light. Dr. Roberts says that's bullshit. Judging by your face, I'm inclined to agree with the doctor.

—Nia was protecting me. Spur of the moment.

—So you really did this to yourself. On purpose. Made yourself permanently blind. Can you give me a reason?

—To find peace.

—I see. And have you found peace?

—Not with you shouting at me.

—Very well. I'm calm now. Can you elucidate?

—It took me forty years to find the answer, Shannon. I needed to be punished, and no one was doing it. The answer was to make the punishment fit the crime.

—What crime?

—That's a long story, which I'll be happy to tell you another time. I'm feeling rather exhausted to go through it right now.

—Well, you sound sane enough.

—Now is the time for you to pace around the room, pondering.

—Damn right. Except I can't pace. Has blindness destroyed your memory as well? You've forgotten my chair just because you can't see it?

—No. But I've sometimes wondered why you hit that tree.

—Because I wasn't paying attention, and I was going too fast. Why are you bringing that up?

—It happened right after the *Time* article. Beautiful rising oncologist — one of America's many hopes for curing cancer. That must have been a hell of a lot of pressure.

—Don't be absurd. I could have continued my work in this chair.

—But you accepted the switch to administration. To head the hospital.

—When did you become a shrink, Michael?

I hear a hint of tears in her voice.

—Shannon, I didn't mean to hurt you. The point is, our minds and psyches work in mysterious ways. Yours, mine, everyone's.

—Don't you think I haven't wondered about that a thousand times? Talked to a shrink about it? Sometimes a cigar. . .

— . . . can burn the house down.

We pause. I can hear Morgan's slow, regular breathing. I can almost hear Shannon's heart beating.

—Very well. What's done is done. I will always owe you and the sergeant for saving the hospital. But you sure have screwed up my ophtho department.

—Sorry about that.

—It's not your problem. Though actually, it is. At the parade the other day, during the speech I never made, I was going to make an announcement. That's why I wanted you there. Last week the board chose you to be Chairman of Medical Services.

—And I went and screwed it up for you.

—On the contrary. Did you think you were going to keep doing surgery without eyes? I would have had to let you go, despite all your experience. But for administration, as you so disdainfully put it, you don't need eyes. Just a good secretary, which we already have in that office, and a voice-operated computer, which I can get here in two days. It will be in your new office when you're ready to move up there.

—Shannon, don't be silly. The board won't approve that.

—The board has already chosen you. They won't be asked again. We'll make the announcement immediately, before they hear about your . . . accident. And think of the publicity. Cal Coastal is now run by two handicapped doctors. Physically challenged? Whatever the hell is pc these days. We'll be the poster hospital for the handicapped. A double example of beating the odds. If you hadn't done this to yourself, maybe I'd have done it for you. . . . Look, a smile. I'm glad you didn't stab that away. I'm excited, Michael. We'll make a great team. They'll probably demand that you meet with Dr. Worthington, though, to get his opinion.

—The head shrink?

—Director of Behavioral Health, he prefers to be called.

—As our ex-president famously said, Bring 'im on. But perhaps I could work for a week or two first, to prove my capabilities. In case Worthington is narrow minded about self-mutilation. Most suicides are not crazy. This was far less than suicide.

—It should be an interesting session, you and Worthington. But I like your idea. Your first assignment, of course, is to find a replacement for yourself in ophtho.

She wheels closer, takes my hand in hers. Her voice softens to almost a whisper.

—Michael, I can't say I understand what you did. Maybe some day I will. But I just had a thought. Between us we make one whole person. In the sense that you can push my wheelchair, and I can tell you in which direction. At home, I mean. You're welcome to move in with me. My home is already handicapped accessible. No door jambs. Ramps instead of stairs, and so forth. Just what you're going to need. In case you haven't thought about practical things like that. You'll have lots of decisions to make. Whether to rely only on a cane, or get a trained dog, for instance.

—One thing I never thought about is driving. For my reading, almost every book comes on tape these days. I never watch television, rarely see movies any more. But I won't be able to drive.

—I have a limousine and driver on call. It came with the job. If we try this, and it doesn't work out, the raise you'll be getting as Director of Meds will cover many amenities.

—I don't know. I don't want to be a burden on anyone.

—Sometimes living alone gets lonely. And Michael — in case you're wondering — I'm still functional in the important ways. You can discover that while sober this time.

She squeezes my hand.

—I don't expect an answer now. It just occurred to me. But think about it. We've always liked each other, you and I, in our ornery ways.

—There's Morgan.

—Yes. There's Morgan. I'm not proposing marriage. But how long are you going to allow her to run your life, practically from the grave?

—You can be harsh sometimes, Madam President.

—It's the truth.

I wince, if you can wince without eyes. I squeeze her hand, hard, then fiercely.

—What's wrong? I don't think that's a friendly squeeze.

—My eyes are starting to hurt like hell. Where's the bell for the nurse? I need more painkiller.

Yet the pain is the point, is it not. The pain is the first punishment. Perhaps the Tetravisc was a mistake. But jabbing that blade into an untendered eye, the pain would have been so excruciating I would have gone into shock. I would not have been able to finish. I would still have full sight in one eye. A one-eyed man can see as well as a two-eyed man, except for depth perception. So what would have been accomplished? The painkiller was necessary to allow me to complete what I intended.

She fumbles along my arm to find the button. Pushes it. A high-pitched buzzer begins that alerts the nurses' station. A nurse arrives almost immediately. Perhaps they know the president is here.

—Nurse, Dr. Lee needs more painkiller. Quickly.

—Coming right up, doctor.

Her footsteps hurry away. I place my hand on my face.

—What the hell have they got on my eyes? This is not a bandage. It feels like breasts.

—Get your mind out of the boudoir. It's two black eye patches. Dr. Roberts says the tissues will heal better if exposed to the air. You can sleep without them. The patches are for the comfort of your visitors. You can do without them any time, if people can stomach looking at the white globes with the strange name.

—Hydroxyappetite.

—Where the hell did they get that from?

—I have no idea.

— Roberts says it will take a few weeks for the artist to finish the contact that replicates your right eye.

—What you mean, my right eye. They took both.

—They didn't. The left . . .injury . . . missed the ocular nerve. Your sight will return in that one. After some surgeries, of course.

I'm not sure if I'm disappointed or elated. Or even awake.

—In the old days they just popped in a glass eye. A lot simpler. I've got a whole collection to choose from.

—So I've heard.

Footsteps return, the nurse jabs me with morphine, or something. I don't care what. My eyes are burning like the fires of Hell.

—What do you mean, matches my right eye? What about the left?

—Roberts didn't order that yet.

—Why not?

—Don't get your hopes up, Michael. She says your aim was lousy, the blade in the left missed the optic nerve and didn't reach the retina. You lacerated the cornea, and will need a transplant, plus cataract work. But there's a chance you'll regain some sight.

—That was not the point!

—I will ignore your lousy pun.

She presses my wrist. I missed the optic nerve? Did Nia grab me at the last instant, twist my arm away? Or did I chicken out?

A new obsession. Will I ever know?

—By the way, about the sergeant's cover story, an exploding gas grill. It won't wash. You're not burned enough. I asked Dr. Roberts to come up with a better one. That spunky intern said, I'm a doctor, I do truth, I don't do cover stories. So I told her, I'm the hospital director — and I do. And you will, too, to protect Dr. Lee. She was quick about it then. She said someone rear-ended your car, and the airbag exploded and blinded you. It's been known to happen.

—My sweet protégé, I murmur hazily, as the morphine pulls me under, away from the lie.

What happened next I did not understand until Rachel Weitz, the psychologist turned rabbi, turned the myth of my life upside down. But that was a week later.

Today I was coming up from drug-induced sleep — I don't know for how long the morphine had put me out — when I heard a voice I had not heard in two years. Morgan. I was shocked, disbelieving. She told me I was blind. I said I know that, dear. She said she did not mean only now, that I had been blind ever since we met. And a fool. What are you talking about? I asked. You come out of your coma to tell me that? The sunglasses, she said. You've spent forty years agitating about the sunglasses. Those sunglasses you stole did not mean a thing. What are you saying? I asked. I'm saying I was there, behind a tree. With an experimental laser I borrowed from work. When the bus came around the curve I zapped the driver with the laser. Burned out his eyes in an instant. Blindness and pain is why he lost control of the bus and plunged into the river. If he were wearing his sunglasses they would not have saved him. The glasses would have melted in a nanosecond before the laser destroyed his eyes. The police report never mentioned the term, of course. Lasers were not yet known to the public.

—This is nonsense, Morgan. Why would you do such a thing? Murder twelve innocent people, with malice and intent.

—Think, she says.

—You come out of a two-year coma to tell me that?

Then a delayed reaction — out of her coma! I fumble for the assistance bell. After a minute or so a nurse comes in to see what I need.

—My wife, nurse. She's alive, I mean, she's awake. She's come out of her coma, she's talking to me. Get a doctor. Max Klonsky, if he is around.

—I don't think so, Dr. Lee.

—What do you mean, you don't think so. We were just having a conversation. Check her vital signs. Get a doctor in here. It's amazing.

The unhurried nurse is straightening the pillow behind my head.

—Keep calm, doctor. When was this conversation between you?

—Just now. Two minutes ago. Morgan, tell them.

No response.

—Is there a curtain around me? Please pull it open.

She swings the curtain open. I hear it on its tracks.

—I can't see, of course. Is she sitting? Are her eyes open?

—Dr. Lee, I'm sorry to tell you this. But there is no one in that bed. Morgan Albright passed away two hours ago. You were deep in a morphine sleep, so we did not wake you. There seemed no point.

—How do you know she passed away?

—She stopped breathing. Her heart stopped beating, she had no pulse. Her brain flat-lined. There was no brain activity whatsoever. We did all the usual checks. We waited fifteen minutes. Then in fact we did call in Dr Klonsky. He verified that she was dead. He signed the certificate. Death came at 2:20 p.m., October 16, 2009.

—Where is she now?

—In the basement morgue. If you want to see her . . . that is . . .

—But she was just speaking to me. Minutes ago.

—Drugs can cause all sorts of abnormal reactions in the brain. You know that, doctor.

I suppose I do. But I don't believe for a minute that I was hallucinating. Damned if I do. This was different in kind than the dead women in my patients' eyes. More palpable. A clearer voice.

—Is there anything else, doctor?

—Did you say today is the 16th?

—Yes, sir.

The very anniversary. I had no conscious idea when I was jabbing myself. I should be home playing the drums, as I do every October 16th. Beating up a storm. Drums I can still play while blind.

— I need to think, nurse. I'll buzz if my eyes start hurting.

—We'll be listening.

I can't do anything for the pain in my chest, my stomach. The anxiety ridden agony of losing Nia — a new life with her, a fantasy that seemed not worth living without. My incomparably joyful and passionate third act. Now I will have a different third act. An ultimate distraction from the pain of Nia. The pain of learning to be blind.

I could have practiced beforehand. Walking the house again and again with eyes closed, learning where the things are that go bump in the night. I did not think of it. Oedipus, the fraud outside the bank, would have had no need. For Oedipus, the King of Thebes, to have done so would have been unseemly.

Sounds I hear as a patient, which I never noticed before. The beep of nurses being summoned. Gurneys being rolled down the corridor. Larger metal cabinets, perhaps filled with empty food trays, rolling by sounding like caissons. The mumble of relatives outside the rooms of patients, sometimes talking on cell phones. The PA paging a doctor. Vital signs equipment being rolled into my room.

—Not again, I say to the nurse.

—It's required, doctor.

She puffs a rubber sleeve around my arm for blood pressure. Clip attached to my finger for blood oxygen level. Thermometer under my tongue.

—You seem to be doing fine, Dr. Lee. There's no reason not to send you home fairly soon. Dr. Roberts will decide.

How will I find my way around the house?

I hear a slight sniffle at the foot of my bed after the nurse leaves.

—Michael, are you awake?

—Victoria?

—It's hard to tell with your eyes covered.

Her slim body depresses the side of my bed, but does not tilt the mattress much.

—Thank you for coming.

—I watched the surgery. Dr. Roberts is good. Then I came here four times. There was not much else to do, we canceled your surgeries for today of course. You either had a visitor, or were asleep, or your wife was being taken out. My condolences, Michael, I'm sorry about Morgan.

—It's for the best. How long would anyone want to live like that? But I have to tell you something. Before I did this, there were two things I didn't take into account. The first, as I was telling Dr. Kelly, is that I forgot I would not be able to drive. The second thing is that never again would I see your lovely face. Your beautiful hair.

—But you can. Whenever you want.

She takes my right hand in hers, loosens the fingers that I didn't realize were clenched with nerves. Places my fingertips on her forehead. Moves them down slowly over her closed eyes. Over her small nose. Her cheek bones, her cheeks. Her soft lips. Her chin. The back of her neck, where her hair flows smooth as obsidian.

—There. That's my face. The lips are hardest to remember.

She returns my fingers to her lips. Presses them firmly against her.

—Some day will you explain to me why you did this? Some reasons I know. The faces of the dead women were taking a toll on your nerves. I could see that. Your love for the sergeant, who was engaged to your son. How could you not fall for this gorgeous young woman who was living with you? That must have been excruciating.

—She's breaking off with him.

—So you took the opportunity to press your suit. And she turned you away. That much I can guess at.

—You see a lot that no one else notices, Vicky. I guess I've said that before.

—You probably feel guilty about the scar on her face.

—I nearly got her killed!

— To save the hospital. Save hundreds of lives. Which the two of you did. You take blame for everything, and credit for nothing.

—That's in my genes.

—Congratulations, by the way, Director of Meds. It was just e-mailed to every department. I should have congratulated you right away. You'll do great.

I realize she is still holding my hand. Pressing it to her lips. I feel a tingling in my crotch.

—I'm sorry we won't be working together any more, she says. But perhaps we could have lunch together in your office sometimes, like we used to do.

—I'd like that.

—The thing that troubles me most is what to tell Maya. She really likes you. With all the violence going on around her, this might freak her out. Really affect her. How could she possibly understand a thing like this? It's hard for all of us to understand.

—There's a cover story floating around. About a car accident. Why not tell her that?

—I hate to lie to her. I rarely do. But in this case I probably should. By the way, thank Sergeant Ruiz for me, if I don't see her. That was so nice, what she did with the press. Keeping Maya out of the story. Thinking of Maya so quickly. I can see it would be hard not to love her.

—I fell hard, Vicky. Like an old fool. No one else knows, I don't think. But I have to get over it. The blade was my first step. With two jabs I made her invisible, and myself undesirable.

—Let me know what I can do to help, Michael. Drive you home, bring you meals.

—Kiss your fingers? That is already calming. Meanwhile, Nia's still here to help at home.

—That will make it difficult to forget her.

—Yes. I do have another idea.

I hear the heavy fall of combat boots near the doorway.

—Oh, I'm sorry. I didn't realize Michael had a visitor.

—That's all right, sergeant. I was just leaving. I have to pick up my daughter. And thank you — I was just telling Dr. Lee — thank you for protecting her from the press.

—No problem. Anyone would have done it.

—Few people would have thought of it so quickly. Thought of the child, after what you had done, while you were hurting. I can see why Dr. Lee likes you.

I wonder if Nia is blushing. One of a thousand things I'll have to learn to do without. Reading people's faces.

—I have to go, Vicky says. I'll leave you two alone.

Much to my surprise, and knowing what she knows, she has the audacity to kiss my cheek before leaving.

Nia's faint perfume mixed with her sweat after a day at the recruiting office clutches at my chest. Enucleation doesn't affect the sense of smell. Nor does it diminish my mournful joy at the sound of her voice. I am not over loving her in a day. I may not be over loving her in a life. The physical pain after the car crash, the fractured pelvis, the fractured vertebrae, induced her to move in with me while Mickey was overseas. Having confessed my infatuation could very well lead her to move out. Cutting Mickey out of her life could very easily lead her to move out; it would create gossip about us living together that was not there until now. With the MVR blade I have made myself helpless. Is that what this was truly about, subconsciously? An attempt to induce her to stay, to take care of me, out of guilt? This did not occur to me until now. I shudder. My action was rooted in consequences much larger than that. The need for penance for the dead women, for justice. The need to change my life in this last phase. I cannot allow her to stay on my account. She takes on guilt like a sponge absorbs water. As do I. She has to get out in the world, see other men, now that Mickey has been banished. Yet the thought of her seeing other men, sleeping with them, is a far greater anguish than if she had returned to Mickey, with whom she had already done that. No other men, Nia! I am the heir to your throne, after Mickey. I truly feel that. Some kind of reverse primogeniture. The thought of others with her makes me want to die. Which I considered before the blinding. I certainly cannot deal with that while she is living with me. Do I throw her out? The town hero? The woman I love?

—Nia. You've come because you've repented. You've changed your mind. You've seen the light! You miss me. Come, crawl into my bed.

I can tell without seeing her that she is grinning.

—Don't put your hopes in that, Michael. I've come because I just got off work. How are you doing?

—Blind as a bat, but otherwise okay.

Blind, I don't see her clothing. Only her nakedness.

—I've been worrying about you all day. About how you'll manage around the house, even if you get rides back and forth to work. Because Michael, I have to move out. Not because I don't love you, I do, in my nonromantic way. Like a favorite uncle. But the way you feel, I think you need a break from me. I'm not worthy of the kind of love you profess, but no matter. You have to let it die, for your own sake. So you can get on with your life. And your feelings are not likely to die with me in the house, sleeping, showering, whatever it is about me that turns you on. I hope that out of some reasoning I don't understand, you didn't blind yourself because of me. I'm afraid you did, and that thought is hard to bear. So I have to move out, for both our sakes.

—I know you do. I was preparing to kick you out, if you didn't go voluntarily. Which is a lie, I still love your voice, your very being, being around you. I was stupid, engaged in a fantasy that was so real to me I could eat it like chocolate. It's not your fault. I fell in love because of who you are, not because of anything you did. You're a very special person, Yessenia Ruiz.

She sits on my bed, a heavier presence than Vicky was.

—But what are you going to do, until you learn the ways of the blind? I'll stay the first few days, of course. I'll need to find an apartment anyway. Probably one nearer to San Jose. But then what?

—I'll herky-jerk around, uncertain which way to turn, like a mouse in a maze, till I learn the lay of the land. So to speak. Or like three blind mice. How the hell did those mice go blind, by the way? The farmer's wife? No, she cut off their tails — after they were already blind. Perhaps I could have helped them. I remember asking my mother when I was a kid why the mice were blind, how they got that way. By the third time I asked she told me stop asking foolish questions. Personally, I still think the question is valid. Anyway, if I find I need assistance, I can hire someone to chauffeur me around, cook meals. But I've had a better idea. Annabel. Her car is falling apart. She can have my Camry. Plus a salary for moving in with me, driving, cooking sometimes. Though I don't mind frozen pizza, as she does. She'll have room and board. She can bring her loom out here, I'll get rid of my drums, she can set up her studio in the garage. She'll have plenty of time to weave without going out hustling to sell her stuff if she isn't ready. Or maybe she'll catch on in one of the galleries around Carmel. Big Sur. What do you think?

—I think she'd jump at the idea. She hates Santa Fe right now. She told me that last week. She said everybody's a phony. She has no real friendships. The men are afraid to commit. She tends to get attached quickly. She's got someone there she needs to get away from.

—Or some two.

—Or some two. This would be perfect for both of you. I'm not sure about the Camry, though. She'd want to trade it in for something cool.

—It would be hers, she could do whatever she wants with it. This would be just until we see how things shake out. Once I'm more self-reliant, she could stay or go.

—Call her, Michael, she'll be thrilled. And she'll keep things lively for you. She's a kick. We have such different personalities, me and Annabel — yet we've gotten very close very quickly.

—She's a joy to be around.

— And listen. You didn't need to blind yourself, Michael, to hide from my scar.

— I should swat you for that.

—We need to start loosening up about both — my scar and your eyes. I told you, I like the scar. It beats a tattoo nine ways. I hate my clean-cut image. The scar makes me look like a tough broad who's been around. As for you, okay, you didn't do it on account of me. I'll try to accept that. You want to hear what I think might be the real reason, with my junior college psychology? Don't get mad. I think maybe you see yourself as a tragic hero, like in the ancient Greek plays. Or would like to be one. Blinding yourself announces it to the world.

Her perspicacity astonishes me. I have noticed that more in Vicky.

— I'll have to think about that.

—One last thing, which occurred to me today. In all the months we've been together, you've never asked me what Yessenia means.

—What it means? Do names have to mean something? Michael, Vicky, Shannon, they don't mean anything.

—Well, Spanish names often do.

—And Yessenia means?

—God Sees.

I try to blink but have no eyes. I try to close the eyes that are not there.

—That's a joke, right?

—It's not a joke among us Mexicans. Or half-Mexicans.

—God does not exist. If he does, there is much evidence that he, too, is blind.

I feel her weight shifting on the bed, her breath coming towards me. Her light perfume. Her lips press against mine. A firm, hard kiss. The first. The only.

—Thank you, Nia.

A gift for my memory banks.

Chapter 19: Murder

I'm allowed to return home the next day. Vicky drives me, turns me over to Nia, who leads me around the house, makes me count steps from room to room, again, again. I bang my knees and ankles many times, even while wielding a blind man's cane. She arranges the clothing in my closet to be color-coordinated, though with solid chinos, solid shirts, solid blazers, I can never go too far wrong. My predecessor in the top doc job wore ties but I have no need to adopt his way, this is California. Why add a daily problem that isn't necessary? I could wear clip-on bow ties but I hate them. Annabel accepted my offer in an instant, flew on my credit card with her necessaries crammed into a duffel bag, arranged to have a friend with a pickup drive out soon with her loom and her boxes of yarn. After two days Nia found a loft she liked near San Jose, and the transition was complete. As we hugged goodbye we vowed to keep in touch. We'll see.

The office is an alternation of frustration and success. Like stepping on the bathroom scale every day when you're dieting and cheating. Talia Rice, the secretary I inherited, is even better than Shannon had said. By the time I got there she'd rearranged parts of the office to be more convenient for me, getting rid of unnecessary obstacles. A voice operated computer was there in two days, as Shannon promised. Talia had the operator's manuel overnighted to her and was well acquainted with the machine by the time I arrived. She teaches me the basics. Patiently. She goes over the most pressing problems I need to deal with, then some of the long range projects already underway. The first thing I act on is dictating an ad for a new cataract specialist, to be placed in newspapers in San Francisco, LA, Denver, Chicago, New York. When I pause, finished with the ad, Talia asks, how about the Internet? Yes, the Internet too, I say. You'll have to keep reminding me of that. I'm Peking Man in that area.

I'm not sure if she knows that Peking Man was a fraud. It doesn't matter, I know it.

Getting used to the voice computer is strange — rather like an arranged marriage. To ask a question of the air and have a metal voice like Hal in *2001* tell you the answer. Talia says there is a choice of voices, which amazes me. I tell her to find one sort of like hers. Blindness doesn't castrate you. She's already, with Shannon's permission, ordered a Braille printer. Now all I have to do is learn Braille. I hope with my surgeon's sensitive fingers I can pick it up quickly. I ask Talia how much money she is making, and immediately put through a ten percent raise. I'll be leaning on her a lot.

Shannon comes by to visit each of the first few days, Maxie, Lacey and Vicky more than once a day. When the police captain, Stenny Doyle, drops by, it's awkward. We avoid the subject of my eyes, mostly we talk about his boy. He's doing well in basketball, which is good to hear. It is rare that you get feedbacks in ophtho. The Marine with the anchor in his head will be going home in a few days, Maxie says, not much the worse for wear, except for his missing eye. He's been given a medical discharge, with no official investigation into how his wound occurred. It was an accident after all, even if the guys had been drinking. Speaking of Marines, still no word from my son, unless he's made contact with Nia via e-mail in the last few days. Stupid shit.

My one disappointment in the realm of visitors is Rachel Weitz. The rabbi does not come by or even call, which surprises me, and hurts a little. I'd thought we liked each other. My accident — as everyone is starting to refer to it, for lack of a better word — had not been in the newspapers. The hospital, which does major advertising for its senior plan and other programs, may have had a hand in that. I'm not sure. But certainly Maxie would have told Rachel. I asked him. He said he had, a few days ago.

Then she calls. Monday afternoon, a week into my new job. She sounds awfully hesitant. Apologizes for not having called or come by sooner.

—I've discovered some things you don't know, she says. I've been debating for days whether to reveal them to you or not. You might be devastated. Or you might be thrilled. I'm not sure. Finally I decided that both as a psychologist and a rabbi, I believe in truth. As a scientist, you must also. So I've come down on the side of candor. I don't want to spend my days, and especially my nights, knowing more about your life than you do.

A worrisome feeling nestles in my gut at this odd little speech.

—Is today a good day to come by?

—You've got me on edge now, rabbi. The sooner the better.

—I can make it at 4:45. After my Hebrew School class.

I send Talia home early, she's done more than enough work. Try to relax in my leather swivel chair, hands hooked on my belt. I have no idea what the rabbi wants to talk about. Finally I hear her footsteps, the sexy hard click of heels coming down the corridor, pausing outside my open door.

—Rabbi? Come in.

I stand and offer my hand, which she shakes. I tell her to sit where she likes. She chooses the nearest seat on the leather couch.

—I won't ask about your eyes, she says. We can discuss that another time, if you like. Or not. For now I need to give you information I've discovered. I hope you won't hate me afterward.

—I can't imagine hating you for anything. What have you discovered?

She shifts in her seat, perhaps smoothing her skirt under her. The rustle of an envelope is clear. I'm getting better at identifying little sounds.

—I could tell you the essence in one sentence, Dr. Lee.

—Call me Michael.

—Michael. But you would not believe me. I prefer to tell you step by step. The way a prosecutor does in court. Not that anybody is being prosecuted. It's just the logical order, the way I acquired the information. It kind of builds the case.

—What case? You've got my attention, Rabbi. Please get on with it.

So she does. As follows:

After I told her, that Sunday in her office, how I had killed eleven nurses — and now bring them back to life in my head — she was very curious. She'd never heard of the terrible bus incident, though of course she was not yet born in 1969. So she went online and Googled Dead Nurses. There were many, but not eleven in one bus crash. Bus Crash Kills Nurses. Bus Plunges Into River. She found plenty of those, mostly in Mexico or the South, but none off Riker's Island, none with eleven nurses. She tries every combination of key words she could think of. No mention of it. Google did not find the story. She decided to Google the New York newspapers for October 16 and 17, 1969. They had to have it. In the New York *Daily Mirror* she found the short bulletin I had told her about. It mentioned the crash, but gave no other details. There were lots of stories and pictures about the New York Mets' World Series victory, a smaller one about the peace march in Washington. The next day's *Mirror,* she expected, would have a complete story about the nurses. But there was no mention of them. Nor the day after that. This was becoming a puzzle. She called up the web site of the paper of record, *The New York Times.* Found a big story on the peace march. Many stories on the Mets. Nothing anywhere on a bus crash that killed nurses. Not that day, or the next. Frustrated, she went to the *New York Daily News,* the largest circulation paper in the city. Nothing.

Now she knew something was wrong. Amiss was the word she used. Like in a P.D. James mystery. But her Internet skills are limited, like mine. She decided to call in a favor. A youngish reporter at the *San Francisco Chronicle,* Jack Diamond, who had started on the police beat but now covered religious issues, was an acquaintance of hers. He'd call her whenever he needed quotes from Jewish leaders, or background on Jewish issues. Diamond had grown up with the Internet. She told him her problem. There were a lot of search engines and data bases besides Google, he told her. He'd call back. When he did, several hours later, he told her the bus crash story did not appear anywhere. Either it somehow had been purged from the public records, or it had never happened.

— Rachel, none of this makes sense. I was there. Why would anyone purge it from the records?

—Let me continue, okay? Jack had comp time coming, he'd just finished a long series on the Middle East. And he was getting intrigued by the missing nurses. He agreed to repay his favors from me big time. I gave him the names I'd written down of four of the nurses you had mentioned. He wanted to check them out.

The first thing he did was obtain a duty roster of all the nurses working at the Rikers Island hospital in the fall of 1969. Two of your nurses were on it. But two were not. If they did not work there, why were they on the bus that day? He went back a year, to the 1968 roster of nurses. There he found all four names. Two had left that spring.

—This was 1969, rabbi. No one was celebrating the Mets in 1968.

—I know. We put our heads together. Jack, a natural born cynic, decided to research the four individuals. Mona, Janelle, Ginger. I forget the other.

—Addie.

—No, Addie was not the one I wrote down, I wasn't taking notes yet when you spoke of her. It took him two days. He e-mailed me his report. Mona Drew is not singing in Paris.

—I know that, I told you I made up their new lives.

—Mona in fact returned to upstate New York in 1983. She died in a car crash on an icy road in 1987.

—Not possible! She was dead, what, eighteen years by then.

—I'll continue. According to Jack, Janelle Williams is working in a home for the elderly in Baton Rouge.

—Is working?

—Jack spoke with her last week. A nice lady, he said. Virginia Soto, called Ginny, left Rikers in 1979 to return to her clerical order. She died of stomach cancer in 1991.

—Rabbi, I don't believe a word of this. What you're saying is that the bus crash did not take place. At least not with these nurses.

—Exactly.

—That can't be. I saw it. I can still see it. I will never forget the yellow bus being lifted from the river, water running down the sides, into the hair of the dead nurses hanging out the windows. Let me get Maxie down here. He saw it, too.

—Don't bother, Michael. I've already spoken to Dr. Klonsky. That was my next step. I told him it was interesting how you two met that day at the scene of the bus crash. Dr. Klonsky looked puzzled. He said he had never been on Rikers Island in his life.

—He's lying! But why?

—Then where did you guys meet, I asked. He said you met as interns at Stanford in 1971. Hit if off right away. Began talking about exploring the visual pathway, you working from the retina back, him working from the brain down.

—He was there!

— You can argue with him if you want. But let me finish first.

—Hold on a minute, Rachel. You're making me sound crazy. Like I made this all up. But three months later I visited Addie Judd's grave. On Long Island. The stone had her dates etched in it. The date of death was October 16, 1969. It must still be there.

—I'm sure it is. Because Addie Judd did die on Rikers Island that day. But she was the only one. And it was not in a bus crash.

—You've really got my head spinning, Rabbi.

—I can imagine. But just hang on. When I looked again at the list of nurses who did work there in 1969, the name Addie Judd rang a bell. She was your sweetheart. Your secret sweetheart at the time. You were going to meet her that night, celebrate her birthday, your first reunion since London. Probably you would make love for the first time, you said. So I Googled Addie Judd, expecting nothing. And a mass of material came up. Mostly from *Newsday*, the Long Island paper, where Addie Judd's parents lived. Her absence from the bus that day was not particularly noted by the other riders, people often changed their routine. You probably know this, I didn't, but often nurses work twelve hour shifts. Three days on and four days off. It so happened Addie was not scheduled to work again for the next four days. So her absence at the prison hospital was not noticed until then. When she did not show up, and did not call in sick, her supervisor telephoned her apartment repeatedly, and got no answer. This was before cell phones, of course. He called her parents' home. They had not heard from her in a week, which was not too unusual. Only then was she reported as a missing person. That was the first mention in the paper, in *Newsday*. Long Island Nurse Reported Missing, a small item. The next day, the 22nd, the body of a nurse washed up against pier pilings in lower Manhattan. It proved to be Addie Judd.

—So she did drown!

—Actually, she did not. This is what I hate to tell you. An autopsy was performed. Ms. Judd had been stabbed repeatedly in the chest, in the heart. The first cut probably in her larynx, so she could not cry out. This was all after she had been rendered defenseless by acid thrown in her eyes. The medical examiner could not determine what type of acid. But he said the small but deep stabs into her body seemed to have been made by a blade used by eye doctors — an MVR blade, he called it, which left distinctive cuts because of the shape of the point. Like an arrow head. With a confirmed murder on their hands, the police went to work. They interviewed nurses who remembered Addie not being on the bus on the 16th. They asked if she had a boyfriend. No one knew, but two people recalled seeing a tall young man speaking with Addie as she left the nurses' quarters, possibly on her way to the bus. She walked behind the building with the man. That was the last known sighting of her, until her body was found. The witnesses described this man as white, tall, thin, wearing a white lab coat and a New York Giants baseball cap — even though the Giants had moved to San Francisco more than ten years earlier.

—Rachel, that's a description of me back then. You're saying I killed her and don't remember? That's crazy. I loved that girl. I had no reason to kill her. This whole story is getting insane.

—Actually, you were investigated, and cleared.

—I was investigated? Never.

—A few days after the body was found, a bloody lab coat was unearthed in a garbage scow that collected refuse from the trash cans on Rikers. The blood type matched Addie Judd's. In the pocket of the coat was an MVR blade, just as the ME had suggested. Blood caught in the flanged tip also matched Addie Judd's.

Also found there was a Giants baseball cap. In mint condition, except for garbage stains, suggesting it was newly bought.

—What do you mean I was investigated? I was never questioned.

—Once police found the coat and blade, they decided the most likely suspect would be a medical student. Detectives began by going over class records for October 16th in every medical school in and around the city. At the alleged time of the killing on Rikers, you were taking a major exam at Columbia. You had signed in for the test in the morning, along with twenty other students. The doors had been locked all day, to prevent cheating. The professor vouched that he himself had seen to it that no one left the room. He had even accompanied those who did to the rest rooms and waited outside. There was a lot of tension in the exam room, he told police, because you guys wanted to be watching the World Series on TV. You all signed out of the room around 6 pm. Given it would take at least half an hour to get from Columbia to Rikers Island, this would have been long after the man in the Giants cap was seen with Ms. Judd. Back then med students didn't choose their specialties, like ophthalmology, until they were interns in a hospital. No viable suspect was ever found in the killing.

That was faulty reasoning by the police, I told her. It's possible an MVR blade could be in a med school, but they're definitely in hospital ophthal departments. That's where they should have looked.

—Apparently someone set them straight, because that's where they looked next. Plus private eye doctors. Medical supply stores. Anyone could walk in off the street and buy that kind of blade. They got nowhere. Not one real suspect. Forty years later, it's still technically an open case.

—But . . .

I was flabbergasted, my mind racing for an explanation, around and around like a stupid NASCAR race.

—The bus, the water, I saw it all. I even dove in and got soaked.

—At that time you were in class at Columbia Med School. Dr. Ralph Franken's class. The records prove it. The signatures match yours.

—Are you trying to make me lose my mind? Of course, half the staff here believes I lost it already, when I blinded myself. Do you have an explanation for any of this? Because I sure don't.

—I have a theory. But I'm parched from talking so much. Could I have a glass of water?

I stand and rather expertly find my way in my new state of perpetual dark to the water cooler in the corner. I fill a paper cup and hand it to her. Fill one for myself.

So the rabbi has a theory. Einstein had a theory. Now it is just called Relativity. Whereas Darwin's Theory is still labeled just that by those who will not admit to the myriad facts of its proof. Did Newton ever have a Theory of Gravity? If so, I never heard of it. Just Gravity. My own theory of my life at this moment as I sit in self-induced darkness in my leather swivel chair is closest to the attitude of the anti-evolutionists. I believe what happened on Rikers Island that day is exactly what I have believed for nearly forty years. Sunglasses, bus, crash, eleven women dead. Those facts have been the skeleton, the weak backbone, of my existence, from the moment Addie died until the moment I fell in love with Nia. For weeks while mourning Addie and the others I used to wait for a bus outside Columbia Med — but not at a bus stop. In between bus stops. Telling myself to hurl myself under a bus as it was speeding by. Let the punishment fit the crime.

But I never did.

With one exception, everything else in my life has carried no more weight than a Christmas ornament. A glass angel hanging by a thread. The exception of course being our breakthrough, mine and Maxie's, into the visual pathway, so long ago. Like the anti-evolutionists — what do they call it, Divine Intelligence? — I have heard the rabbi's evidence that it did not happen, and I cannot give it credence. I know what I did, I know what I saw, I know that the dead are dead. But as a man of science, in the face of her investigations I must keep listening to her theory.

—Do you know the word confabulation, doctor?

—I've heard it. I suspect I knew its meaning once. I don't now.

—Confabulation means false memories. Also defined as choice blindness, with supportive bias. Sometimes called an availability cascade — a self-reinforcing process in which a false belief gains plausibility through increasing repetition.

—In other words, your theory is that I made this all up. That I chose to live my life suffering under a nonexistent burden.

—No. No. Not at all. You couldn't have made it up by yourself. Mainly because you had no reason to.

—You're losing me, Rabbi.

—You can still call me Rachel. I'm not a threat to you. Well, perhaps I am. But let me proceed. When you went off to Oxford for the summer, Morgan told you to come back with a British accent. Like her favorite actor, Lawrence Harvey. A slim, handsome fellow. Do you know what Harvey's most successful film was?

—Sure. It's a classic. Came out long before we met, but is still shown in reruns all the time at two theaters near Columbia, the *Thalia* and the *New Yorker*. *The Manchurian Candidate*. Morgan saw it half a dozen times, at least. I went with her twice.

—Do you recall the story?

—Angela Lansbury as an evil society mother. Her son is captured fighting in Korea, is brainwashed by the Communists, comes back to this country as a sleeper assassin. He's supposed to kill the president. The one thing I can never remember, it's been so long since I saw it, is who the brainwashed assassin was, Lawrence Harvey or Frank Sinatra.

—It was Lawrence Harvey.

—And this movie is relevant how?

—Only in the context of other details. Did you ever meet Morgan's father?

—Of course. He gave her away at our wedding. A few times before and after that. We were not close.

—Do you know what he did for a living?

—He was a psychiatrist.

—Do you know what his specialty was?

—Not really. Mostly we met at fancy dinner parties. Shop talk was frowned upon.

—Let me tell you. His specialty was hypnotism. After the Korean war, when brainwashing became a household word, he was fascinated by it. Intrigued by the possibilities. He interviewed some of the returning servicemen. Conducted experiments. He wrote a scientific paper on the subject that was published in American Science in 1967, exploring the methodology of long-term hypnosis. He even referred to the fictional *Manchurian Candidate.*

Cold sweat appears on my forehead like dew. My open collar feels too tight. The room has gotten warm. Anxiety crawls along my arms like ants.

—I don't like where this is going, Rabbi. You're telling me that someone, Morgan, I suspect, fed into my mind all the details of a nonexistent bus crash? Not possible. Even if she had a reason.

—When I described the tall, thin probable killer, you said it sounded like you. Who else could look like that — with her hair pushed up under the cap?

—You're saying Morgan murdered Addie?

—Don't be in denial, Michael. I can give you a hundred classic quotations on her motive. Let's settle for one: Hell hath no fury like a woman scorned. You had just jilted Morgan. Broken off a very public engagement. In favor of Addie, whom you were crazy about. Morgan wanted you. Perhaps she loved you, as much as she could love anyone. With Addie out of the way, she figured, she could get you back. As she did.

I'm shaking my head no even as I explore yes. This is making my teeth ache.

—Let's say that's true. Let's say she killed Addie. Christ, how her death that day still torments me. But let's say it was Morgan — stabbing, torturing her with tiny cuts. Jesus! I'm beginning to visualize it without any eyes. But where did I get the bus crash into my head? How? Why?

—If the truth of how Addie Judd died had come out quickly, you might have suspected Morgan at once. She had a clear motive. She was the only one who did. She fit the description of the killer. The unidentified acid thrown in Addie's face — Morgan worked for a laser company. She hit Addie with laser beams to her eyes to make the repeated stabbing simple, before pushing her into the river. Lasers were not introduced to the public until 1972 — three years later. You know how? In supermarket checkout stands, reading bar codes. Anyway, hearing how Addie really died, you would have gone to the police — if you didn't kill Morgan yourself in a rage. She wanted to blur your mind. Turn suspicion away from her. If she could make you believe the bus crash story, which she totally concocted, then Addie was not singled out to die, was not murdered, just one of eleven women in an accident. Morgan put you at the scene with the sunglasses story, to have a hold over you. Only she knew that you were partly responsible, in her scenario. This secret between you was a leash on you. To keep you in the marriage.

—I think you've been reading too many mystery stories, Rabbi.

—Fair enough. I have an envelope here with all the news stories about the murder. Mostly in *Newsday*, as I said, which did circulate in downtown Manhattan back then. You were in medical school, you had no time for the news anyway. Also in the envelope are tapes of the phone conversations Jack Diamond had with the living nurses who supposedly died on the bus. Also her father's paper on hypnosis. The question remains, how did she accomplish this complete and lasting brainwashing, if we can call it that. First of all, she was a child at home when her father was really into the brainwashing stuff. He must have talked about it, she must have heard things. Years later, when she decided to kill Addie, she put all of that to use. Was Morgan by any chance a gardener?

—That was her one hobby, besides spending money. She used to tell me that as a child she wanted to play in the dirt with seeds and flowers, but at their estate on Long Island they had a professional gardener. She was not even allowed to get dirty. When we moved out here, a requisite for a house was a large lawn, so she could grow her flowers, putter around.

—I didn't know that, but I suspected it was the case. Her repressed childhood desire coming out in a diverted psychological way. Years ago I came across a phrase in a text that I've always remembered, it was so vivid. The landscaping of the mind. I think that's what Morgan was doing with your head. Planting seed after seed, bush after bush.

What my head is doing now is wanting to spin in all directions. I grab the chair arms tight. The room is not spinning, without eyes dizziness is more like an internal carousel. But just as unnerving.

—You mean she made up the whole bus crash? How could she come up with such a complicated idea? That's madness.

—Well, Jack discovered a pretty likely source. Let me read you something he found on the Internet.

She lifts a piece of paper with computer print on it. And reads:

—*On March 4, 1963, a bus belonging to the Department of Hospitals of New York City suddenly left the road on Welfare Island and crashed into the East River. In addition to the driver, the vehicle carried ten persons employed by the Department. Of these, six, including the driver, died immediately by drowning, one succumbed one-half hour after the accident, and four survived. One body has not been recovered.*

My mouth is so dry I can barely rasp my words.

—Welfare Island, not Riker's Island? In 1963? I don't remember that.

—Well, Morgan clearly did. She killed off the four survivors and made it eleven dead, just for the fun of it. Her fake story was based on a certain reality. Just not yours.

—You're saying I've carried guilt for nearly forty years when I was totally innocent?

—Let's go back to that night, that week. It was Addie's birthday. You two planned to meet for dinner and then — who knows. Maybe whoopee. In Morgan's version, you decided to surprise Addie, you went to Rikers Island to meet her as she got off work. Maybe you carried flowers. You took the sunglasses from the dashboard of the bus, missed the bus, it went into the river, and so forth. You've spent your life repenting. But let's see what fits with the facts. Where were you supposed to meet, if you did not go to Rikers?

—Mr. Laff's. A bar on the East Side, owned by a ballplayer with the Yankees. Or former player. Phil Linz. A big baseball hangout. I figured we'd have a drink or two there, pick a place to eat, and so on. To whoopee, in your choice word.

—Okay. But Addie never showed. Because by 6 o'clock she was dead and in the river, probably weighted down with a cinderblock or something. So you're at the bar, waiting for her, the whole city is celebrating the lowly Mets winning the World Series, the streets are crowded, traffic is slow, you figure she went home from work to shower and change, maybe was having trouble getting a cab. After half an hour, you call her apartment. No answer. There was no voice mail back then. You have another drink, keep looking for her to come walking up the street, this girl of your dreams, whom you have not seen in over a month, not since London. Every time the phone in the bar was free you dialed her number. No answer. Either she'd stood you up, which would be unbearable, or something happened to her. She's hurt or something. Another few drinks and you can't stand it any more. You decide to go home, maybe she's been calling you there. Or left a note. But in your apartment there is no hint of her. So what did you do? Perhaps you called a few hospitals to see if she had been admitted, but she had not. Then you did same thing you did in Morgan's story. You started drinking everything you had, to still the pain in your gut, that feeling of wanting to cry. Maybe you did cry. When you ran out of booze you were in no condition to go downstairs and buy more. What to do? You called your old buddy, Morgan. She had taken the breakup so well, why not? Sure, she could come over, bring more booze. On the way over she picked up a copy of the *Daily Mirror*. She asked if you had seen this. The front page was all about the Mets victory, inside more Mets, plus the peace march in Washington. But there was a small bulletin on page three about a bus going off Rikers Island with eleven nurses and the driver aboard, and no known survivors. That was the kernel of reality that set up everything else, that made the whole story logical. You probably screamed, bawled. Addie was on that bus, that's why she didn't show! You were crushed, sobbing. Morgan holds you in her arms, but there is no comforting you. You remained drunk for a week, that's what you told me, and then had to make up the missed work. Did you ever get so drunk, Michael, aside from this time, that you couldn't remember much the next day?

—If I mix drinks, and really go at it, it happens. It seems I fathered a baby — a fetus — in that condition about ten years ago. I never knew about it until recently.

—Well, there you are. I don't know what kind of suggestive techniques Morgan might have used. Stuff she'd heard from her father. Straight out hypnotism. Brainwashing — a term not in favor anymore. But she planted the bus story in your mind, and she was good at it. She planted it in a way that you would never forget it. Hardy as a Russian olive tree. You could even see the image of the dead nurses hanging from the bus. But it never happened, Michael, not that night. Confabulation. False memories. Repeated to you and by you again and again while you were in a diminished capacity from excessive alcohol. A while back there was a rash of false accusations of alleged molestations by fathers against their children when the kids were little. Some were real. But others turned out to be false — not necessarily intentional lies, but false memories. Perhaps implanted by angry divorced wives, perhaps not. I mentioned availability cascade — the self-reinforcing process in which belief gains plausibility through increasing repetition. Jack Diamond used to be on the police beat, as I said. Cops use it a lot. In a lineup, or a photo lineup, there are subtle and not so subtle ways they can indicate to a witness which suspect they want them to select. The witness identifies that person, and at an arraignment repeats the identification, and at a hearing, and by the time the trial comes along and he or she is on the witness stand, they are accusing the wrong person, under oath. They're not intentionally committing perjury. They've come to believe completely that this was the man they saw at the scene of the rape, or murder — because they have repeated it so many times. They've become wedded to it, even if at first they were not sure. A lot of innocent men are in prison — some on death row — because of just such sworn but false identifications. With Morgan, a kind of home-schooled student of psychology intentionally manipulating you, it's not hard to believe. With her little game she was surpassing her father. There have been articles in the journals just recently that suggest the brain desperately wants explanations for things it doesn't understand — like why Addie stood you up. When Morgan offered an explanation, your brain grabbed it and held tight.

—What about Maxie? If I did not know him back then, where does he fit in?

—I'm just guessing here, but I suspect that once you moved to California, Morgan wanted to test whether your false memory was still holding. So she inserted Max Klonsky back there, handing you the sunglasses in a bar. It took hold.

I'm worn out. I've been locked in a spinning washing machine — brainwashing machine — for forty years. There's one flaw in her theory, though. The bulletin in the newspaper.

—Yes. Jack and I puzzled over that. That was hard to explain. It really was in the paper, Morgan did not have one of those phony newspapers made up. It still shows on the Internet, as I said. So. How to find out why. *The Daily Mirror* went out of business more than thirty years ago, no way to find out there. But Jack is good, as I said. When a newspaper folds, the reporters and editors flee to whatever papers will have them. Some sign on with the competition. Jack called the *New York Daily News*, which was the *Mirror's* main competitor. He wanted to speak with someone who had been around — who might remember something back then. Newsmen cherish fake stories, and classic typographical errors. Do you know that at most newspapers it is forbidden to refer to a blond child as towheaded? Because nine times out of ten it will appear in the paper as two-headed. Anyway, Jack got to speak with the managing editor, an older guy named McKendrick, Paul McKendrick. Jack asked if by any chance he remembered that bulletin, and why the alleged bus crash never again appeared in any newspaper. McKendrick said that as a matter of fact he did know that story. It seems the *Mirror's* deadline for the first edition — often called the Bulldog Edition, heaven knows why — was 6 PM.

On that day of the Miracle Mets winning the World Series, the first edition was about to be put to bed, as they say, and most of the staff was drinking champagne or stronger booze to celebrate the Mets. Some were out on the street, or looking out the windows. The phone on the city desk rang. With nobody of authority answering or caring to, a young news clerk took the call. It was the paper's chief police reporter, Myra Goodall, with an exclusive story. Myra dictated the bulletin about the bus crash and the eleven nurses feared dead. She told the clerk to rush it to the composing room, they'd beat the whole city on the story. The paper was to lock up in three minutes and no sober editors were to be found. The news clerk figured his job was on the line. He raced down to the composing room and got the bulletin inserted onto page three just as the paper was going to press. That was one happy news clerk, according to McKendrick. Maybe he'd get a bonus. Well, the paper was not on the street for ten minutes when the real Myra Goodall called and asked what the hell that bulletin was all about. She'd checked with police headquarters and with Rikers Island. There had been no such crash. The paper pulled the false bulletin from their next edition, of course, and published a brief correction, but that edition did not hit the streets until after 11. The correction doesn't appear on the Internet, because only one edition of each paper is on line — at least of defunct papers.

—How did this McKendrick fellow know all these details? No, don't tell me. He was the news clerk who screwed up.

—Exactly. He didn't know Myra Goodall's voice, just that she had a lot of clout. So he did what he thought was best for his career. The odd thing is, it turned out that it was.

—How do you figure that?

—He was fired that very night for his excessive enthusiasm. He drank a lot of beer and the next day walked a few blocks to the *Daily News* and applied for a job. At the *News* they'd been chortling over the *Mirror's* screw-up. To them it was hilarious. They hired him on the spot, with a warning not to let it happen to them. McKendrick was a better reporter for the incident, learned to double check every fact. Now he's the managing editor. An unlikely story, but true. Jack checked it with the publisher.

—That was a hell of a lot of planning Morgan did, if I'm to believe all this stuff.

—It certainly was. It probably was the genius of madness. She may have been temporarily insane, judging from the brutality of the murder. Her cleverness in selling you the bus crash story, keeping you drunk for a week while repeating it over and over, was perhaps a triumph over her father, as I indicated. He had not much use for female children, I would guess. And she got what she wanted — you. That probably restored her sense of balance.

—And ruined my life. Maybe her spell was finally wearing off, with the women coming back to haunt me.

—That was all in your psyche, of course, since we know the crash never happened. You were in no way responsible for a single death.

—You know something, Rabbi. Last week, right after my — operation — when I was lying in bed across from Morgan and her coma, she started speaking. She didn't talk of a stabbing murder, but she did mention a laser. She said she had been behind a tree and had shone the laser into the driver's eyes, burned them out so that he lost control and crashed. The sunglasses I stole would not have mattered, she said, because they would have melted instantly. They would not have protected him. She was confessing to being involved. But when I called in nurses to say she had come out of her coma and talked with me, they said that had not happened. Morgan had died two hours before our conversation. She was not even in the room. What do you make of that?

—I'd guess that your unconscious was finally beginning to break into the sleeping part of your brain that knew the truth. You were beginning to suspect that she was involved, that she was the guilty party. Maybe it all would have come back to you, the way it really happened, with a little more time. It's too bad you felt the need to punish yourself so severely before that occurred.

—The last two times I saw Nia, Addie was in her eyes. Drawn in blood. But in death Addie had no eyes.

—Your psyche was working on it. The spell was unraveling. You were asking yourself, in imagery, was it the bus driver Morgan had blinded with a laser, or was it really Addie? Perhaps, like Romeo and Juliet in death, you needed to join Addie in blindness — to share her last torment before the fatal cuts.

—So I've been blind all my life. You've made that clear. I've suspected that in other areas of my life. Maybe that's why blinding myself felt right. The immediate trigger was to escape the pain of Nia. No doubt. Now I'm too busy learning to be blind to agonize so much over that. Still, I'd give anything to hold her in my arms, of course — the luscious third act of my life, as I used to hope. The third act turns out to be blindness. It's a good thing Morgan died. Because hearing your facts, I surely would have strangled her, coma or not. And that would have been murder, coma or not. I'm a lifelong baseball fan, never mind the steroids crap, and my favorite quotation about death compares it with baseball. It's from August Wilson's play *Fences*, which I saw up in Seattle once. Wilson wrote, *Death is just a fastball on the outside corner*. The thought has always comforted me. But it clearly does not apply to death by violence, from the guns of a gang, as Laurette Dubal died, or by four dozen stab wounds in the chest with a small blade, as Addie appears to have suffered — been tortured by. For the crime of loving me. May a hundred million gods damn Morgan's soul. But what you just said resonates. Joining Addie in her final moments of life — blindness.

Silence. As in a courtroom. I'm waiting for the bailiff to read the verdict.

—You know something, Rachel? You've been sitting here for what, maybe an hour? And I haven't once looked at your legs.

I can't divine her expression. As a joke I suppose it is sick.

—Getting back to the past, she says, the one thing that still puzzles me is how Morgan knew about Addie in the first place. Your relationship was supposed to be a secret from everyone.

My head drops into my hands. I want to cry, scream, blind myself again, this time without the painkiller.

—Oh, fuck! Jesus! I told her.

—You told her?

—When I was breaking the engagement.

Without eyes, I discover, the tears remain in your brain.

—I had to give a reason. I told her the truth. I was in love with someone else. She asked who. This girl I met in England, I said. Addie. She's a nurse at Rikers Island.

Rachel inhales sharply.

God forgive me, she says. Sometimes out of curiosity I ask one question too many.

The tension in my office has become a hangman's noose. Silence, the pause before the guillotine falls. My voice is weak, I struggle forming words.

—So I did kill Addie, after all. I put a target on her back.

—Michael, you had no way of knowing.

The rabbi's voice trails off in despair.

The telephone on my desk is ringing. I ignore it. It continues to ring. I'm in no mood to speak with anyone. I explain this to Rachel. My intercom buzzes.

—Hey, Michael are you there?

—I'm here, I have a visitor, what is it Maxie?

—Is your phone ringing?

—Yeah, my phone is ringing.

—You know what you're supposed to do with a ringing phone? You're supposed to answer it.

— I don't feel like talking to anyone right now. It's one of the few freedoms we have left. Not to answer a ringing phone.

—Michael, pick up the fucking phone. Now.

—Why the fuck should I?

—Why the fuck should you? I'll tell you why the fuck should you. Because I just got off the same phone call. Because it's fucking Stockholm on the line.

When I fumble to hang up the receiver, dazzled, Rachel stands, bubbling with congratulations, and shakes my hand. I stand and we hug like old friends or lovers and she kisses my cheek. Her husband won't mind she says, she's never kissed a Nobel Laureate before. My head is a simmering stew of the good, the bad and the ugly — the Nobel Prize, which is as close as a doctor can come to immortality, the death of Morgan, her despicable murder of Addie forty years ago, and my blindness for forty years, and now my real blindness. How long it will simmer like this before settling down I cannot say. Madam President offers congratulations over the intercom, trying ladylike to conceal her joy, says my presence is required in the Community Room at once. I walk down there on Rachel's arm, and when we enter, several dozen people who have been able to leave their posts for a few minutes break out into a discordant but loud rendition of *For He's a Jolly Good Fellow*. My face reddens, I can tell. The rabbi tells me Maxie is standing sheepishly in a corner surrounded by admirers. She points me in that direction and I stride forward. When he sees me he's suddenly rushing at me, I can hear his sloppy shoes and the rush of air that surrounds him and he's in front of me and he says son-of-a-bitch, and I say son-of-a bitch, because what can you say at a time like this? We embrace in a bear hug, chest to chest, arms tight, as if we are trying to crush each other. The dozens in the room cheer and applaud our embrace, and as we break apart he says slowly son of a bitch, and I say slowly son of a bitch back, the goddamn Nobel Prize. Shannon Kelly wheels up, I can sense the waters of people parting before her like the Red Sea. She manages to stand — she can do that for a few seconds if she does not have to walk — and she joins our embrace and kisses each of us on both cheeks, French style, and in separating brushes her lips against mine as if no one will notice or if they do will think it an accident. I told you Vegas knows, she says, and looking around she calls out, more champagne! I hear a metal cart rolling into the room like field artillery, to even greater applause. Housekeeping starts popping corks, cold bottles of champagne are being passed around. You really did buy champagne weeks ago, I say to Shannon, and she says, of course. Someone hands her a bottle. She gives it to Maxie who slurps right from the bottle's lip, I hear it gurgling down his throat. He hands it to me and I do the same. It's cool, wet, nice. I try to savor the taste, dry, not fruity, the coldness, the moment. I hand it to Shannon as if we are in college sharing a joint. I hear her sink into her wheelchair before tilting the bottle up to her lips. How the hell did you keep it cold? I ask. In the morgue, she says, where else?

People begin to swarm around us, docs, nurses, aides, techs, housekeepers. I shake hands I cannot see, am kissed on the cheek by lips I do not recognize. Though some I do. One pair belongs to Lacey Roberts, smelling like daisies, and I don't let her get away with that. I put my arm around her waist, pull her to me, her chest against mine, plant a sticky but sweet champagne kiss on her lips. Something to tell my grand kids about, she says, The Kiss of the Wounded Laureate. Vicky rushes up breathless, she'd been finishing with a patient, and hugs me, her diminutive form holding back a bit, she is shy in public. I want to find a chair and have her sit on my lap, but she is content to say without words, *Wait until later.*

The celebrants have to get back to work, but a shift breaks and dozens more docs, nurses, aides swarm into the room — I can hear their striding or shuffling feet — to offer handshakes and sip champagne from plastic cups that housekeeping has broken out. When do you get the money is the most common question — when do you receive the prize comes from the more sophisticated. December tenth, in Stockholm, I have been told. Waltzing in through the outside door, singing, comes Annabel Lee, she'd heard the bulletin on the local radio station while driving and U-turned straight to the hospital. The only person missing is Nia.

I don't know how long this goes on, through several glasses of champagne at least, then Vicky tugs on my arm and whispers in my ear. That's great, I tell her, that's fine with me, and I find my way to Shannon in her chair, where she is buzzing to some docs about how great this is, what this will mean to the hospital in terms of donations and expanded services. If she is thinking at all back to the past, that one day she was supposed to be celebrated like this, for insights about cancer that she never got to prove, she does not show it.

I tell her I have to leave now. She asks why, the party has only started, it will continue in a while at her home, she's invited the board of directors to share champagne with Maxie and me.

I tell her I'm sorry, I do have to leave, and she asks, On the biggest day of your life? I assure her we'll have plenty of time to celebrate in the weeks ahead, but now I have to go, Vicky's daughter Maya is making a victory dinner for me.

—That's why you have to go, because a kid is making you dinner?

—She's a special kid, I say.

● ● ● ● ● ● ● ● ● ● ● ● ● ● ● ●

Books by Robert Mayer

Fiction

Superfolks

The Execution

Midge and Decker

The Grace of Shortstops

Sweet Salt

The Search

I, JFK

The Origin of Sorrow *

The Ferret's Tale *

Danse Macabre *

Confessions of a Rain God *

Non-Fiction

The Dreams of Ada

Notes of a Baseball Dreamer
(First published as *Baseball
And Men's Lives*)

* Available in print and e-book at www.Combustoica.com

www.ingramcontent.com/pod-product-compliance
Lightning Source LLC
Chambersburg PA
CBHW020746250626
47155CB00003B/947